CONTENTS

New York Times bestselling author **Janet Tronstad** grew up on her family's farm in central Montana and now lives in Turlock, California, where she is always at work on her next book. She has written more than thirty books, many of them set in the fictitious town of Dry Creek, Montana, where the men spend the winters gathered around the potbellied stove in the hardware store and the women make jelly in the fall.

Books by Janet Tronstad

Love Inspired

Dry Creek

Dry Creek Sweethearts
A Dry Creek Courtship
Snowbound in Dry Creek
Small-Town Brides
"A Dry Creek Wedding"
Silent Night in Dry Creek
Wife Wanted in Dry Creek
Small-Town Moms
"A Dry Creek Family"
Easter in Dry Creek
Dry Creek Daddy

Visit the Author Profile page
at Harlequin.com for more titles.

CALICO CHRISTMAS AT DRY CREEK

Janet Tronstad

In the beginning of time, it was said that
"...God created man in his own image,
in the image of God created he him..."
This was written in the Holy Bible,
the book of Genesis,
the second chapter, and the twenty-seventh verse.
And then, many generations later,
it was also said that
"God made me an Indian."

This was spoken by
Chief Sitting Bull
Lakota Medicine Man
1831–1890

This book is dedicated with love to my grandfather,
Harold Norris, who loved nothing better than
a good Western novel. I wish he were alive
to read this book.

Chapter One

Fort Keogh, Montana Territory, 1879

Elizabeth O'Brian heard voices outside her tent and thought it must be Mr. Miller coming to see if she was dead yet. It was a cold November day and she'd been sitting in her tent for eleven days now in this desolate land. It had only taken her husband, Matthew, and their baby, a few days to die from the fever so Elizabeth couldn't fault the blacksmith for being impatient.

"Mrs. O'Brian," a man's voice called in the distance.

Elizabeth ignored the voice. Mr. Miller knew she was still waiting for the fever to come upon her. He would just have to be patient a little longer. It wasn't as easy to die as it looked.

She supposed he was nervous because she was so close to the fort. No one had thought her tent would be here for this long. She had used the canvas from her wagon to make a tent in this slight ravine that stood a good fifty feet east of the mud-chinked logs that made up most of the buildings at Fort Keogh.

The canvas stretched from the back of her wagon to

the only tree here, a squat cottonwood that had looked tired even before she'd tied her rope to it. She had made sure the tree put her far enough away from the fort to prevent the influenza from striking anyone there while at the same time still being close enough that Mr. Miller wouldn't have to walk far when he came to bury her.

The fort was a noisy, smelly place and Elizabeth wanted to die the way she had lived, quietly and alone.

"Mrs. O'Brian," the same man's voice called out. He was closer now.

She frowned. It didn't sound like Mr. Miller calling her.

She'd given the blacksmith her team of oxen in exchange for his promise to dig a proper burying hole for her next to the one that held Matthew and their baby, Rose. Once Mr. Miller had pledged himself, she believed he would do what was necessary when the time came. Still, she wanted her tent to be in sight of the man when it was time for him to do his job. She didn't want to give him any excuse to forget about the deal when she was no longer able to remind him of it. Men, she'd realized in her twenty-eight years on this earth, weren't always reliable.

Elizabeth got to her knees and crawled to the opening in the tent. She hadn't been out of the tent since dawn when she had gotten water from the barrel that was attached to the side of her wagon. She had added another piece of wood to the smoldering fire just outside her tent and boiled water for tea. Someone had left her a plate of hardtack biscuits yesterday. A morning frost had already covered the biscuits before she saw them, making them so brittle she had to dip each one in her tea before it was soft enough to chew. She'd had no appetite, but she'd forced herself to eat two of them for breakfast anyway.

After she ate, she had checked to see that the handkerchief was still securely tied around the back of the wagon seat. When she had refused to stay inside the fort, the doctor had insisted she have a signal for when the fever came upon her. She was to exchange the white handkerchief for a small piece of blue fabric at the first sign of heat. She'd ripped the cloth from the back of one of Matthew's shirts and had it, folded and ready for use, lying beside the old blankets on which she slept.

"Who is it?" Elizabeth peered through the canvas flap that was the closest thing to a door that she had. She saw two men standing a proper distance away. The canvas was stiff in her hands and still half-frozen from the night's cold. She could see her breath when she spoke.

Even with the white handkerchief up, the people who left food and firewood didn't try to speak to her. She had started leaving jars of her preserves on the wagon seat to repay them. She was always glad to see the jars were gone when she walked the few feet back to the wagon. She didn't want to be beholden to anyone when she died.

She wondered who wanted to talk with her now.

"Sergeant Rawlings, ma'am."

Elizabeth nodded. She had seen the man at the blacksmith shop. "I'm sorry, but tell Mr. Miller that it's not time yet."

She moved the canvas in her hand slightly and felt the brush of a freezing wind. She tightened her blanket around her. She'd thought she'd never feel this kind of bitter cold again. Suddenly, she wondered if the blacksmith wanted more payment now that the temperatures were dropping, making it harder to dig in this gray dirt. She hoped not. A deal was a deal.

"We're not here about that. Could you come out here so we can talk?"

Elizabeth hadn't talked to anyone in days and she wasn't in a hurry to do so now. Besides, she wanted to study the men a little before she went out to meet them.

"Give me a minute."

She could see Sergeant Rawlings plainly, but the other man had his back to her. Initially, she thought he was one of the soldiers from the fort, too. But when she looked at him more closely, she realized he couldn't be a soldier. He wore a buckskin jacket and he had a black fur of some kind wrapped around his shoulders in a sling.

She shivered, and this time it was not from the cold. He must be an Indian. She'd seen Indian scouts coming and going from the fort, but this man looked like one of those wild Indians, the ones who killed people. She'd heard they did unspeakable things. Things she shouldn't even think about—like taking a lone woman's virtue and then, most likely, her scalp.

Elizabeth reached up to touch her hair. She suddenly wondered if Mr. Miller was planning to use the Indian to scare her into giving him more payment to dig her grave. Maybe Mr. Miller could threaten to have the Indian do the digging if she didn't cooperate. Her breath caught at the thought of a heathen preparing her grave.

Elizabeth kept count of the days, using a stick to mark their passage on the ground outside her tent. She should be in her grave by now, but she wasn't. She didn't know what was wrong. She supposed God was giving her more time on this earth in hopes she would repent of the anger she felt toward Him, but, if that was what He was doing,

He might as well move things along. She knew who had taken her baby away from her and more time wouldn't change that.

She couldn't afford to lie in a grave dug by a heathen, though. What if God used that as an excuse to shut her out for all of eternity? She had been careful not to say a single word of complaint against God during this whole time—not to Matthew as he lay dying, not to the doctor, not to anyone—but an unholy grave might turn God from her anyway. She couldn't risk that; the only consolation she had left was the promise that she would see her baby again in Heaven.

She closed her eyes and tried to remember her exact words to the blacksmith, but she couldn't. Matthew had always said she didn't know how to drive a good bargain, and he was right. She should have made it clear to Mr. Miller that he was to handle the shovel himself. Over the past few days, she'd started to feel the cold seeping into the ground beneath her, but she hadn't realized what it might mean. She hoped God would let her die quickly before everything froze deep enough to trouble the blacksmith.

A horse neighed somewhere and Elizabeth opened her eyes again to look at the two men. Something was wrong. Maybe it wasn't Mr. Miller who wanted what was left of her possessions. Maybe it was the two men in front of her who were going to try and steal everything. They were certainly talking about something more serious than shovels as they waited for her. She swallowed. She would be no match for them if that's what they decided.

Elizabeth reached behind her for the old rifle she had, but then stopped. She couldn't shoot someone, not even if they were intent on stealing every last thing she owned.

She moved her hand and leaned forward to look more closely at the men. She did not see any sign of greed on the sergeant's face as he kept talking to the Indian. Neither one of them looked as if they were thinking of robbing her.

"It must be the preserves," Elizabeth suddenly muttered to herself in relief.

Of course, that was it. She'd forgotten they were in the wagon. The army man probably wanted the Indian to help him carry the rest of the preserves to the fort before the jars got so cold they cracked. Matthew had loaded the bottom of their wagon with things for the new store he planned to open, but Elizabeth had known she wouldn't be able to rely on Matthew to feed her and the baby, so she had canned everything she could before they left Kansas.

She'd even poured a mixture of beeswax and beef tallow on top of her jellies and apple butters so the ones they didn't eat on their journey would keep through the winter. Now, the last of the preserves were lying cradled on top of the woolens at the back of the wagon.

Well, she told herself after a moment, the sergeant had the right of it. Preserves were scarce out here. These soldiers lived on their rations of salt pork, dried beans and green coffee. She'd seen the men coming and going from the fort and none of them looked well-fed. She should have hauled all of those preserves up to the wagon seat before now, anyway. Even her pickled things, like her red beets and sour cabbage, shouldn't go to waste just because she was dying.

It wasn't until the man in the buckskin moved that

Elizabeth saw the Indian girl sitting on the pinto pony near the fort. She must be about nine or ten years old and she had a blanket wrapped around her. Edges of a faded calico dress showed through where the blanket didn't cover and animal pelts were tied around her legs. Elizabeth couldn't imagine why the girl was watching them so intently.

"Could you just come out here, please?" Sergeant Rawlings called out again.

Really—men, Elizabeth thought to herself. She supposed it never occurred to any of them to let her die in peace and worry about the preserves later. That was men for you. Always thinking about their stomachs. Matthew had been like that, too. He had always expected her to have a meal ready even when he didn't provide her with a scrap of meat or a handful of flour to use in the making of it.

But, oh, how she missed him and Rose. Matthew hadn't been much of a provider, but he had treated her well enough. She had been learning to please him, too, and, if they'd been given a little more time together, she was sure she would have succeeded in making him happy with their marriage. He was the first family that was really her own. And he'd given her Rose. Her baby only had to be herself to melt everyone's heart.

Elizabeth wrapped a blanket around her like a shawl and stepped out of the tent. The ground outside was slippery from frost and she felt the cold deeply as she walked toward the sergeant and the Indian. She had taken several steps when the man in the buckskin turned around and she saw him fully for the first time.

"Oh, dear, I'm sorry." She stopped and stared. Why, he wasn't an Indian at all. His eyes were blue and the skin around his eyes, the part that was wrinkled from squinting, was undeniably white. His nose wasn't flat like some of the Indians she'd seen and his cheekbones were high. Even with that knowledge, though, she wasn't quite sure about him. Up close, he seemed larger than she had expected. And more fierce than a white man should be. He looked like a warrior no matter what color he was.

"There's no need to apologize," Sergeant Rawlings said stiffly. "We're sorry to trouble you."

Elizabeth nodded and tried to think of something to say to cover the erratic beating of her heart. "It's no bother. It just took me a while because—because I wasn't prepared for company."

She was still staring at the other man. She'd never had this kind of breathless reaction to the sight of anyone. Of course, it probably wasn't really the sight of him that was causing her heart to continue racing. It was only that she had thought he was a savage capable of doing anything.

Even now that Elizabeth knew the man she was looking at was a white man, she was still uneasy around him. He was nothing at all like Matthew. Nothing like any man she'd ever seen before.

Oh, dear—whatever he was, he was looking straight at her and frowning.

Then he spoke. "There must be some mistake. She doesn't look like a widow—just look at her."

Elizabeth had expected his voice to be harsh, but it wasn't. It sounded kind and, if she was hearing right, a little discouraged. Although why the man would be feeling that way was beyond her. If he was worried about the way anyone around here looked, he should be worrying about himself instead of her. The soldiers here dressed better than he did. And that wasn't saying much.

She'd noticed right off that the dye in the men's uniforms was poor and some patches of wool were a darker blue than others. The buttonholes were fraying, too. That's what came of using indigo for dye; everyone knew it ate away at the cloth. She would have used dyer's woad if she'd been charged with making the garments, although the leaves of the plant did take longer to prepare.

Even with all of that, though, none of the soldiers wore buckskin the way this man did. One army man she'd talked to said he'd gladly wear a buffalo coat in winter if he had one, but he'd rather wear the blanket from his bed than dress like an Indian.

Elizabeth looked at the man in buckskin. The furs the man wore over his shoulder formed a pack of some sort that he kept close to his chest.

Elizabeth let the blanket she wore as a shawl slip away from her. The air chilled her skin, but she didn't want to feel she was hiding anything. In her childhood, she had learned that a soft answer would smooth away most unpleasantness and that she was the one always expected to give it.

"Please, don't let my appearance concern you. I normally do better," she said.

The wind blew a strand of brown hair across her cheek and Elizabeth knew what the men saw. The mosquito bites on her face had faded, but the freckles she'd gotten from neglecting to wear her sunbonnet on the dreadful journey here were still plain. By now, the icy wind would have drawn all of the other color from her face, as well, so the freckles would stand out like tiny pebbles scattered on a bank of fresh snow.

And she still wasn't wearing a hat; the only one she owned was that worn-out yellow sunbonnet and she refused to wear it ever again. She might even burn it in the fire one night before she died. Everything about it reminded her of the journey here and she wanted no part of those memories.

Elizabeth lifted her head high. She'd grown weary of trying to please others. She'd been orphaned young and spent her childhood being passed from household to household whenever extra help was needed. She'd never been asked to sit at the family table in any of these places where she worked, but she'd earned a measure of respect with her cooking and with her clever ways of dyeing cloth.

She was wearing her best dress, even if there was dirt on her skirt after crawling to the opening in her tent. Her hands brushed at the folds of the gray silk garment that she'd been given by the last family she had worked for. It had been damaged when they had given it to her, of course, but it was still the only silk dress she was likely to ever own. And it was twilled silk. Elizabeth had put the dress on last week when she realized she could hardly expect Mr. Miller to change her clothes for her burial.

"I never said there was anything wrong with the way you look." The man's eyes softened. "I just expected someone older. And not so pretty."

Elizabeth watched in horror as the man reached out and touched her chin as through she was a child to be consoled.

"I'm hardly pretty," Elizabeth said, a little more

sharply than she intended. She moved her face slightly to discourage him, although his touch on her chin had been gentle and, surprisingly, pleasant.

She'd heard enough warnings in her life to know handsome men couldn't always be trusted, especially not when they were talking to females who had no protectors. And this man was certainly trying to turn her up sweet for some purpose of his own. Matthew once said she looked nice, but that wasn't the same as saying she was pretty. No one ever called her pretty and Elizabeth was sensible enough to know not to expect it. It wasn't true.

She wondered for a moment if the man was delusional and then she remembered the fever. She always did look better when her cheeks had some color in them. Maybe the fever was already on her and she just hadn't noticed it. She put her hand to her forehead.

"Well, I can't expect you to help me." The buckskin man finally said before turning to the sergeant as though he hadn't just been smiling at her. "There's got to be someone else."

Elizabeth was ready to leave when the sergeant spoke urgently. "There's nobody else. You've got to ask her—for the baby's sake."

"What—" Elizabeth looked around. Her hand dropped away from her forehead. There was no fever heat unless, of course, she was the one who was delusional. "What baby?"

There were no babies at the fort. She had asked. Mr. Miller thought she wanted to save herself the pain of seeing a living baby, but that wasn't it. Babies were so innocent. If there was a baby around she would have asked to look at it, from a distance, of course, so as not to risk giving the fever to the little one.

She saw the buckskin man's hand go to the bundle he wore across his chest.

"This baby," the man said.

"Ohhh. Can I see it?"

The man started to turn the bundle toward her.

"I'll keep back so you won't have to worry about it getting sick."

The man stopped his turning and looked up at the soldier. "I thought you said she didn't have the fever."

"That's right," Sergeant Rawlings said and then looked at Elizabeth. "The doctor said you'd be dead by now if you were going to get it. I was just coming over to tell you that when I ran into Jake here."

"We can't always time our deaths perfectly," Elizabeth said. It wasn't up to the doctor when she died. "I'm sure I'll die soon enough."

"But you don't have the fever now?" the buckskin man asked.

"No, not yet, Mr....ah... Mr...."

"It's just Jake," the man said.

Elizabeth frowned. After he had touched her chin, she should have known he had no manners. If she could be courteous when she was dying, the man could at least be polite when he stood there in vigorous health. He might dress like a heathen, but he didn't need to act like one. A full name was not too much of an introduction to ask.

"How long do you plan to wait for this fever?" Jake asked.

Elizabeth lifted her chin. If he wasn't going to show her the baby, he could just say so. And he could keep his hands to himself. "I'm sure I don't know, Mr...."

She didn't know why she bothered with the man's manners. She just wanted him to relent and show her the baby. She'd love to see a baby.

Jake was looking at her impatiently. "If you need the full name to feel better, it's Jake Hargrove."

"Well, Mr. Hargrove." Elizabeth nodded her head in acknowledgment. There. That had made her feel better. "I'm Elizabeth O'Brian and I plan to be here as long as it takes to die. Did you need this land for something?"

It wasn't only the preserves that might interest the men, Elizabeth had realized. They could also want the very ground under her feet. God might not even leave her with that.

Except for the lone cottonwood tree, the piece of ground where she had her tent didn't have anything on it, not after she'd pulled up the few scraggly thistles that had managed to survive the scorching heat of this past summer. There were more cottonwood trees farther up the ravine, but she doubted even a jackrabbit wanted the barren piece of land that was now her camp. Although she did know there were men who would lay claim to something just because someone else had their tent pitched on it already. Maybe this buckskin man was one of them.

"No, no, it's not that," Jake said and then he hesitated. "It's you. Women are scarce out here and it's hard for a man to find one when he needs her."

Elizabeth blinked. "I beg your pardon."

Sergeant Rawlings spoke up. "It's not what you think, ma'am. It's on account of the baby being hungry is all."

"Oh." Elizabeth breathed out in wonder. She knew in that moment she was going to see the baby.

Jake hesitated and then finished unwinding the furs from his shoulders.

The baby was so tiny and its eyes were shut. Elizabeth thought it must be sleeping until the baby opened its mouth and yawned. Her Rose used to yawn like that.

"There's no one to feed her," Jake said. "I asked all around Miles City before I came out to the fort."

"Miller thought he might be able to milk one of your oxen," Sergeant Rawlings said. "But it didn't seem like it would work."

"I should think not," Elizabeth said as she stepped closer to the baby. She left enough room so that she wouldn't pass on any sickness just in case. "It's a little girl then, is it? If I could, I would feed her."

The baby started to give a weak wail.

Elizabeth felt her breasts grow heavy with milk. "Where's her mother?"

"Dead," Jake said flatly and then repeated what the soldier had said. "The doctor says you're not going to get the fever." He looked square at her. "You're her last hope. She'll die without something to eat."

"But still…" Elizabeth knew she would not have let anyone who might come down with the fever touch her Rose. This baby here was frail and reminded her of how Rose had been when she was dying. If Elizabeth closed her eyes, she could still see the image of Rose lying so still after she took her last breath.

Suddenly, the baby stopped its wail.

"I can't…" Elizabeth started to say, but her arms were already reaching out.

God would have to forgive her if that doctor was wrong, because she couldn't let this baby die without trying to help it.

Jake held out the baby. Elizabeth wrapped a corner of her blanket around it and bent down to go back inside her tent. She supposed the two men would just stand outside and wait, but she didn't care. She had a baby to hold again.

Once they got started, Elizabeth was surprised at how easily the baby fell into the rhythm of nursing. Even when the baby had finished eating, Elizabeth just sat there for a while with the baby at her breast. The little one's hair was black and soft. She was an Indian baby, of course, but she looked like Rose all the same.

The baby didn't seem as heathen as a warrior would, though.

She had heard that some of the white men who came to the territories took Indian wives. She wondered briefly if Jake Hargrove had married the baby's mother in a church ceremony.

For a moment, Elizabeth was glad Matthew wasn't here to see her nursing the infant. From the day he had proposed to her, Elizabeth had tried to be the wife Matthew had wanted. He had married beneath himself; there was no question of that. A lady would never nurse another's baby and Elizabeth felt sure Matthew would refuse to let her do so if he were here, especially because the baby was not white. And probably irregular in its birth, as well.

The sun was almost setting when Elizabeth opened the tent flap again. Sergeant Rawlings had gone, but the other man was still there sitting on the ground near her wagon. The Indian girl had come closer to the wagon, as well, even though she still sat on top of her pony.

When she opened the tent flap, Jake stood up and walked over to her.

"What's the baby's name?" Elizabeth asked as she knelt at the door of her tent and lifted the baby up to the man.

"She doesn't have a name yet." Jake took the baby and began to wrap it back into the furs he wore over his shoulder.

"Oh, surely she has a name," Elizabeth said as she stood up and hugged her blanket around her. Hoping for a girl, she and Matthew had picked out the name Rose before their baby was even born. Rose had been the name of Matthew's mother, but Elizabeth had liked the name for its own sake, too. "She'll sleep for now."

"The Lakota wait to name their babies," Jake said as he adjusted the baby inside his makeshift sling. "She hadn't earned her name yet when she was brought to me."

"My sister will be called the Crying One," the girl on the pony said. "For the tears of her people."

Elizabeth was surprised to hear the girl speaking English. Her words were not easily formed, but Elizabeth could understand what she was saying.

"Your sister doesn't belong to the Lakota anymore," Jake said. "She belongs to the people of her grandfather."

The girl didn't say anything. She just sat, facing east. She didn't even seem to look at the man. Her face was smooth, devoid of expression.

Elizabeth had heard arguments like this before.

"Your dress is beautiful." Elizabeth smiled up just in case the girl looked over at her. The faded yellow tones of the calico looked almost white in the rays of the setting sun. A good boiling with some of the dried marigold petals Elizabeth had in her wagon would bring the color back, though. "Your sister is fortunate to have a big sister like you to take care of her."

"I cannot take care of her." The girl turned and looked at Elizabeth for the first time. "She needs you."

"Oh."

Elizabeth saw the girl's face crumble. Resentment and pleading both shone in the young girl's eyes. How she must hate asking for help. And how desperately she wanted it.

Elizabeth nodded. "Of course, I—I will do what I can until some other way is found."

"What other way is there?" Jake asked. His voice was strained, too. "The baby sickens on cow's milk. I tried to buy some of that canned milk in Miles City— the kind they gave our men in the war—but none of the stores sell it. Most of them hadn't even heard of it. You are our only hope."

If things had been different, she and Matthew might have eventually owned a store like the ones that the man mentioned. That had been Matthew's dream. They probably wouldn't have canned milk, either, at least not in the beginning. But, in time, who knew?

Matthew always said he would tend the store while Elizabeth tended Rose. He had all those things in the wagon to sell. A fierce sadness rose up in Elizabeth just thinking about it. Those dreams and hopes were all dead. It didn't seem fair that the peace of her passing should be disturbed with memories of things that would never come true. Matthew had died so fast, he hadn't even had time to mourn his lost dreams.

Death had been taking its time with her, though. Without her Rose, she wanted to die. She had no family and she would not go back to being an outsider in other people's homes. She was ready to die. She did not need two pairs of eyes watching her and demanding that she stay alive. She wished she could just close her eyes and keep them closed until she was done with this life.

But, Elizabeth admitted, the doctor in the fort had been a cautious man when he treated Matthew and Rose. A professional man like that wasn't likely to make a mistake about the fever. She wondered if the doctor had seen the Indian baby. Elizabeth knew most people wouldn't think it was a tragedy if one more heathen baby died, but she found she did. She had nursed this one. This baby reminded her of Rose. She wanted it to live.

"Of course, I will do what I can," Elizabeth finally said. She looked over at the baby, snug in the man's arms. "But if the doctor is wrong and the fever comes, you must leave. If you stay, the baby will die anyway."

Elizabeth knew she could not bear to watch another baby die. Surely there were limits to what God could ask of any person, even of her.

Chapter Two

It was night when Jake Hargrove returned from the fort and laid himself down on his buffalo robe. He was bone tired. He'd stood off Indian raids and packs of starving wolves, but he'd never been more worried than he was now. He had no idea how to keep the baby alive if this Mrs. O'Brian wouldn't stay with him through the winter. The men he'd talked to inside hadn't been encouraging; they'd said she was one powerfully stubborn woman and she was set on dying.

Still, for now, she was doing what she could for his niece, Jake told himself. And a woman needed to be stubborn to survive in this land so he didn't begrudge her that. He just needed to turn her mind around to match his. That was all.

He could see her tent clearly in the moonlight from where he lay. He'd put his bed a few yards from it. The baby was sleeping inside the tent with the woman and Spotted Fawn was lying next to the wagon, close enough so she would hear if her sister cried. The two girls hadn't slept that far apart since Red Tail, his half brother, had brought them to him, begging him to raise his daughters in the white man's world so they would live.

Jake had accepted the girls, knowing there was no other way for them. Sitting Bull and the rest of the Lakota Sioux were starving in Canada. Once Red Tail had said goodbye to his daughters, he had gone back to do what he could for the rest of his tribe. He told Jake not to expect to see him again in this life.

Jake put his rifle next to him on the ground. He'd checked earlier and seen that the woman had a rifle in her tent, as well. It had to be the one the blacksmith said he'd given her when she refused to stay inside the fort, claiming the noise and dirt were troublesome to her.

When Jake first heard about the woman, he was surprised no one had made her go into Miles City and take a room at the new hotel there. The bare land around here was no place for a woman from the East. The town was on the other side of the Tongue River, but it was only a few miles away from here.

Of course, now he knew the men at the fort had tried to reason with her. When Jake had talked to the blacksmith, Mr. Miller had said it was all he could do to get the woman to promise that she would run to the fort if she heard a warning shot being fired. The blacksmith didn't look Jake in the eye when he told him that. They both knew a raiding party could be so quiet there would be no warning shot, at least not one that would do the woman any good.

Not all of the Sioux had fled to Canada after their battle with General Custer. Some of the younger braves were still in the territories, their hearts set on vengeance and thievery. As determined as they were to kill all of the white people they could find, these renegades were also looking for extra horses. That was one reason why Jake kept his rifle close. The easiest place to find horses was to rob an army corral, which meant they would need to come to the fort. Once the raiding party got to the fort, the loaded wagon standing outside would be a temptation. As would the woman inside the tent.

Jake shook his head just thinking about that woman. She should be sitting in a parlor back East somewhere. He didn't know what her husband had been thinking to bring her out here; she didn't belong in a land like this. But, as surely as Jake knew she didn't belong, he wasn't going to suggest she go back. Now that she was here, he was going to ask her to stay with him for the winter.

She likely hadn't faced up to it yet, but she had a problem as big as his. She couldn't winter where she was. The winds from the north had been damp lately and that meant winter would come early and it would bring enough snow to bury that makeshift tent of hers. At least, she would be warm and dry if she was with him and the girls.

Unfortunately, for the woman to stay with them, Jake would need to marry her. He'd known that before he met her. Miles City was an unforgiving place these days and he had the girls to consider. They were already viewed with suspicion because of the color of their skin. They would be true outcasts if people found out he was not married to the woman living with them. And, there would be no way to keep the woman a secret. He'd be a fool to even try.

Of course, when he'd first heard of the widow, he'd assumed she would be older and practical enough to make an arrangement with him. Jake looked up at the sky searching for stars. He hadn't counted on Mrs. O'Brian

being young or having eyes that made him want to protect her from things he didn't even see.

The truth was he couldn't even protect her from the
things he could see coming. He and the girls were going
to have a battle finding acceptance in Miles City and
any woman he married would be in the battle with them.
There was no limit to the mean-spiritedness of human
beings and Jake figured his little family was going to
see their share of it this winter.

It made him weary just thinking of it. If he had a fire
going, he would read some from the Bible his mother
had given him as a boy. It never failed to comfort him.
His mother had been a fine lady. Of course, she'd been
totally unsuited to the roughness of life out here. He relaxed just thinking of his old home, hidden on the side
of a mountain northwest of here by the pines growing
thick and tall all around. His father had brought them
there, not believing the reports he'd heard that the trapping days were almost over. He thought it was all just
rumors spread by the Hudson's Bay Company. He pictured getting rich on furs once the other trappers gave
up, but he barely managed to feed his family.

Jake had grieved when his mother died a couple of
years after they came West. The crude cabin where they
lived seemed to shrink and grow empty without her. He
and his father never talked about his mother after her
death. They had both felt too guilty for failing her. His
father hadn't even put a marker on her burial place. The
last thing Jake had done, before he left to go out on his
own, was to find a smooth slab of rock and place it in
front of his mother's grave with her name scratched on it.

By that time, his father had married again, this time
to a Lakota squaw. Red Tail was their son.

If he didn't have the girls, Jake would not consider marriage—especially not to a woman like Elizabeth O'Brian. She reminded him too much of his mother. This land had changed in the almost forty years he'd lived here, but it still wasn't a place for pretty, young white women. He didn't want to watch another one of them grow bitter and fade away here. He didn't have much choice, though. Not if he wanted to keep the baby alive.

Elizabeth wasn't sure if it was the pebble under her back or the smell of frying salt pork that woke her the next morning. She could see out the flap in her tent well enough to know there were heavy gray clouds hanging low in the sky. There was also a biting cold to the morning air. Winter was coming. The low bluffs in the distance might even have snow on top of them by now.

Elizabeth hadn't slept well and it was later than she'd planned to waken. It had taken her hours last night to coax the older girl close enough to the tent so that Elizabeth wouldn't worry about her. Finally, Spotted Fawn had agreed to sleep beside her tent when Elizabeth said she might need help with the baby.

Fortunately, the baby only stirred twice during the night. Elizabeth had fed her both times and the little one was doing better. Maybe this man, Jake, would be content to spend a few more days near the fort so Elizabeth could nurse the baby. That should give him enough time to find someone else to take care of the infant.

In the cold light of morning, Elizabeth accepted the fact that she was going to live. She looked down at the sleeping infant. Maybe God was keeping her alive to save this Indian baby. That was the only thing that made sense, even though she couldn't help but wonder why

He saw fit to worry about this little one when He had not hesitated to take her Rose away.

Elizabeth knew no one was supposed to question the ways of God, but she couldn't help her thoughts. It would be a wondrous, as well as a bitter thing, if God used her to save this heathen child's life when she had not been able to do anything but watch her own baby die.

Unfortunately, no matter what her thoughts, she could not spend her day hiding inside her tent. Whether or not she wanted to see him again, Jake Hargrove was out there and he'd naturally want to know about the baby.

Elizabeth pulled the blankets closer to the sleeping infant before she tried to smooth back her hair. Maybe she could slip around to the wagon without being seen and get her mirror. She didn't want anyone accusing her of being untidy again. Maybe if she rubbed her cheeks with a damp cloth, the color on her face would even out, as well.

When Elizabeth opened the flaps to her tent, she could see that Jake wasn't the one frying the pork. There was a layer of frost on the ground and someone had hollowed out a place in the dirt to build a cooking fire, even though the blackened ashes from her own fire were only a few feet away.

Elizabeth didn't recognize the man who crouched by the fire's coals, although he was wearing the usual army uniform so he clearly belonged to the fort. She took a quick look at the ground around him and didn't see any signs of his belongings. She did see that the man had a coffeepot settled at the edge of the fire and was heating a rock that looked as if it had some biscuits warming on it.

She took a deep breath. The coffee didn't have the faintly bitter smell of green coffee, either. That's what she usually smelled around the fort. No, this was the kind of coffee a man would buy special in the mercantile. That soldier had probably been hoarding that bit of coffee for months. And now he was celebrating something.

Elizabeth frowned. The only thing around here to celebrate was his new camp. Why—she drew in her breath as she finally understood. That man wanted her place. Elizabeth's needs had been pushed aside by others all of her life, and she'd accepted it. But now that she'd been cheated out of death too, something rose up inside of her. She refused to be pushed any longer. She didn't care what her hair looked like.

"This spot's taken," Elizabeth said as she stepped out of her tent. The canvas had kept the frost away from the ground inside, but the icy cold outside made her gasp when her foot touched the ground. She had worn a hole in her left shoe from all of the walking she'd done on the way here and the cold went right through her stocking. She saw her breath come out in white puffs again today.

But she ignored all of that. As cold as she was on the outside, she felt a growing heat inside. For all this man knew, she was still dying. People needed to wait for the dead to be finished with their business before they took everything from them. She liked the spot where she was camped; she intended to keep it.

"If you're planning to set up a camp, you might try a little farther down the ravine. There are more cottonwoods and dry thistle down there anyway so it will be easier for fires and all." Elizabeth forced herself to smile. If she stood in one place, the ground under her shoes grew a little warmer.

"I'm not setting up camp." The man stood up indignantly. His nose was red from the chill of the morning and his hair was slicked back with some kind of grease. He looked vaguely familiar. "I'm cooking you breakfast."

"Me?" Elizabeth was astonished. She forgot all about her manners and her cold feet. "Whatever for?"

What would possess the man to do something like that? No one had ever cooked breakfast for her, not even the morning after she'd given birth to Rose. Maybe the doctor had decided she was going to die after all and this soldier had been sent to prepare her last meal. Really, that was no way to break the news to a person.

"Who told you to cook me breakfast? That doctor?"

"Nobody told me to do it. I just know women like to have breakfast cooked for them once in a while."

The man smiled, even though he didn't look too happy.

Elizabeth took a closer look at him. The man had shaved this morning. It wasn't Sunday. Outside of God's day, the men at the fort only shaved for special occasions like Christmas, the occasional dance and, of course—funerals.

She swore she'd never listen to a doctor again. The man couldn't even keep a proper log of days. He had probably lost track of time and, when he recalculated, discovered his error.

"I'm still dying, aren't I? Just tell me the truth. I won't make a fuss."

Elizabeth braced herself even though it was what she had suspected all along.

"No one's dying. The doctor told me you were as healthy today as you've ever been in your life."

Elizabeth wasn't really listening to the man anymore. She was looking around. The man cooking breakfast wasn't the only soldier here. There were actually several soldiers standing to the left of her. They'd been hidden from her view when she was in the tent. They were certainly standing quietly. And they all seemed to be carrying big, tall bunches of dried weeds.

"Is something wrong?" Elizabeth asked. Surely, the men would be worrying about their rifles and not those weeds if something was really wrong.

The first man in the line stepped forward. The gold penny buttons on his uniform were all in place and his posture was straight. He'd recently shaved, as well. She could tell that by the whiteness of his skin where his beard had once been.

Surely the doctor wouldn't lie about whether she was expected to live.

"I was hoping you'd like these flowers," the man said as he handed her what looked like dried cottontails. Then he took a deep breath and recited something he'd obviously memorized. "They should be roses to match the roses in your cheeks."

The man gave an abrupt bow and turned to the side.

"But Rose is—" Elizabeth swallowed. She hadn't even said the name aloud since Rose died. She'd scratched it in the dirt several times when her longing had overcome her, but she'd never spoken it again until now. "That's my daughter's name."

The men weren't listening.

"Roses aren't fair enough to compare to your loveliness," the second man said as he thrust another bunch of weeds in her direction. At least, he'd had the foresight to tuck in a little sage so it smelled better. "I'm saving to buy some land when I finish up here at the fort. I've got prospects. This is going to be cattle country soon. You'll see."

The third man stepped forward.

Elizabeth finally realized what was happening. "You can't be here *courting* me."

She wouldn't have been more surprised if they had shown up to tar and feather her. She supposed it was flattering, but— "I'm afraid there's been some misunderstanding. I'm not—that is, my husband and my baby, Rose—they're, well…"

Elizabeth gave up and pointed. Surely they could see the mound of fresh dirt near the edge of the ravine. She had carried over the biggest rock she could find to mark the place so the grave wouldn't be lost in the vast expanse of land here. But now that she looked again, it didn't seem as if it would be enough. The weather here would wear the rock down or someone would move it not knowing what it was.

The third man took off his hat. "It's sorry I am for your loss, but I was hoping you'd be willing to be my wife."

"Your wife! But I don't even know you."

Never, in all of the years that Elizabeth had longed for a family, had she imagined that a man she didn't even know would want to marry her. It didn't seem quite decent, somehow. Matthew had taken her to church for months before he proposed. That was the way civilized men courted their wives.

Elizabeth hadn't seen Jake coming toward her until he was suddenly there. The sight of him, standing so solid before her was reassuring. He might have surprised her yesterday, but today he felt like safety itself. At least he could explain that she was not looking for a husband.

"Tell them," Elizabeth said to Jake. She could hardly think of what to say so she just gestured to the men.

"You're going about it all wrong," Jake said to the men. "She sets a great deal of importance to names. You might want to introduce yourself before you propose."

"Well, it takes more than a name to—" Elizabeth stopped as she looked up at Jake for the first time. "Surely no one expects me to get married *now*."

Elizabeth didn't know what to do. Maybe Jake didn't understand the problem completely. She was going to explain it, but she noticed he had changed out of his buckskins and stood before her in a blue shirt and black wool pants. It didn't seem right that the blue dye of the shirt should match his eyes so exactly. And, the color was evenly spread so she knew someone had used dyer's woad to get the blue. It had probably been one of those big factories that dyed the cloth, but it was the same process and it looked good. Not that the man probably knew anything about how his shirt was made. Men never did.

Elizabeth noticed her breathing was betraying her again as she looked at him. She realized she was actually gawking at the man.

"I could still be dying," she finally muttered and then turned to face the soldiers. It wasn't all she'd meant to say, but that piece of information alone should put the men off the idea of marriage. "The doctor could be wrong. It's a bad death—influenza. I'd probably pass it along to any man I…ah…married."

There. Elizabeth crossed her arms. She'd said enough. She'd be left in peace.

Jake should have realized what would happen. He'd gone to beg some hot water off the blacksmith so he could shave again without needing to build a fire and, when he had gotten back, he'd seen the men. He wouldn't have taken so long, but he had a new razor strap and he felt a wedding proposal deserved a careful shave. While he was gone, the men had gathered.

He knew right away what that meant. It hadn't taken long for word to get around that the woman was going to live. There weren't many women at the fort and it wasn't often an opportunity to marry presented itself to these soldiers. If the men hadn't been so scared of the fever, they would have been lined up to court Elizabeth before now.

Jake couldn't blame them for taking any chance they could. He knew how tired a man got of his own company. He just wished they were not lining up for this particular woman. Jake could see the men looking at each other and wondering if the doctor really had miscalculated how long it would take for someone to come down with the fever.

"I can't marry one of them," Elizabeth said as she turned to Jake. Her eyes were wide. "I've never even seen most of them until this morning. They're absolute strangers."

Jake wished he could ease the panic he saw in Elizabeth's eyes, but he knew he wasn't going to. "Given that you've known me a bit longer, maybe you should marry me instead."

She just stared at him as if she hadn't heard him right. Jake figured he better add some more persuasion. "You're going to have to do something before winter comes anyway."

Jake could hear Elizabeth's breathing as she considered his words. He'd heard the same shallow breaths from wild horses that had been corralled for the first time. He would have put his hand on her arm to soothe her, but he thought it would have done the opposite.

"But what if she does get sick?" one of the soldiers called out. "You'd likely die, too, if you married her."

"I'm not worried. She looks healthy enough to me. And pretty, too."

Ah, good, he thought. She wasn't looking so scared now that she was a bit angry again. He found it hard to believe Elizabeth was a widow when she blushed up pink the way she was doing.

"They're right. If the doctor's wrong, I could be dying any day now," Elizabeth said. Jake thought she sounded downright hopeful. "You need someone else for your daughters."

"They're my nieces, not my daughters."

"Oh."

"The doctor's not wrong," he said. She looked so troubled that he decided to reach out to touch her arm anyway; he only pulled back when he saw her move away. "If you're waiting to see if you get the fever, you could wait just as easy if you are a married woman."

"I *am* a married woman. At least, I—I was."

Jake nodded. He'd expected that. She was still in love with her husband. Well, it was probably better that way. All he really needed was someone for the girls. "I'm not asking for myself. It's for the baby."

"I don't need to marry you to help with the baby. Of course I'll help with the baby."

Jake nodded. That was something. "I can't keep the girls here at the fort all winter, though. We have to go back to my place and folks won't understand us living under the same roof and not being married."

Jake didn't add that the girls wouldn't be welcome at the fort. The only Indians at the fort were the Crow scouts and the Sioux who were here against their will. The girls would be treated like captives and he couldn't do that to them. They would have a hard time gaining acceptance with civilians; but they would have no hope of finding it among the soldiers and their families. The girls' tribe had fought General Custer and his men. No army man would forget that defeat soon.

"I could take my tent with me," Elizabeth said.

"You would need to be with the baby at night. The baby can't sleep in your tent when it gets colder." He wondered if the woman had any idea what winters were like here.

Elizabeth nodded. "Still, we don't need to get married."

"The people of Miles City will see it differently."

"I don't care about gossip."

"Neither do I, but Spotted Fawn needs to go to school."

"Ah." Elizabeth nodded.

She still didn't look convinced. And she was looking at him as though there was something lacking in him.

Jake had known a woman from back East would have a hard time with the land out here. But he'd never quite considered that she might have an even harder time with him. He'd changed out of his buckskins, but he knew he didn't look like what an Eastern woman would expect in a husband. Well, he decided, it was best she know the truth about him.

Jake wasn't the man his mother had hoped he would grow up to be. He didn't much care for big cities. Or small ones, either. He was wearing wool now, but he preferred buckskin. Still, he was a fair-minded man and he didn't expect more in a bargain than someone should have to give. "It can just be a piece of paper between us. All I need is someone for the baby."

She was silent.

"My girls, they're good girls."

"Oh, I'm sure they are."

Jake could see he wasn't making progress. Her eyes still seemed drawn to that grave, as if she was afraid the ones who were dead and under the ground could hear what she was saying and would rise up to accuse her of disloyalty.

"It wouldn't need to be a real marriage," Jake made his words even clearer. "You'll be able to get it annulled in the spring if you want."

He'd do whatever she wanted in that regard.

Elizabeth just stood there looking sad. "I just buried my husband. I don't need another one."

As a boy, Jake had watched his father trading pelts. Everyone, no matter their tribe, had something they wanted. A good trader just watched until he figured out what that was. It didn't take long to figure out what Elizabeth really wanted.

"I can make you a marker for that grave if you agree to help me. We can get a good-sized piece of granite sent down from Fort Benton. It'll last forever."

Elizabeth was looking at him now.

"I'm a pretty good carver. I'll set their names on it and anything else you want to say. There won't be a fancier headstone in the whole territory." It was the best he could do.

"Oh." Elizabeth breathed out. "Matthew would like that, but—"

"And an angel. I could carve an angel on the corner of it for your daughter."

Jake hadn't carved anything but letters on his mother's stone. But he whittled some in the evenings and he'd carved shapes of most of the animals around here. He could do an angel.

Elizabeth just stood there, blinking.

"Don't cry," Jake said.

"I never cry," Elizabeth whispered and then took a deep breath. "You have yourself a deal."

Now it was Jake's turn to be surprised into silence.

"You can't marry him," one of the soldiers in line protested. "I haven't had a chance to read you my poetry. I wrote a poem for you and everything."

Elizabeth turned to the soldiers in line and squared her shoulders. "I'm sorry. I haven't thanked any of you properly. You've paid me a great compliment. I'm honored, of course. Could I give you each a jar of sweet pickles? I canned them myself."

"Well, that'd be nice of you," the soldier who had removed his hat said. "I haven't had anything like that since I was back home."

Jake helped Elizabeth hand out four jars of pickles.

After the soldiers left the campsite, Elizabeth turned to Jake. "This marriage—it's only for the baby?"

"I'll bunk down in the lean-to and give the rest of the place to you and the girls."

Elizabeth nodded. "I gave Mr. Miller my oxen in exchange for his promise to bury me when the time comes so—well—I expect him to do what he said. Even if he has to come to your place and get me."

"You don't need Mr. Miller now. You have me."

"Oh." Elizabeth looked at him skeptically. "Are you a God-fearing man, Mr. Hargrove?"

Jake was a little taken back. "Yes."

She still looked suspicious. "The God of the Bible?"

Jake smiled. "Yes."

"Well, then…" She paused as though weighing his words. "Do you promise to dig the burying hole yourself?"

"If that's what you want."

"I don't want any easy promises here. I know I can't come back and make sure you've done that particular job properly so I'd be relying on your word. I want you to dig the hole yourself and do it with prayer in your heart."

"You've got my word." Jake had seen peace pipes passed with less resolve than Elizabeth showed. "I'll take care of you in good times and bad times. Dead or alive."

"When I go, I'll want to be buried beside my baby."

"I'll see to it. I'll even leave room on the headstone for all three of you."

Elizabeth nodded. "Then I think we should ask for the oxen back."

Jake knew a battle could be lost if a man didn't act quickly to secure his victory. "I'll get the oxen and then we'll head out. I know the minister in Miles City. The Reverend Olson. He'll say the words for us."

"Matthew and I never did get as far as Miles City. But I heard they had a fine preacher there. Mr. Miller promised to ask the man to come and say a few words over my grave when I—you know—" Elizabeth nodded to the grave "—when I died—which I guess isn't going to be as soon as I thought."

Elizabeth pressed her lips together firmly.

Jake hoped that meant she was accepting her new life. "The reverend's a good man."

"If we're going to see him about getting married, I'd like to have some time alone with him before I take my vows."

Jake figured that meant she wasn't accepting her new life at all. She was probably going to ask the minister about her funeral. He didn't know what the Reverend Olson would think when Jake rode into town with a bride who was more intent on her funeral than she was on getting married to him.

Of course, she probably wouldn't be content with just talking to the reverend about her worries. She might mention it to anyone who would listen until finally even the old trappers would hear about it. They'd have a fine time telling about the woman who'd rather go to her own funeral than marry up with Jake Hargrove.

Oh, well, Jake told himself with a wry grin; he never was one to begrudge others a good laugh around their evening fires. He just hoped they got a few things straight. Like the fact that his bride's eyes were some of the most beautiful eyes a man was likely to see this side of the Missouri. He hadn't expected that. They reminded him of the moss that grew on the side of those ponderosa pines high in the mountains where he'd lived as a boy.

Being married, even temporarily, to a woman with eyes like that couldn't be all bad. He'd just have to think of ways to keep her happy until she decided to leave. Even his mother had taken a few months to judge this land before she decided that she hated it. His mother might have gone longer before making her decision if she'd had something to distract her. Women always liked new clothes. Maybe he should buy the woman a new dress to match those eyes of hers.

And a pretty brooch. His mother had set great store by her few jewels. Jake stopped himself. He wondered if he should offer to pay the woman outright. Eastern women were touchy about money, but even he wasn't so sure about paying a woman to marry him. Of course, he'd see that she had plenty of money for her trouble; he'd panned a modest amount of gold in the Black Hills southeast of here this past spring so he had enough. But it just didn't seem right somehow to bring up money quite yet.

Chapter Three

There was a cluster of cottonwood trees leading into the small town of Miles City. The trees were slender and not rooted very deep in the gray alkali soil, but they gave some relief from the vast emptiness that seemed to echo back and forth in this part of the territories. Elizabeth hadn't been prepared for all of this vastness. It felt as though God could look right down and see her, not because He was searching her out, but just because there was so little else in sight. Well, if He wanted to look, she couldn't stop Him. It did make her nervous, though.

She sat on the wagon seat next to Jake. It had rained some on the way here and the dampness had turned the ground dark. It wasn't wet enough to slow down the wagon wheels, though, so Elizabeth had been holding the baby in her arms to protect the little one from the worst of the jostling as they bumped along the rough road. She looked down and smiled.

Elizabeth might not want God looking at her, but she was glad He knew about the baby. She adjusted the blanket covering the infant and, when she looked up again,

Jake had turned the oxen team slightly to enter the town and she could see the main street for the first time.

The trip to Miles City had been slow. Jake had his horse tied to the back of the wagon, and Spotted Fawn had ridden her pony as far away from the wagon as she could while still riding with them.

"Why, it's full of people." Elizabeth couldn't believe it. There were people everywhere and dozens of wagon wheels had made tracks down the street. Her first feeling was relief that she and Matthew hadn't come through this town before he got the fever.

Matthew had everything so well planned. He'd told her it would be okay if he started his store by selling things from the back of their wagon. He figured most of the buildings would be thrown together with bits of canvas and mud-chinked logs so people would not expect to shop in a regular mercantile as they would if they were back East.

But Matthew had been wrong. There were no canvas and rough-hewn huts to be seen. The frame buildings were neatly painted and laid out on two sides of something called Richmond Square. There was even a sign naming the place. That meant someone had money. Miles City was not like the gold-mining towns Matthew had heard about that were thrown together haphazardly because everyone was looking for gold. The gnarled branches of the cottonwoods weren't the kind of trees used to make the plank boards in these buildings.

"Somebody hauled in a lot of lumber." Elizabeth wondered if maybe the town had been rough earlier, but had grown up without Matthew hearing about it.

Jake nodded. "It came in on the steamboats. I brought some of the lumber down from Fort Benton myself. I was going to add onto my place, but I gave it to the school instead."

Elizabeth was glad no one could see the flannel union suits and unbleached muslin Matthew had packed so hopefully in the bottom of their wagon.

"We couldn't afford to take a steamboat," she said. "Not with all the goods Matthew wanted to bring. That's why he got us our wagon. Fortunately, we found a few other wagons still going this way, so we came together."

Elizabeth wondered what she would do with all of the things Matthew had packed in that wagon. Most of it was rough fabrics with little value. The best cloth they had was the red calico cotton she'd dyed herself. It was one of the few things in the bottom of the wagon that truly belonged to her.

Most people wouldn't even have attempted what she'd done, but an old woman had told Elizabeth about the dye process and she'd decided to try it. She liked the name of it—Turkey red oil-boiled dye. It had all sounded so grand and exotic.

She'd been pregnant at the time and wanted some bright red yarn so she could knit a blanket for their baby's first Christmas. Matthew had said it was foolish to give a present to a baby, but she didn't think so. Most of the reds that were dyed in other ways would fade or bleed with each washing and she wanted a blanket that would hold its color for generations to come. She had pictured her baby showing the blanket to his or her own baby in the distant future and telling the little one that Grandma had made the red blanket for a very special Christmas years ago.

A lone rider passed their wagon and Elizabeth was jolted out of her memories. She'd gotten so caught up in thinking about the Christmas yarn that she'd forgotten that her whole reason for making it was now gone. She had no family. No husband to worry about pleasing. She had no use for a red blanket that held its color for generations.

Her life had changed once again and an unbleached gray was enough to mark her endless days. She was sure she could sell the red yarn, and the fabric she'd dyed, too, but she doubted there would be much of a market for the other things she and Matthew had brought west. The people walking in and out of the stores here were not wearing poor clothes. It was mostly men walking around, but there were women, too. And they were clearly used to getting good fabrics.

Matthew hadn't had the money to buy any but the lowest quality. He thought that, by the time people demanded better goods, he would have the money to buy them. His heart would have been broken if he had lived to see his dream fall apart.

Nothing was turning out the way they had planned, Elizabeth told herself as she looked away from the busy street and back at the man sitting beside her on the wagon seat.

She couldn't believe she was going to marry this man. She still felt married to Matthew.

She, Jake and the girls had left the fort before midday. She had put everything back in the wagon and Jake had managed to convince Mr. Miller to return the oxen that were now pulling it. The blacksmith had even thrown in a bag of oats for good wishes on their life together. Elizabeth hadn't known what to say when the man carried out the oats so she'd unpacked six jars of her best canned green beans and given them to him in appreciation.

Jake grunted as he turned and motioned for Spotted Fawn to come closer.

Then he turned to Elizabeth. "This town gets busier every day. Someone put up that hotel hoping that the railroad will stop here. All of the surveying the army is doing has people on edge wondering what route the railroad will take when it comes this way. I tell people it's years away, but no one knows for sure."

Elizabeth thought Jake wanted to say more about the railroad, but he didn't do it so she kept looking around. She noticed that the hotel was only one of several two-story buildings on the street. The rain had turned the top of the ground into a thick mud. Several horses and a buggy were making their way through the street. The wheels didn't sink in far, but the boots of the men walking seemed to pick up a layer of mud.

"Maybe Matthew could have gotten a job clerking in one of these places," Elizabeth said looking down the length of the street. In her heart, though, she knew he would have refused to work for someone else. He would have given up. They would have been even poorer here than they had been back in Kansas. She would have had to take in laundry again and there would have been no one to watch the baby while she lifted the tubs of scalding water.

The laundry itself would have been difficult, too. No one seemed to be wearing simple clothes. The woman hurrying across the street in front of them was holding up skirts that showed lace-trimmed petticoats. Ruffles like that required a hot iron at the end of it all. And the skirt over the petticoats looked as if it was made of blue French serge. It would take extra brushing to keep the double weave looking nice. And no one wanted to pay extra for any of it.

A modest blue hat sat atop the woman's brilliant copper hair. Elizabeth looked at the hair closely. The hair was so colorful she wondered, at first, if it had been dyed with henna. But surely the woman could not get those tones with the dye, so the hair must be natural. Elizabeth almost envied her until the woman lifted her head and finally saw Elizabeth and Jake. The woman glanced up with a vague smile, but as she looked fully at Jake, her expression turned to shock and then to an indignant frown. Elizabeth wondered if the woman was angry with them for some reason, but she hurried off before Elizabeth could ask Jake about her.

"I'll send a note down to the reverend while we buy a few things at the store," Jake said as he slowed the wagon.

Elizabeth forced her attention back to the man beside her. "Oh, you don't need to do that—buy anything, I mean. Not for me."

"You'll still need things for the girls. Dresses and all."

Elizabeth wondered if Jake knew how much things like that cost. A man who wore buckskin wasn't likely to know how dear fabric was. If it was gingham or calico, the price might not be too bad. But a twill silk or French serge material was impossible. Still, it was nice of him to think of what they needed. It was more than Matthew had ever done. "I know how to get by. We won't need much that's store-bought."

"I want the girls to look like ladies."

"Surely they won't need to—" Elizabeth stumbled when she saw she was giving offense. "Not because they're Indian girls. That's not what I meant."

"They have white blood in them, too. Red Tail was half-white."

"Of course. It's just that they're only girls."

"I want them to have the best dresses possible. We'll order from San Francisco if we have to."

Elizabeth nodded. Now she'd gotten his pride involved. He was probably going to spend money on dresses that they should be saving for winter food. But she knew men well enough to know that she'd only make matters worse by continuing to press him on it. She would sew the dresses herself, of course, and she'd only pick out the cheaper fabrics. Maybe she could even use some of the muslin they had in the wagon. The bark of an oak tree made a light yellow dye that would set the muslin well and the girls wouldn't even notice the material wasn't store-bought.

"You should get a new dress, too," Jake added. "Maybe something in a deep moss green to match your eyes."

She didn't have any dyes that went to a deep green. She had the leavings of some indigo that she could mix with wood ash to make black, but she'd have to buy bolted material to have any kind of a green. "I'd rather have some tea. And maybe a lid to cover my pan so I can steep it properly."

Tea was cheaper and more to her liking than color-pressed fabric anyway. She'd had the luxury of real tea for a week or so now. A tin of it had been left on the seat of her wagon one morning with the hardtack. She hadn't been able to brew it properly because she only had an open pan to hold it, but she'd enjoyed it immensely. Her conviction that she was dying had made her reckless and she'd used more of the tea than she had intended so she didn't have much left.

Elizabeth felt Jake pull the wagon to a complete halt in front of a building with a large sign that read The Broadwater, Bubbel and Company Mercantile. The store was fronted by a small section of wooden walkway and she could look right into the windows. She had never seen so much merchandise, not even in any of the stores she'd gone to back in Kansas. She was glad she was still wearing her gray silk dress even though she didn't have a proper hat to wear with it.

Jake jumped off the wagon and walked around to take the baby. He slipped the baby into his fur sling before reaching up with the other arm to offer Elizabeth help in stepping down from the wagon. Elizabeth was grateful for the assistance, more to impress anyone who might be watching them than because she needed the help. If they were going to do business in this town, Elizabeth wanted them to look respectable.

The warm smell of spices greeted Elizabeth when she walked through the door that Jake had opened for her. This time Elizabeth didn't want to take any chances on unintentionally offending someone. She smiled at the woman behind the counter. She did not get a smile back. Spotted Fawn had not come in with them so Elizabeth wondered if it was the Indian baby that was causing the upset look in the woman's eyes.

But that couldn't be right, Elizabeth told herself. The furs covered the little one so completely that no one could even tell a baby rested in Jake's arms. The woman was definitely staring at the furs, though. She must have been watching them through the windows.

"Good afternoon, Annabelle," Jake said.

The woman did not answer. Her skin was flushed and her chin defiant. Her face looked kind, even if her eyes were braced for battle and focused on a spot to the right of the doorway. She was past middle-aged and some gray showed in the light brown hair she wore pulled back into a bun. Her white blouse was freshly pressed and her black wool skirt was proper.

Elizabeth thought the other woman wasn't going to answer Jake, but finally she did.

"Good afternoon to you, as well."

Only then did the woman meet Elizabeth's eyes.

Elizabeth forced herself to smile. Even if the woman wouldn't want to socialize with them for some reason, surely she would be polite. And, if Elizabeth were even more polite in return, the woman would need to continue answering back.

"You have a good store here. Your shelves are completely full. I see coffee and spices. Flour, too," Elizabeth said. "You must be proud."

The store looked well enough stocked to meet anyone's needs. The front counters, showcase and shelves were a dark wood made shiny from repeated rubdowns. To the left, there was a tobacco cutter. Behind the woman there were tins of face powder and hand mirrors with matching brushes. A cracker barrel stood in front of the case. A few leather-bound books lay on the top of the counter.

Farther back, Elizabeth saw a tin of tea that was the same kind that had been left at her wagon. Beside it was a china teapot with lovely pink roses painted on its side.

"It's not my store. I just clerk here," the woman said stiffly.

"Still, you must make recommendations and I can't think of anything your shelves are lacking."

"We do have a good selection," the woman admitted. By now her face looked pale as though she needed to force herself to stand by her words. "For our better customers."

Elizabeth could see Jake's jaw clench.

"I didn't know you had different kinds of customers," Jake said.

Annabelle was silent for a minute. "Your friends were here this morning, after you left."

"Higgins and Wells?"

Annabelle looked miserable, but determined. "Our other customers complained."

"I know they can be a little loud," Jake said. "But I've never known them to mean anyone harm."

The store clerk's face tightened.

"I...ah—" Elizabeth tried to think of something to say to relieve the tension "—I am surprised to see such a fine store. Back in Kansas, we hadn't expected to see something like this way out here. My husband would have—"

Elizabeth faltered to a stop, but then continued. "My husband wanted to own a store like this someday."

Annabelle took her eyes off Jake and turned them toward Elizabeth. Something flickered in the woman's eyes, but she didn't say anything.

Jake looked at the shelves behind the counter and then turned to the clerk. "We need to buy a wedding ring."

Oh, dear, Elizabeth thought. She was not sure she could marry another man who wanted to spend money so freely. She accepted that she would be the one responsible for providing most of the food and clothing. She had always had to do for herself and those around her. But cash money was hard to come by and she didn't like to see it slip away no matter who had worked for it.

"I don't need a new ring," Elizabeth whispered as she leaned closer to Jake. She had no desire to embarrass him in front of the store clerk, but they needed to come to some understanding. "We can use the one I already have."

"I won't use your husband's ring."

Elizabeth watched as the clerk turned to look for something on the shelf behind the counter. Elizabeth figured the woman was giving them some privacy. She smoothed down the skirt of her dress.

"The ring was my mother's," Elizabeth murmured quietly. She'd been given it at her parents' funeral and had kept it all the years since. Matthew had been relieved that he didn't need to buy a ring for her. "And it's an expense that we don't need."

Elizabeth watched Annabelle turn around and set a tray on the counter. The woman's face softened slightly as she studied Elizabeth. "You're that woman, aren't you? The one out by the fort who lost her husband and baby?"

Elizabeth gave a jerky nod. So that was the problem. "The doctor says I'm past the time of getting the fever, though. You don't need to worry."

The woman reached over and set her hand on Elizabeth's arm. "I felt so sorry for you. I sent a tin of tea out with one of the soldiers. I hope you got it. Tea always soothes me when I don't feel good."

Elizabeth relaxed. Maybe the woman was just cautious with strangers. Or maybe Jake's friends had upset other customers by cursing or something. It was likely a misunderstanding of sorts. Annabelle seemed to be a nice person.

"That tea was such a lovely gift," Elizabeth said as

she smiled at the other woman. "I don't know when I've had tea that I've enjoyed as much. I had some sassafras bark in the wagon with me, but I used most of it up when my husband was sick."

Elizabeth didn't think she'd ever be able to drink sassafras tea again without picturing Matthew dying. Even the smell of it made her feel ill.

The woman nodded. "That tea was from England. We got it with our last shipment."

Elizabeth thought the woman was going to say something more, but instead she glanced up at Jake and all of the friendliness in her face drained away. She looked worried and afraid.

Jake didn't see it because he was looking down at the rings, but Elizabeth did.

"We'll want a gold ring, of course." Jake was looking at the tray of rings the woman had set on the counter. Dozens of rings were lined up in shiny rows.

Annabelle bit her lip and, when she didn't move, Jake looked up.

"Perhaps you would care to wait outside while she tries on the rings," Annabelle suggested softly.

Elizabeth could see the woman had needed to brace herself to say those words.

"Some women like to try on several," Annabelle added as her face flushed.

Jake nodded, although he looked doubtful. "I guess I should see about sending that note to the reverend anyway. Otherwise he'll probably leave the schoolhouse before we get there."

The store clerk watched Jake walk out of the store and close the door before she turned to Elizabeth.

"I can't let you do this," the woman whispered in a

rush. She had bright spots of color on her cheeks. "I'm a widow, too. I know what it's like. And he is a striking man. But, surely you're not so desperate that you'll marry him."

Elizabeth stiffened. "I know it's unusual. And I haven't known him long, but he seems like a good, God-fearing man."

Elizabeth saw no need to tell Annabelle about the arrangement she and Jake had made.

Annabelle pursed her lips. "A man like him needs to fear God a little more if you ask me."

A man like what? Elizabeth wondered. "If it's the girls. I know they are Indians, but I understand that Mr. Hargrove is not. Besides, I believe we are all God's creatures."

Elizabeth knew that was stretching the truth. She wasn't sure what she thought about God and the Indians. But she wasn't going to admit that to a stranger in this town where the girls needed acceptance. She owed them that much loyalty at least.

"It's not the girls. It's him."

"Oh." Elizabeth felt herself go cold. "What do you mean?"

"I mean he's a *wolfer.*" Annabelle's lips deepened in a disapproving line. "At least those friends of his are. They were in today and, well, it's no conversation for a lady. It's disgusting what they do. Even the Indians are better."

Elizabeth swallowed. "He mentioned that he had done some prospecting for gold and some trapping."

The woman nodded grimly. "The trapping days have been over for years. Even the buffalo are thinning out. What trappers that are left have turned to wolfing. His friends wanted to put in an order for that poison—

strychnine—this morning. A big bag of it. I told them no. As though we'd carry that. They kill a buffalo and sprinkle the dead animal with it."

"Oh, dear, you're sure?"

The woman nodded. "I used to think that the one, Higgins, was a good God-fearing man. A little rough in his manners maybe, but he told me he prays and—he even asked if he could walk me home from church if he came someday. I said yes, but then—"

The woman crossed her arms. "Then he started bragging about how he can poison up to sixty wolves in one night the way they do it. And no holes in the pelts, either, so they get top dollar on the furs. All they do is go out and pick up the dead wolves the next morning. With unblemished pelts just like the folks back East want them."

Annabelle paused and looked a little sad. "He's got all the money he needs now, of course. But…to die of strychnine poisoning. Even for a wolf, well, I simply can't condone it. The convulsions. The foaming at the mouth. Besides, other animals die, too—it's not just the wolves. And, birds. I love birds, even the vultures. It's not fair to the animals, they don't have a chance."

"Oh, dear." Elizabeth couldn't believe it. She hadn't known Jake for long, but he didn't seem like a cruel man. She had a bit of poison in her wagon, of course. All dyers did. The indigo leavings used to make a strong black dye were poisonous. She was careful with it, though, and always kept it in a lidded jar so no animal could mistakenly eat it.

"Jake lives out there on Dry Creek by those friends of his. I talked to the manager and he agrees with me. I'm not going to sell the men poison. Decent folks are trying to make Miles City a good place to live. There's talk all the time that someday the railroad representatives will come to town and look us over. I don't want to be selling strychnine to wolfers when that happens."

"So it's not the girls?"

The woman shook her head and then gave a small smile. "Folks around here might shoot an Indian, but they'd spit on a wolfer. If they had the nerve, that is."

"Oh."

"I'm just giving you a word of caution."

"I'm grateful."

Elizabeth realized she was in trouble. She wanted to help the baby, but she didn't see how she could marry someone like Jake. Even if the marriage wasn't real, she would be out there alone with him and the girls— and his wolfer friends. What if they put poison in her tea some morning? She had been willing to die, but she didn't want to be murdered.

"I don't suppose there's any jobs available in town."

The woman frowned. "Virginia Parker got a job recently working at the saloon down the street, playing piano."

"Oh, I couldn't work in a saloon. What decent woman could?"

"I'll not hear anything said about Virginia. She's a fine young woman. There's just not much work around here and most of it's in the saloons."

"Surely there are other jobs. I could teach a little school. Not Latin or anything fancy. But I'm good with numbers."

"The Reverend Olson already teaches school. He even knows Latin. But, between that and his preaching, he barely makes enough to keep body and soul together for him and his wife. The town hasn't exactly gotten around to paying anyone for the school yet. The parents are going to meet to see what they can do about it. My son, Thomas, goes to the school."

"I wouldn't need to make much. It's only me to support."

"Could you sew enough to be a dressmaker?"

"If the styles were simple."

The woman shook her head. "You'd need ruffles and hoops to please this crowd. Most of the regular women make their own dresses. It's the women in the saloons— not Virginia, of course, but the other women—they are the ones willing to pay someone to make dresses for them. But they want French lace and that new kind of shimmering braid they've been asking for. In silver and gold both, mind you. We stock some of the best silks in the world just for them. But, what's a good fabric if the thing doesn't fit right? A handy seamstress could make a good living if she knew fashion."

"I could learn. I'd just need to buy some patterns."

"We don't have any of the new styles yet. The owner hasn't even sent off for them. We have some old ones, of course, but—"

"Oh, well. I suppose I could take in laundry for a while." Elizabeth squared her shoulders. She'd do that if she had to and keep the Indian baby with her for the winter. "I'm used to washing men's shirts and woolens."

The woman shook her head. "Sam Lee does that. You may have seen the sign on your way into town— Good Washing and Fireworks Here? He's a Chinaman who docs thc laundry for most of the town. He'd be hard to beat."

Elizabeth heard the door to the mercantile open.

"Who'd be hard to beat?" Jake asked as he walked inside and up to the counter. He had the baby in the sling next to his chest. He didn't know what had Annabelle in such a contrary mood, but she couldn't have picked a worse time. He'd come to know her because she went to church most Sundays just as he did. He'd always thought her to be a sensible woman and Higgins had praised her extravagantly the last time Jake had shared their evening fire.

Maybe that was the problem.

"I don't suppose it's Higgins?" Jake asked Annabelle directly. Higgins had been a trapper for decades, as Jake's father had been. The man was said to have wrestled a grizzly once and gone back to chopping wood afterward as if like there had been nothing to it. But for all of the man's courage, he had even less of an idea about how to act around refined women than Jake did.

"I was speaking of the man who does the laundry," the store clerk said stiffly. "Mr. Higgins is none of my concern."

"All right then," Jake said slowly. That should be good, he thought. He turned to Elizabeth. "Did you find a ring that fit?"

"Not quite." Elizabeth hesitated. "Maybe we could use my mother's ring until we find exactly what we want."

Jake searched Elizabeth's face. "If you're sure. Most women like new things."

Something was wrong. Annabelle had stared at his shoulder most of the time she was talking to him and Elizabeth could barely look him in the eye. He supposed she was finally realizing what she was about to do. Not that he could blame her. He knew he had no business marrying someone like her and dragging her into the problems he'd probably have with the people of this town.

Of course, why would that make Annabelle so unfriendly? Maybe it did have something to do with Higgins instead.

"Higgins didn't propose to you, did he?" Jake suddenly asked. Annabelle had been in town for several months now. Her husband had been a miner over by Helena until he'd been shot and killed. But maybe she'd lived back East before that. "I know things are different out here. Most men don't feel they have the time to spend courting, so they just get to the point. But they don't mean any harm by it."

Jake figured he was speaking for himself as well as his friend.

"Mr. Higgins most certainly did not propose," Annabelle protested. Her face had gone a bright pink and she looked indignant. "He knows better than that. He's never even come calling. I'm a widow in mourning. A decent women wouldn't—" Annabelle stopped and looked at Elizabeth. "Oh. I didn't mean—"

Elizabeth waved the words away. "Don't worry about it."

Jake didn't know what had happened to his Elizabeth. All of her indignation was gone. She looked tired. For the first time, he felt the urge to put his arm around her shoulders. He didn't deserve this woman, but he did plan to protect her with all of his might. The problem was he wasn't exactly sure how to protect her from the discouragement Annabelle was causing her.

"You won't need to see Higgins if you don't want to," Jake said quietly to Elizabeth. "I usually just go over and sit with him and Wells at their place anyway."

It was probably best if he kept his old trapper friends away from her.

He could see Elizabeth straighten her shoulders. "Your friends will always be welcome at your home. I wouldn't stand in their way. It's your house."

"It will be your house, too."

Now that they were talking about it, Jake wondered what Elizabeth would think of his house. They were mentioning it as though it was a grand place, but it wasn't. It wasn't even really a house. He supposed it would be considered a cabin if a man were generous in his judging. Jake had given all the smooth lumber he had to the school when they were building that. He was due to get lumber in return when the school had some money, but he planned to let the debt pass. The children needed books more than he needed a better cabin, especially since it was just him.

Jake stopped himself. Of course, he wasn't alone anymore. He had his nieces and now this woman. The next thing, he'd be getting a dog. He should have built a better place. But, it was too late now. The smooth lumber was gone and his cabin already built.

He had used the logs from some of the cottonwood trees that trailed along the Dry Creek when he built his place. The logs weren't big enough to make a full cabin like they made back East. Folks here dug a trench and put the logs in it upright and then chinked it all together with mud, lime and twigs. They'd done that at the fort. Still, he'd put in a window of real glass opposite the fireplace when he could have just stretched a greased deerskin over the opening. He hadn't bothered with a proper floor, though. Instead, he'd packed the earth down and spread some buffalo hides around.

What had looked to him like a snug home for wintering would not appeal to a woman who'd known better. He was a fool if he thought otherwise. Maybe Annabelle had heard about the house from Higgins and warned Elizabeth about it. Something was upsetting the woman he was planning to marry.

This time Jake did put his arm around Elizabeth's shoulder. Her muscles were tight. He couldn't tell if it was because she was forcing herself to stand there without pulling away or because she was trying not to give in to his embrace. Neither thought comforted him much.

"I don't need your house. I still have my wagon," Elizabeth said as she pulled away slightly and then turned around to start walking out of the store. "Thank you for your help, Annabelle. I appreciate it."

The other woman nodded. "Stop by any time and God's best to you."

Well, if that didn't beat everything, Jake thought. If he'd heard right, his bride was still thinking about wintering in that wagon of hers instead of in his cabin. That didn't make any sense at all, not even for an Eastern woman who didn't know these parts. He still had some things to buy before he left the store. Maybe if he gave her some time alone, the woman he was going to marry would tell him what was wrong.

Elizabeth wondered what she was going to do. She opened the door and took another good look at the streets of Miles City. There were no Help Wanted signs in any of the windows. Maybe the preacher would have some words of advice.

Elizabeth was glad Jake had stayed in the store after she went out on the street. She needed to think. There was a bit of a breeze outside, but Elizabeth scarcely noticed it. The woman with the red hair and blue serge skirt was standing in front of a store on the other side of the street. She had her head bent and was furiously talking to two other women who were both wearing simple calico dresses with sunbonnets. It was good to know there were some plain people in this town. The other women's faces were weathered and pinched.

Whatever the women were upset about, Elizabeth figured it was not as bad as the predicament she was facing. It took a moment for Elizabeth to realize the women across the street had stopped talking and were staring at her. No, it wasn't her. She looked to her left and saw Spotted Fawn.

Jake's niece hadn't moved an inch since Elizabeth first went into the store. Not unless it had been to push farther back into the shadows of the overhang that covered the boardwalk in front of the mercantile. Spotted Fawn might be very still, but she could hardly miss the antagonistic looks those women were sending her.

Elizabeth stepped over to stand beside the girl. "Don't pay them any attention. They're just curious."

Spotted Fawn shrugged. "It does not matter."

Elizabeth recognized that tone of voice. She had said the same kind of words when she was made to feel awkward in her place as the unpaid servant of the houses where she worked back in Kansas. One needed to feel some power in a situation to protest. Without that, a person merely endured.

Just then, Jake came out of the store and started to usher Elizabeth and his niece down the street. He told them they were headed to the schoolhouse.

Elizabeth didn't say anything to Jake about the

women. She told herself that they might have been just curious. And they could have been staring at her more than Spotted Fawn anyway. It wasn't often that a woman who was supposed to be dead came to town to go shopping. Maybe one of them had seen her outside the fort and was worried about the fever. That made sense.

They came to a saloon and Elizabeth happened to glance into the half-draped window. She saw a woman standing beside a piano. Her blond hair was swept up and she was wearing a fresh white blouse and a gray skirt. "That woman works there?"

"Only because Colter is a soft touch. Virginia's brother was one of the soldiers killed a few weeks ago so she needs the work. Her other brother is off somewhere prospecting for gold."

"She's not dressed like I would expect."

Elizabeth wasn't sure, but maybe she could work in this saloon if she were allowed to dress like a decent woman and stay in the back of the place. A couple of used glasses were sitting on the counter as the bartender poured whiskey for some man. "Do they pay someone to wash dishes?"

"Usually there's a kid, Danny, who does that, but he's been in jail for a few days. He stole a man's watch," Jake said as he turned to look at her. "But Colter wouldn't hire you, if that's what you're thinking. A lady doesn't belong in a place like that, especially not washing dishes."

"I'm not a lady. Besides, there's nothing to be ashamed of in washing dishes," she continued. "People are entitled to a clean glass no matter what they're drinking."

Jake was looking at her skeptically. "I'd say a woman is entitled to a wedding ring, too."

Elizabeth didn't have anything to say to that. She

didn't want a new wedding ring. She didn't want a new husband. But, she had to admit, she did want to spend more of her days holding a baby. And she wouldn't mind seeing a smile on Spotted Fawn's face. She wasn't sure what she'd say when the minister asked if she'd take Jake as her husband.

"What do you do for a living?" Elizabeth suddenly asked as she looked up at Jake.

She saw his jaw tighten.

"I'm not a banker, if that's what you're asking," he said. "I don't rightly know what I am. I panned some gold in the Black Hills, though, and I've got enough to stake myself to some cattle when the time is right. This country is changing and I figure that's the next thing for a man to do."

"You don't poison wolves?"

Jake shook his head firmly. "I don't poison anything."

Elizabeth let out the breath she was holding. Well, that was that. Not that he might not have some other dark secret he was hiding, given the friends that he had.

Elizabeth wondered if there would be any witnesses to the marriage if it did take place. She didn't know anyone she could ask to do it. Those women she'd seen staring at them earlier might be following to see what they were doing, but she couldn't ask them. She even refused to look behind her to see if they were following her and Jake.

Elizabeth reached up to pat her hair. She'd washed herself as best as she could in her tent before folding up the canvas and storing it on top of the wagon earlier. She was glad now that she was clean even if she was rumpled. She might not be good enough to go calling on people, but she was wearing her gray dress. It had been suitable in Kansas; it should be good enough for the streets out here.

Those women could stare at her if they wanted, but she dared them to find genuine fault. Her dress was so neatly mended that no one could tell where the spark had settled on the skirt or the seam had parted under the arm. And her hair might be slightly damp from the rain, but it was firmly anchored behind her head in a bun.

Footsteps made their own sound in the mud, but Elizabeth didn't pay any attention to them until she heard someone muttering behind her. She looked back and saw the women she'd seen earlier marching straight toward her.

The women did not wait until they were even with Jake before they started talking.

"Where did you get her?" the woman in the blue skirt demanded of Jake.

Elizabeth was taken aback by the hostility in the woman's voice. They must think she was still carrying the fever. Surely it must be fear that brought out such antagonism. Then she felt Jake tense up beside her. The woman was not looking at Elizabeth; she was looking at Spotted Fawn.

"Good morning, Mrs. Barker," Jake said. "This is my niece."

"She's just a child," Elizabeth added. *Who could be afraid of a child?*

"She's a heathen," Mrs. Barker said as though that settled everything. "She needs to be sent back to her people."

"I am her people," Jake said.

"Nonsense. Anyone can look at her and see she doesn't belong with you. You might have lived with some of those people, but that doesn't make you one of them. Take the girl back to her own kind. She belongs with the other heathens out there." Mrs. Barker vaguely waved her hand to the vast unsettled land outside of town.

"She's not a heathen. She believes in the same God that you and I do," Jake said.

"I doubt that very much. You listen to me and you listen good, Jake Hargrove. This town is no place for her kind. God doesn't want people mixing. Everyone should keep to their own kind. That especially goes for the heathens."

"It doesn't say that in the Bible."

"Well, then, it should. We won't stand for it. Mark my words on that."

The women gathered up their skirts and stomped past them, their skirts all swaying as they went.

Elizabeth watched them walk down the street.

"Sorry about that," Jake muttered.

"It's not your fault."

Elizabeth was angry. Even the women who had looked down their noses at her back in Kansas hadn't been this rude. No one should treat anyone as Mrs. Barker and her friends were doing. Before her recent tragedy, Elizabeth would have shrugged off their behavior. But not anymore. She might be all alone in life once again, but she wasn't going to let those women treat an innocent young girl as if she was a criminal just because they didn't like the color of her skin.

Elizabeth knew enough about dyes to know that a piece of cloth could turn out red or yellow or blue and still be the same fabric, woven on the same loom. Dyeing was just something the maker of a garment did. It didn't make the cloth itself better or worse.

Besides, Spotted Fawn might be an Indian, but she had a family. She had her uncle, Jake. They shared the same blood. He was her people. Elizabeth didn't want to see anything happen to this new family, not if she could help it.

Standing right there, Elizabeth made her decision. She was going to get married. Higgins might put poison in her tea and those women might drive them all out of town, but she'd stand up for Spotted Fawn and the baby until that day. If anyone knew what it was to be all alone at Spotted Fawn's age, Elizabeth did.

"Don't pay them any attention," Elizabeth said in a furious whisper to Spotted Fawn. The girl didn't look as though she'd heard Elizabeth any more than she'd heard the women speaking earlier. If Elizabeth didn't know Spotted Fawn spoke good English, she would have thought the girl hadn't understood what had been said.

They didn't stop walking until Jake brought them to the steps of a white frame building. More humble than the stores and with no walkway out front, the building did have a landing at the top of the steps large enough for a dozen people to stand. They climbed the steps, Jake knocked and a man's voice told them to come inside.

"School is out for the day. The reverend will be expecting us," Jake said as he opened the door.

Spotted Fawn stood to the right of the doorway just as she'd stood beside the door of the mercantile. Elizabeth finally realized the girl didn't feel welcome.

"I hope you'll come inside with us," Elizabeth said to her.

Spotted Fawn made no move.

"You can hold the baby," Elizabeth added softly. "I

don't know if there's any place to lay her down inside. Wait a few minutes and come when Jake comes, please."

Spotted Fawn nodded. "I will come."

"Thank you," Elizabeth said as she turned.

She looked back at Jake. "You said I could have some time with the pastor before—"

Jake nodded.

Elizabeth hoped the pastor had some comfort to give to her. It wasn't right to marry another husband when she hadn't made her peace about losing her first one. Granted, it wasn't a real marriage that Jake was offering. And she'd already decided to do it, even if she had a feeling it would cause more trouble for everyone than they would know what to do with. But, still, she'd like to confess what she was doing to a minister. She hoped he understood about the baby.

Chapter Four

The inside of the schoolhouse smelled of damp wool. The children must have played outside and gotten wet before they left this afternoon. Light streamed in the three windows, two located on each side wall and one by the door. There was a glass-fronted wood case beneath one of the side windows and it held plants and leather-bound books. A map was tacked to the wall beside one potbellied stove. Another small stove sat in the opposite corner. Elizabeth could imagine children being very happy here. She took one step into the room as the man in front stood up from his desk.

"You must be Elizabeth," the man said with a welcoming smile. "I'm Reverend Olson. I got Jake's message that you were coming."

The man walked down the aisle between the rough-hewn log benches. Each bench had a long, thin table in front of it. There were inkwells and small pieces of chalk to show the places where students sat. She supposed the children kept their lead pencils with them; they wouldn't want to lose those.

Jake had kept his word and hadn't followed her inside the schoolhouse so Elizabeth had closed the door behind her.

The reverend stopped when he was a few feet away from her. "I only wish I'd been in town when your family had the fever. I was up at Fort Benton picking up some books I'd ordered for the school."

Elizabeth shrugged. "There's nothing you could have done."

She'd guess the man was about fifty years old. His brown wool suit was well-worn, but his white shirt was crisply ironed. His hair was a thick gray and his eyes looked at her with sympathy.

She didn't want sympathy.

"I could still go with you and pray over the grave if you'd like. If you'd find that comforting."

Elizabeth shook her head. "Maybe later. Jake's going to make a marker. Maybe then it would be good to—" Her voice trailed off. She swallowed, but continued in a whisper. That was all she could manage. "Maybe by then I will be able to do it."

She hadn't realized she'd neglected to give a prayer at the burial. The doctor from the fort had read some scriptures over the grave and he had said a prayer. But Elizabeth had been silent. She hadn't cried, either. Not even after everyone else was gone. She hadn't grieved for the ones she'd lost, she'd merely waited to join them. But now—

The reverend nodded. "It's always hard when someone we love dies."

"They were all I had and God took them away for nothing."

"I know it feels that way."

Elizabeth looked up sharply. "Do you have a wife?"

The reverend nodded.

"Then you don't know how I feel." Her whisper was gone. Anger filled her voice. "I had no family before I married Matthew and now—" she spread her hands "—I was trying to be so good. So careful. But now I'm alone again."

"God is with you," the reverend said.

Elizabeth didn't know what to say.

Reverend Olson smiled encouragingly at her. "I know it's not always easy to see His hand in our lives, but He loves us all the same."

Elizabeth couldn't keep silent. She'd kept the words inside until now, but it all came bubbling out of her. "I don't care if He loves me. I don't love Him anymore. He took my Rose. That's the end—"

Elizabeth stopped. Her cheeks were burning. She'd been right earlier when she had begged God to let her die. If He'd done it when she asked, she never would have spoken this blasphemy aloud. She could have saved them both the accusation in her voice and the pity on the reverend's face. She wondered if she had damned her soul forever.

The reverend put his hand on her shoulder. "He understands how you feel."

Elizabeth just stood there. If God understood her, He understood more than she did. She just wanted time to go backward to those days when her family was alive. Her only consolation had been the hope of being with Rose and Matthew soon in Heaven and God was not even giving her that comfort. He might never give her that blessing now, not when her feelings were out in the open where everyone could see them. How was she going to live without her baby?

* * *

Jake stood outside of the schoolhouse door. It had been almost half an hour since Elizabeth had gone inside. Spotted Fawn had wanted to hold the baby and he had given the little one to her. He couldn't hear anything inside the schoolhouse. He wondered if Elizabeth was changing her mind about marrying him.

Well, if she was, he couldn't blame her. It wasn't just the harshness of the land that might deter her. Mrs. Barker had just demonstrated the extra problems any woman would have in this town if she married him. A woman who was used to the ways of the polite world couldn't be faulted for wanting to avoid that.

And Mrs. Barker had been more charitable than she might have been. Jake suspected there were people in this town who would say he belonged with the heathens as much as the girls did. To them, it didn't matter what a man believed; everything turned on the way someone looked and he still looked more like a mountain man than a gentleman.

Jake was questioning whether he should open the door and tell Elizabeth he understood. He might as well save her the agony of admitting she was going back on her decision. Besides, he had an ominous feeling about Mrs. Barker. He was half-surprised that the woman hadn't followed them to the schoolhouse to complain to the reverend that he and Spotted Fawn were dirtying the steps by standing on them.

Mrs. Barker liked to believe the church could not go forward without her guidance, but she held things back more than drove them forward. And it wasn't just the church that suffered. It was the whole town.

If it weren't for her talk about the railroad, people

wouldn't listen to her. In Jake's opinion, the railroad was fool's gold. It might or might not ever come by here. Unfortunately, Mrs. Barker had a cousin who worked for one of the big railroads back East and somehow she'd used that to make herself the local judge of what a railroad wanted in a town they'd consider for a regular stop.

If she and her Civic Improvement League said one of the saloons needed to wash their windows every week, the windows were washed. If they said the hotel needed to get more bathtubs for their guests, the order was sent back East. Everyone wanted Miles City to be a railroad stop and they were willing to obey Mrs. Barker to see that it happened.

Just then the door opened and Reverend Olson asked Jake and Spotted Fawn to come inside. Jake let his nieces go into the schoolhouse and then stepped inside himself, wondering what he would find.

Elizabeth stood at the front of the room. The afternoon sunlight was shining through the window and surrounding her with its glow. She had a small red flower in her hand.

Jake was stunned.

"It's a geranium," Elizabeth said when she saw him looking at it. "The reverend had a plant and he offered me a bloom for my bridal bouquet."

Jake felt suddenly conscious of the dried mud on his boots. And the creases in his shirt. He'd tied his hair back with a string of rawhide, but he smoothed it down anyway. He should be wearing a suit. Not that he owned one, but he should have tried to borrow one from the officers at the fort. Sergeant Rawlings probably had one.

Elizabeth was smiling at him. Not a big smile, granted.

But she looked as though she was well enough pleased to be standing where she was.

"I should have gotten you a ring. If you wait a minute, I'll go back and get one." Jake realized with a start that he was as nervous as an untried colt. Until this very minute, part of him had assumed Elizabeth would have the sense to back out of their agreement. He'd even given her a half hour with the reverend. Surely the good man had talked some sense to her.

"Or flowers. Maybe I can find some proper flowers." He could almost see his mother shaking her head over that little geranium blossom.

Elizabeth shook her head. "We don't need to fuss."

Jake didn't agree. Elizabeth looked like a bride. Not just because of the flower, but also because her face was all pink and glowing. She looked very pleased with herself. And beautiful in that quiet way she had.

"You're okay with all of this?" he asked her. He needed to give her one last chance to change her mind.

But Elizabeth nodded. "Reverend Olson made me realize that, if I had died before Rose, she would have needed another woman to help her live. The fever could have taken me as easily as it took Matthew. So I'm doing this for Rose in a way. I consider it an honor to help."

Jake felt her words like a kick to his stomach. He didn't know what he had been thinking. Of course, this wasn't about him. He wouldn't be able to please this woman any more than he'd pleased his mother. Elizabeth wasn't marrying him with any hope in her heart related to him. She was being a dutiful martyr, giving herself up to keep a helpless baby alive.

Well, Jake decided, he couldn't complain. That had been their agreement.

He glanced over to where Spotted Fawn sat on one of the benches with the baby on her lap. Those two were all he needed to worry about.

"Ready?" Reverend Olson asked as he walked over to look out the window. "I see my wife and her sister coming. They've agreed to be witnesses."

"We decided to do the minimum." Elizabeth looked up at Jake. "None of the sickness and health—just the 'I dos.'"

"Is that legal? I don't mind promising to take care of you."

"Well, but it doesn't mean anything, does it? Not when we're already planning to annul the marriage in the spring."

Jake felt his frown deepen. He turned to the reverend. "Are you okay with that? An annulment?"

"All I ask is that you give God time to work in your hearts," Reverend Olson said as he opened his Bible. "There's the baby to think about, and besides He might surprise you."

Jake felt Elizabeth flinch beside him. Then he heard the door open and the footsteps of the two women as they walked forward.

"Can we begin?" Elizabeth asked.

"Of course," Reverend Olson said as walked to the front of the aisle and looked down at his Bible. He began to read.

Elizabeth tried not to listen. She didn't want to hear about anything but the good thing she was doing for the baby. If she kept remembering that it could be some other woman doing this for her Rose, she felt good. If she thought about getting married, she felt a little, well, panicked.

Elizabeth calmed herself. She knew how to be a servant in someone else's house and that is the way it would be for her in Jake's. The reverend had been right when he pointed out that she needed Jake's provision as much as he needed her help. It was an agreement much like the ones she'd made with those families when she'd been a girl. She knew what to expect with those arrangements; she'd be fine until spring. Living in those households hadn't made her part of a family any more than living in Jake's house would make her his wife.

"It's time," the reverend whispered to her and Elizabeth realized she'd missed the reading of the vows.

"I do," she said. It didn't matter if she had missed everything. She knew what her job would be. Cooking, cleaning and taking care of the baby. Really, it wouldn't be so bad. She'd get to hold the baby whenever she wanted and she wouldn't need to winter in the wagon.

It would be better than washing glasses in some saloon in town. If the truth were told, she wasn't so sure she could have wintered in a saloon, even if she was in the back where she didn't have to see the customers. She wondered how life would be for that woman who was playing the piano in that place.

Elizabeth forced her mind back to the present. She'd just heard Jake make his own vow to take her as his wife.

It was quiet for a moment. Then one of the women standing behind the reverend cleared her throat quietly.

Elizabeth was going to turn to leave but the minister continued.

"You may now kiss the bride," Reverend Olson announced firmly.

Elizabeth looked at the minister in astonishment. He knew it was not that kind of a wedding. But there was no missing the hope on the older man's face. Or on the faces of his wife and sister-in-law. Elizabeth was going to protest, but she already felt Jake's hands on her shoulders.

Oh, my. She looked up and his eyes darkened. Maybe it was the shadows inside the schoolhouse, but he looked as if he meant something by the way his hand was tipping her chin up to meet his lips.

Elizabeth didn't have time for her back to stiffen. She told herself that was why her knees felt a little weak. Jake was thoroughly kissing her. Oh, my. Even Matthew hadn't coaxed her lips apart quite so sweetly or slipped his hand around to the small of her back as though he knew she needed a little support.

Jake had been hit over the head once. He hadn't passed out, but he'd seen a star or two floating around while he caught his breath. He never knew a man could feel the same way after a simple kiss.

He'd have to have a word with the Reverend Olson. The man had meant well, but he had set in motion something Jake did not want to think about. Of course, Jake didn't want to think about much of anything. He'd rather share another kiss with the surprising Elizabeth O'Brian. He wondered if she knew he could feel her melting into his arms.

Jake heard a woman's indignant gasp and he thought it was Elizabeth until he realized she couldn't be gasping and kissing him at the same time. He lifted his head just in time to see the pink rising in Elizabeth's cheeks. He was tempted to leave his gaze there, but he looked higher and saw Mrs. Barker standing in the doorway of the schoolhouse with one arm pointed heavenward like an avenging angel.

"This is outrageous," the woman said. Her hat was halfway off her head, but she didn't hesitate. She bristled as she led her charge into the schoolhouse. Her two friends meekly followed her, looking around, unsure if they should be there.

Mrs. Barker stood at the front of the church and glared at the reverend's wife. "I didn't expect to see you here at this—this—"

"A man's entitled to kiss his wife," Jake interrupted mildly.

"I don't care who you kiss," Mrs. Barker spat out as she put her hands on her hips. She turned her frown to Jake. "But I'll have you remember this is our children's schoolroom."

"I'm sure Jake is well aware of that," Reverend Olson said.

"Just so he knows he doesn't have the right to interfere with the education of our children."

"School's not in session," Reverend Olson said. "This is also the church and, as such, the proper place for two people to be married. My wife and I will have everything back in place and ready for school tomorrow morning in plenty of time for the children. You don't need to worry."

Mrs. Barker walked halfway back down the aisle until she was standing next to the bench where Spotted Fawn sat. "There won't be any children here tomorrow until we get one thing settled."

Jake took a few steps closer to his nieces so he was standing between them and the woman. "We'll settle it later and alone."

Mrs. Barker didn't stop. She leaned around Jake and pointed at Spotted Fawn. "This school is for the children of this town. Not for heathens like her."

Elizabeth gasped. "She's not a heathen."

"She is an Indian. And I want it to be clear that she won't be going to school here. Not with my children or any other children of Miles City."

Jake grunted. If he were facing a man, he'd know how to handle him. Mrs. Barker required something else. It took him a second to think of what it was. "You're forgetting that I own half the lumber in this school. Spotted Fawn will go to school here if I say so."

Even Mrs. Barker couldn't argue with that.

"Is that true?" Mrs. Barker turned to the minister.

The Reverend Olson nodded, his satisfaction evident. "Don't you remember, we thanked him at the dedication of the building?"

"Well, that doesn't mean he has any say over the whole school. You'll see. The Civic Improvement League won't stand for it. Will they?" Mrs. Barker turned to the two women who had followed her inside and they shook their heads dutifully.

With that, Mrs. Barker gave a curt nod to the reverend's wife, turned around and righted the hat on her head before marching out of the schoolhouse. Her two friends followed in her wake.

There was a moment of stunned silence after they were gone.

"She'll calm down," the minister said. "That Civic Improvement League of hers can't even agree on what kind of flowers to plant beside the schoolhouse."

"Rosebushes," his wife said. "Virginia Parker needed someplace to transplant them after she left her lodgings at the fort. The council finally voted to accept them."

"Good choice," Jake said.

"They weren't too sure since Virginia plays the piano in that saloon now."

"Virginia Parker is the same woman today as she was when she lived at the fort with her brother," Jake said. "I know for a fact she's not doing anything in that saloon she couldn't do in church. For pity's sake, she spends the afternoon playing hymns and Colter sends her home before it gets dark. Some people in this town are just too close-minded for their own good. Make that everybody's good."

With that, Jake gathered up his new family and wished the reverend and his wife a good day. His home might be humble, but Jake wanted to walk through his own door with his family and shut the rest of the world out.

Miles City was not the place he wanted any of them to be right now.

By the time they were getting close to his cabin, though, Jake wished he hadn't left town in such a hurry. If he had waited for a couple of hours, it would be dusk when they came upon his cabin. He should have taken everyone to dinner in the hotel dining room. Then it would be sundown and the shallow light would hide some of the flaws of his place. Spotted Fawn and the baby had been staying in his house, of course, so they were comfortable there, but he wasn't sure what Elizabeth would think of it.

He'd built the cabin into the side of a ravine close to the creek. The back wall was made with cottonwood logs, but he'd dug out a space in the ravine so that only half of the wall showed aboveground. The Lakota didn't bother him because of Red Tail and the Crow knew him from the times he'd scouted for the army. He hadn't wanted to announce his cabin's presence any more than necessary, though, because the Blackfeet sometimes came through here. A few trees blocked the view of the cabin so no one would see it until they were almost upon the place.

The lean-to was built into the ground next to the cabin, the logs standing upright in a deep ditch he'd dug for them. He kept his horses there and he'd made the place almost as big as the cabin. He was glad he'd done that now that he'd be spending the nights there with the animals. He'd even had the foresight to build a small loft over half of the space so he'd be able to sleep in peace.

Elizabeth had been quiet for most of the trip out of Miles City and Jake suddenly wondered if she was as nervous about seeing his house as he was about showing it to her.

They were almost close enough to see the cabin now.

"It's built tight," he said. "I chinked and daubed the walls myself. And, being close in to the ground like it is, it stays a little warmer in bad weather."

He'd mixed a good amount of lime with the clay mud he'd used in the daubing and taken only the best twigs for his chinking, too. No one could say his place wasn't well built even if it was humble.

"I've read about sod houses," Elizabeth said quietly.

"It's not really sod." Jake was miserable. He was thinking what Mrs. Barker or even Annabelle would think if he offered them up a sod house. Women expected more. "It's mostly logs."

The cabin came into full view just as Jake had known it would. The window was dirty. He should have cleaned it after the last rain, or at least the rain before that. The ground in front of the door was packed down. He'd meant to put some logs in that place to make a sitting porch, but it looked more like a dried mud puddle than anything at the moment.

His horse, tied to the back of the wagon, saw the lean-to and gave an excited snort. He knew they were home.

"I haven't had a chance to do much cleaning," Jake muttered as he took the baby and then helped Elizabeth down from the wagon. Spotted Fawn was wisely staying on her pony and keeping her distance. Jake wished he could let Elizabeth go into the cabin alone, but he wasn't a coward. He had to admit he'd rather face a charging bear than follow her into that house, but he'd do it anyway.

When she stepped inside the door, Elizabeth smelled sage. She'd never known a man who kept herbs. A large stone fireplace stood on the wall to her right. A black cast-iron hook reached out of the fireplace so a pot could be hung for cooking even though there was also a fine-looking cookstove sitting in the corner. Several pots were scattered on shelves next to the fireplace.

A large table stood in the middle of the room. The legs were made of slender logs with the bark peeled away. The surface was planed lumber, one board lined up next to another so it was smooth. A coal oil lamp stood in the middle of the table with a glass globe that would do justice to a parlor back East. Three straight-backed chairs sat around the table. She thought they were made of oak.

On the far side of the room, Elizabeth saw a bed piled high with blankets and furs. She quickly looked away from that. Midway down the side wall was a rope ladder hooked over a peg in the wall. The ladder led up to a loft area.

The most surprising thing in the room was the rocking chair that sat beside the fireplace. It was a dark wood, she'd guess it was mahogany, and the sides were well-rubbed with some kind of oil so the whole thing had a soft sheen. It was as fine a chair as Elizabeth had seen in the houses where she worked back in Kansas. All it lacked was a back cushion.

"I can bring your things inside," Jake said from the doorway.

Elizabeth turned around to face him. "Thank you. Just the satchel, please. Your place is lovely."

Jake grunted. "There's wood to build a fire."

Jake left the cabin before he could do any more damage. He should have more to say to his new wife than to ask her to build a fire. Maybe he could think of something more pleasant to say when he brought her satchel inside. Something about the color of her eyes or the shine of her hair. Women set great store by compliments.

He usually wasn't so tongue-tied, but nothing had prepared him for a wife who made him nervous. That kiss had been his undoing. There was a sweetness inside Elizabeth that reminded him of all he was missing in life. Maybe, even if she was new to this land, she could come to be content living here. With him.

Chapter Five

Elizabeth couldn't go to sleep even though it was past midnight. The coals from the banked fire cast a dim light around the cabin and everything was quiet. Spotted Fawn was asleep in the loft and the baby was curled up in the rough wooden crib that Jake had fashioned beside the bed.

Everything was peaceful, but Elizabeth was restless.

Maybe it was that she was lying in a bed, she thought to herself. On the way here, she'd spent so many nights stretched out on the ground and then she'd slept on even harder ground outside of the fort. Her body had forgotten how nice it was to have some softness to lie on as she slept.

Besides, it was her wedding night. She smiled in the darkness. The marriage might not be real, but the night seemed momentous nonetheless. She had been pronounced a wife for the second time in her life. She'd felt a little skittish today until she was sure Jake was going to abide by his agreement.

After seeing how fiercely protective he was of his nieces, she had started to trust him, though. She hoped he had enough furs in his lean-to. He'd said he would be fine out there and she was going to take him at his word. He'd been a real gentleman about giving up the cabin and she appreciated it. If nothing else, she needed some privacy to nurse the baby.

For the first time since she'd agreed to Jake's suggestion that they marry, she thought everything might work out fine. She would stay until spring. She'd spent longer than that working at different homes as a girl. Back then, she'd figured out how to work in the midst of a family and still keep her heart separate. She could do the same now.

This was a good place for her. Not only would she save the baby's life, but she would have some time to decide what to do next. She wondered if, come next spring, she could go to a town smaller than Miles City and open the store she and Matthew had envisioned. Maybe she'd ask Annabelle the next time they were at the store. She might know of a community that would welcome cheaper goods. She might even be able to dye some of their goods to make them more appealing.

Elizabeth had managed to drift off when she heard the first yell.

"Ahhh," she squeaked as she bolted straight up in bed. She wondered if she'd imagined the yell, but then she heard the banging of tin—*was it tin cups?* And then another yell. And some heavy bells. *Were they cowbells?*

Elizabeth stood up and pulled a blanket off the bed to wrap around herself. She'd heard similar sounds not so long ago when the men got paid at the fort. There must be a bunch of drunken soldiers outside. She couldn't begin to guess what they were doing here, but she intended to find out.

Elizabeth was at the door of the cabin when she heard Spotted Fawn climbing down the rope ladder. The girl had slept in her clothes.

"Don't open the door," Spotted Fawn whispered as she reached the floor and then looked around wildly before racing to pick up one of the cast-iron skillets from the shelves.

"It's okay," Elizabeth said as she arranged the blanket around her so that none of her nightclothes showed. "It's just some foolish drunks."

Elizabeth figured the soldiers would be sick as dogs come morning, but she couldn't do anything about that. She'd put a stop to their noise tonight, though. She opened the door and stepped outside.

"Oh." She almost turned to go back inside. The moon was shining and she could make out two hulking men sitting atop two equally massive black horses. The men were waving their arms and banging on things. The horses were rearing up and stomping their feet. It sounded like a fort full of men and there were only the two of them.

Elizabeth heard the door to the lean-to open and saw Jake step outside. If she hadn't been so worried about those strange men, she would have been concerned about Jake catching a night chill. She could feel the frost on her feet. He must be freezing. Jake had taken time to reach for his rifle, but he hadn't bothered to pull on any of his shirts.

"What do you think you're doing?" Jake yelled at the men.

Elizabeth was mesmerized. She forgot all about the fearsome horses and the men who rode them. Jake was beautiful in the moonlight, the muscles in his arms defined and strong as he moved. She was relieved to see he didn't raise the rifle he held in his hands. That must mean he at least knew these men.

"Heard you got yourself married," one of the men called down from his horse. The man was grinning at Jake. "We didn't have a present handy so we thought we'd give you a proper shivaree."

The horses and the men were all facing the lean-to. Elizabeth was going to turn around and go back inside when the other man noticed her.

"Well, this must be the bride right here," the man said as he turned his horse to face her. He tipped his hat. "It's all my pleasure, ma'am. Jake, here, he'll make a good…" The man's voice trailed off in puzzlement as he looked over at Jake and then back at Elizabeth. "Did we get it wrong? We heard the wedding had happened already."

Elizabeth felt a blush crawl up her neck and she pulled the blanket closer to her. The men were wondering why Jake wasn't sleeping in the cabin with her since they were married. Well, she supposed it was a logical question even if it was none of their concern.

"You heard right." Jake's voice was strong and held more than a hint of warning. "Come back another day and I'll introduce you."

"Breakfast," Elizabeth added brightly. She didn't suppose Jake liked his friends knowing about their arrangement, but it was too late for that. "Why don't you come back for breakfast? I'll make you some raised biscuits."

"With molasses?"

Elizabeth nodded. "All the molasses you want. And jam, too."

"You don't have to ask us twice. We'll be here."

Elizabeth hoped the thought of biscuits would make

those two men forget all about the Hargrove sleeping arrangement. She'd fry up some salt pork, too. And maybe soak some of the dried apples she had in the wagon.

"Just let the sun come up first," Jake called after the men as they started to ride off.

Then he turned to Elizabeth. "You didn't need to do that. We could have just sent them away."

Elizabeth shrugged. "They're your friends. They meant well."

Jake walked closer and grinned. "They meant to wake us up is what they meant. And they did a pretty good job of it."

Jake stood there for a minute, just looking down at her.

"You'll catch cold," Elizabeth finally said. The moon had gone behind some clouds, but she could still see Jake like a shadow in the dark night. If it wasn't so fanciful, she almost thought she could feel the heat of him as he stood there.

He gave her a half smile. "I was just thinking that I never did give you the present I bought for you today."

"You bought me a present?" Elizabeth asked in soft astonishment. No one had ever given her a present. Not even on her real wedding day with Matthew. "Oh, you mean the tea."

Jake shook his head. "There's more. Let me get it. I slipped it into the back of the wagon. Go inside and get warm. I'll bring it in."

Elizabeth nodded. This was a most extraordinary day. Someone had bought her a present.

The inside of the cabin was dark, but Elizabeth could feel her way to the table and then to the fireplace. She reached into the box that sat next to the fireplace and pulled out a short log. She gently placed it onto the fire and sparks flew up and then died down as the fire took hold again. Once she had the fire going, she used a small stick to light the coal oil lamp.

When Jake opened the door a few minutes later, the cabin was glowing with light.

Elizabeth smiled up at him. She had smoothed back her hair and pulled an old calico dress over her night-gown. It might look strange, but it was more decent than just sitting there as she was.

Jake was carefully holding a wooden box as he walked into the room. He set the box on the table and then sat down in one of the chairs himself.

"I hope you like it," he said.

"I'm sure I will," Elizabeth said.

She sat down in one of the chairs and Jake slid the box over to her.

The box was open on the top and newspaper was stuffed in the corners of the box, covering whatever was there.

"Go ahead," Jake urged her.

Elizabeth pushed the paper aside and there it was— the round china teapot with the delicate pink roses that she'd seen in the mercantile earlier. She'd never had a teapot before in all her life. She pulled the pot out of the box. It even had a lid that fit right on top so she could brew her tea properly. She'd never touched anything so fine and it was hers.

Jake figured he had done it now. His bride sat there looking as if she was on the verge of tears. "Don't cry."

"I never cry," Elizabeth whispered and then she cleared her throat. "Never."

"I shouldn't have gotten the one with the roses," he said. "I didn't mean to remind you—I thought you'd like it best."

"It's beautiful."

"You're sure. We can take it back. They had one that was plain."

"I love roses."

Jake smiled. There was no mistaking the sincere gratitude in his bride's eyes. "Oh, well, then—I'm glad you like it."

Elizabeth put the teapot back in the box. "I'll treasure it forever."

She started to replace the paper that had been packed around the pot.

"You are planning to use it, aren't you?" Jake had felt something inside him relax when he knew she liked his gift. But now he had the feeling that she was going to keep the teapot in a trunk somewhere.

"But I don't want it to break," she protested.

"If it breaks, I'll buy you another one."

Jake watched Elizabeth's face color up in astonishment and then go flat again.

"Yes, of course," she said, the joy gone from her voice. "I'll leave it on the shelf."

"You can make tea in it whenever you like."

Elizabeth nodded. "It is a great addition to the kitchen here."

Jake wished he knew a little more about women. He was beginning to think his mother wasn't the best example to go by. This woman didn't fret about the things that had upset his mother. He'd given Elizabeth a gift and she'd accepted it with pleasure. And then—

"What's wrong?" he asked softly.

She looked up at him and her eyes were stricken.

"I'll need to leave it with you when I leave," she said. "It'll only break on the road and—I don't even know where I'll be and you'll be—"

Jake grinned. "It doesn't matter where you are. Just get me word if the thing breaks and I'll bring you a new one."

"But I could be miles from here."

Jake nodded. "Still, you have my word. I've got a couple of good horses. I'll bring you a new one."

He would do it, too. He liked thinking Elizabeth would call on him someday in the future if she needed something. "You can call on me for anything."

"Well, thank you then. Instead of setting it on the shelf, I might leave it out on the table. That way the girls can enjoy the roses, too, and—" Elizabeth stopped and looked around. "Oh, dear—"

Elizabeth pointed to the window. It was partially opened. "I think Spotted Fawn—"

"Spotted Fawn," Elizabeth stood up and called toward the loft. "Spotted Fawn, are you there?"

There was no answer from the loft.

"She must have gone outside," Elizabeth said. "She was frightened by your friends."

Jake stood up, too. "I should have thought of that." He started to walk toward the door. "It must have reminded her of being with the tribe when—" Jake looked at Elizabeth. He didn't want to upset her any more than she was already. "Stay here. I'll find her."

Even though Jake had asked her to stay in the cabin, Elizabeth would have gone to help him look if the baby didn't need someone to stay with her. How had she forgotten about Spotted Fawn? The girl had been so upset, Elizabeth knew she should have checked on her the first thing when she stepped back inside the cabin. That's what a mother would have done.

A mother would have known what was bothering the girl, too. She should have known the terror in the girl's eyes earlier was enough to make her bolt.

Elizabeth had usually worked as a cook. Of course, she'd also done more than her share of laundry and scrubbing floors. But she'd never been in charge of children before. Or small animals, either. For some reason, it had never occurred to her that she'd avoided taking care of anyone or anything that needed mothering—until Rose.

She wondered if that was why God had taken Rose from her. Maybe He knew she wouldn't do it right. Being a mother required constant attention. The worst that would happen if she was inattentive in her cooking was that something would burn. But being a caretaker meant something serious could happen if she was day-dreaming about teapots instead of making sure someone was where they were supposed to be.

Elizabeth knew Jake needed a mother for the girls more than he needed a cook, but she wished she was only in charge of feeding this family. She would have to do better if she hoped to keep up her end of the bargain. She had known the baby would need her help, but she hadn't thought about the girl.

The fire had burned down to embers before Jake brought Spotted Fawn back. He was carrying the girl and, if it wasn't for the shivering, Elizabeth would have thought the girl was asleep in her uncle's arms. Her calico dress was too light for the night air and she wasn't wearing the animal pelts around her legs as she had been earlier in the day.

"I should have seen to it that she had a blanket with her, at least," Elizabeth said. She'd make sure of it next time, somehow. "Here, let me get the fire going better."

Elizabeth stood up and put a small log in the fire before walking over to the bed and pulling some of the covers off of it. "These will help."

Jake took the blankets she handed to him and set himself in the rocking chair, with Spotted Fawn in his arms. He covered the girl. "We'll just sit here for a while until everyone is warm."

Elizabeth sat back down at the table and watched Jake rock his niece. She felt miserable. If she had failed so completely at a task for one of the families who had taken her in when she was Spotted Fawn's age, Elizabeth would be packing her mother's old satchel about now, getting ready to move on to the next family.

But there was no next family here. She'd be here for the winter.

Elizabeth wondered now if she had chosen to spend her time in the kitchens of those various homes so she wouldn't be called upon to take care of the children of the households. Elizabeth knew her heart had been broken when Rose died, but she was beginning to wonder why she hadn't had a lesser heartbreak years ago when she left the children of some household. She couldn't even remember being sad about leaving a kitten behind. She had never let herself be responsible for any living thing. The closest she had come was tending her garden every summer. But then, no one grew overly fond of a carrot or a tomato.

Elizabeth looked over at Spotted Fawn as she cuddled

against Jake's shoulder. The girl was gripping Jake's buckskin shirt even in sleep. Whatever was troubling her, it probably didn't have an easy solution.

No child except Rose had ever clung to Elizabeth.

Not that it would be wise to become attached to this family. They had more problems than she could solve. Elizabeth reminded herself that she was only here because the baby needed to nurse. Spotted Fawn resented her and Jake had been all too willing to say she could leave in the spring. No, this was not the place to form any attachment, but when she left here she might just look for a simple family who had children who needed care.

The floor of the cabin was nothing but hard dirt, but that suited Elizabeth. She walked back to the bed and leaned down by the head of the bed so she could draw a series of lines in the floor. She would mark her days in this household. Four months should be enough for the baby. Elizabeth guessed the infant was already a few months old. It wouldn't be long before it could survive on soft food like well-cooked potatoes and mashed carrots.

Elizabeth would set aside the canned goods that could be used for the baby. And, when the time came, she would start to look for an uncomplicated family who needed someone for their children.

She glanced back at Jake and his niece. She still didn't know what had upset Spotted Fawn and it didn't look as though she'd learn anything tonight. They were both sitting in the rocking chair, dozing. The blankets had fallen to the floor. She walked over and picked up the heaviest blanket, tucking it in around them both.

She hated to say it, but she was bound to this family for the moment. Until she left, she'd do her best to take care of them.

Chapter Six

Mr. Wells was sincerely interested in breakfast, Elizabeth decided as she slid a second batch of biscuits onto the tin plate she'd found on the shelf. It turned out most of the bulk she'd seen on him last night had been from his buffalo coat. The man himself was tall and something in the way he moved reminded her of a stalk of wheat, bending this way and that with his head looking down half of the time. She decided the man must be shy. Or just not used to being around women. Or maybe not interested in talking to anyone, period.

Jake's other friend, Mr. Higgins, was definitely not shy. He reminded her of a grizzly, both because of the size of him and the kind gruffness that was evident in his voice as he talked and laughed. He didn't just talk to her, either, for which she was pleased. He also included a few comments to Spotted Fawn, trying to get the girl to smile back at him. For that alone, Elizabeth forgave him for interrupting their sleep last night.

The men were sitting at the table in the middle of the room. Spotted Fawn was in the rocking chair, holding the baby. Elizabeth was moving between the stove and the table.

"The apples are almost ready," Elizabeth said. She had crushed some cinnamon to put on the sauce she'd made of dried apples and walnuts. She'd cooked the soaked apples, but she wanted to be sure the spices didn't overpower the taste of the fruit so she'd waited to add the cinnamon until she pulled the pan off the stove.

She'd gotten up at first light and started the fire so she'd have the stove hot enough to make her biscuits. She'd pulled an apron out of her satchel to cover the old calico dress she had been wearing.

"It sure smells good," Higgins said.

Elizabeth nodded and tried to smooth down her dress with her free hand. She didn't want Jake to be ashamed of his new wife so she had planned to change into her gray dress before the men got here. She'd practically slept in the old calico one and it was wrinkled. But the stove had given her some problems. And she hadn't found any flour so she'd had to go out to the wagon and get some of hers.

And then she had remembered that the men who were coming to breakfast were wolfers. Biscuits and applesauce didn't seem like enough to feed men like that, not even when she added some salt pork to the frying pan. In the end, she'd pulled out a jar of her sour cabbage to use with the salt pork in case the men wanted more than biscuits. This was the first meal she'd made in Jake's house and she wanted him to be proud of her.

"Yes sir, this is a mighty fine meal, ma'am," Higgins said. He lifted his shaggy head and looked at Elizabeth as she set the applesauce on the table. "I don't know when I've tasted anything as good as what you've got right here."

"Thank you," Elizabeth said quietly. She was wondering if she should have forgotten about the sour cabbage and changed her dress. Jake was scowling. Oh, he was sitting at the table as if everything was fine and, when she looked at him square on, his face was pleasant enough. But when she turned, and he couldn't see that she saw him, he was definitely scowling.

It had to be the dress. Matthew had never liked it when she wore old clothes, either. She should have invited the men for dinner instead of breakfast. At least then she would have had all day to prepare the food and make sure she was well-dressed.

Elizabeth lifted her head. Men never did understand the work that was involved in seeing to their comfort.

"It's my pleasure to feed someone like you," Elizabeth said to Higgins. At least someone appreciated the fact that she'd cooked the biscuits and put up jam last summer so they could eat it now. She hadn't worn her silk dress when she'd picked those wild strawberries, either. "You're a real gentleman about it, too, Mr. Higgins."

Mr. Wells gave a snort of amusement.

But Mr. Higgins reared back in astonishment. "Me? You think I could pass for a gentleman?"

"Well, I… Of course." Elizabeth remembered that she was speaking to a wolfer. Still. "A man can be as much of a gentleman as he chooses to be."

Jake should have known a woman would be trouble. He'd no sooner gotten married than Higgins was eyeing his wife. Oh, the other man probably thought Jake didn't know what was going on, but Higgins hadn't taken his eyes off Elizabeth since he had come in the door this morning.

Of course, Wells hadn't been much better, but it was pretty obvious that when Wells had been looking at Elizabeth and salivating like a lost dog, he was really more interested in the biscuits that she had been holding than the woman herself.

Higgins, though, hadn't eaten enough to feed a grasshopper. Elizabeth probably wouldn't know it, but Higgins didn't consider six biscuits to be a full breakfast, not even when he had spread a fair bit of jam on each one of those biscuits and eaten some of the sour cabbage besides.

The problem, Jake realized, was that his friends knew his marriage to Elizabeth was a sham. They'd seen that he wasn't bedding down with her and they had sense enough to figure that, come spring, Elizabeth would be looking for a new husband.

A woman who could cook as fine as Elizabeth wouldn't need to look farther than this table for a husband to replace him.

It was all Jake could do to sit and act as if nothing was wrong.

And Elizabeth wasn't helping any. She kept bringing this to the table and that to the table. She should be sitting down beside him and showing the world that they were bound in holy wedlock. He had left the chair to his right free for her and he'd had to pull up a stump for himself to do so.

Obviously, his bride wasn't one to settle in quickly, though.

"Have a seat before the biscuits get cold," Jake finally said. If Elizabeth was going to marry a trapper come spring, it would be him. He might be willing to let her go to a rich man in some city who could give her all the comforts she deserved, but he wasn't willing to let her go to someone like him unless it *was* him.

"But—" Elizabeth started to protest.

"If there's anything else that needs to be brought to the table, you can tell me where it is and I'll get it," Jake said as he stood up. He thought he heard his new wife gasp in amazement, but he wasn't sure. He was too busy pulling the chair out for her so he could show Higgins how a real gentleman acted.

Elizabeth sat down. She wasn't used to sitting down with company. When she'd cooked for Matthew, they had sat together. But for years, she'd been working in the kitchen, or serving at the table, until the family meal was over and then she'd just eaten a few leftovers as she heated water to wash the dishes. She looked at the two men who still sat at the table and then at Spotted Fawn over by the fireplace. Elizabeth wasn't sure she knew what to say to any of them.

"Do you think I could learn?" Higgins asked.

It took a second for Elizabeth to realize what the man was talking about. "To be a gentleman? Of course."

"Teach me." Higgins asked and then seemed to reconsider. "I mean, I'd appreciate it mightily if you would be so kind." He stopped and then added, "Ma'am."

Higgins looked at her triumphantly.

"Well, I—"

"What kind of nonsense is this?" Wells demanded. He looked bewildered. "You planning to take up banking or something?"

"Women appreciate gentlemen," Higgins stated calmly.

Wells just looked at his friend. "What women?"

"Women. That's all. Just women."

"Women appreciate the kind of money we're making, that's what women appreciate."

"Not all women," Higgins said.

Elizabeth finally understood. "I'd be happy to give you some pointers." Somehow that didn't seem to be enough. "And I must say I think your efforts will pay off."

"You do?" Higgins looked over at her with the most hopeful look on his face.

Elizabeth nodded. "I most assuredly do."

The room was very silent. Elizabeth realized that not everyone knew about Annabelle Bliss or, if they did, they hadn't made the connections. She didn't want to give away any secrets. "Any woman would be pleased."

By now, Higgins was beaming.

Jake dropped a plate. Fortunately, it wasn't anything but a tin plate. He couldn't believe his ears. He'd taken Elizabeth for a quiet, serious-minded woman. She hadn't seemed to want to take a second husband when she'd taken him. And here she was lining up another one—Higgins.

"We have a busy day ahead," Jake finally said. He didn't want to suggest Higgins and Wells leave, but he didn't want them to stay right now, either.

All pairs of eyes turned toward him. He'd just put a bit more wood in the stove.

"We have to unload the wagon," he explained.

"Oh, we could help with that," Higgins offered. "Sort of a thank-you. Nothing to it."

Jake clenched his jaw. "I can unload the wagon myself."

"When we get it unloaded, I thought maybe we should go back into town to the mercantile," Elizabeth said. "We'll need some things for Spotted Fawn before she goes to school."

Jake noticed his niece flinch at that news. She looked at him pleadingly.

Suddenly, it didn't seem so important whether or not he could show Higgins who was the better gentleman. Elizabeth wouldn't be settling down with either one of them anyway. If she had any sense, she'd be looking for some refined man from town by the time spring came.

The new Miles City banker, Harold Walls, was a widower and likely open to the prospect of marrying again. Or the man who had come here to open the hotel. What was his name? Well, it didn't matter. Both men were rich and traveled back East whenever the fancy took them. Jake couldn't compete financially with either one of them.

Then he looked at his niece. He had other things to worry about anyway. "Maybe we could get some lemon drops, too. I've heard the children in school all like lemon drops. They probably wouldn't say no if someone were to offer them one."

"I don't need to go to school," Spotted Fawn said. "I can talk English."

"You'll want to learn how to read," Jake said softly. "I know you have your father's Bible."

His niece didn't answer.

"I wish I knew how to read," Higgins finally said.

"You don't want to pass up a chance to learn something like that."

"It won't be so bad," Elizabeth said. "You'll get used to it."

Spotted Fawn nodded slowly. "I'll try."

"Maybe we all should go into town," Elizabeth said brightly. "I didn't ask the reverend what you'll need for your first day in school. I'm sure they'll know at the mercantile, though."

"Well, let's get the wagon unloaded then," Higgins said.

Jake didn't refuse the offer this time. If Higgins was determined to help, he would let him. At least, he'd be able to watch the man if they were unloading the wagon together.

Elizabeth was worried. Jake said there was room in the lean-to for most of the goods in her wagon. But, as she recalled what she had there, she tried to remember where she had packed her sewing needles. It would take her at least a day to make Spotted Fawn ready for school. The girl would need to wear pantalettes instead of those pelts she had wrapped around her legs. The mercantile might have some ready-made ones that weren't too dear. And she'd also need shoes and stockings. Hopefully, they would have some that fit.

But a new dress for the girl would require some sewing. Even if Elizabeth only put tucks in one of her dresses for the girl to wear, it would take time. She might think of a dye to freshen up the one dress the girl did have, too.

It wasn't until everyone was ready to leave for Miles City, that Elizabeth remembered Annabelle, and Higgins's plans to be a gentleman.

"Maybe you should stop by the barbershop first,"

Elizabeth said to Higgins as Jake was helping her into the wagon.

The man was on his horse, preparing to ride along with them. "Why?"

"Women like a man with tidy hair," she said.

"I've never been to a barbershop," Wells offered with a frown. "Your hair just grows back if you get it cut, anyway."

"Yes, but it grows back more neatly. If you can't find a barber in Miles City, I'll cut your hair for you."

Elizabeth had cut Matthew's hair for him. She wasn't as good as a barber, but she'd managed.

"Maybe some other day," Wells said hesitantly. "Higgins is the one who wants to get all fancy. Me, I'm heading back home."

Jake wondered how he could have been so blind. It only took one look at Elizabeth bending her head toward Annabelle in the mercantile to know that something was up. Another look at Higgins's intensely still face as he watched them through the window told Jake all he needed to know. Higgins wasn't aiming for Elizabeth; he had his heart set on the woman behind the counter inside.

Jake felt relieved for himself, but more than anxious for his friend. He remembered when the three of them—Higgins, Wells and him—had fought off some hostile Blackfeet. They'd been holed up in the Paha Sapa, what some called the Black Hills, for several days and they were running out of ammunition and water. But, even facing death as they were, Higgins hadn't looked as miserable as he did now as the two of them stood on the porch outside the mercantile and tried not to look in through the window.

That, Jake told himself, was what a woman could do to a brave man.

He took another look at the inside of the store to be sure Spotted Fawn looked comfortable where she sat in the corner with the baby. Elizabeth had already told him she'd need a good hour to finish her business. Then he turned to Higgins.

"Come on, let's go find out if there's a barber in this town." Jake put his arm around his friend's shoulders. "How bad can it be to get a haircut anyway?"

A half hour later, Jake and Higgins walked back out on the street. The morning was almost over and there were people stepping every which way, going into one shop or another.

"I've been scalped," Higgins protested as he reached up to touch what little hair he had left. They still stood under the overhang that covered the walkway in front of the barber's shop.

Jake had to admit Higgins looked awfully pink all of a sudden. The man hadn't done more than trim his beard in the years Jake had known him. Now he was fresh-shaven and short-haired. Why, the man's forehead was pure white because it hadn't seen the sun in decades.

"You look younger," Jake offered by way of consolation. He decided not to mention the fact that the man's nose was a lot darker now than the rest of his face.

"Who wants to look younger?" Higgins bellowed. "Women are supposed to like a man who's been around awhile."

That stopped half of the people walking down the street. At least five women turned around and looked at Higgins. The man turned beet-red, which apparently didn't make him any more appealing to the women since they all turned back around and continued on their way a little faster than before.

"Neatness. That's what women like," Jake said as he rubbed his own neck. He was used to his hair being back there and now there was only air. His hair was cut short enough to compete with that new banker. Of course, Jake's neck was cold and probably white, too.

Higgins grunted. "I suppose I'll need to get new boots."

Jake nodded. "And a new hat."

Rightfully speaking, Higgins didn't have a hat now. It was little more than a buckskin bandana he'd used to tie his hair back. It had looked fine when the man had long hair, but it did look odd now.

"It's an expensive business—" Higgins frowned "—being a gentleman."

"I can't argue with that."

Somehow, though, Jake thought the other man didn't really mind.

Elizabeth had to look twice before she recognized Higgins when he stepped into the mercantile. If it weren't for the size of him, she might have needed to look a few more times. No one else was as massive and his height gave him away when his face didn't.

"Clarence?" Annabelle whispered from where she stood behind her counter.

Higgins's face went so pale even his nose was white. "I told you I don't use that name anymore."

Then Jake stepped into the mercantile, too. He chuckled. "I always wondered what the *C* stood for. I didn't think it was for Captain."

"It could have been," Higgins protested. "I helped the army out some."

"Oh." Elizabeth stared at Jake. It had taken her a minute to find her voice. "You cut your hair, too."

Jake's hair was still shining black, but now it had a few waves in it and it framed his face. Someone needed to smooth the strands into place, Elizabeth thought, but it wouldn't be her. She held her hands firmly at her sides.

Jake looked at her and smiled. "I figured I couldn't let Higgins make a fool of himself all alone."

"It's not foolish," Annabelle protested hotly from where she stood. "Good grooming is the mark of a gentleman."

Elizabeth took her eyes off Jake long enough to see Higgins swell up like a peacock. She'd noticed Annabelle had added a pretty brooch to her dress today, too. And set the bun on the back of her head a little higher so she'd look a little younger. The other woman had also greeted Elizabeth as if she knew she would be here today so she may have been hoping to see Higgins, as well.

"Thank you for noticing," Higgins finally said to Annabelle.

Jake gave a soft snort, not loud enough for Annabelle to hear, but he'd walked close enough to Elizabeth so she heard it.

"Do you need more time?" Jake asked as he stepped closer yet.

"No, but thank you for being gentleman enough to ask," she replied softly with a grin and watched Jake's eyes light up with laughter.

Annabelle and Higgins were having a moment of their own.

"You're just afraid of what Higgins and I would do if we had more time in town."

Elizabeth laughed. "Even so, I've finished with my shopping."

"You got the lemon drops?"

She nodded. "And a paper tablet with some lead pencils."

Elizabeth didn't mention that Annabelle had whispered to her that Mrs. Barker had been in with a petition, trying to get as many parents to sign it as she could. She wanted to prevent Spotted Fawn from going to school with the other children. Fortunately, she hadn't had many signatures when Annabelle saw it. Maybe the other adults in Miles City would decide it was only fair that Jake's niece have a chance to have the same kind of schooling that their children had.

The parents would think that, too, if they could have seen the girl earlier as she sat in the mercantile waiting patiently for Elizabeth to finish talking with Annabelle. It wasn't until they were almost done that Elizabeth noticed the girl had been holding open a small Bible. She clearly couldn't read, but she seemed to be trying.

Elizabeth wondered how many of the white children in Miles City had that much of a longing to read God's Word. She was glad Annabelle had seen the girl, too. Maybe that information could circulate around the town along with the petition.

Chapter Seven

Jake was happy as he sat near the fireplace and whittled. He couldn't help but notice that his wife looked happy, too. Elizabeth never referred to herself as his wife, but he found he liked calling her that, even if it was only in his mind. He had begun praying that Elizabeth would grow content with her life here.

He was watching her now as she stood in the light of the coal oil lamp and twisted pieces of old rags into Spotted Fawn's long black hair. The baby was already in her crib sleeping. Maybe it was all of the effort Elizabeth was putting into getting the baby fed and Spotted Fawn ready for school that was causing the good feelings he was having.

Marrying Elizabeth O'Brian was the best thing he'd ever done, Jake told himself as he paused in his movements. Four different hair ribbons were spread out on the table. The final decision had not yet been made on which one they would use. He doubted Spotted Fawn had ever worn a ribbon before and he knew he wouldn't have thought to get her ribbons if it wasn't for Elizabeth guiding them.

It didn't matter if this woman had come from the East or the West, whether she was used to a soft life or a hard life. She was the woman his family needed; she belonged with them.

Even his niece seemed to know it.

"You'll be the prettiest girl in school tomorrow," Jake said as he smiled over at Spotted Fawn, who was sitting in a chair pulled up to the table. She had an old apron tied around her shoulders. She was the only one in the room who didn't look happy.

"She's better off not being the prettiest," Elizabeth said mildly as she wrapped another strand of hair. "She doesn't need to call any attention to herself. We've already talked about it and, the first day, she's just going to smile a lot."

Spotted Fawn looked up at him and gave him a smile that was almost a grimace.

"She should just be herself," Jake said. "The other kids will like her when they get a chance to know her."

"I'm sure they will."

Elizabeth didn't look at him when she said that and Jake had a sinking feeling that his wife didn't think Spotted Fawn would have an easy time of it in school. Elizabeth had told him about the petition Mrs. Barker had been passing around, but he assumed the woman hadn't gotten many signatures or someone would have been out to his place to tell him about it by now.

"We'll take you to school and see that everything's okay," Jake said.

Elizabeth looked over at him.

"We'll stop by after Spotted Fawn has settled in a bit," Elizabeth corrected him as she made one last knot in a rag and patted the girl on the shoulder. "There, you're all ready for bed now. Have sweet dreams and don't worry about anything."

Spotted Fawn looked over at Jake with a question in her eyes.

He nodded. "I'll be up in a minute to say your prayers with you."

Red Tail had always said evening prayers with Spotted Fawn and Jake knew that was the time when his niece missed her parents the most.

Spotted Fawn stood up and Elizabeth took the apron off of the girl's shoulders. For a second, Jake had thought Elizabeth was going to bend down and kiss the top of his niece's head. But she didn't.

Spotted Fawn was waiting for something, though.

Elizabeth looked down at the girl. With her hair in rags and the worried expression on her face, Spotted Fawn looked a lot like Elizabeth had felt at her age when she needed to walk to a new household to see if she could work there for a while. Everything always depended on the kindness of the women in the new place. She supposed it would be the same for Spotted Fawn.

"The day will go fast," Elizabeth said softly as she reached over to smooth down a stray piece of the girl's hair that had escaped a knotted rag. "And I'm going to bake some molasses cookies to put in your lunch pail."

In the two days that she and Spotted Fawn had been getting ready for school, Elizabeth had discovered that the girl liked cookies. Elizabeth planned to bake some before the stove cooled off tonight.

Spotted Fawn nodded to Elizabeth before turning to the ladder that led up to the loft.

Elizabeth watched as the girl climbed the ladder.

"Here." Jake walked over and pulled out a chair for Elizabeth. "Rest a bit before you worry about those cookies."

Elizabeth nodded as she eased herself into the chair. It had been a long day. "I hope—" She looked at the loft above. Spotted Fawn was already up there.

Jake nodded. "Me, too."

Elizabeth could hear Spotted Fawn moving around in the loft.

"We can't go with her to school, though," Elizabeth murmured quietly so they wouldn't be overheard. "The other kids will tease her if we do."

"Well, what do other parents do?"

Jake looked so bewildered, Elizabeth started to giggle. "I'm sure I don't know."

Elizabeth couldn't get her breath. She knew it was half from exhaustion, but the more she giggled the more Jake's eyes danced along with her. She liked watching the lamplight flicker on his face. He was standing beside her chair, looking down at her, and then—

Oh, my, Jake had bent down and was kissing her. She should pull away and say something, but she couldn't think of anything coherent to say. This kiss was—no, she was. Everything stopped. Yes, she was a bad woman.

"You're not supposed to do that," Elizabeth finally whispered as she managed to pull away slightly.

She remembered, of course, that he had kissed her when the minister pronounced them married, but that had been a kiss with a purpose. A wedding kiss had a certain dignity to it. But this—this kiss was something a grieving widow should never be part of.

Matthew and her baby had only been dead for fifteen

days. What was wrong with her? They were cold in the ground and she was—she'd never felt this way before.

Elizabeth couldn't look at Jake, but she saw him stand up anyway.

"Don't worry," he said. "I'll leave—I—"

"You can't leave. You have to pray with Spotted Fawn."

Elizabeth kept her gaze on the table, but she eventually saw Jake start walking toward the ladder that went up to the loft.

Elizabeth was glad when he'd climbed to the top.

She wanted some peace while she contemplated what was wrong with her. Maybe all the time that Matthew had been grumbling because she wasn't enough of a lady to suit him, he wasn't talking about her hair or her clothes. Maybe he had been able to see inside of her and he realized she was a wanton. A loose woman.

She had never suspected. She had known she had to be very careful in the households where she worked. People all too often assumed servant girls had no morals. But she had always thought the problem was with other people. She had never expected to feel this heat rising up within herself.

Elizabeth listened to the sounds of Jake and Spotted Fawn praying together. How could he talk to God after this? He had promised to respect her grief. She had been Matthew's wife and she'd been on the verge of betraying his memory. The worst of it was that she had never been stirred like this with Matthew.

It wasn't until she heard the voices upstairs fade away that she stood up. She had cookies to bake before she went to bed. It was her gift to Spotted Fawn—something to give the girl comfort in the middle of the day tomorrow. It would remind her that people were at home thinking of her.

Jake sat up in the loft until Spotted Fawn closed her eyes. He could hear Elizabeth moving around downstairs and he thought he should give her some peace. He had blundered badly. He had seen the shocked distress on her face.

The problem was he'd neglected to court his wife. He was feeling married to her, even if he had no right to it. But he should have remembered she didn't feel the same about him.

He had noticed earlier in the afternoon that she was marking the days beside her bed as she had done beside her tent. He'd even counted the days she had there, but he had not realized what all of those lines in the dirt meant. Elizabeth still marked her life by the death of her husband. God might not be sending her the fever, but she considered herself tied to that family she'd buried in a way that left no room for him and his nieces.

He slowly climbed down the rope ladder. Elizabeth stood by the stove. The room smelled of ginger and molasses.

"Thank you for all you did today," Jake said quietly. Even if she didn't have room in her heart for him and his nieces, she was doing her duty by them. That was more than a lot of women would do. Come spring, he'd have to find a way to let her go if that's what she wanted.

Elizabeth didn't turn around as Jake walked out of the cabin. She was ashamed to face herself; she certainly didn't want her emotions to be seen by anyone else.

She finished baking the cookies. Then the baby woke up, hungry to be fed.

Elizabeth held the baby as it nursed. Everything always seemed better when she had the baby in her arms. The little one was gaining weight and making happy gurgling sounds that made Elizabeth smile.

The baby fell back asleep before Elizabeth returned her to the crib.

The house was warm and quiet again before Elizabeth went to bed. She didn't sleep well, but she hadn't expected to. Finally, she got up early. She wanted to make certain that the cabin was warm for Spotted Fawn when she dressed. Elizabeth had already decided that she would react to Jake as though nothing had happened last night. She didn't want Spotted Fawn to be any more worried than she already was.

Besides, the problem didn't lie within Jake; it lay within her. She was the one who had forgotten her husband.

When Spotted Fawn came down the ladder, Elizabeth put all worries out of her mind. Yesterday, she'd helped Spotted Fawn try on each new piece of clothing. Now, of course, the girl didn't like anything she was supposed to wear.

"I'll be cold," Spotted Fawn complained as she stood by the bed. Elizabeth was holding out the white linen pantalettes. Fortunately, the mercantile had some that were only a little large on the girl.

"You'll have an extra petticoat."

Black lace-up boots were sitting on one of the table chairs and the blue calico dress that Elizabeth had cut down from one of hers was hanging on the back of the rocking chair.

"I'm sorry, but you can't wear your leggings," Elizabeth said when Spotted Fawn kept frowning at the pantalettes.

Leggings wasn't the right term, but Elizabeth refused to call them animal pelts although that was what they really were. They had been Elizabeth's biggest challenge. She knew Spotted Fawn didn't stand a chance of being accepted by the other children unless she dressed like them and the leggings were the most obvious difference in her usual clothes. To make matters worse, the pelts had been rubbed with bear grease, probably to keep out the dampness, and had a strong animal smell.

When they'd gone to the mercantile earlier, Elizabeth had picked out a length of yellow calico to make another dress for Spotted Fawn. She'd start sewing on that this afternoon. And she'd see about dyeing the girl's old dress. Elizabeth had enough dried leaves and things to work with until she could grow the plants she usually used for her dyeing.

"Why don't you pick out your ribbon while I get the biscuits out of the oven?" Elizabeth suggested. The ribbons were the one thing that Spotted Fawn had liked about her new wardrobe.

Elizabeth wasn't surprised when Spotted Fawn picked the red one. The girl loved that color. After Jake came inside and they ate breakfast, Elizabeth tied the ribbon around Spotted Fawn's hair.

They had agreed they would all ride into Miles City in the wagon early enough to get Spotted Fawn to school on time. But Jake and Elizabeth would wait a couple of hours before stopping by the schoolhouse to see how things were going for the girl.

It was almost two hours after the school bell had initially rung that Jake looked up from the newspaper he was reading. He was sitting on a chair in a corner of the mercantile while Elizabeth stood over by the counter, looking at some dress patterns and chatting quietly with Annabelle. Fortunately, someone must have explained to Annabelle that Jake wasn't a wolfer because she had been cordial to him this morning.

"Do they ring the bell again for recess?" Jake asked as he stood up.

"Sometimes," Annabelle said. "I think it's up to the reverend."

"Is it time for us to go over?" Elizabeth looked up at him.

"I'd guess they are out to recess about now so it'd be as good a time as any to say hello to her."

Elizabeth nodded and put the pattern she was looking at back in the box on the counter. They both said goodbye to Annabelle and then they walked out of the store.

Jake heard the sound of children laughing as they walked down the street toward the schoolhouse so he figured he'd timed it about right for recess. Maybe if all of the kids were outside, he'd be able to ask the reverend how Spotted Fawn had done this morning. She knew how to speak English, but she'd be at the beginning of the McGuffey Reader they used in the school. He wondered if he shouldn't have tried to teach Spotted Fawn how to read a little bit before she went to school.

Jake heard a girl's scream and then a yell— *"Ho'ka hey."*

"What was *that?*" Elizabeth asked as she looked around.

Jake started to run. "The Lakota battle cry."

He heard Elizabeth's footsteps following him.

The reverend was coming out of the schoolhouse as Jake reached the steps.

"Where's Spotted Fawn?" he asked the other man.

"Behind the school with the other children. It's recess."

"Not any longer," Jake said as he started to run around the school.

Jake came to a stop when he reached the area behind the school. There were a few scrub trees close by, but the children were all standing still as though they were afraid to move. In the middle of them all, Spotted Fawn was crouched down with a wild look in her eyes and a small branch in her outstretched hand.

"What happened here?" Jake asked as he slowly walked toward Spotted Fawn. He knew she had times when she remembered her village being burned by some soldiers, but he hadn't expected this.

"My ma says we don't need to go to school with no Injuns," one of the taller boys said. He had flaming red hair which could only mean one thing: he was a Barker.

Jake didn't pay him any attention. He squatted down to be level with his niece. "Spotted Fawn?"

His niece looked up at him and, as she moved her arms, he saw the egg that had been thrown at the front of her new dress. Her face was dirty and she had a bruise on her cheek. Her red ribbon was missing and her hair swung around in disarray, the curls all gone.

"Elias Barker, you go inside this minute," the Reverend Olson's voice thundered behind Jake. "Mary, you go get Mrs. Barker for me. We're going to get this settled right now. I won't have my students caught up in a brawl."

"Well, it was her fault," Elias said.

"I doubt that very much," the reverend said as he pointed to the schoolhouse. "And if I find out that you're the one that started this, you're going to be cleaning blackboards for the rest of your natural life."

Jake saw Elias walk back to the schoolhouse at the same time as Elizabeth bent down beside him. She'd found the red ribbon somewhere.

"Here, let's get you cleaned up," Elizabeth said as she offered a hand to Spotted Fawn. "I'm sure Annabelle will let us use her room so you can get rid of this dirt."

Jake had thought Elizabeth had taken care of his nieces earlier. But it was nothing compared to what she was doing now. She helped Spotted Fawn get up and put her arm around the girl's shoulder as if they were going for a stroll somewhere. She made everything look so dignified.

Elizabeth turned to look at the reverend. "We'll be back as soon as we can."

The reverend nodded. "Rest assured, I'll have the class ready to apologize by the time you do."

Elizabeth nodded as she walked away with Spotted Fawn.

Jake still felt like pounding something. He settled for glaring at the two older boys who stood there smirking.

"What was that?" a nearby girl asked Jake and he wondered what she meant.

"That thing Spotted Fawn said," the girl persisted. "What does it mean?"

"That it's a good day to die. The Lakota Sioux say that when they ride into battle." Jake looked over and noticed the boys weren't smirking any longer.

"That doesn't make them come here, does it?" one of

the boys asked. "The Indians, I mean. It's not like *calling* them here, is it?"

Jake hid a grin as he shrugged. "You'll have to ask Spotted Fawn."

Jake wished adults could be told to stay after school the way their children could. Mrs. Barker wasn't doing anything to encourage peace in the classroom. Fortunately, the Reverend Olson had asked the rest of the children, even Elias, to stay outside while the adults had their meeting.

"I told you there would be trouble," Mrs. Barker said the minute the three adults were inside and the door was closed. "That girl doesn't belong here."

"Your son started the trouble."

"Indians have no place in the Miles City School."

"You don't own the school," Jake said.

"Neither do you."

Mrs. Barker stood in the school aisle with her hands on her hips and Jake felt his temper rising.

"Now, now," the reverend said as he came back from closing the door. "We need to talk about this rationally."

"I am being perfectly rational," Mrs. Barker said as she pointed at Jake. "He's the one who isn't moving ahead with the times. This isn't Indian country any longer. Those savages have no place here."

"My niece is going to this school and if you try to stop it I'll call in my loan on the lumber."

Mrs. Barker turned to the reverend. "Can he do that?"

Reverend Olson nodded. "It's his right. Half of the lumber in the school is his."

The woman turned around to face Jake. "The school can't afford that."

"I know."

"Well, your niece can sit on *your* side of the school then, but my son will sit on the town's side."

With that the woman turned and walked out of the school.

"Well, I guess that is a compromise," the reverend said hesitantly. "Or at least moving in that direction. She said Spotted Fawn can be here."

Jake grunted. He wasn't sure what was going on in Mrs. Barker's head, but he didn't think it was compromise.

Chapter Eight

Elizabeth used her fork to pick up a piece of cooked carrot. Jake had invited her to have a roast beef dinner with him in the hotel. Of course, she knew the invitation was just an excuse for them to linger in town until it was time for school to be dismissed. Neither one of them had wanted to return Spotted Fawn to school unless they were close enough to help if there were problems later.

"We should have pie, too," Jake suggested. His new hat sat on the chair next to him and Elizabeth sat across the table from him. He didn't even seem to notice that the waitress had stopped to ask several times if he'd like her to put his wonderful new hat on the rack by the door. *Wonderful,* Elizabeth thought sourly. That was the waitress's exact word. A hat wasn't wonderful.

"Pie would be nice," Elizabeth said. She needed to forget about Jake's hat and enjoy herself.

The hotel had maroon rugs spread along its floors and white linen napkins on the tables. The silver was heavy and well-polished. Elizabeth had never been in such a fine place to eat. Then the waitress came back. It seemed she was not only worried about Jake's hat;

she also seemed to be offering him more coffee than the other diners.

Not that Elizabeth was jealous, she assured herself. She just didn't want the young woman to exert herself for nothing. Elizabeth put her hand on top of the table and turned the ring on her finger slightly so it would catch more of the light shining in the window.

There—by the look on the woman's face, the waitress had finally noticed.

Elizabeth put her hand back on her lap. She liked the feel of the wedding band on her finger, although she was no longer sure if the ring reminded her of Matthew or of Jake. Not that it mattered. She planned to give Matthew the widow's respect that he was due. Not that she wanted women flirting with her other husband, either.

Oh, dear. She winced as she heard herself thinking. Was she that confused?

"I suppose you'd like to read some this winter," Jake said.

"What?" Elizabeth looked up from her plate. Why would he ask that? "I've always worked hard. Summer or winter."

She couldn't blame the waitress for noticing that Jake was the most handsome man in the room. He'd shaved again this morning and his short hair was falling into place nicely. The waitress was probably not the only woman here who had wondered about him.

Right now, he was leaning toward her, though. "I'm just saying that we could buy a book or two at the mercantile. This might be a good time to see what they have in stock. A home should have a few books for reading."

"Oh." Elizabeth guessed that made sense. She'd never had any leisure for reading anything but the Bible.

"Maybe there'd be a book we could read with Spotted Fawn."

"And poetry. We could get some poetry, too—that is, if you'd like it. I know women like their words."

"Yes, yes, of course." Elizabeth tried not to let her dismay show. She had learned how to read here and there in her life, but she'd never sat down with a book of poetry. She wasn't even sure she could read all those fancy words if she saw them. "If that's what you'd like."

"I…" Jake opened his mouth and then closed it again.

Elizabeth thought he looked frustrated. "I suppose you're worried about…things."

"What things?"

"Well, I imagine me and the girls are keeping you from your work."

"It's winter. I don't prospect in the winter. I think the Black Hills are pretty well played out anyway."

"Well, that's too bad." Elizabeth reached for the water glass at the top of her plate. "I guess."

Just then the waitress came to ask if they'd like some apple pie. At least this time she offered both of them cream on their pie.

They ate for a few minutes in silence.

Jake lingered over his dessert. He was trying to think of ways to court Elizabeth and he wasn't being too successful. He tried to remember if there had been any romantic gestures between his parents. He knew his father had gone to great trouble to bring a few of his mother's possessions out West with them. It was her rocking chair that Jake had in his cabin now. His mother had been very grateful to his father for keeping the chair with them. And his father had sent back East once for some lilac perfume that had delighted his mother. She said a

lady needed her perfume. Even if his mother returned
to her unhappiness, those presents brightened her life
for a time.

Maybe that's something he could do. "Is rose your
favorite scent, too?"

Elizabeth looked up from her plate. She'd just taken
the last bite of her pie.

"I mean, I know you're partial to the flower," Jake
continued. "I was just wondering about the smell of
them. Like in perfume."

"Rose water is lovely," Elizabeth said hesitantly.

Jake nodded. "We'll get some of that, too, then."

Elizabeth looked puzzled now. "You mean for Spotted Fawn? I'm not sure girls would wear rose water. Especially not to school. Mostly they just wash up good."

"No, I mean for you."

"Me? But I—I—"

Jake could tell he'd gone about this wrong. "You smell
wonderful all by yourself. I just thought you'd like a
present."

Now Elizabeth was looking at him suspiciously. "You
already got me a present. The teapot."

"Well, but Christmas is coming up. The teapot is
your wedding present. It can't be your Christmas present, too."

"Oh, I forgot. Yes, Christmas. It must almost be December."

All of Elizabeth's reserve melted away and she
beamed at him with pure delight on her face.

"It's December third." He wondered what she'd be
like on Christmas Day if the mere thought of the holiday brought out such sparkle to her eyes.

"Well, some rose water would be very nice then,"

she agreed. "I'll need to get you a present, too. And the girls, of course."

Jake nodded. He wished someone had told him how hard this courting business would be. He suddenly had a lot of sympathy with his father as he tried to please his wife. He wondered if he should warn Higgins.

Just then the man himself appeared.

"Annabelle told me where to find the two of you," the man said as he drew up a chair and sat down at the table with them. "She also told me what those kids did. Those boys should be turned over someone's knee. And I wouldn't mind doing the turning."

"Reverend Olson will handle it," Jake said.

Higgins snorted. "The Reverend doesn't stand a chance with boys like that. I know, I used to be one of them. They'll convince him to forgive them and then they'll be at it again."

Jake didn't answer. He wasn't sure if the reverend would be able to persuade the boys to behave or not. The reverend was a peacemaker and sometimes that didn't work so well with bullies.

"At least Annabelle asked her boy, Thomas, to look out for Spotted Fawn," Higgins said. "He told her what had happened when he came home for lunch."

"Thomas isn't big enough to face those boys," Elizabeth said. "He's only ten. Some of those older boys are thirteen or fourteen."

Jake stood up. "Then maybe we should go see for ourselves."

The schoolhouse door was closed when Jake, Elizabeth, and Higgins walked down the street toward it. It was midafternoon and the sky was gray. The streets of

Miles City were quiet. There weren't even any riders coming into town.

"We'll just peek in the window," Elizabeth said. None of them had gone up the steps yet. "I don't want the children to tease Spotted Fawn."

"Sounds to me like those boys already did that." Higgins grumbled.

"But no one has teased her about her parents yet," Elizabeth said. "And I don't want them to tease her about me."

Jake turned in astonishment and pushed his hat up so he could see his wife more clearly. She shouldn't be worried about people thinking badly of her because of him and the children. "How in the world could they tease her about *you?*"

Elizabeth raised her chin just a little. "The children might know I'm the woman who was supposed to die of the fever. And, I was camped out in that tent by the fort. Who knows what people are saying about me? They probably think I'm crazy. And no girl that age wants anyone to think she can't make a move without her parents watching her."

Jake jammed his hat back down on his head. Now, if that didn't beat all. "Well, I'm going to be watching no matter what she wants."

"Of course," Elizabeth said as she stepped up on the porch and slid closer to the window. "I never said we shouldn't watch over her. We just need to do it so no one notices. You know, tactfully."

"I can be tactful," Jake growled as he followed her up the steps.

Higgins snorted.

Elizabeth was the first one to peek in the window

of the schoolhouse. Jake and Higgins stood to the side of her.

"Oh," she breathed softly when she got a clear view.

Elizabeth's heart sank. Spotted Fawn and Thomas were sitting all alone on one side of the classroom. The other children were all pushed together on the benches on the other side. The Reverend Olson was not looking happy, but he was pointing to something on the map.

Elizabeth stepped away from the window.

Jake didn't even ask what she'd seen. He just took a look himself. His face was grim when he stepped back to where Elizabeth was standing.

"It'll get better," Elizabeth whispered hopefully.

"It will after I go in there and talk some sense to those kids."

"That might make it worse. It's Friday today. By Monday the children will probably have forgotten all about this. But if we stir it up even more, it'll take longer to fix it."

"I suppose you're right," Jake said softly as he rubbed a hand over his head.

Neither one of them had noticed that Higgins had stepped away until they heard him knocking on the school door.

"What's he doing?" Jake turned to whisper.

Elizabeth could only shake her head. Whatever it was, they were too late to stop it.

"Hello, everyone," Higgins said as he opened the door to the schoolhouse. Elizabeth and Jake could hear him clearly as he walked into the room. "I'm here to sign up. I figure it's time I learned to read."

Elizabeth and Jake were silent for a moment.

"Well, at least he's not her parent," Jake finally said.

"And she'll be safe," Elizabeth added.

They just looked at each other for a moment before they turned and walked back to the mercantile.

They didn't talk much as they rode back home in the wagon. Then Jake went to check the animals and Elizabeth brought out the yellow calico she was going to use in Spotted Fawn's new dress. If she worked on it this evening and all of Saturday, she should have the dress ready for the girl to wear Sunday morning.

Elizabeth picked the sharpest one of her needles and set it beside the fabric. Then she bowed her head. She hadn't been praying much lately. But she felt helpless in light of what she'd seen today. *Dear Father,* she prayed. *Help me to know what to do. Help me know what to say to Spotted Fawn. Don't let the bullies win.*

Elizabeth knew that the heartache she felt over Spotted Fawn was an echo of the things she had suffered in her own life as a child. The Bible said that God took care of the orphans, but she wasn't so sure. If He really cared so much, there wouldn't be any orphans to begin with. Or widows, either. Or mothers who lost their babies.

Her anger at God felt like ashes in her mouth. How could she be angry and need Him so much at the same time? She shook her head. She had no answers.

Spotted Fawn looked tired when she came home from school. Higgins walked her to the door and Elizabeth thanked him.

"My pleasure, ma'am," he said as he tipped his hat to her.

"How was the rest of the day at school?" Elizabeth asked Spotted Fawn after Higgins left.

The girl didn't say anything.

"Well, it'll be better on Monday," Elizabeth finally

said. "Would you like some biscuits? We have some left from breakfast."

Spotted Fawn nodded as she sat down at the table. Elizabeth opened a jar of rhubarb jam and set it beside the girl with her biscuits. The girl made no move to eat, so Elizabeth sat down beside her.

Only then did Spotted Fawn pick up the biscuit.

Dinner was late because they were waiting for Jake. Elizabeth had fried some potatoes and salt pork.

"I want to go home," Spotted Fawn announced after they had all finished eating.

"But you are home," Jake protested.

"I want to be with my people."

"Oh, dear," Elizabeth said. She looked up and met Jake's gaze.

Jake cleared his throat softly. "I know it was hard for you today, but you can't go back to your people."

"The Crying One and I will go," the girl insisted. "I have my pony. My father taught me like the son he did not have."

"Well, you're certainly not just going off by yourself," Elizabeth said. That much she knew. "Who knows what kind of people you'd meet out there."

"I'd meet my people," Spotted Fawn said. "I'm not afraid."

"Your father knew you'd need to be brave to live in the white man's world," Jake said. "But he wanted you to live. Both you and your sister."

Spotted Fawn was silent.

"Please, give it another chance," Elizabeth said. "I know it's hard, but we'll think of a way."

Spotted Fawn nodded and left the table. She went to sit by where her sister was lying in the crib. The girl picked up the baby and hugged her before returning her to the crib.

"There's church on Sunday," Jake said as his niece walked toward her rope ladder. "Maybe by then people will have calmed down a bit. The kids will forget all about which side of the room they're sitting on."

Elizabeth nodded as she looked over at Jake. She wondered if he really believed that or if he was just saying it to give Spotted Fawn hope. Elizabeth knew how it felt to be unwelcome in a place. She had needed to work hard in some households to find any measure of acceptance. Of course, she had always softened people's hearts first with the food she cooked. People always seemed friendlier if they were biting into a biscuit or a fried apple doughnut.

Jake had been in the lean-to repairing his traps and, when he came next door, he smelled a mouthwatering aroma. There were jars on the table and the smell of cinnamon in the air. And something else.

"Doughnuts!" Jake couldn't believe it. Sometimes for breakfast, one of the restaurants in Miles City served doughnuts but they weren't anything like the perfectly round golden things that were sitting on several plates on the table. Spotted Fawn was standing beside the doughnuts, her dress covered by a large white apron that was too big for her. She had a cup of what looked like sugar in her hand and a streak of flour on her face.

She reached for a plate and held it out to him. Jake took one of the doughnuts and bit into it. He'd never tasted anything so good. There were pieces of apple in the dough. And the cinnamon and sugar that his niece was sprinkling on them gave each one an extra something. They were wonderful.

"We're making fried apple doughnuts," Spotted Fawn said proudly.

Elizabeth looked up from where she stood by the stove. "I thought we could take a big basket of them to church tomorrow to pass around. It might, you know, help people get along better."

Jake decided the doughnuts were not the sweetest thing in this room.

"I think that's a fine idea," he said, grinning.

Even Mrs. Barker wouldn't be able to make progress against a campaign like this. The adults in Miles City, most of them men, would rather eat a doughnut than sign a petition any day. And the children—Jake would bet even Elias might be willing to sit on the same side of the schoolroom with Spotted Fawn if he got to eat these doughnuts.

Chapter Nine

Jake reined in his team of horses, pulling the wagon off the street near the schoolhouse. When they had built the schoolhouse, they had placed it on the edge of Miles City so there would be room behind it for the children to play. It was Sunday morning and he, Elizabeth and the girls were preparing to go inside for the usual preaching service. It had snowed a little last night and the air was still moist, but he could already see smoke coming out of the chimney on the building's roof so it should be warm enough inside.

Someday, Miles City hoped to have its own church, but for now everyone sat on the benches the children used during the week for school. It was a little crowded and occasionally someone would get ink on their clothes, but no one seriously complained. It was better than meeting in a saloon as some of the churches in other small towns had to do.

Jake walked around the wagon and lifted his niece to the ground before giving the baby to Spotted Fawn so he could help Elizabeth climb down.

"Wait," Elizabeth said after she shook out her skirts

and took the baby back. "I want to be sure everyone is buttoned up and spotless."

Elizabeth gave Jake and his niece a final inspection that would have made the sergeants at the fort proud.

Jake had shaved earlier and he was wearing the blue shirt Elizabeth had washed and ironed for him. Spotted Fawn had a red ribbon neatly tied in her hair. The girl's new dress wasn't ready, but Jake thought the made-over calico looked respectable enough on her thin frame. And the bruise on her face barely showed now. She didn't have a coat, but Elizabeth had given her his best blanket to wrap around like a shawl.

In Jake's opinion his niece looked pretty good. She would look even better, of course, if she didn't have that haunted look in her eyes. Earlier, when they had sat around the table before eating breakfast, he'd prayed for all of them. He asked God to make the doughnuts a true peace offering to the children and parents in Miles City.

Jake said another quick prayer now. Spotted Fawn had seen too much violence in her young life. Any kind of anger made her withdraw; he prayed God would help her feel safe.

Right now, his niece was standing very still while Elizabeth did her inspection. It was clear Spotted Fawn wanted to please the woman who was helping them all.

Elizabeth brushed a speck of something off Spotted Fawn's shoulder and then bent quickly to give the young girl a kiss on her forehead.

Spotted Fawn smiled slightly.

"We look fine," Elizabeth announced as she stood back up and gave a nod to Jake.

Jake couldn't agree more and he was only looking at one person. Elizabeth's gray dress made her eyes turn a deeper green and the resolve on her face moved his heart. He'd been wrong about her. She was nothing like his mother. She was already teaching Spotted Fawn some important lessons on how to face adversity. Elizabeth leaned into life, she didn't back away from it the way his mother had.

Jake took the baby so Elizabeth could carry the basket. He was proud of his family as they all walked up the steps of the schoolhouse. The sounds of voices reached them so he guessed a fair number of people were already gathering for the service. Normally, people kept their voices more subdued as they readied themselves for church, but it might be best if people were more relaxed today.

Even in the damp air, Jake could smell the doughnuts that Elizabeth was carrying in the basket. She had put a piece of red gingham on the bottom of the wicker basket and another one over the top. With her gray dress, it made everything look like a picnic.

When they reached the door, something about the voices inside the schoolhouse made Jake pause. The Reverend Olson had an early service for the soldiers at the fort so he wouldn't be here yet to do his civilian service. Generally, people did talk before he came, but these voices sounded sharper than usual. Instead of ushering Elizabeth in as he normally would, he stood in front of her as he opened the door.

"Whoa!" Jake recoiled as he saw what someone had done. The people inside were all standing around the edges of the room, looking uncomfortable and staring because, right there in the center of the schoolroom, from the front of the room to the back, someone had painted an ugly black stripe. The stripe divided the room in half. On one side, the painter had crudely lettered *Miles City.* And on the other, he or she had painted the words, *Dry Creek.*

Jake closed the door as quickly as he could and faced his family. "We're going home."

"What's wrong?" Elizabeth asked as she turned with him.

Jake shifted the baby he was holding so he could guide Spotted Fawn and Elizabeth with his other arm. "I'm taking all of you to the wagon. You can wait there while I talk to some people about something."

Elizabeth hesitated for a minute and then reached out her arms to take the baby from Jake. "We can manage. I'll take the girls and we'll wait for you there."

By now, Jake saw his friend Higgins riding into town at a slow gallop. Then he saw Wells, pounding hard behind him. They were clearly heading for the schoolhouse, even though they'd never shown any interest in going to any of the church services that had been held there in recent months.

Virginia and Annabelle were starting out into the street, but they held back to let Higgins and Wells pass.

"Go to Elizabeth," Jake called out to the women as he pointed to his wife.

Then he turned his attention to the men.

Higgins pulled his horse to a stop beside Jake. "You been inside?"

Jake nodded. "Enough to see what's been done. How did you know?"

"Annabelle sent Tommy out to tell us. He's putting his pony away now. We figured you might need some help."

Jake looked over at the wagon. He couldn't make out what any of the women were saying, but his heart sank when he saw the hand gestures Annabelle was making. She was clearly telling Elizabeth about the black dividing line. His earlier words about half of the school lumber being his must have prompted someone to do this. Even without the hand gestures, he would have known what was being said by how stiff Elizabeth's back became.

Higgins and Wells both climbed off their horses.

"Well," Higgins said as he rolled up the sleeves on his shirt. "Do we divide the room into three? I'll take the men on the right. Wells can take the middle. We'll show them what Dry Creek people are made of."

Jake shook his head. "It's a church. Besides, violence isn't the answer."

"Violence was sure the answer when it came to the classroom," Higgins protested. "I told Elias Barker that he'd be sorrier than a treed cat if he ever did anything to Spotted Fawn again. Then I gave him my grizzly growl. The boy turned white enough that I figure he got the message."

"He might have heard what you said, but it didn't change his mind so it didn't really solve anything," Jake said as he pointed to the wood-frame structure in front of them. "Just like all the talking I've been doing. And now we've got the line right across the room in there."

All of the men stood and looked at the building.

"Don't seem fair that we can't fight because it's a church," Wells finally said. "It's a schoolhouse most of the time."

"You shouldn't fight in a schoolhouse, either," Elizabeth said as she walked up behind them. "Besides, it's nothing to be afraid of. It's only a bit of paint."

Jake hadn't realized Elizabeth was there. He turned to look at her.

"Oh, I know it's meanness and spite at the same time," Elizabeth added. Her jaw was set and her eyes blazed with determination. "But we can't just go home and let them win. What kind of a message does that send to the children of this town?"

Jake realized he hadn't been thinking about the other children. He just wanted to protect Spotted Fawn. Like it or not, though, those children would be his niece's classmates. And maybe her neighbors for the rest of her life. Letting someone get away with that black line was bad for the whole town.

"Hey, something sure smells good," Wells said.

Spotted Fawn had just walked up with the basket of doughnuts. Annabelle and Virginia were walking beside the girl.

"It's our doughnuts," Spotted Fawn said. "Elizabeth says they're a peace offering."

Spotted Fawn looked up at him with a fragile hope in her eyes and Jake realized he needed to say something to encourage his niece. "If Elizabeth thinks they'll bring peace, we'll give it a try, won't we?"

Spotted Fawn gave a slight nod and then she looked over at Elizabeth.

If Jake hadn't seen it with his own eyes, he wouldn't have believed it. But he watched as Spotted Fawn squared her shoulders and then lifted her chin in the exact same way Elizabeth had done just seconds ago.

Jake might have a dozen enemies on the other side of that school door, but his heart was warm just the same. Maybe an Eastern lady had something to offer his nieces that he hadn't expected. He knew she had plenty to offer him.

This time, Jake opened the door so that he and Elizabeth could enter the schoolhouse together. Elizabeth carried the baby and Spotted Fawn, with her basket, followed close behind. By now, folks had sorted themselves out and were sitting on the Miles City side of the stripe. The benches were empty on the Dry Creek side.

Usually, people didn't even seat themselves this early. They stood and talked with each other until the reverend came. Jake would guess the good man wouldn't be here for another five minutes and maybe longer the way the roads were since the light snow that fell last night had already melted and turned the ground soft.

There were muddy footprints on the floor and the smell of wet wool in the air. Someone would have to scrub the floor before school tomorrow, but that wouldn't do anything to help that black painted line now.

Elizabeth put her hand on Jake's arm to caution him or he would have started to demand some explanation of how anyone could have let this happen. A wave of muffled voices greeted them as they walked up the aisle. Jake wasn't feeling too kindly toward his neighbors, but he tried not to show it. He even nodded to a few of the men; they didn't bother to nod back. Then he ushered Elizabeth and Spotted Fawn to a bench near the front on the Dry Creek side. He heard Higgins and Wells slip in behind him.

At least, Jake thought to himself, he knew who his friends in this town were. He looked across the aisle. Most of the men over there were merchants, except for Mr. Walls, the banker. All of them wore suits, though, even the barber who'd cut Higgins's hair. Jake hadn't really noticed before that none of the rougher element in town came to church. There should be some down-on-their luck miners somewhere. And the man who ran the livery stable. He knew dozens of Psalms by heart and was always quoting them. Where was he?

There was some rustling of skirts and Jake turned around to see Annabelle join Higgins and Wells on their bench.

There was more talking on the other side of the aisle. Jake smiled at his friends. "Thanks for joining us."

"No need to thank me and Wells," Higgins said. "We both live on the creek, too. It's our home as much as it is yours."

Wells nodded.

Jake looked over at Annabelle. The store clerk's color was high.

"You live in town," Jake said to her softly. "You don't have to do this. I know you don't like trouble."

"Injustice is what I don't like."

Jake smiled. "I guess that means we're all forgiven?"

Annabelle nodded. "Mr. Higgins tells me he's giving up wolfing and I'm not one to hold a person's past against them once they've turned over a new leaf. Besides, if I can stand up for a wolf, I can certainly stand up for a little girl."

Jake turned to Higgins. "You've given up wolfing?"

Higgins cleared his throat uncomfortably. "Now that I'm getting some learning, I figure I can do something else."

Jake nodded. "Good. That's, well, good."

Times were definitely changing here in the Territory.

Elizabeth looked around her. She was stunned by Annabelle's decision to sit with Higgins. The woman was still wearing her mourning black. Her husband hadn't been dead for all that long. The other woman didn't look guilty about it, either. Of course, sitting with a man wasn't the same as marrying one as Elizabeth had done. And Annabelle's husband had been gone for a couple of months instead of a couple of weeks. No, Elizabeth decided, it wasn't the same at all.

Just then a man stood up on the other side of the room. The man was well-past fifty, bald and he wore a vest that stretched over his large stomach so tightly that the buttons were in danger of coming loose. The man's suit was gray and Elizabeth watched in fascination as he pointed a finger across the room. "Annabelle Bliss, I believe you're sitting in the wrong place."

Oh, dear. Elizabeth saw Annabelle press her hands together until the knuckles were white. There was still a pale strip on her finger where she'd taken off her wedding ring.

Annabelle whispered. "That's my boss. Mr. Broadman. He's the manager of the mercantile."

"Maybe you should go over," Elizabeth whispered back. She didn't want Annabelle to lose her job over this. After all, the other woman didn't have a husband to support her now so she needed that income to take care of herself and her son.

Annabelle just shook her head, took a deep breath and then stood up. "You know I can't abide injustice, Mr. Broadman. If you want to fire me over that, then you're welcome to do it right now. Just remember, I'm a good employee and you—you won't have anyone to open the store tomorrow if I'm not working."

Elizabeth decided Annabelle was the bravest woman in the room. She stood there in her black wool dress, the material so heavy that it fell limp from the waist. The dye in the cloth was uneven and there was no sheen to the black like most mourning dresses would have. She must have made the dress hurriedly from what material she could find at the time. There wasn't even a touch of lace anywhere to relieve the somber lines of it. And yet Annabelle's shoulders were straight and her eyes challenging, even if her breaths were quick and shallow.

A brown-suited man stood up on the other side of the aisle. "If you want to talk injustice, you need to talk to my sister. She lost her husband to them Indians." He pointed to Spotted Fawn. "And my sister isn't the only one to lose a loved one to the savages. Decent folks shouldn't have to be reminded of that sadness when they sit down in church."

"These are only two little girls," Annabelle shot back. "And one's a baby. They haven't done anything to anybody."

A woman in a feathered hat stood up on the other side. "Haven't done anything! That one there almost scared my little Susan to death, carrying on like she did behind the school. Giving some wild war cry and waving that piece of branch around. It's heathen ways is what it is—heathen, I tell you."

Just then there was a loud bang from the doorway.

"Enough!" Reverend Olson roared. He stood in the open doorway, with the gray overcast sky behind him and his black coat jacket moving slightly from the breeze coming through the door. "Is this any way for the children of God to act? And on the day of the Lord! You should be ashamed."

Everyone grew silent, even the children. Elizabeth looked at Jake sitting next to her. He certainly seemed relaxed in the midst of all of this shouting. Didn't he know fistfights could break out at any minute? Matthew would have left the room by now, or crawled under the bench.

Elizabeth gasped. She was horrified at her thoughts. Men were brave in different ways. She shouldn't compare one to the other. She was being disloyal and it was shameful. She needed a new dress. A nice black dress would do, something like the one Annabelle wore. The dead deserved some respect and she intended for Matthew to get what he was due. A person shouldn't just slip out of this life without someone grieving for him.

She moved a little farther away from Jake, just in case anyone was paying attention to how close she was sitting, which she could see no one was.

If Jake hadn't felt Elizabeth move a little farther down the bench, he would have clapped his hands after the reverend's speech. He didn't want to embarrass his wife with his actions, though. Not that everyone else wasn't staring at the minister just as much as Jake was. Even Spotted Fawn was caught up in it. Reverend Olson took his time looking over the crude line that had been painted down the middle of the room and the markings on the wall telling people where to sit.

"I want to talk to whoever did this after the service," the minister said. "In the meantime, I want everyone to know it will not be tolerated, especially not in the house of the Lord. Now, I'm going to ask everyone to get up and change the place where they are sitting. And I expect a goodly number of people to be on both sides of that line when we're finished, just like it used to be."

No one moved.

"You can't tell us where to sit," a woman's voice called out from the Miles City side.

The room was silent for a moment. Jake thought he recognized the voice and he was right. It was Mrs. Barker who stood up and adjusted her hat.

The reverend looked over the people again before finally saying, "If you're not willing to sit with your neighbors, no matter what the color of their skin, I'm going to ask you to leave the house of the Lord today."

Jake heard a series of gasps from men and women on both sides of the aisle.

"You can't ask us to leave church," Mrs. Barker finally said. "This is—well, it's *church*."

Reverend Olson smiled a little sadly. "I'm not asking you to leave. I'm asking you to stay in the grace of God and in good fellowship with your neighbors."

"I've never heard of such a thing," Mrs. Barker protested as she stepped out into the aisle. "This is our church. It belongs to this town."

"It's God's church," the minister replied. "It belongs to Him."

"Well, God's church will be empty then," Mrs. Barker said indignantly as she walked down the aisle to where the reverend stood. "You can't have a church with no people, remember that. And don't come complaining to me when the parents vote not to pay you for your work at the school, either."

Mrs. Barker turned to those still sitting on the benches and pointed her finger at them. "The rest of you, if you care about the future of this town, you'll get up and follow me out of here right now. We can't have Indians walking around like they belong here. If the railroad people see that, they'll never make us a stop. They're looking for civilized towns where their passengers will feel safe. No one feels safe with Indians sitting right next to them. Besides, it just isn't right."

With those words, Mrs. Barker walked straight out of the church. A flash of lightning streaked across the gray sky that showed through the open door, but no one paid it much attention, not even when the thunderclap followed. It only took a few minutes for most of the rest of the people to follow her out. Some of them stopped to murmur a few words to the reverend on their way, but none of them turned back to sit down again.

"Poor fools," Jake muttered to himself as the last Miles City person closed the door on their way out of the building.

Jake looked around and counted a total of nine people still inside. The reverend, himself, Elizabeth, Spotted Fawn, the baby, Annabelle, Higgins, Wells and Virginia Parker. The young woman surprised him. She was sitting in the back on the Dry Creek side, looking unsure of herself. Jake started to say something to her when the door opened again.

Annabelle's son, Tommy, walked in. The boy's hair was wild and his shirt had come untucked from his pants. Jake didn't know where the boy had been, but he could see his eyes grow wide as he walked down the aisle and looked around.

Jake was prepared for a question about where the people had gone, but the first thing the boy said was, "Do I smell doughnuts?"

Jake grinned. At least some things never changed. "You sure do. And we have plenty to share, too." Jake looked up at the minister. "After the service, that is."

The Reverend Olson walked forward, too. He looked tired. "I think we have a few minutes for the boy to eat a doughnut before we begin the service. I wouldn't mind sitting a bit myself and having one, either. My wife wasn't feeling good so she didn't come this morning."

"Come, sit with us," Elizabeth spoke as she stood up and then looked at the girl next to her. "Spotted Fawn, can you help me pass out some of our doughnuts?" Elizabeth glanced back at the reverend. "You're sure there's time?"

He looked to the back of the room and addressed Virginia. "Does that work with your solo?"

"I'll be ready to sing whenever you want me to," the young woman said from where she sat. "Any time is fine."

Jake thought Virginia still looked a little unsure of herself, sitting alone in the back. He supposed she hadn't trusted her welcome enough to sit with the people of Miles City, not now that she was playing piano in that saloon of Colter's.

He nodded and smiled. She was welcome to sit with them—that much was for sure.

"I always look forward to your singing," the reverend said as he sat down on one of the benches. "You've got a lovely voice."

Jake was glad Elizabeth wasn't as fragile as Virginia. Once Elizabeth had gotten past her determination to meet the angels right away, she'd always seemed to have her feet planted squarely on this earth. He appreciated that.

"Can I go get my friend?" Tommy asked after he'd taken a bite of his doughnut. "He won't want to miss out on this."

The reverend nodded. "Just get him back here quickly."

The boy started running down the aisle.

"Tommy!" his mother scolded him. "No running in church."

By then the boy was already outside. Annabelle turned to the reverend. "I'm sorry about that. I try to teach him better, but...without a father, I—"

Jake noticed Higgins go red in the face. No one else seemed to see it, though.

"After what this church has seen today, a boy running in the aisles is refreshing," the reverend said as he held up a half-eaten doughnut. "These are wonderful, by the way."

"They were going to be our peace offering," Elizabeth said as she quietly asked Spotted Fawn to pass the basket back to the man. "We thought maybe people would..." Her voice trailed off. "Well, I guess it didn't work."

Reverend Olson shook his head. "Now, we don't know that. It's still an act of faith. Sometimes faith takes time."

Just then Tommy burst back into the church. "They're coming."

"Who's coming?" his mother asked as she stood up, looking a little alarmed.

Tommy just turned to grin. He still had sugar on his face. "I told them there were doughnuts and that Miss Virginia was going to sing. They like to hear her sing."

Jake's heart lifted when he saw who was coming through the door. The first man had the look of a hard-luck miner. The second was a soldier from the fort. The third was a drifter and the fourth looked like a trapper. None of them wore suits and they all needed a shave. But, they all stepped into the room with reverence, taking off what hats they had on their heads.

The last two through the door were Colter and the

boy, Danny. Apparently, the boy had been released from jail. His light brown hair was newly cut and the wool pants on his lanky frame looked clean. Colter still had a hold on his collar, as though he didn't quite trust the boy yet.

Jake didn't blame him. The boy looked a little older than Spotted Fawn and full of vinegar. Colter appeared as bewildered about parenthood as Jake felt. Maybe more.

"Welcome," Jake said.

"Come have a doughnut—or two," Elizabeth said as she moved so Spotted Fawn could get to the aisle to pass the basket.

Jake watched over Elizabeth and Spotted Fawn until they had given out all of the doughnuts and grains of sugar was all that was left at the bottom of the basket. But by then, there were a good forty people in the church and none of them cared which side of the room they sat on.

When Elizabeth settled in next to him, Jake was content. Now that the folks who worried about appearances were gone, he could relax. It seemed the most natural thing in the world to put his hand over Elizabeth's hand as it lay on her lap. He snuggled the hand a little closer to him and she didn't object. He decided she was beginning to accept him as her husband and it made him feel good inside. He'd never expected being married would feel like this—as if the world was a better place just because someone else was in it.

Chapter Ten

Elizabeth felt the heat rush to her face. She supposed Annabelle meant well with her comments, but Elizabeth felt strange talking about Jake. So she bent her head to concentrate on the scrub brush she had in her hand. The church service was over and the women were all down on their knees trying to get rid of that black line while the men were out cutting firewood for the upcoming school week. The reverend had started to feel unwell and he was home now, hopefully eating some of the soup Annabelle had sent over for him and his wife.

"Well, anyway, I thought it was sweet," Annabelle finished up her thought as she leaned back. "The way your husband was holding your hand in church."

Elizabeth suddenly realized that Annabelle had been saying the word *husband* for the past ten minutes and the only face that had come into her mind had been Jake's.

"My husband's dead," she said in a twist of guilt.

"Oh," Annabelle said in surprise.

"Oh," Virginia echoed. Her blue eyes were wide with confusion, but she didn't say anything.

"Besides, it was chilly," Elizabeth finally added as she leaned into her scrubbing.

The women were silent after that.

Annabelle had lent both Elizabeth and Virginia old dresses to wear while they cleaned. The dresses hung a little loose on both Elizabeth and Virginia so they'd tied them tight with the strings of the aprons she'd also given them. They'd started by washing the mud off the entire floor so by now they were wet and dirty as they worked on the black line.

Spotted Fawn sat in the back of the room, playing with the baby.

Elizabeth didn't want either woman to think she was unfriendly. She paused in her scrubbing and leaned back to wipe her forehead.

"Have you noticed this isn't milk paint?" Elizabeth finally asked. That seemed like a safe topic. "I wish it was—it'd be easier to get off."

Milk paint was what poor people generally used. Elizabeth hadn't stirred up any for a few years, but she knew how to search out the right clays to give the mixture color. But she doubted many people here still made the lime and milk paint. It was too messy. And, like dyeing one's own cloth, it was going out of fashion.

"I suppose everyone buys that new oil paint now," Elizabeth continued. "I miss the colors of the milk paint, though. It makes such lovely soft, rich colors."

"I know what you mean," Annabelle said. She tucked a few strands of her hair back into place. "We have some of that oil paint at the store, of course, but it's not the same. I forgot you'd mentioned you made your own colors. With that and the dyeing both. I've never done that."

"You do your own dyeing?" Virginia asked.

Elizabeth nodded. "I even made my own Turkish red calico last year. Oil-boiled, of course, and with wax for the pattern on the cloth. That was just extra, though. What I wanted most was to dye enough yarn for a small blanket."

"Really?" Virginia said. "I was thinking I might try to dye some of my old dresses." She flushed. "Nothing as complicated as an oil-boiled dye, of course. They're just getting faded and—well, I can't…"

The young woman let her voice trail off.

"No need to be shy about money with us," Annabelle said as she put her brush back in the rinse water. "Both of us are widows. We understand it's not easy for a woman to make her way without a man."

"That's true," Elizabeth added.

"I don't know what I would have done when my brother died if I hadn't gotten that job at Colter's saloon." Virginia wiped her reddened hands on her apron. "I wrote to my other brother, but I don't really know where he is. He hasn't written in years. And I couldn't stay at the fort. I'd applied everywhere else for a job and didn't find anything except with Colter."

"Well, I hear the man runs an honest place," Elizabeth said. Jake had told her that much.

"The men there respect him."

"Well, I'm glad he has the good sense to send you home before dark. That's all I've got to say," Annabelle declared.

Elizabeth noticed the light in Virginia's eyes when they talked about the saloon owner. She wondered if the young woman had any idea that she was in love with the man. It was too bad, really, Elizabeth thought. She didn't suppose there was much to recommend a marriage between the two. Not even the way they looked together.

Virginia looked like a seashell, all white and pink and shiny clean. Colter was dark and lean. Elizabeth supposed he was handsome enough, but he reminded her more of a stormy day than a sunny one.

"I was pleased to see him come to church this morning." Elizabeth thought she should say what positive things she could about the man. Everyone deserved a chance. "And he brought the young boy with him— Danny."

Virginia nodded. "He keeps telling Danny to improve himself so he doesn't get sent back to that jail. That's why he brought him, I'm sure." She looked at Annabelle. "I'm glad Danny has made friends with your Thomas."

"If he wants to improve himself, Danny should be going to school, too." Annabelle put her brush down. "I know he doesn't, but Tommy must know him from somewhere and—" She stood up suddenly and put her hand to her heart. "Don't tell me Danny's been hanging around that—that place!"

"No, no," Virginia reassured her. "Colter doesn't let boys near the saloon. Well, except for Danny and he's in the back room washing dishes. I think the boys met at the sheriff's when Danny was in jail. The sheriff let them play checkers through the bars."

"In the *jail*. My baby's been going to the jail!" Annabelle walked over and sat down on the nearest bench. "I'm sorry. I just had no idea it would be so hard to raise a boy without a man to help. And me working all day."

"Higgins might help you out," Elizabeth said, a slight smile on her face.

"Why I'd never—" Annabelle started and then looked

at Elizabeth. "No fair. I never said I was interested in Mr. Higgins. He's just a—a friend."

Elizabeth grinned. "I know."

Annabelle looked at her and started to smile back. "Okay, no more encouraging remarks for you, either. Although I am anxious to know how you and Jake are doing. I mean, I hope it's okay. I feel guilty for trying to talk you out of it earlier."

"You were trying to be helpful," Elizabeth said. She felt bad now for being so short with the woman earlier. If she'd known it was guilt that was prompting her comments, she would have assured her that things were fine.

"Like we all know, it's just hard for a woman alone," Annabelle said. "I was worried about you."

"I appreciate that," Elizabeth said. "But you can ease your mind. Jake is a perfect gentleman."

"I wish Colter were a perfect gentleman," Virginia said, and then blushed. "I mean, he doesn't even know I'm there and I'm playing the piano so everybody should know I'm there. Why I've played 'Amazing Grace' several times and he hasn't even moved. Some of those men in there have wept when I've played that song, especially when I sing it, too. And he doesn't even blink an eye."

The young woman bristled with such indignation that her smooth blond bun quivered slightly on the back of her neck.

"I think he was half-asleep," she continued. This time her voice wavered a little.

"Well, he might not know the song," Annabelle said kindly. "He's wearing a suit now, but I'd guess Colter had a rough life before he got that saloon of his. He's probably not too familiar with hymns."

"I guess," the younger woman said and then sighed. "I just don't understand men."

"If it's any consolation, neither do I, dear, neither do I," Annabelle said. "And I've been married twice before."

"Twice?" Elizabeth asked.

Annabelle nodded. "I've buried two husbands. Tommy's dad and then my last husband."

"I'm sorry," Elizabeth murmured. It didn't seem fair that a woman should have to bear that grief twice. And Annabelle was only ten or so years older than she was.

The three women sat and looked at each other for a minute or so. Elizabeth thought it was a nice silence. It occurred to her that she was actually making some new friends. She wasn't going to want to leave this place in the spring.

"I could help you if you want to dye some things," Elizabeth said as she turned to Virginia and then looked back at Annabelle. "And you probably have some things of Thomas's that you'd like dyed."

Both women nodded.

"I'd like that," Virginia added.

"Could we do it before Christmas?" Annabelle asked.

"I don't see why not," Elizabeth declared. She had presents to make, as well. "Although we still need to figure out what to do here."

"I suppose we could paint the whole floor black," Annabelle said dubiously. "But we only have one can of black paint in the store right now and that wouldn't be enough. Besides, even if we could get it covered, it wouldn't be dry before school tomorrow. Not with the amount of paint we'd need to use."

"I have the afternoon off," Virginia offered, "but if the paint won't dry…"

"We don't need to paint the whole floor," Elizabeth said. "I have an idea."

Jake shifted the trunk of the tree he was carrying over his shoulder. He and the other men had walked toward the fort far enough to come to the wooded area that the soldiers used when they needed firewood. Higgins, Wells and Colter each had an old cottonwood on their shoulders, too. They'd only bothered to strip the bigger limbs off the trees and one of the remaining smaller branches of his tree was scratching Jake on the back of his neck.

"Explain to me again why these trees will burn so slow the reverend will hardly ever need to feed the fire," Jake said as he stopped to set his tree down so he could break off the offending branch. Then he turned to the men behind him. "You're the one who said it, Higgins."

"Well, I didn't say no one would ever need to feed the fire," Higgins objected as he let his own tree slide to the ground. "I just said it should burn longer because these pieces will be so thick."

"They're thick all right," Wells said as he let his own tree fall to the ground. "And heavy."

Jake rubbed the back of his neck. He wouldn't have those tree scratches if he'd kept all his hair. Oh, well. "I'm not sure anyone will show up for school Monday anyway so it might not even be worth it to have a fire."

Jake knew all of those responsible citizens filing out of church this morning were bound to make some changes. He figured school is where they'd start.

"Let me know if they don't come." Colter let down

his own burden. "I'll send Danny over if I know—" The man broke off.

"I'm sure there's room for Danny even if everyone else is there," Jake said as he sat down on his tree just as Higgins and Wells had done with theirs. "The reverend invites all of the children to school."

Colter turned around. "I haven't sent the boy before because I was worried the kids would make fun of him. His mother used to work in one of the other saloons, you know."

"And his father?" Jake asked.

Colter snorted. "See, that's the kind of thing he'd face. Some folks assume I'm his father—poor kid—but I only met his mother a couple of years ago. And then only to say hello. She died soon after and, well, there was no place for the boy to go so I figured working in a saloon was better than starving to death."

"Don't worry about him," Jake said. "Higgins will be there so he'll see that things go okay for him."

Colter looked over at Higgins in surprise. "You're teaching school?"

"Not teaching. Going," Higgins said proudly. "I aim to learn to read."

"A man doesn't need to know how to read," Wells protested. "Knowing how to read won't get these logs to the school any faster, now will it?"

"Well, maybe not," Jake said as he stretched out his legs. "But it would be mighty nice to sit by the fire that comes from these logs and read a book some evening."

"Women like that, don't they?" Colter asked. "Reading by the firelight?"

Jake nodded. "Most women, I'd say. They think it's romantic."

Jake was reminding himself to buy a book of poetry for Elizabeth. He kept remembering that the soldier at the fort had written his own poem for Elizabeth, but Jake didn't know if he could do that. A nice leather-backed book of poems should convey his feelings just as well.

Then Jake realized it was someone else who had thought of the romance of words first and he looked at the saloon keeper more closely. "You got some particular woman in mind for your firelight reading?"

Colter shrugged. "Maybe."

Jake frowned. He shifted his weight on the tree in case he had to stand. "Well, I hope it's not Virginia Parker. She's a decent woman and—"

"Don't you think I don't know that?" Colter interrupted in disgust. "Why do you think I make her leave my saloon before my business even starts?"

"I don't know. I never did understand why you hired her in the first place. The only kind of piano playing she can do is hymns."

"I know. She's chased away most of my customers. And the ones who haven't gone have either sworn off their whiskey or they sit there, sobbing into their drinks and talking to their dead mothers. Even my bartender is threatening to quit. He says it's depressing to watch grown men behave that way."

"Well, there must be some other job for her in a town the size of Miles City."

"She's already got a job," Colter said as he stood up. "At my place."

So that's the way it was, Jake thought as he stood, as well. "A woman like that deserves a home and marriage and—"

"I know, I know," Colter said as he walked ahead a bit

and kicked a couple of rocks out of the way. Jake thought the man did it with more force than necessary, but he supposed it was just as well. It was a hard thing when a man set his eyes on a woman who was out of his reach.

"Well, let's get started again," Jake said as Higgins and Wells both stood up. "We've got to get these trees back to the school so we can take an ax to them."

"Isn't this Sunday?" Higgins grumbled as he lifted his tree. "It's supposed to be a day of rest."

"Well, this Sunday isn't," Jake answered as he lifted his, too. He hoped the women were having an easier afternoon than the men were. "Whose idea was this to bring in these trees anyway?"

No one owned up to it.

By the time the men carried their old trees into the school yard, the afternoon was starting to fade. They pulled the trees around to the back of the schoolhouse to where the woodpile usually was.

"Looks like the reverend has enough wood to keep the fire going for most of a day," Jake said. "Maybe I'll just wait until tomorrow to come around and chop this log up for him."

It would give him a chance to check on the students, Jake thought. Even Elizabeth couldn't accuse him of not being tactful if he was chopping wood while he was looking around.

"I can come over in the afternoon to help, too. There isn't anything happening at my place anyway," Colter offered. "Besides, well, I'd just feel better keeping an eye on things."

Jake looked at the man. "You know something or is it just a hunch?"

Colter shrugged. "A little of both. Danny said he

thought he overheard some of the boys talking about doing something Monday."

"Well, why didn't you say anything before?"

"I'm saying it now," Colter protested. "Besides, he wasn't sure. He was slipping around to enter the saloon by the back door when he saw a couple of the older boys sitting there. They stopped talking while he walked by, but he thought he heard them say something about school or Sam Lee's laundry. He wasn't sure which."

"I can't imagine what they'd want with Sam Lee. I don't see those boys being overly concerned about clean clothes."

"Boys sometimes just talk big," Higgins said. "Maybe those boys didn't mean anything."

Colter nodded. "That's one of the reasons I didn't say anything earlier."

"And the other reason?" Jake asked.

Colter looked him in the eye. "I wasn't sure anyone would believe Danny anyway. Not after him stealing that watch."

"Does the boy make a habit of lying?" Jake asked.

"I've never known him to. Boys are hard to know sometimes, though. I get the feeling he's at one of those places in his life where he could go either way."

"Well, the boy's had a hard life," Higgins said.

Colter nodded. "I'm the closest thing he has to a parent and I don't really know what to do for him."

"You feed him, clothe him—you brought him to church," Jake said. "That's a good start."

"Well, I only got him to come to church because he knew Virginia was going to sing. He worships that woman. Says he's going to marry her when he grows up."

"Oh," Jake said in surprise and then he thought about it a minute. "Oh."

"I know," Colter said wryly. "Any other competition I wouldn't mind."

"Well, what'd the boy say he heard?" Higgins asked impatiently. "That's the important thing."

"He just said they were talking about showing them Indian lovers a thing or two." Colter looked chagrined. "Sorry. Those aren't my words. Danny also said they were going to pound the mountain man. I wondered how they could describe Sam Lee that way, but now that I know Higgins is going to school, I figure they must mean him."

"Well, just let them try!" Higgins bellowed.

"Keep your voice down," Jake said with a look at the schoolhouse. "We don't want to get the women all worried."

The men were silent for a bit. They were at the back of the schoolhouse so Jake listened for the sound of the front door opening. He didn't hear anything.

"I guess we might as well see how the women are doing anyway," Jake said.

"I doubt they could get that paint off with those brushes of theirs. I don't think it can be done," Colter said.

Jake was of the same opinion, but he wasn't about to say anything. He'd come to realize that women had their own way of solving problems and he wasn't betting against them. Not anymore. Especially not when Elizabeth was involved.

Chapter Eleven

Jake walked into the schoolhouse and stopped. If it wasn't for some old cards his mother had kept in a box by her bed, he wouldn't recognize what he saw. It was Christmas. Yellow stars were painted on the black line in the middle of the floor and red-berried holly twined around them both. The women had their backs to him and hadn't heard him come inside. They were standing at the front of the room painting Merry Christmas on the Dry Creek side of the wall. There were even red-painted bells ringing over the words and more stars falling everywhere.

"You've been busy," Jake said as the other men crowded into the room behind him. He glanced over and saw his nieces were curled up together, sleeping on a blanket in a corner of the room.

"Don't walk on the line," Elizabeth said as she turned around. "It's not dry yet."

Jake grinned. His beautiful wife had a dab of yellow on her cheek and a streak of red on the back of her hand. And she looked happy. "We'll be careful."

"I guess you decided not to scrub it all away," Colter

said as he carefully walked closer to the line and looked down at all of the painted stars and berries.

Jake wondered if the other man recognized what he saw.

"Christmas," Jake said quietly and the other man nodded.

"We came up with a different plan." Virginia turned around and smiled at Colter. Well, actually, she beamed at the man. Jake was surprised Colter managed to sit down on one of the benches before his legs gave out. Jake was only getting the reflection of the look and it knocked him back a little, too.

It was hard to tell if Virginia was beaming because of the man or because of her excitement over what she was doing. She held a paintbrush that had been dipped in yellow paint and she waved it around freely as she spoke.

"It was really Elizabeth's idea but everyone, even the reverend, thought it was wonderful," Virginia continued, with such enthusiasm a man could only conclude it was the painting that was the cause of her exuberance at the moment.

Jake saw Colter's jaw tighten a little and he almost felt sorry for the man. It must be a disappointment to lose out to a holiday the man probably didn't even celebrate.

"All kids love Christmas," Elizabeth explained as she carefully put her paintbrush down in an empty tin can. "So we decided to remind everyone that the season of goodwill is coming soon. There'll be time enough to paint over the whole floor after Christmas. And the front wall, too."

The men were silent for a moment, letting everything sink in.

"Well, the stars are real nice," Jake said. "I'm partial to them myself."

He always had liked reading about how the star guided the wise men on their trip. He could relate to men like that. Not to the value of their gifts, of course, but he knew many men who traveled in search of something they weren't sure they'd find.

Men like Higgins, for instance. Jake noticed that the man had quietly made his way up to the wall where Annabelle was painting a sprig of holly.

His partner, Wells, though, appeared to be looking for treasure of a different sort. He eyed the empty basket that Spotted Fawn had carried around this morning. "I don't suppose you'll be making any more of those doughnuts? To celebrate the goodwill and all."

"I plan to make another batch for the children," Elizabeth said. "Most of them didn't get any this morning. And we want to have lots of good things for Christmas."

"Could there be pies, too?" Wells asked. "My mother used to make the best pecan pies for Christmas."

Jake had never heard the man mention a longing for pie before. Or a mother, either.

"Pies, too," Elizabeth agreed. "I even have some pecans in a box just waiting to be used."

The years rolled away and Jake remembered his mother trying to make a pie once. He'd picked some berries for her; he'd long since forgotten what kind they were. But his mother had spent the morning making a crust and finally had slipped the pie into the oven. The heat had been too hot, or the plate too full, because the berries juiced up and spilled over and onto the bottom of the stove. It had taken the rest of the day to get the smoke out of the cabin and his mother had declared the pie too ruined to eat. She'd never tried to make another one.

Jake brought himself back to the present. One thing he knew was that Elizabeth wouldn't have given up after one try.

"We talked to Reverend Olson," Elizabeth was saying, her voice quietly excited. "And we're going to work with the students to put on a Christmas pageant."

"For the whole town," Virginia added as she spread her arms out and twirled around. "Isn't that wonderful? The children are going to be angels. And sing."

Jake exchanged a worried look with Colter and then asked. "All of the children?"

"Of course," said Virginia.

"I'm not sure the older boys will——" Colter began until Virginia started to look disappointed. "I mean, they may need to have special costumes. The little children can wear a man's shirt or something, but——"

"We've got the costumes all planned out," Virginia said as she brightened again. "Elizabeth said we can use the old union suits that are packed away in the things from her wagon. We can put something with them if we need to make them whiter. Or dye them if we want, although then I'm not sure she'll be able to sell them afterward. Anyway, they'll be big enough to fit the boys so they're perfect. In fact, we'll need to cut them down for the younger children." Virginia stopped to take a breath.

She looked right at Colter.

"I'm sure they'll be grateful for the ah——" Colter cleared his throat "——for the opportunity to perform."

"And it's not like they'll have wings or anything," Jake added hopefully. Someone needed to say something and it was obvious Colter wasn't able to get the words out. If there were no wings, the boys might be able to tell themselves they were trees or rocks or something.

"Wings!" Virginia exclaimed. "Of course, we'll need to make wings."

Jake had a sinking feeling. "What time are you planning to announce this to the kids?"

"Tomorrow morning just after they finish working their sums. About ten o'clock." Elizabeth walked over and stood beside Virginia. "We wanted to wait until they finished so the excitement wouldn't distract them from it."

Jake nodded. He looked over at Colter and the other man dipped his head in answer. They'd both be outside the schoolhouse cutting wood about then. They knew those boys wouldn't agree to wear wings without a fight. Fortunately, the women hadn't mentioned halos yet. Jake knew he wasn't going to even say a word about that.

"I don't suppose some of the boys could be innkeepers or something?" Jake asked. He guessed they'd rather sweep the floor than flap their wings with the girls, but he wasn't too sure. "Or maybe shepherds? Shepherds would be okay."

It wouldn't be the cowboys these boys dreamed of becoming, but at least being a shepherd was a man's job and they would be proud to do it.

"Well, we should have a Joseph, I suppose." Elizabeth bit her lip in thought. "And a Mary and the Baby Jesus."

"Mary and Joseph could be adults." Annabelle turned around finally to join the conversation. "It is supposed to be a pageant for the whole community. Adults should do their part."

Jake wondered what Mrs. Barker's Civic Improvement League would think of the pageant. On this issue he might even agree with her. He sympathized with any boy that had to wear a halo or wings or pretend to be married to someone he probably didn't like.

But, even if they had Mrs. Barker behind them, these boys would have a hard time going against Christmas. Not because they cared whether they were holy or not. No, it would just eventually become clear that, if there was no Christmas, there'd be no doughnuts. He was sure rumors of those doughnuts had reached all the boys in town by now.

Elizabeth felt tired and happy as she rode home in the wagon with Jake and the girls. She had the baby in her arms and Spotted Fawn was sitting on the seat between her and Jake. It made Elizabeth feel as though they were a real family, sitting together after all they'd been through that day.

There was little more than a rut for the wagon wheels to follow as they drove home. After the overcast skies that morning, the afternoon sun had come out and dried the dirt so the wheels turned smoothly.

"I'm glad it's not raining still," Elizabeth said. "It's going to take most of the night for that paint to dry as it is. If it rained, I don't know if the floor would be ready for school in the morning."

"It wouldn't be such a bad thing if school couldn't meet for a day or two." Jake pulled on the reins slightly to signal the horses to make a wide turn. They were almost to the last small rise before they dipped down and could see the first signs of home.

"Oh, but the children have to go to school."

"I know, but a day or two wouldn't matter much."

They were both silent for a bit.

"Do you think we did the right thing?" Elizabeth finally asked. "Leaving the Miles City side of the room bare for the others to paint? We didn't want to look like we were taking over everything. I mean—maybe they don't want to wish anyone Merry Christmas."

"It wouldn't be very neighborly not to say Merry Christmas."

Elizabeth nodded. She supposed so. It bothered her that, even though they had painted things over that line on the floor, the line was still there in her mind. It was now Miles City and Dry Creek; everyone made the distinction. Annabelle, Jake, Higgins, even Wells. When they had left for church this morning, they were one community and now, only eight hours later, they were two.

Elizabeth wondered if that was progress or not. She supposed it was too early to judge that really. So far, Dry Creek didn't have much to recommend it. There was no good road to where Jake had his cabin. No school. No hotel. Nothing but a flat stretch of gray dirt with a few ripples in the landscape and those cottonwood trees. In time, though, things could change. Maybe a little community would grow here someday and have some of the same kind of heart the Dry Creek side of things had shown this morning.

But she doubted she would be around to see it. Even with all of the friendship she'd seen today, she didn't feel easy in her heart about staying here. She didn't know what she would do in the spring.

"We're home," Jake said softly and Elizabeth noticed that Spotted Fawn had gone to sleep next to her uncle. The baby was sleeping, too.

"It's been a long day," Elizabeth whispered back.

Jake bedded the horses down for the night and fed the other animals before he started toward the cabin for supper. It was dusk. He stopped a moment to look around his land. The cottonwood trees sheltered him from the east. The ravine that dipped down to the creek was close enough that hauling water was no problem. The emptiness that stretched in all directions made some people uneasy, but it gave him peace.

This was a good place to live. He would improve on it over the years, of course. Maybe he'd send a telegraph and order another load of lumber for when the Missouri river opened up again and the steamboats were able to make the trip up to Fort Benton. Whether or not Elizabeth stayed with them, the girls needed a better home. He might as well start on it this summer.

In the meantime, he reminded himself to buy more coal oil for the lamp. One nice thing about having a family was he was using the lamp more often in the evening. He felt satisfaction just walking to the house and seeing the warm glow coming from the windows. One day soon, he'd see about getting some new books, too.

The smell of fried onions greeted him when he stepped in the door. Two plates had been set on the table and Elizabeth was standing by the stove. She'd worn the dress she'd used for scrubbing the floor home, but had changed into one of her own dresses. It wasn't any newer than her scrubbing one, but it was clean and dry.

"Spotted Fawn already ate and went to bed," Elizabeth said. "And I fed the baby, so she's sleeping, too."

Jake glanced up to the loft and stepped closer to Elizabeth. He kept his voice low. "Did Spotted Fawn mention wanting to run away again?"

Elizabeth shook her head and whispered. "I think the

promise of celebrating Christmas will keep her here for a while. She could barely keep her eyes open while she ate and she was still asking questions about it."

"She likes the story of it all. She used to sit and listen to the old people of her tribe tell stories for hours," Jake said before he turned to look at the stove. "That smells good."

"It's just fried potatoes and onions. Annabelle mentioned it to me. It's one of her son's favorites. She gave me a couple of onions from her root cellar. I'll have to plant some in my garden this year. She also gave me a recipe for elk stew and I gave her mine for stewed tomatoes."

Elizabeth took the frying pan off the stove and walked to the table. "I'm thinking I'll have some use for the elk one."

"I should go hunting soon." Jake turned toward the table, too. He had been pleased to see how much Elizabeth enjoyed the company of Annabelle and Virginia. His mother had always complained of her solitude. Maybe the territory had grown up enough in the years since then that a woman could find some social life even if it was only exchanging recipes and painting stars on the schoolhouse floor.

Elizabeth spooned the potatoes and onions onto their plates.

"I never knew you could do so many things," Jake said as he sat down. "Virginia said you even know how to make soap. And your own dyes. I didn't know ladies back East knew how to do any of those things."

Elizabeth set the spoon back in the pan. She supposed, at heart, all men were the same. "Not every woman can be a lady, you know. Not when it takes so much work to run a household."

Jake gave her a look of surprise.

Now, she'd done it, Elizabeth thought. "I'm sorry to be snappish. I just—I just—well, I guess I'm tired."

They were both seated at the table by now, but neither made any move to say a prayer so they could eat. Jake was looking at her as if he was expecting her to say more.

"Of course, you are," Jake finally said. "And this afternoon probably brought back lots of memories."

Now it was Elizabeth's turn to look at him. What did he mean?

"Of Christmas," he explained. "My mother always was a little sad when she looked through her Christmas things. Too many memories, I suppose, along with the trinkets and cards she'd kept from her childhood."

"I'm fine with Christmas," Elizabeth said and bowed her head. It was true; she always had been fine with Christmas as long as she didn't let herself dream about it being special.

Jake looked at her a moment and then bowed his head, too. "Thank you, Father, for this day. And for our neighbors. May you show us how to live peacefully together. And, thank you for this food Elizabeth has made for us. May You keep us in Your hands. Amen."

"Amen," Elizabeth echoed as she reached for her spoon.

"I suppose you have some Christmas things in your boxes," Jake said as he started to eat. "Things from your childhood."

"No."

Jake stopped eating and looked at Elizabeth. He knew

how much his mother valued her Christmas things. They made her sad, but they had also made her happy reliving the memories. "I suppose your husband didn't think there was room for them in the wagon."

Jake never had liked Matthew. Which was a terrible thing to say about a man who was dead in the ground, but there it was.

"I didn't have anything to bring," Elizabeth said. "I mean—I do have some yarn I dyed bright red so I could make Rose a blanket for her first Christmas present, but that's all."

"But you must have memories, too." Jake persisted. Even he had some memories of holidays when his father had whittled him a horse or a grizzly and his mother had given him hard candy she'd hoarded from the last time his father had been to a trading post.

Elizabeth was looking down at her plate as though like she'd just as soon avoid this conversation. Maybe she didn't want to remember because she knew it wouldn't be the same this year.

"I'm sorry. I know memories can be best left alone," Jake finally said. "I don't mean to pry."

Elizabeth finally looked at him. "There's nothing to pry into. I didn't have time to celebrate Christmas as a child. There was too much to do getting everything ready for the family. I had to scrub all of the windows so someone could put pine boughs over them. I had to chop nuts and knead dough for the fruit buns people wanted. And then there were the pies and the puddings. I was usually allowed some time off after Christmas dinner was served, but I was so exhausted all I wanted to do was sleep."

"But surely your parents—"

"My parents were dead." Elizabeth had only taken a few bites of her fried potatoes, but she pushed her plate away.

"I'm sorry," Jake said as he pushed back his chair and stood up. "I didn't realize—"

"Of course not," Elizabeth said as she stood, as well. She gave a forced little smile. "And I can't say I never had anything of Christmas. When I was real little, the cooks almost always saved me something good to eat. If a gingerbread cookie was broken, it would be set aside for me. Sometimes I had an orange of my own to eat. And new shoes. One year, the family I was with got me new shoes for Christmas. That was in my agreement with them. I was to get a pair of shoes and a new dress for my work that year, so I would have gotten them anyway, but it was nice they did it on Christmas."

"How old were you when your parents died?"

Elizabeth shrugged. "I've tried to figure that out myself. I can't remember. There didn't seem to be any marking of the time. It feels like I was with them one week and the next I was working at my first house, expected to go on like it was just the passing of one week to the other."

"That must have been hard."

Jake decided that some days a man needed to hold his wife for his own comfort as much as hers. He held out his arms and Elizabeth walked into them. She was stiff as though she'd come to him reluctantly.

"Anything wrong?"

"I—I," Elizabeth stepped back from him and looked at his chin. She looked miserable, but determined at the same time.

"You can tell me," Jake said. "Whatever it is, it's okay."

She looked at him square this time. "I'm sorry, but I want to wear mourning for Matthew."

Jake tried to keep the flinch he felt inside from showing on his face. "But Matthew isn't your husband anymore."

"I know. It's just that it's like with my parents. Just because someone moves me to a different house, that doesn't mean I should erase all my memories of who I used to belong with."

"I'm sure no one meant for you to do that with your parents."

"Maybe not. But there was no room to grieve for them. No way to mark their passing. I don't want to do the same thing with Matthew. He was a good man. He deserves to have someone pay attention to his death."

Jake nodded. He might not like it, but he could almost understand it. "How can I help?"

"I'll need to have a black dress," Elizabeth said hesitantly. "Usually, I would dye some fabric, but with all we need to do to get ready for Christmas, I—"

"Buy what you need."

"I'm not asking you to buy me a dress. I have some red calico I'm pretty sure I can sell or trade for enough black cloth. This is something I need to do myself. All I really want is your blessing."

Jake looked at her for a full minute before he nodded.

"Thank you," Elizabeth said and then turned back to the stove. She felt more tired than she had when she was lying in her tent waiting to die. She had not realized when she agreed to Jake's suggestion that marrying him would be so hard for her. She hadn't given up her life with Matthew and Rose; it had been jerked away from her. She needed time to grieve before she could open her heart to a new family.

She heard the door close as Jake let himself out of the house.

Chapter Twelve

Jake had never expected to have his wife dress up like a widow, at least not while he was alive, but that's what was happening. It hadn't taken Elizabeth long to start looking for a black dress. He and Elizabeth had both come into town Monday morning to be sure that Spotted Fawn was at school on time. Even before school was scheduled to start, however, Elizabeth had walked into the mercantile with some brilliant red cloth and asked Annabelle to put it up for sale or trade so she could buy a black mourning dress.

"I'll walk Spotted Fawn to the school," Jake said when he heard Elizabeth ask her question. He wanted no part of that black dress. He had the baby with him and the fresh air would do them both good. He'd bring the baby back before long so she could take her morning nap at Annabelle's.

Annabelle watched Jake and Spotted Fawn leave the mercantile before she turned her attention back to Elizabeth. "What are you doing? Jake's your husband. He's not dead."

"But my other husband is," Elizabeth protested. "I

don't know how you do it. I can't just walk away from my old life. Everything's happening too fast."

Annabelle put her hand on Elizabeth's arm. "You poor thing. It has been fast. I keep forgetting that. It's just that you and Jake seem so right together."

"It was okay at first, I mean we only got married to take care of the baby, but—"

Annabelle smiled. "It's becoming real."

Elizabeth looked up at her new friend. "I just don't know anymore. If I'd been the one to die from the fever, I hope Matthew would grieve for me. At least for a little while. A person should leave a mark on someone's life when they leave this world."

"I remember feeling that way when Tommy's father died. I was alive and he was dead and there was no rhyme nor reason to it all. I was full up with guilt inside. Thought I should have done more for him when he'd been alive. Wished I had just one more minute with him to tell him how sorry I was for always fussing at him over his muddy boots."

Elizabeth nodded. "Matthew was terrible with his boots, too."

The women were silent for a bit.

"Well, if it's a mourning dress you want, you're welcome to have mine," Annabelle said. "The old thing itches and it's the ugliest thing around, but you're welcome to it. I can't wear it for work anyway and it seems foolish to wear it to church when I don't wear it for the rest of the week."

"You'd let me have your dress?" Nothing had ever sounded more comforting to Elizabeth than to wear her friend's mourning dress. "I'll trade you for it, of course. You can have the red calico if you want—to sell or use."

"I won't take anything for that old mourning dress. A friend of mine in Helena gave it to me so I didn't pay anything for it, anyway." Annabelle looked at the fabric Elizabeth held in her arms. "Is this the cloth you dyed yourself?"

Elizabeth nodded as she took a lingering look at it.

"You should keep it," Annabelle said. "You've put a lot of work into that cloth."

"I need to give up something that means something to me to get a mourning dress. It doesn't feel right not to have something taken away."

"Well, I'll keep it for you for a while, if that's what you want. We'll talk about what to do with it later." Annabelle reached out to touch the cloth. "It's so pretty. It gives the whole place a Christmas look."

"Thank you," Elizabeth said.

Annabelle nodded.

"Here, let me close the store for a minute while we go in the back and get the dress for you," Annabelle said as she reached under the counter and brought out a silver bell. "One of the nice things about this job is being able to slip back to our rooms when I need to."

"It is a good job for you," Elizabeth agreed as she followed Annabelle to the back. "You're sure things are okay with Mr. Broadman? He's not still threatening to fire you, is he?"

Annabelle shook her head as she unlocked the door leading to her quarters. "He already stopped by. He's calmed down by now. He just gets riled up when Mrs. Barker claims someone needs to do something to be sure the railroad comes through here. I think he'd jump off a bridge if that woman told him it would bring the railroad. He always settles down later, though."

Annabelle opened the door to a small parlor.

"Well, she might be right in some of the things she says," Elizabeth said as they both walked into the room. "I don't know anything about what would make the railroad chose one place over another."

"I'm beginning to realize that we need to live in this town whether the railroad comes or not. We need to be a good town, no matter what comes."

The furniture in the parlor was well-worn, but sturdy. An ivory wallpaper covered the walls and light brown curtains hung over the windows.

Annabelle helped Elizabeth try on the mourning dress. It was a little loose on her, but they both decided it would do fine.

"It needs a good washing," Annabelle said.

Elizabeth nodded as she started to remove the dress.

"Just don't put it in water that's too hot," Annabelle added. "I made that mistake and the black color faded so bad it isn't worth much anymore."

Elizabeth examined the dress as she stood there in her chemise and petticoats. "It looks like whoever dyed it didn't set it properly. It's easy to forget that the water needs to be boiling when you add the soda ash."

The bell rang out in the front of the store.

"Oh, I've got to go," Annabelle said. "Take your time. And I can't wait to hear how excited the kids are today when you and Virginia tell them about the pageant. I didn't tell Tommy so he can hear it with the others."

Elizabeth nodded as she finished putting her regular dress back on. She'd go over to the school and wait for the children to finish their sums. Virginia said she'd meet her there.

* * *

Jake felt the ax sink into the side of the log. He and Colter had a rhythm to their chopping even though they were both working on different logs. Jake found himself thinking about that dress his wife was wanting and he started bringing the ax down faster and with more force with every thought he had. Then he realized Colter was matching his pace.

"What's ailing you?" Jake stopped chopping to ask.

The other man might be a business owner, but he didn't lack staying power when it came to work. Colter had taken off his vest and rolled up his sleeves. His shirt was drenched in sweat. He stopped swinging his ax and put his arm up to wipe his forehead.

"Business," Colter said.

"Losing money, are you?"

"It's my employees if you must know. Someone's taking money from the till."

"Ahh."

"I think I know who it is, but—"

"I hope you don't think it's Virginia Parker. She wouldn't take a dime that didn't belong to her."

"I know, I know. The woman's a saint. No, I think it's the guy tending bar. But—"

"But you don't know for sure."

"And it could be Danny."

"Ahh." Jake sympathized with the man. "I don't know what I'd do if Spotted Fawn started stealing things. Not that—I mean, the Sioux don't really see possessions like we do, but if she was taking money I'd need to put a stop to it somehow. It could be a problem."

Colter nodded. "I don't know what real parents do."

"You might ask Annabelle. Her son, Tommy, seems like he's turning out all right."

"I might do that. If I can think of a way to ask without sounding like I'm accusing anyone of anything. I don't want people to say I think Danny is thieving." Colter put his ax up to make another swing. "Folks get their minds around something like that and they don't let go even if it turns out not to be true."

Jake pulled his ax up, as well. He wasn't about to be outdone by a businessman.

It wasn't two minutes later before both men stopped chopping. They could see Elizabeth and Virginia walking down the street, getting ready to turn into the walk that went to the schoolhouse.

"Did you get a chance to tell them how few kids are in school today?" Colter asked.

Jake shook his head.

"Well, at least we don't have to worry about those boys today," Colter said. "I can't see why they'd want to make trouble in a classroom when they don't even need to go near the place."

"That makes sense." Not that it was good news when a man looked at the whole picture, but there was nothing to be done about it at the moment.

"In that case, maybe it wouldn't hurt to go in and hear what the ladies have to say," Colter said, trying to appear casual about it.

"They'd probably appreciate the company."

Jake heard the door to the schoolhouse open. He was looking at the back of the building, but that must be the women going inside.

Elizabeth stood in the open doorway. She took a deep breath as Virginia waited by her side. There were exactly five people in the schoolroom. The reverend, Spotted Fawn, Thomas, Danny and Mr. Higgins. Of those, Spotted Fawn was the only one who probably had any interest in being an angel in a Christmas pageant.

"I guess all of our painting didn't work," Elizabeth whispered to Virginia. "None of the kids from Miles City are here. And I know the reverend was going to ask Mrs. Barker over to see everything this morning."

The yellow stars and the trailing holly weren't as shiny today as they had been yesterday. Even with fires in both stoves, the room was chilly. Elizabeth supposed it was because the heat from all of the other children was missing. She even missed the musty smell of the damp wool scarves and mittens that were usually drying on a chair near the stoves.

"We can't force people to be nice to each other," Virginia said.

"That's what laws are for," Elizabeth said. "To keep people civilized."

"Well, we can't arrest people for not saying Merry Christmas to each other."

By now, Reverend Olson had looked up and seen them.

"Come on in, ladies," he said with a welcoming smile. "We're just finishing our sums."

Elizabeth nodded and she and Virginia stepped farther into the schoolroom.

"The ladies have some exciting news for you," the reverend said, with as much enthusiasm as he would have used if the room had been filled with children.

"Well," Elizabeth began. "Miss Virginia and I are here to see if you'd like to put on a Christmas pageant.

There would be lots of angels and Miss Virginia would lead them in singing songs and—"

A hand went up.

"Yes, Danny?"

"Can I be one of the singers with Miss Virginia?"

Elizabeth nodded. She felt much better now. If even Danny was glowing with excitement about their news, the others would soon realize how much fun it could be. "I think that can be arranged."

Jake and Colter opened the schoolhouse door and slipped into the last bench. Virginia was singing one of the songs the women planned to use in the pageant and her voice rose and dipped over everyone like a flock of songbirds coming home to rest. When Virginia had finished singing, Colter gave a deep sigh.

Jake knew it wasn't the music that moved the other man and he could have sighed right along with him. Neither one of them was doing very well with the women they wanted to impress.

Wham! Jake heard the sound of some kind of bullet right outside the schoolhouse. Then there was another one.

"Everyone down!" Jake ordered as he, Colter and Higgins fanned out and each slid toward one of the windows. Colter had his pistol drawn and Higgins had stopped to pick up a good-sized piece of firewood. Jake put his hand on the knife he had strapped around his thigh. His rifle was out by the woodpile behind the school.

Wham! There was an explosion on the other side of the schoolhouse.

Jake looked at Colter. "That doesn't sound like a bullet."

"It's firecrackers," Higgins said. "Made by Sam Lee, I expect."

Just then, Jake saw a flash of blue as a boy took off running.

"Elias Barker," Jake muttered. He should have known.

Higgins must have seen him, too, because the man gave his grizzly roar and took off out of the schoolhouse shouting, "I'm going to catch that boy."

Jake started to chuckle. The day was getting better all ready. Most people didn't think Higgins could move as fast as he could because he was so large, but the man used to say he'd learned to run by racing grizzly bears and Jake thought it just might be true.

Twenty minutes later Higgins was back holding a white-faced Elias Barker by the collar of his jacket.

"Now," Higgins said as he hauled Elias into the schoolroom. "You need to apologize to all of these good folks for scaring them."

"It wasn't only me," Elias protested.

"The others will apologize when I catch them," Higgins assured him. "This is your turn."

Elias muttered, "I'm sorry."

"There now," Higgins said as he gave the boy a little shake. "You sit down where you belong and pay attention to your schooling."

The boy's face went white. "I can't. My ma will tan my hide good. I'm not supposed to go to school with—" Elias stopped and swallowed.

The boy didn't finish his sentence, but he didn't need to for Jake to know what he'd been going to say. His mother didn't want him to go to school with Spotted Fawn.

"You leave your mother to me," Jake said as he started for the door.

"Wait."

He turned to see Elizabeth walking toward him.

"I'm coming with you," she said as she came even with him.

Jake liked having Elizabeth at his side as they went to talk to Mrs. Barker. She might be in mourning for another man, but she was standing by him in the ways she could. That had to count for something.

Chapter Thirteen

Mrs. Barker lived in a two-story frame house off the main street in town. Jake wondered if Elizabeth was comparing the woman's house to the one where they lived. He hoped not. Several loads of lumber had been used in the building of this house; the schoolhouse alone would have taken less than a third of the wood. And there were beveled glass windows in the front of the house that were for decoration alone. It made his house look damp and dark in comparison.

That being said, he didn't envy the Barkers. Not when he had Elizabeth by his side.

"Oh," Mrs. Barker said when she opened the door and saw who was there.

A man didn't need to know anything about elegance to know that the glimpse he had into the foyer of Mrs. Barker's house was about as fine as any sight he'd see around here. Even the banister on the stairs gleamed with polish.

"May we come inside?" Elizabeth asked.

Jake glanced down at his wife and noticed she wasn't looking to the inside of Mrs. Barker's house the way he was. No, Elizabeth was very proper. If he didn't know better, he would think she was on a social call. She had a polite smile on her face and a voice that sounded very formal.

"It's not really convenient right now," Mrs. Barker said as she crossed her arms.

Jake didn't much like the look of triumph on the older woman's face.

"It's about Elias," Elizabeth continued smoothly, however, as though she hadn't just been asked to leave.

"If it's about him going to that school, he won't be there until it's a fitting place for children to be." Mrs. Barker started to close the door.

That was enough, Jake told himself as he put his foot in the door. The time for politeness was over. "Is it fitting that the boy is running around almost getting himself shot?"

Well, that got Mrs. Barker's attention. She swung the door wide again. "What do you mean?"

"This nonsense has gone on for too long when a boy like Elias is setting off firecrackers to try and scare people. You know as well as I do, there are enough nervous men with guns in this town that the boy could get himself shot pulling stunts like that."

Mrs. Barker's face went a little pale. "He's all right, though, isn't he?"

Jake nodded. "Higgins ran him down and brought him back to the schoolhouse. Which is where he belongs."

"The children do need to be in school," Elizabeth added softly.

Mrs. Barker looked at them for a minute.

"I saw what you did with the schoolroom," she finally

said with a sour twist to her mouth. "All those Christmas decorations."

"You're welcome to add some more to what's there," Elizabeth said. "The reverend has what's left of the paint we used. And there's lots of wall left."

"I did think you could use some more holly," Mrs. Barker said.

"Christmas is the time for goodwill," Elizabeth said. "Children especially always like Christmas. I know you don't want to ruin it for them. Can't we wait until after the holiday to sort everything else out?"

Mrs. Barker sighed. "I just want to make this a better town. I know it might not mean much to people like you, but having the railroad come here would make a big difference to most people in this town."

"The railroad won't mean anything if we don't find a way to get along better," Jake said. "Towns have split over things like this."

Mrs. Barker was quiet for another minute then she looked over at Elizabeth. "I suppose you're right. We can settle everything after Christmas. I'm sure no railroad representative will be out traveling this close to the holiday, anyway."

"Would you mind coming over and telling your son that?" Jake asked. "He can let his friends know and, my guess is, they'll all be back in school this afternoon."

Mrs. Barker nodded. "I'll be over as soon as I get my hat."

"We'll see you there," Jake said as he took Elizabeth's arm. He didn't figure there was any need for her to be looking inside Mrs. Barker's house any longer than necessary. If he wasn't mistaken there was a window in the foyer that did nothing but look into another room. Who had so much money they could buy a glass window when they didn't even need to keep out any rain?

But Elizabeth must not have seen the window.

"She listened to us," Elizabeth said in amazement as she let Jake lead her down the steps of the Barker house. "I didn't think she'd listen to anyone."

"She cares about her son," Jake said.

"Well, of course, I can see that," Elizabeth said as they kept walking back to the schoolhouse.

"She's not giving up, you know," Jake added. "She just doesn't want to fight the children over Christmas."

Elizabeth knew how the woman felt. Every child deserved a happy Christmas.

The schoolhouse was noisy and crowded by the end of the day. Since so few of the children had been there in the morning, the reverend suggested Elizabeth and Virginia repeat what they'd said earlier about the pageant. By that time Elias was already rather loudly declaring that it was a dumb idea and Higgins was giving him his grizzly roar as a reminder to be polite—or, at least, silent.

"I still don't want to be no angel," Elias muttered, looking up at Higgins. "And nobody can make me be one, either."

Higgins snorted. "I can see that, boy. Only a fool would think you could behave well enough to pass for an angel. I'm just trying to get you to quiet down so people don't take you for something else entirely."

Elizabeth stepped closer to the man and the boy. She hadn't fully explained the pageant, but she didn't want any of the other children hearing the quarrel right now to follow Elias's lead. "If you don't want to be an angel, you can be something else then."

"Like what?"

Elizabeth looked to Virginia for help. "Ah, you could be a shepherd—"

"Nah, I don't want to be a shepherd, either. Sheep are dumb. Besides, I have a horse. Shepherds don't have horses."

"Well, then," Virginia said as she looked around the schoolroom. "Maybe you could be a star."

"Like in the sky?" Elias asked, obviously thinking about the idea.

"Even bigger and brighter than the ones you see in the sky now," Elizabeth said. "The Christmas star was a special star. Kings—remember 'We three kings from Orient are'? Well, these kings followed the star because it brought them to the Christ Child."

"So the star gets to tell the important people how to find things?" Elias asked. "Like a map for hidden treasure."

"In a way." Elizabeth paused. "I guess you could say Jesus was a hidden treasure at first because no one knew where He was."

"Good," Elias said. "Could I ride my horse when I'm a star? He's a bay so he's kind of yellow."

"The pageant is inside. You know you can't ride your horse."

Several children rode horses to school each day and there were several posts at the side of the school where they could tie them.

Elias grinned. "It doesn't hurt to try. That's what my dad always says. If a man's got a good horse, he can do anything."

Elizabeth grinned back. "Even your dad knows a horse can't come inside the schoolhouse."

"I suppose."

Elizabeth decided Elias wasn't as much of a problem as she had thought. She looked at all the children. "We're going to have a wonderful Christmas. We'll enact the story of the birth of Jesus, we'll sing songs, we'll have—" She looked over at Virginia for help.

"We're hoping to have a tree, too," Virginia announced with delight. "You children would love to have a tree to decorate, wouldn't you? The school has to look like Christmas for our pageant."

The children were nodding and Elizabeth agreed. She'd love to have the inside of this room shining with Christmas cheer.

Mrs. Barker hadn't arrived yet to paint more decorations on the Miles City side of the wall, but Elizabeth intended to offer to help her when she showed up. And if they were going to decorate more, they should have a tree.

None of the children had any reservations about having a Christmas tree. Almost all of them had heard about making ornaments even if they hadn't made any themselves.

"We'll ask the men to help us find a tree," Elizabeth said. "I'm sure whatever they find will do nicely. After all, the important thing is the joy we take in Christmas."

With that triumphant remark, Elizabeth and Virginia decided to let the children get back to their lessons. The two women walked out of the schoolhouse and stood on the steps.

"Well, at least they seem to like Christmas," Virginia said wearily. "I never knew a classroom of children could be so hard to manage."

"They'll do better when we start practicing," Elizabeth said as she put her hands on her back and stretched. She was a little sore from all of that scrubbing and painting yesterday. Her muscles weren't used to working after she'd lain in her tent for almost two weeks, doing nothing.

"We'll start in on the trees tomorrow," Virginia said. "I better get to Colter's place and start playing the piano."

Elizabeth nodded. She had things to do at home, as well.

Jake took Elizabeth and the baby home in the wagon and then rode off to go see Wells.

Two hours later, Elizabeth sat down in the rocking chair by the fire. Her hair was falling down and her clothes were all wet. She'd just finished washing that black mourning dress and she'd rather scrub the old canvas on her tent before she took her washboard to the dress again. The wet wool was heavy and it smelled bad.

Added to that she had made the mistake of using water that was hotter than she thought it was. The black dye turned her rinse water gray almost immediately. She'd had to wring the water out of the dress before she draped it over a chair that she'd placed close enough to the woodstove so the dress would hopefully dry before tomorrow.

As odd as it was, Elizabeth admitted, she had an immense feeling of relief as she worked on that dress. She wanted to wear mourning. She wasn't ready to move on with her life and the dress helped her show that to everyone. It marked where she was. Somehow the dress slowed everything down so her feelings were once again equal with her life.

She would know who she was when she started wearing that dress. A wound needed a scab before it could heal properly and that dress was her scab.

Elizabeth sat and rocked for a few more minutes before she stood up and walked back to the stove. While the dress had been soaking earlier, she had started to bring in her canned goods from the lean-to and stack them against the far wall in the cabin. All of those jars of canned vegetables and preserves reminded her of who she was, as well. She was a strong woman who could provide for herself. She'd survive her mourning.

While she was bringing in the jars, she also brought in the red yarn and slipped it into her satchel that she kept at the foot of the bed. She had decided to use the red yarn to knit Christmas scarves for the baby and Spotted Fawn. The older girl took such delight in her hair ribbons she would surely like a bright red scarf to wear around her neck. And babies always liked bright colors.

She hadn't thought about what to get Jake for a present, but she planned to ask Annabelle's advice. She was almost certain the other woman was getting Higgins a Christmas present so she'd probably given the matter some thought.

Elizabeth almost envied Annabelle. The other woman seemed to accept things better than she did.

Elizabeth was not naive. She knew women often had to marry quickly to survive out here in the West. A man and a gun were almost necessary. But she did not want to be one of those women who married from necessity. She and Jake had an agreement that would be in place until spring, but she already knew he would let her stay and become a real wife to him if that's what she decided to do.

But she didn't want it to be that way. She wanted to

be chosen. Oh, Jake had chosen her after a fashion. But he had been thinking of his nieces and not of himself. He would have married her no matter who she was. And he was much too kind to do anything but throw himself into their bargain.

She could spend the rest of her life with him and not know if he really wanted to be with her. Or she with him. She didn't want to risk that. She had learned with Matthew that it was very hard to live with a man she could not please. If she really got married again, she wanted the man to want to be with her. She didn't want to be some compromise he had made in life.

Besides, it would be good for her soul to grieve. She had lain in her tent, frozen in her anger at God, and now that she was out of her tent, she felt adrift. It's not that she'd forgiven God. She'd just kept going because there was nothing else to do.

She wasn't praying, not the way Jake did. He prayed as though God were his friend. When she started to pray lately the words stuck in her throat. She'd worn out her anger and it no longer felt as white-hot as it had. It had not gone away, though. It had just changed form into something cold and heavy and uncomfortable. In fact, it was very similar to that old mourning dress.

Just thinking of the dress reminded Elizabeth she should go turn the chair by the stove a little. She'd have to keep moving that chair all night if she expected the whole dress to be dry by tomorrow.

Well, supper would be coming before tomorrow, Elizabeth told herself as she stood up. She'd set some beans to soaking last night and they were ready to be cooked. She'd like to put a small jar of her tomatoes in with the beans. If she also chopped up another one of the onions Annabelle had given her, she'd have a good soup.

She'd noticed Jake liked his food spiced up with onions and maybe some black pepper flakes. She'd make him some corn bread, too. She had to admit she liked cooking for the man. Maybe it was because he never seemed to just assume there would be food on his plate as Matthew had done.

She shook her head. Is that what her days would be like, always comparing one man to the other? Surely, her heart should give her peace eventually.

Chapter Fourteen

The next day, Jake drove Elizabeth and the girls into town before it was full light. The frost was growing heavier each morning and he figured it would be good to get a stack of wood for the schoolhouse before the snows started. The reverend wasn't looking well enough to be out in the winter cutting firewood himself, anyway.

Besides, Jake felt like chopping wood today. He was trying to avoid looking at that mourning dress of Elizabeth's, but it was hard not to see it. He wondered if he was supposed to stop speaking to her while she was in this mourning of hers. It was a peculiar feeling to have his wife acting like a widow.

He knew right then that he had a problem. He needed to stop thinking of Elizabeth as his wife. They'd said their vows, but they'd only made a commitment until spring. He shook his head. He didn't know what to do with the mess he'd made of things. He never should have offered to let her go, but then she might never have agreed to stay.

He looked over at her and Elizabeth pulled her shawl

more closely around her. She was moving away from him already.

Elizabeth could sense Jake was looking at her, but she didn't look up to meet his eyes. He hadn't said anything about the mourning dress even though she'd put it on for the first time to wear today. She'd taken a hot iron to it first, but it still looked a little rumpled. And it was itchy.

She knew it was unattractive. It was probably a good thing Matthew wasn't alive to see the dress; he would have made her tear it up for rags. Men could be so particular about things.

She quickly glanced sideways at Jake. "It's just for a season—the dress."

Jake grunted.

She was glad he didn't ask her how long the season would last. She wasn't sure what she would say. She had some things she wanted to finish with Matthew and she wasn't even sure what they were.

At least the brown shawl she wore covered most of her dress. She had unpacked the shawl yesterday; it was a thick winter one she'd used when she did her heavy work back in Kansas. She hadn't needed it on the journey and, when the fevers started, it had been easier to use a blanket. When she had lifted it out of its box she could almost still smell the dye she'd put into it early last fall. She'd boiled black walnut husks with a few late-season marigolds and the shawl had turned out a rich golden brown. She was grateful to have it now.

The schoolhouse was chilly when they all arrived. Spotted Fawn had been sitting in the back of the wagon with the baby so she was the last one to climb down from the wagon and go inside the schoolroom. No one else was there yet. Jake had said he wanted them to get there early so they could start fires in the two stoves so the reverend wouldn't need to do it before classes started.

Elizabeth held the baby inside her shawl while she bent over the book Spotted Fawn was showing her. The girl was already learning to read a few words and was carefully pronouncing them.

"That's wonderful," Elizabeth said and then beamed up at Jake as he closed the door on the second woodstove. "Spotted Fawn can read!"

Jake walked over and put his arm on his niece's shoulder. He looked as if he was going to say something, but just then there were the sounds of footsteps on the porch.

"Someone's already here," a boy's voice protested from outside as something dropped on the wood.

Elizabeth looked at Jake. "That has to be Elias."

Jake nodded grimly. "I'll go see what he's up to."

Before Jake got to the door, however, it opened.

"Why, whatever—" Mrs. Barker said as she stood there in surprise. She had a handkerchief wrapped around her copper hair and a bucket of paint in one hand. She looked at Jake and Elizabeth. "What are you doing here at this hour of the morning?"

"Starting the fire," Jake said.

"I didn't think anyone would be here," Mrs. Barker said. She had a blanket draped around herself and a well-worn work dress showing under that. "I don't normally go around looking like this."

"Don't worry about it," Elizabeth said. She was glad to see the other woman wasn't always so proper. "No one dresses up when they go to paint. I'm so glad you decided to help with the wall."

"Well," Mrs. Barker said with a twist to her lips. "It is Christmas. And Elias is quite taken with all of the stars.

He wanted to add a couple of constellations to the wall. It won't be much paint so we thought it would be okay if we did it before school today."

By this time Elias was inside the schoolroom, as well. He carried a couple of small paintbrushes. For once, he wasn't scowling.

"I thought maybe the Big Dipper," Elias said. "I like that one."

"I like it, too," Jake said as he walked over to the boy. "If you want any help getting the distances right, let me know."

Well, Elizabeth thought, a person just never knew what would happen in a day.

Elizabeth helped Mrs. Barker get the paint opened and stirred while Jake and Elias marked the places on the wall where they wanted their stars.

"It was good of you to do this," Mrs. Barker finally said. "All of the stars and other Christmas decorations are nice."

Elizabeth nodded. She refused to ask the other woman if she was the one who had painted that awful black line. It had to have been her. Who else would have done it? But if Elizabeth asked the question she was pretty sure it would destroy any fragile truce they had managed.

"We'll wait until after Christmas for—" Mrs. Barker said with a nod of her head at Spotted Fawn.

"She is not harming anyone," Elizabeth said, trying to keep her voice low and mild. She didn't want to let the remark pass, but she didn't want to distress Spotted Fawn, either, so she didn't want the girl to hear their voices.

"We've got the places marked," Elias called out excitedly.

Mrs. Barker took the paint over to Elias and Jake.

"He's having fun," Elizabeth said when the other woman returned to where they had been standing.

Mrs. Barker nodded. "It's good for him to spend some time with a man. Boys like that and his father has been away for such a long time."

"Oh, I'm sorry. I didn't know."

"He's off prospecting again. He made one big strike. You'd think that would be enough for the man. We have everything we need, but he's off again. Someplace over by Helena, the last time he wrote."

"Well, I'm sure he'll be home soon," Elizabeth said. She didn't want to feel sympathy for the other woman, but she did.

"I keep thinking that, if the railroad comes, there would be a good job that would keep him here. A boy needs his father."

And a wife needs her husband, Elizabeth thought, until the irony of it struck her.

By the time the reverend got to the school, several constellations were painted and the chill had been taken off the morning air.

"Oh, the children will be so pleased," the reverend said as he admired the additional stars. "That's excellent work, Elias."

The boy ducked his head. His face was pink with pleased embarrassment.

"I think everyone would agree that Miles City is keeping up their end of things," Mrs. Barker said proudly.

"It's not a competition," Elizabeth protested. "It's Christmas."

"Still, people have certain expectations of the people

of Miles City that they naturally don't have of the people of Dry Creek."

"I don't think—" Elizabeth began.

"Ladies," Reverend Olson interrupted hastily. "You have both given us wonderful decorations. And the children are so excited about the Christmas tree you mentioned."

"There's going to be a Christmas tree?" Mrs. Barker frowned. "Elias didn't tell me there was going to be a tree."

"It won't be a big tree," Elizabeth said. "Jake says he thinks there are a few short pines not too far east of here, down some ravine. He's going to bring a small one back for us."

Elizabeth had been delighted when Jake had heard them talking and offered to bring them the tree. She had never known a man before who bothered with the dreams of children.

"Well, if we have a tree, we want to have a proper one. My husband used to say there were some fine-looking pines north of here someplace. He and Elias saw them when they were out riding one day. I'm sure Elias remembers. It's quite a ways from here I think, but maybe he could tell one of the men where it is and—"

"I'm sure Jake will talk to him," Elizabeth said. "But it's likely too far. I'm sure if there's anything close, Jake would know about it. Besides, a simple tree is fine. Just something so the children can make ornaments."

"Oh, dear, no," Mrs. Barker said. "I don't think we want a small little tree to represent our town. We have a certain reputation, after all."

Elizabeth figured the other woman would stop worrying as the day went on, but she was wrong. By the time Elizabeth and Virginia were ready to help the students make ornaments, Mrs. Barker was back at the schoolhouse, this time dressed in a mauve silk dress and matching hat.

Annabelle had offered to keep the baby at the store with her while Elizabeth and Virginia worked on Christmas with the children so Elizabeth was able to give her complete focus to the ornaments. Unfortunately, focus hadn't been enough.

"I guess people generally use red paper," Elizabeth said as she and Virginia looked at the rope of white paper that the students had made. The decoration was sitting on top of the teacher's desk. The loops in the rope were uneven and, instead of looking charming, it gave the whole thing the appearance of being fought over by a couple of dogs.

"I don't suppose we could paint the paper with something," Virginia asked.

"Oh, of course not," Mrs. Barker said as she walked over to where they stood. "Any kind of paint we have would wrinkle the paper even more. You need to let me buy us some decorations. The children have better things to do than decorate a Christmas tree, anyway."

"We can't buy Christmas," Elizabeth protested. "The children have as much right to decorate a tree as anyone here."

"Ladies," the reverend interrupted gently.

Elizabeth looked behind her to see the children all looking at her and Mrs. Barker. Some of the younger girls had big eyes and even the boys were looking a little stunned.

"Of course, the important thing about Christmas is

that we all get along," Elizabeth said as she forced a big smile onto her face.

Then Elizabeth walked right over to Mrs. Barker and gave her a hug.

The other woman gasped, but Elizabeth knew there was nothing Mrs. Barker could do but adjust her hat and smile back.

"And, don't worry," Elizabeth said to the children as she turned to face them. "Miss Virginia and I are going over to the store right now to see what we can get to use to make better ornaments. We'll be back."

With that Elizabeth swept out of the room, with Virginia following her.

"Do you think Annabelle will let us owe the money for a week or so?" Virginia asked as they started walking down the street. "I don't make enough to do more than pay for my room and board. Although Colter has said all along that I could use the piano to start giving lessons to people. Maybe then I'd have extra—"

Elizabeth stopped. "The piano in the saloon?"

It was the middle of the afternoon and the streets of Miles City were dry, but quiet.

Virginia nodded. "So, of course, it would have to be an adult for them to have the lessons."

Elizabeth shook her head. "We need to find you a different job. I'm sure you could find children who would want to take piano lessons, but their parents will never send them to that place to take them."

"I know," Virginia sighed. "But, even if I had a room someplace, I would need a piano. I've been praying, but—"

"I know." Elizabeth pursed her lips. Finally, someone else understood. "God just doesn't answer."

Virginia looked startled. "That's not what I was going to say. I was just going to say He hasn't told me my next step yet."

"Oh," Elizabeth said.

"I can understand how you feel," Virginia said softly. "I'm still grieving for my brother, too."

Elizabeth nodded. "I can't get past it. The whole thing is just a knot inside of me. That's why I'm wearing this mourning dress. I need to find a way past everything if I'm going to stay with Jake."

"Well, I'll pray you do that then," Virginia said as they reached the boardwalk in front of the mercantile. "It's not everyone that gets a second chance at happiness."

When they walked inside the store, Annabelle walked out from behind her counter and greeted them. "The baby's asleep in the back if that's why you've come."

Elizabeth shook her head. She'd already been over to nurse.

"We want something to make into Christmas ornaments," Virginia said.

Annabelle motioned for them to follow her over to a shelf. "We do have some of the most beautiful hand-blown ornaments, if you decide not to make them yourselves."

Annabelle pulled a box off the shelf and opened it.

"Ohhh," Elizabeth said. Beautiful glass apples shone there. And shiny pinecones. And clusters of red berries.

"They're expensive, of course. The owners ordered them from the Greiner's factory in Germany. They were supposed to be on our shelves last Christmas, but they got stuck in the docks in New York and missed some railroad connection so we saved them to sell this Christmas."

The ornaments were molded into the shapes of fruits and nuts.

"They're lovely," Virginia sighed.

"But we're thinking more of something to use so the students here can make their own ornaments." Elizabeth added.

"Well, if that's what you want, the best thing is right here."

With that, Annabelle went behind the counter, reached down inside the clerk's space and pulled out the Turkey red calico cloth that Elizabeth had dyed.

"I know this cloth has special meaning to you," Annabelle said. "But ornaments wouldn't use much of it. And it would make lovely ornaments—it's got that strong Christmas red color."

"Oh, that's the perfect thing to do with it," Elizabeth said.

"I still don't know how you managed to get it so the color would stay," Annabelle said.

"It was simple enough." Elizabeth grinned. "I boiled the cloth in alkali and let it sit in a tub of soured oil before I dunked it in the dye."

Virginia wrinkled her nose.

Elizabeth nodded. "I had to do it outdoors. Matthew refused to walk near the tub. It did smell pretty bad."

She might wear this mourning dress in memory of Matthew, but her heart would ease some on her daughter's death if the children made Christmas ornaments out of Rose's cloth. She knew the bright red cloth ornaments would have delighted Rose if she could see them.

"Still, Matthew must have been proud of you. Knowing how to do something like that," Annabelle said.

Elizabeth shook her head. "It embarrassed him that I was doing what he called servant work."

"I didn't know you had servants."

Elizabeth laughed. "Oh, we didn't have the money for something like that. Matthew just wanted us to live like we had servants. Which meant I had to do so many things when he wasn't looking. Unfortunately dyeing wasn't something that could be done when he was away for an hour or so."

"Well, he should have been proud of you for doing what you did," Annabelle protested staunchly. "Not every woman knows how to dye her own cloth."

"It wasn't just that the smells were bad," Elizabeth said. "He didn't like that my hands sometimes wore a stain for days afterward. I tried to be careful, but it is hard to dye things without getting any of the dye on you."

"Well, Jake would have been proud," Annabelle said. "It's quite something what you can do."

Elizabeth smiled. "I used to be so taken away when I was dyeing things. To be able to turn something plain into something beautiful is—well, it's hard to describe. One good dunking and everything looks different."

"It's like getting a second chance," Virginia said. "Like with redemption. You know, in the Bible."

"I suppose it is at that."

When they got back to the schoolroom, Mrs. Barker had gone. Elizabeth showed the children the cloth and Virginia started to cut some of it into strips so the children could make bright red Christmas braids for the tree.

When Virginia told everyone that Elizabeth had dyed the cloth herself, the children were impressed.

"Maybe we can dye some of the costumes for the pageant," Elizabeth said, looking to Reverend Olson for approval. "We'd have to do it outside, of course, and only the adults could actually do the dyeing. But it is interesting."

The reverend nodded. "I'm sure my wife would like to see this, too. Not too many people dye things anymore. It's quite the art."

Elizabeth beamed. No one had ever called her dyed fabrics art before.

She'd thought about what Virginia had said earlier, about her dyeing cloth being like a redemptive second chance. She wondered if God ever felt the way she did after she'd taken something gray and sorrowful and given it a new life. She hoped He did. Maybe He could do that with the angry hurt inside of her.

Chapter Fifteen

Two days later, Jake was chopping wood again behind
the schoolhouse. He had found a small pine tree the
day before and dragged it up from the ravine. The tree
wasn't higher than four feet tall. He knew Elias was convinced there was a ten-foot tree out there somewhere, but
Jake knew there wasn't a pine tree that tall closer than
the ponderosas in the Black Hills and even the soldiers
weren't making that trip right now.

There were rumors that the renegades were banding
together to make some final attacks before winter set in.
Of course, everyone was probably safe this close to the
fort. There were not that many renegades even if they
all came together for an attack.

Jake told all of that to Elias, but the boy repeated his
claim with a fervor made more adamant by his obvious
wish that his father was here to back him up and his
mother's misguided statements that even an eight-foot-
tall tree would solve everyone's Christmas troubles. She
considered the four-foot-tall tree they had in the schoolhouse to be no better than a bush.

Jake had no patience with any of it. He knew no tree

would solve his trouble. Unless, of course, he could chop it up into kindling and use it to burn that old mourning dress his wife was wearing.

"Here, let me carry that," he said as he saw Elizabeth walking around the side of the schoolhouse pulling an old scrubbing tub.

"Thanks," Elizabeth said as she stopped and tried to catch her breath.

"You should have called me earlier," Jake said as he picked up the tub and balanced it on his shoulder. "That's what you have a husband for."

"Oh." Elizabeth was still wearing that drab mourning dress, but she blushed like a young girl.

Jake didn't even try to hide his grin. "I'm guessing this tub has something to do with Christmas?"

Elizabeth nodded and her eyes lit up. "We're going to dye some of the costumes for the pageant. I thought it would be a good chance to show the children how clothes are dyed. Some of them have never seen it done."

"You know, I don't think I've ever seen it, either," Jake said. He needed a break from chopping wood about now anyway. "Maybe I could use a little education, too."

"You're interested in dyeing?" Elizabeth asked, the delight evident in her face. "Most men don't pay any attention to that kind of thing."

"Out here, men need to know a lot of different things."

Elizabeth nodded. "You can help me build the fires then. We'll need three of them. One for the yellow. One for the brown. And the tub of soda ash for getting the angel costumes a little more white. Well, and setting the other colors, too."

Jake nodded. It was a good thing he and Colter were

chopping firewood the way they were. They were going to need it.

Elizabeth walked back into the schoolhouse and stood for a minute in the doorway. The children had spent so many hours making ornaments lately and practicing their songs for the pageant that they had spread out to cover both halves of the room. She had noticed the young Larson girl was even chatting away with Spotted Fawn yesterday during recess. Elizabeth figured it was difficult to continue being afraid of Spotted Fawn when the children saw how much effort she was putting into pronouncing the names right in her McGuffey Reader.

Jake had watched Elizabeth walk around the schoolhouse before he turned and looked for several good places to put her dyeing tubs. The schoolhouse was on the edge of town and, standing behind it, a man could see for miles. A few cottonwoods were scattered here and there and there was a fair-sized ravine that ran fairly close to the school. He suspected the boys had some good games with each other, hiding in that ravine.

Jake decided to set the tubs up a few yards from the school. He had barely cleared the second spot of dead grass when Colter walked around the schoolhouse carrying his ax. Jake glanced up and knew something was wrong. He'd seen the other man frown a fair amount, but he'd never seen him looking so thunderous.

"Problems?" Jake asked.

Colter grunted as he walked past Jake and went to a log that was lying near the woodpile.

Jake followed the other man over. "You didn't overhear any other pranks the boys are planning, did you?"

Colter shook his head as he positioned himself in

front of the log to take a swing with his ax. "Nope. But I found out who's been robbing the till."

Jake watched as the other man took a powerful swing at the log with the ax, chopping it cleanly into two pieces.

"The bartender?"

Colter shook his head as he moved to take another swing. "Danny."

Jake stood there in sympathy as the ax hit the wood. "You're sure?"

Colter turned and looked at Jake fully for the first time. "I caught him at it. He didn't deny it, either. He told me he was taking the money so he could buy Miss Virginia her own piano." Colter's lips twisted into a bitter smile. "That's why he stole that watch, too. It seems Danny doesn't think Miss Virginia should play the piano in my fine establishment. He thinks she should have her own place where she can give piano lessons to people without them needing to come to a saloon."

"Ahh," Jake said.

Colter glared at Jake. "I suppose you agree with Danny."

Jake shrugged. "A woman like Virginia knows how to behave no matter where she is, but I do think she'd get more students if she was in her own place."

As the two men stood there for a minute longer, the fight went out of Colter.

"Don't you think I know that?" Colter said. "But she doesn't have money to buy her own piano. How's she going to set herself up in business?"

"Maybe some of us could get together and loan her the money," Jake said.

"You know she'd never take it," Colter said. "Before she even started working at my place, I offered to give her some money. She was so indignant you'd have thought I was offering to buy her virtue."

"Were you?" Jake asked softly. He knew the way men like Colter operated.

Colter shook his head. "I didn't intend it at the time, but, well—I've never known a woman like Virginia before. She's—" Colter swallowed. "The truth is I don't know what she is, but I do know Danny is right. She doesn't belong in my place playing piano for a bunch of depressed men who've got nothing better to do than drink themselves into an early grave. She doesn't belong anywhere around men like that—or, ones like me."

With that, Colter sank his ax into the tree log and stomped off.

Give the poor man grace, Lord, Jake prayed as he watched Colter walk around the side of the schoolhouse. He figured Colter knew he didn't stand much chance with Virginia, but the man still wanted to help her to a better life. A man who didn't know how to help the woman he loved was a miserable man indeed.

Jake decided he could use some of that grace himself. He had spent more time these last few days resenting that old mourning dress his wife was wearing than asking himself how he could help her with her grief. Whether she decided she wanted to be married to him or not, he owed her the concern he would give to anyone else who had seen someone they loved die.

It was afternoon before Elizabeth had everything ready for the children to watch their costumes being dyed. Before she had left the house that morning, she'd put all of the old union suits in the back of the wagon so she'd have them in school today. There were nineteen union suits and seventeen children in the pageant. Some of the union suits needed to be cut and some cinched with a rope so they'd stay on, but each child had their own and brought it out behind the schoolhouse to be dyed.

The sun was shining today and the children were comfortable outside.

"Stand back," Elizabeth said as the children came too close to the tub she had boiling. "This first dye is yellow for the stars."

"Take mine first," Tommy said.

Elizabeth accepted Tommy's union suit and put it in the boiling water. She had dried petals of goldenrod and marigolds in there.

While Elizabeth was dyeing the yellow suits, Jake put up another tub a few yards away. Soda ash was stirred into the boiling water in that tub. The limestone-and-salt mixture would help set the yellow dye and whiten the angel costumes.

The last tub, filled with water and the husks from black walnut shells, was boiling away. That dye would make the shepherd's costumes a nice brown.

It would take most of the afternoon to finish the dyeing and Elizabeth was amazed that Jake helped her with the stirring. The yellow and soda ash tubs didn't smell too bad, but most people didn't like to go too close to any of it.

Jake was in love. He'd known it before, but watching Elizabeth and her dyes made him proud of his wife. She showed a reverence for the whole process that made the children feel as though they were part of an important moment. And Jake agreed that they were. His wife knew how to change things. She was taking those old union suits and making them into costumes that were exciting the children.

"I think we want a little more yellow for your star, Elias, don't you?" Elizabeth asked as she held up the boy's costume. "After all you are the brightest star in the sky."

Elias nodded.

Jake wondered how his wife had managed to take this schoolroom full of students who just last week were sitting on opposite sides of each other and make them into one excited group of kids pulling together to have just the right colors.

Jake stayed through all of the dyeing and watched as finally each child had a wet union suit in a different color that they were holding close enough to them so they could see what each other looked like.

"Look, Spotted Fawn isn't brown no more—and Elias is yellow," the Larson girl said with a giggle.

Jake almost said something, but he saw Elizabeth turn to the girl.

"That's the way it is with most color," Elizabeth said as she looked over all of the children with satisfaction in her eyes. "Color is usually just on the outside. Inside most things are the same."

"Hair's that way, too," Tommy said. "Elias got his in red and I got mine in brown."

"I've always said God likes color," Elizabeth agreed as she motioned for the children to bring their union suits to the rope she'd tied between two of the closer cotton-wood trees. "We'll just let these dry while we go back inside and practice your songs for the pageant."

Jake watched the children walk around the side of the

schoolhouse. He couldn't help but notice they walked a little closer to Spotted Fawn than they usually did.

Jake realized he'd married a miracle worker. He didn't know if his wife had set out to teach the children a lesson on the color of everyone's skin, but he had a hunch she had known exactly what she was doing. It made him feel humble. And even more sympathetic than before to Colter.

Elizabeth had left some bean soup simmering on the back of the cookstove when she'd left in the morning so, by the time she, Jake, Spotted Fawn and the baby came back to the cabin late that afternoon, supper was almost ready.

"Just let me see to the horses," Jake said as he helped Elizabeth down from the wagon.

Jake guided the horses closer to the lean-to once Elizabeth and Spotted Fawn were inside his cabin. He wanted to unload a few things without anyone seeing. When the wagon was still, he stepped down and folded back the furs that had been lying behind the seat.

He had a mirror and hairbrush for Spotted Fawn for Christmas and a small music box for the baby. Annabelle had wrapped them both in bright pieces of cloth when he bought them in the mercantile this afternoon. He'd searched the shelves for something fitting for Elizabeth, but he hadn't found anything. He had gone to the telegraph office, however, and put in an order for a large piece of pink granite for that headstone he had promised her.

The girls' presents were to be a surprise, but the headstone wasn't. He planned to tell Elizabeth that he'd ordered it; he just didn't want to talk about it in front of the children. He knew that Spotted Fawn had grown close to Elizabeth. He didn't want his niece to worry that, once the gravestone was completed, Elizabeth would leave them.

Although, he had to admit, his niece might be right to think that. Jake spent a few extra minutes taking the presents up to his loft area before walking back to the cabin door.

Elizabeth added a little more salt to the bean soup. She would let the soup finish cooking while she put the leftover biscuits from breakfast into the oven to heat.

"My angel costume is the whitest," Spotted Fawn said as she walked over to the stove. "Even Elias says so."

Elizabeth smiled as she slid the cold biscuits onto a tin plate. "Christmas is not a competition. It's our Lord's birthday. But I am glad to see you are making some friends."

Spotted Fawn shook her head emphatically. "Elias is not my friend, he's my enemy."

Elizabeth opened the door next to the stove's firebox and put the biscuits inside. "Well, sometimes enemies can become friends. It takes more effort, of course, but the Bible talks about it."

Jake walked through the door.

"What does the Bible talk about?" he asked as he took off his coat.

"Making friends out of enemies." Spotted Fawn frowned. "I'm not sure it can be done." She looked up at Jake.

Jake nodded. "You'll even be able to read about it yourself. I'll show you where it talks about it tonight when I come up to say good-night."

"Supper will be ready soon," Elizabeth said as she turned away from the stove.

An hour later, Jake sighed in contentment. They were all seated at the table, although Elizabeth looked as if she was ready to get up again.

Jake stood and put his hand on his wife's shoulder. "You sit a bit more. I'll start the water heating for dishes. You've had a busy day."

Elizabeth nodded. "But you still don't have to—I mean, I'm perfectly able to wash a few dishes."

"So am I," Jake said as he bent down and picked up the dish tub from the bottom shelf. "Maybe they won't come out a different color than they were when I started, like you did today with those costumes. But I can get something clean enough."

"Even the browns turned out pretty good," Elizabeth said as she stood up. "And it's hard to get a true color in browns."

Eventually, Jake and Elizabeth decided to do the dishes together. Elizabeth was washing and Jake was drying the dishes with a piece of flannel. When he'd done dishes in the old days, he'd give them a good dunking in hot water and set them back on the shelves. But drying dishes was nice. He got to stand close enough to Elizabeth that their hips were always touching.

Spotted Fawn was rocking the baby to sleep so Jake kept his voice low so only Elizabeth could hear.

"I lost my mother, you know," Jake said quietly. "I know how it is to lose someone you love."

Elizabeth looked up from the dishwater in surprise.

"If there's anything I can do to help you grieve, let me know," Jake continued. He might not be overly fond of that black dress, but he was surely attached to the woman who was wearing it.

Elizabeth blinked. "Thank you, I—well, thank you."

"I ordered the headstone today. Granite, like I promised."

"Oh."

"It won't be here until after Christmas, but I'll start to carving as soon as it comes." Jake figured that finishing that headstone was the one clear thing he could do to help his wife in her grief.

"I'm obliged," Elizabeth said.

Jake nodded as he went back to drying dishes. He hadn't known what simple pleasures were to be had when there was a woman like Elizabeth in his house.

"You did a fine thing this afternoon," Jake said as he folded his flannel cloth and set it on the shelf. "Dyeing the costumes for the children and helping them to see that God has made us all different and yet the same."

"Well, it's true," Elizabeth said and then hesitated. "Your baby niece taught me that."

"I wish the parents of those children could learn the lesson, too."

Elizabeth winced. "I think Mrs. Barker is getting worse, not better. She was at the school this afternoon and I could tell she was trying to get the children to sit on the Miles City side of the room. The reverend kept them up doing sums at the board and then Virginia had them singing, so we just didn't let anyone sit down much. But we can't keep that up."

Jake nodded. It was hard to worry about Mrs. Barker when he noticed how delicate his wife's neck was with that loose strand of hair falling down like it was. That mourning dress might be all that was ugly, but it showed off Elizabeth's skin for the beauty it was.

Chapter Sixteen

It was Thursday of the next week before the alterations were made on the costumes and the children could all hit the high notes in the Christmas carols they were practicing for the pageant. Sunday had come and gone with no thaw in the line that separated Miles City from Dry Creek in church. Elizabeth was unhappy about that. She didn't like to see conflict in the church and, added to that, there were only a few people who came to sit on the Miles City side. Mrs. Barker and her friends stayed away.

The Reverend Olson just carried on as if the whole church was in attendance.

Elizabeth asked him about that on Wednesday.

"God would rather people speak their minds than just go home and complain about the church's policy on something," he said.

Elizabeth was helping the reverend get ready for school to start. Spotted Fawn and the baby were in the back of the room and Jake was outside getting some wood for the fires.

"I always thought it was disrespectful to show that kind of anger to God," she said, a little hesitantly.

The reverend chuckled. "I'm sure God has seen more anger in His time than any one of us can possibly imagine."

Elizabeth took a breath. This was her chance. "When my baby died, I was afraid to tell God I was angry for fear He'd punish me and not let me see her again, not even in Heaven."

"Oh, dear," the reverend said. "God isn't interested in punishing you for your feelings. He knows you are grieving for your baby."

Elizabeth blinked.

"If you want to cry, that's fine," the reverend said.

Elizabeth shook her head. "I don't cry."

Just then Jake stepped inside and the reverend called him over.

"It's time to comfort each other," the reverend said as Jake stepped closer. "That's what being married is about."

Elizabeth stiffened. But Jake just put his arms around her and drew her to him. He had been outside and his clothes were cold and a little damp. He was wearing his wool shirt, though and, once it warmed up, it was soft and nice.

Jake didn't seem to want anything but to hold her so Elizabeth relaxed against him.

"The reverend and I were just talking," Elizabeth mumbled against Jake's chest. "About Rose and Matthew."

"I know," he said as he pulled her closer. "I know."

"I don't think I can forget about them."

Jake pressed a kiss to the top of her head. "You don't have to. Just add me and the girls to them."

If there weren't more footsteps on the porch outside

the schoolhouse, Elizabeth thought she would never have moved away from Jake's arms. As it was, she took the feel of his arms with her throughout the rest of the day.

Later that day, Elizabeth taught the angels to fly. Colter had given them some smooth wire he had in the back room at his place and Virginia bent the wire into the shape of wings for each of the angels while Elizabeth took the angels, once they had wings, and taught them how to walk without doing damage to anyone passing by. The children called it learning to fly.

"Well, I get to be a blazing star," Elias said as he went over to twist a bit on Spotted Fawn's wings. The girl turned to glare at him.

Elizabeth's heart sang at the sight. Elias was treating Spotted Fawn just the way he treated the other girls. Spotted Fawn might not see his actions as being friendly, but Elizabeth knew it was a big step forward for the boy.

"Now, children," Elizabeth said, her voice all that was proper.

Virginia finished fashioning the last of the angel wings and stepped over to where Elizabeth was.

"I think we're going to be ready," Virginia said.

Elizabeth nodded. It was Wednesday and the pageant was set for Friday evening. "I think it's going to be wonderful."

The angels were in tune, the shepherds had all found an old tree branch to use as a staff, and the stars had practiced looking wise for the procession. Annabelle and Higgins were going to play Mary and Joseph.

The short Christmas tree was decorated with stars and wreaths cut out of Rose's red calico. It might not be a glamorous tree, but it had been made with the love of little fingers. The reverend was calling the class back to attention so Elizabeth and Virginia quietly went outside on the steps of the school. The air was chilly, but not as cold as it had been. The sky was overcast, though, and the whole town of Miles City looked gray and muddy.

"Not very much like Christmas out here," Virginia said. "I keep telling Colter he needs to put some decorations up in his window, but he keeps saying that's not the kind of place he runs."

"I suppose it isn't."

Virginia nodded unhappily. "I wish it was."

"I know." Elizabeth put her hand on her friend's arm.

Just then they both heard a woman's shriek.

"What was that?" Elizabeth said as she started down the steps with Virginia following right behind her.

The two women were at the bottom of the steps and walking toward the street when they saw Mrs. Barker coming straight toward them, waving a small piece of paper in her hand.

"This is terrible," she shouted from the street as she marched her way toward them.

"What did we do now?" Virginia asked.

"Nothing," Elizabeth said. She hoped that was true. "We've done nothing she can object to."

Mrs. Barker's face was red and her breath was coming fast when she got to the schoolhouse steps. Her hat was a little crooked and her eyes were panicked.

"Oh, dear." Elizabeth took an instinctive step forward. "What's wrong?"

Mrs. Barker took a deep breath and then wailed, "He's coming."

Elizabeth looked at Virginia, but the other woman was of no help.

"Mr. Barker?" Elizabeth asked. She couldn't think of

any other man who would get this reaction from Mrs. Barker.

The older woman shook her head. "No, the railroad man. I just got a telegraph from my cousin. The railroad man will be here Friday night. Somehow he heard about our Christmas pageant and he decided it would be a good time to visit."

"He heard about our Christmas pageant?" Virginia said, looking pleased. "Well, isn't that nice?"

Mrs. Barker glared at her. "It's a disaster is what it is."

With that Mrs. Barker started marching toward the schoolhouse door.

"Wait," Elizabeth called after her, trying to stop the woman. "School is in—"

It was too late; Mrs. Barker had opened the schoolhouse door.

Jake was walking back from the mercantile, his Christmas present for Elizabeth securely tucked away in his shirt pocket, when he heard the commotion over at the schoolhouse.

The schoolhouse door was open and Jake walked right inside.

"We're ruined, just ruined," Mrs. Barker said, wringing her hands at the front of the classroom. "Just look at this—we've got paint all over and we don't even have a proper Christmas tree. That railroad man is going to take one look at us and decide not to come near us."

"Surely he knows it's a children's pageant," the reverend said. "He can't expect it to be perfect."

"He'll at least expect a proper Christmas tree," Mrs. Barker wailed. "I had such high hopes for the railroad coming."

Elizabeth stepped over to put her arm around Mrs. Barker. "There. There. It will be fine."

"What do you know?" Mrs. Barker pulled back. "Your husband is here. You don't have to make this a better place so he'll come home."

"I'm sure the railroad man will understand," Elizabeth repeated quietly. "We'll just do what we can to make him comfortable. And I've already planned to make a big batch of my fried apple doughnuts. I've never known a man to turn one of those down. And I promised Wells I'd make some pecan pies. And maybe some fruit bread for everyone."

"See, it'll be a feast," the reverend said as he patted Mrs. Barker on the back. "He probably won't even notice the tree."

With that, Mrs. Barker let out a sob and ran from the schoolroom.

There was silence when she slammed the door behind her.

"Now I don't want any of you children to worry," the reverend finally said. "We're not doing this pageant to impress the railroad man. We're doing it to the glory of God and that's all we need to worry about."

Jake could see right then that the children weren't as worried about the glory of God as they were about pleasing Mrs. Barker. Well, he couldn't blame them. He'd never been inclined to do battle with the woman, either. She could sure take the joy out of Christmas.

That afternoon, Virginia stayed at school to help the children practice and Elizabeth went home to begin her baking. She stopped by the mercantile to pick up the baby, of course, but she also wanted to get a bottle of vanilla to use in her doughnuts.

"What's happening over there?" Annabelle asked when Elizabeth walked into the store. "Mrs. Barker was just here and she bought every one of those Christmas ornaments we had—the imported ones. All two dozen of them. They cost a small fortune."

"Well, I'm not surprised," Elizabeth said as she stood in front of the counter. "The railroad man is apparently coming to see the children's pageant and Mrs. Barker is convinced we'll look so bad the railroad will never come."

"I doubt the railroad is worried about whether or not the children can sing," Annabelle said.

Elizabeth smiled. "I think we'll do all right in the singing. Virginia is singing along with the children and she has the voice of an angel. No, it's the tree and probably the children's costumes that are upsetting Mrs. Barker most."

Annabelle grinned. "Well, I suppose angels don't really wear union suits."

Elizabeth chuckled. "Neither do the stars. Shepherds might, though."

"Well, it will all work out fine," Annabelle said. "Especially now that you have Higgins up on stage to make sure the boys behave."

Elizabeth nodded. "I'm thinking the look of awe in the shepherds' faces will have more to do with Higgins than the devotion the boys have for the Christ child."

Annabelle laughed. "Clarence does enjoy going to school with the boys."

"Clarence, is it now?"

Annabelle blushed. "He's asked me to marry him."

"Oh, I'm so happy for you. He's a good man."

Annabelle nodded. "I know."

Elizabeth took the happiness of her conversation with Annabelle home with her. Her friend and Higgins hadn't publicly announced their plans yet so Elizabeth didn't tell Jake. He'd let Higgins tell his friend. Once Jake did know she planned to ask him if they could shivaree the couple just like Higgins and Wells had done with the two of them.

Elizabeth made enough fried apple doughnuts that afternoon so that she could take some to the children. The pageant was coming tomorrow and she wanted them to relax and concentrate on pleasing their parents with the performance. She realized this would be the first time the adults of Miles City and Dry Creek would sit together since they'd parted over that black line down the middle of the floor. None of the parents would refuse to come to the pageant because of where they might have to sit.

Surely, the parents were more important than some railroad man.

Before she went to bed that night, she baked some ginger cookies, too. She was determined to do whatever she could to make sure the pageant was a success. If that meant she had to stay up late baking, then so be it. She'd cooked for enough people in her life to know that people were more civilized with each other when they were well fed.

She'd have to take a basket of cookies to the school, as well as the doughnuts. Food worked on children just as it did on their parents.

She was slipping the last cookies from the oven when it occurred to her that maybe she had a tendency to rely on her cooking too much. She'd spent so much of her life taking care of herself that she never had found it natural to turn to God with her troubles. And then, after Matthew and Rose, it was even harder.

She'd been seeing God a little differently of late. Maybe if He believed in dyeing people the way she believed in renewing cloth, then maybe He was worried about people getting along as much as she was. Maybe He wasn't just up there with the stars. Maybe He was down here with her, as well.

But, of course, she thought to herself with a rueful smile, that was what Christmas was about, after all. Even Spotted Fawn had been asking more questions about how to make Elias her friend instead of her enemy.

Now, if only the adults in Miles City could ask the same questions, this Christmas would really be a time of love and goodwill.

Chapter Seventeen

Friday morning was overcast. The sky had been getting a darker gray for the past few days and Jake was predicting a snowstorm before Sunday, which was Christmas Day. As long as the snow waited until then to fall, she would welcome it, Elizabeth told herself as she sat by the fire, rocking the baby. The baby had finished nursing and Elizabeth snuggled her closer. The thought of being snowed in with her little family for the holiday sounded very pleasant.

But first, all of the families needed to go to the pageant and, for that, bare ground would be helpful. Elizabeth put the baby in the crib. She had heard enough about the snowstorms that came to this area to realize no one wanted to travel during them. Virginia said the snow could be five feet tall around the fort some winter days.

Elizabeth didn't want to think about any snowbanks that were as high as that. She did make Spotted Fawn take a blanket with her when she rode her pony to school, though. Elizabeth and Jake would be taking the wagon in later so they would bring Spotted Fawn home after school or Elizabeth wouldn't have even let the girl ride this morning.

But Jake had assured them both that the storm was at least hours away and his horses could pull a wagon home through the snow if it came later.

Still, Elizabeth worked quickly to finish baking the last batch of pies.

Spotted Fawn had her angel costume with her in a pouch she carried on her pony. She'd also asked Elizabeth for some yarn to tie things and so she had a ball of yellow yarn as well as some hair ribbons. Elizabeth suspected the girl was putting together some kind of presents. Elizabeth even tucked a small ball of the red yarn in with the yellow in case the girl wanted anything to look like Christmas.

Elizabeth hadn't thought of a gift for Jake yet, so she needed to take some time today to visit the mercantile. She'd finished knitting the scarves for the girls and she'd had enough yarn left to also make some red socks for Jake, but that wasn't going to be her real gift. She knew he'd have fun with the red socks, but she wanted to give him something that would show him what he was coming to mean to her.

She'd held back several of the pies she'd made and planned to give a couple of them to Wells and Higgins. The rest would be for Jake and the girls. She had jars of her rhubarb jam set aside for Annabelle and Virginia.

This was going to be a special Christmas, Elizabeth told herself, as she packed the basket full of the cookies she'd baked last night for the children.

Miles City was busy when Jake drove the wagon down the street toward the mercantile. Annabelle was going to keep the baby for them again today. Elizabeth was looking forward to having the pageant over so she could spend more time at home with the little one.

"I don't see Spotted Fawn's pony," Jake mentioned as they pulled close to the schoolhouse. The children's horses were always tethered on the left side of the schoolhouse, out of the way of the comings and goings from the schoolhouse. There were no horses there today.

"Maybe they moved the horses somewhere because of the pageant," Elizabeth said.

Jake grunted. "They probably didn't look good enough for Mrs. Barker. She's probably got them hidden behind some bush someplace."

Elizabeth grinned. "You could be right. I hope, for her sake, that that railroad man doesn't even come. Her cousin might have been all wrong about it."

"Well, someone from the railroad is going to show up sooner or later. I guess now is as good of a time as any."

Jake helped Elizabeth unload her pies and cookies. They could hear the shrieks of the children playing behind the schoolhouse so the room was empty.

"It must be lunch," Elizabeth said as she walked over to the teacher's desk that had been pushed in a corner.

Elizabeth and Virginia had decided to put the food there so it wouldn't interfere with the performance space being used by the children. The red calico that had been left after all of the ornaments were made was lying there on the desk, ready to be spread over the food. The tree itself had been moved to the side, as well.

Elizabeth had to admit as she surveyed the empty room that a taller tree would be nice. The tree they had lacked majesty. But, Elizabeth reminded herself, it had been decorated with love and that's what the children would remember.

Jake put the last of the pies on the top of the desk. "It's a good thing you're going to cover these up. Even Higgins won't be able to keep those boys in line."

"I don't think Higgins is going to be here today. Annabelle said he was going to be helping her with something at the mercantile."

"Well, then we better be sure everything's covered before everyone gets back from lunch."

Elizabeth smiled. "Virginia keeps those boys in line almost as well as Higgins."

Jake nodded. "That's because they're all half in love with her."

Elizabeth felt her smile freeze. "I suppose all men would—"

Jake didn't even let her finish. He stepped over and gave her a hug that half lifted her off the floor.

"Not all men," he whispered when he finally put her back down.

"Oh," Elizabeth breathed. "Oh."

Elizabeth thought Jake would have kissed her if they hadn't heard the pounding of little feet on the porch of the school.

"I guess lunch is over," Jake said. He didn't move away from her, though.

"Yes, I—" Elizabeth stepped back and smoothed down the folds in her dress. "I should get ready to help with the practice—for the pageant."

Jake nodded. "And there's always more wood to chop."

The children were only starting to come back into the schoolroom when Mrs. Barker marched into the room. "Where's my ornaments?"

Elizabeth watched in fascination as the woman

walked right up to the front. She should have been a drill sergeant. "I suppose you're putting them on that pathetic excuse for a tree."

Mrs. Barker lifted the Christmas tree up by its top and spun it around in front of her nose so fast a few of the pine needles fell off.

"I can assure you, the only ornaments we have are the ones the children made," Elizabeth said as she walked up to the front, as well. If someone didn't stop the woman, they wouldn't have a tree left. "Maybe you misplaced them."

Mrs. Barker humphed, but at least she put the tree down. "No one misplaces ornaments that expensive."

"Well, then, maybe Elias knows where they are," Elizabeth said as she turned around to look for the boy. The children were still coming into the room, but usually the boy was easy to find because of his red hair.

She didn't see Elias and eventually she noticed that what she did see was guilt spread across the face of every child as they came into the room.

"What's wrong?" Elizabeth asked as the reverend came inside the room with the last of the children. Elizabeth looked at him. "Where's Elias?"

"Surely, you don't think my own son—" Mrs. Barker sputtered.

"Elias didn't come to school today," the reverend said. "I thought he must be sick."

"Elias is never sick," Mrs. Barker said and then her face started to change. Fear seemed to be struggling with annoyance. "He's not off on one of those pranks of his, is he?"

Jake was looking over the children, too.

"Spotted Fawn isn't here, either," he finally said.

Dear Lord, Elizabeth breathed. *Have mercy on us.* She was hoping she'd just overlooked the girl as the others came through the door.

"Where are they?" Jake asked, facing the children.

"Did Spotted Fawn do something to my boy?" Mrs. Barker demanded. "I always said we just can't trust those people."

"Silence," Jake roared.

Mrs. Barker stopped, her mouth half-open.

"You're scaring the children," Jake said to her as he turned back to the students. "Now, who's going to tell me what's going on?"

Anna Larson, the girl who had warmed up to Spotted Fawn the most in Elizabeth's opinion, started to whimper. "Spotted Fawn hasn't done anything. She's only trying to—to help Elias."

"My son doesn't need help—"

Jake glared over at the woman until she stopped.

"Now, what are Elias and Spotted Fawn doing?" Jake turned back to the girl and asked, his voice gentle this time.

Anna gulped. "Elias said he was going to get that tree he's seen. He wanted to surprise his mother. You know, like a Christmas present. He even took the ornaments so he could have it all decorated when he brought it back to town for the pageant tonight."

"He went to get a tree for me?" Mrs. Barker looked astounded.

Anna nodded. "We weren't supposed to tell. It's a surprise."

"We understand," Elizabeth said as she stepped forward. "But what about Spotted Fawn? Where's Spotted Fawn?"

"She tried to stop him from going. She said the snows are coming. But Elias wouldn't stay—" Anna lifted her chin proudly "—so Spotted Fawn went after him to save his life like the Bible says she should—on account of him being her enemy and all."

"Well, surely, no one's saving anyone's life," Mrs. Barker said as she looked up at Jake. "There's no danger of him dying out there, is there? He'll just get the tree and come back here."

All of the irritation drained out of Jake's face and he looked at the woman with pity. "There is no tree around here, not like the one he thinks he's seen. But I'll go after them. The ground is bare so I should be able to track them with no problem. I don't expect snow until tonight at the earliest."

"I'll pack up some of the cookies," Elizabeth said as she moved toward the table they'd set up with food. "They'll be hungry."

Jake nodded.

He looked back at the children. "I assume Elias is riding that big bay he has?"

He got a dozen nods.

"Well, that's a blessing at least. That's a fine horse and should do him some good if he does run into snow," Jake said.

Elizabeth bit back her worry about Spotted Fawn's horse. She assured herself that the pony might be small, but it had been trained by the Indians. It should know just as much about snow as Elias's big bay.

Elizabeth looked down to tie the cookies in a piece of cloth and, when she looked up again, Jake was standing close. He opened his arms and she went into them as naturally as she drew her next breath.

"Don't worry," Jake whispered. "I'll get our daughter back."

"Please." Elizabeth nodded against his chest.

This time when Jake bent his head to kiss her, Elizabeth didn't care who was watching them, she kissed him back with all of the love and hope she had inside of her.

Elizabeth blinked a few times as she watched Jake walk to the door.

Jake hadn't gotten off the porch before Higgins came down the street, riding one horse and trailing another one behind him. Jake swung into the saddle of the extra horse and the two men started to ride north.

Elizabeth walked out on the porch in time to see Annabelle and Tommy come walking to the schoolhouse. Annabelle was carrying the baby.

"Tommy told us," Annabelle said as she hurried toward Elizabeth. "Don't worry. Clarence and Jake will find them."

"I know," Elizabeth said as she turned back to go inside the schoolhouse. "They have to find them."

"I wish I could stay," Annabelle said as she took a couple of steps with Elizabeth anyway. "But I have to get back to the store. Send Tommy over to tell me when they come back."

"It shouldn't be long, should it?" Elizabeth stopped walking and looked over at her friend.

Annabelle shook her head. "Elias and Spotted Fawn have probably already turned back. But I'll be praying for them."

"Me, too," Elizabeth said.

Annabelle gave her a reassuring smile before she started walking away from the schoolhouse.

Elizabeth put a confident smile on her face before she

stepped into the schoolroom. God would answer their prayers for safety. Besides, Jake hadn't thought the snow-storm would come for hours so there was really no need to worry.

Elizabeth sat in the back of the schoolroom while the angels rehearsed their songs. Mrs. Barker sat in the back, too, although she was on the Miles City side of the room and Elizabeth was sitting on the Dry Creek side.

An hour had passed when Danny came running up the stairs.

"He's here," the boy announced when the singers stopped for a breath.

"Elias?" Mrs. Barker said joyfully as she stood up.

Danny shook his head. "No, it's that railroad man. He just went into Colter's for something to drink."

"Well, we can't leave him at Colter's," Mrs. Barker said as she waved her hand at Danny. "We want the man to see the best of our community. Take him over to the mercantile."

"Me?" Danny asked in astonishment.

"You're right," Mrs. Barker said. "I'll need to go get him myself. You just run and tell Colter to bring the man outside of his establishment. Maybe I'll take him to the restaurant and buy him a nice dinner."

"It's two o'clock in the afternoon," the reverend said from the front of the room. "He's probably already had something to eat."

"Then he'll have pie." Mrs. Barker pursed her lips.

Elizabeth looked at the other woman and had pity. "He could come back here for pie. I have dried apple, pecan and berry. That way you can be here when the children come back."

Mrs. Barker nodded. "Thank you. That's very...ah... thank you."

As the woman walked out of the schoolhouse, Elizabeth thought Mrs. Barker had lost most of her starch. She didn't even leave any last-minute instructions on how they were to impress the railroad man. Still, Elizabeth knew it was important to the woman and to the town.

Elizabeth stood up and motioned to Virginia.

They sent the children outside for an early recess and the two women set up a nice place for the railroad man to eat. They moved the doughnuts and cookies to the cabinet by the window and put a plate and fork at the teacher's desk with a folded napkin to the side.

"I could make him some coffee," the reverend said. "I have my pot in the back. It's not that green coffee, either. It's good."

"That would be nice."

"I don't suppose you could sing some for him?" Elizabeth asked Virginia. "You have such a lovely voice. That's sure to make a good impression."

By the time Mrs. Barker brought the railroad man back with her, everything was ready.

"Oh," Mrs. Barker said when she stepped in the schoolhouse and saw what they had done. Then she smiled. "Isn't this nice? Mr. Jamison, I'd like you to meet some of my—well, my friends."

Elizabeth didn't listen to the rest of the introductions. She felt pleased that Mrs. Barker had finally decided to call them friends. Spotted Fawn would be happy to know that treating one's enemies as friends did sometimes work.

Thinking of Spotted Fawn made her go to the side window of the room and look out again. The clouds were a little darker than they had been earlier. Even if it didn't snow today, darkness would come earlier than usual. Elizabeth looked out into the vastness, squinting to see as far as she could across the land here. She could see to the squat mountains north of here, but there were no signs of anyone on horseback.

Lord, she prayed. *Bring them all home safe. Please.*

Chapter Eighteen

Mr. Jamison seemed to take a long time eating his pie. Virginia kept singing and the reverend had joined the children outside to organize a spelling bee.

"This is a lovely community," Elizabeth said as she walked to the front of the schoolroom.

"Oh, yes," Mrs. Barker agreed.

Elizabeth thought the other woman sounded half-hearted. And she knew why when the woman took a peek at the watch she wore as a brooch.

"My, it's getting cooler outside," Mrs. Barker said as she stood up from the bench where she was sitting and began to wander the schoolroom as Elizabeth was doing. "I hope that doesn't mean the snow will come earlier than we expected."

"Don't worry about the snow," Mr. Jamison said as he pushed back his empty plate. "Now, that's some of the finest pie I've ever had in my life."

Elizabeth nodded. "Thank you. So you don't think the snow's coming soon?"

"Oh, I expect the snow will come, I just don't think there'll be much of it." Mr. Jamison brushed at his lips with the napkin. "I stopped at the fort before I came over here and they were sending several patrols out. I don't think they'd be doing that if a blizzard was expected."

"No, no, I suppose not," Elizabeth said with a frown. She knew the soldiers didn't go out on patrol in winter unless it was important. "You don't happen to know—"

Just then Colter walked into the schoolhouse. He was wearing a gun belt and carrying a rifle. "A soldier just came to my place and said the patrols are heading north of here."

Elizabeth felt her breath stop. "North of here? That's the way Jake and Higgins went. What's north of here?"

Colter had a trapped look on his face. "Now, there's no need to worry. I just wanted to let Virginia know I was—"

"What's—north—of—here?" Elizabeth barely got the words out.

Colter didn't answer.

But Mr. Jamison did. "I expect it's those renegades the patrols are out looking for."

"Oh, dear," Mrs. Barker said as she sank down to the nearest bench. "My Elias is out there with those savages?"

"Not to mention Spotted Fawn, Jake and Higgins," Elizabeth added.

"Of course," Mrs. Barker mumbled.

"I'm hoping to catch up with Jake and Higgins," Colter said. "They can't have gone far yet."

"You can't—" Virginia started to say.

But Colter had already left the schoolroom.

There was silence for a minute.

"I don't know if the railroad is interested in places

that have this much trouble with the savages still," Mr. Jamison finally said as he stood up.

"Oh, who cares," Mrs. Barker wailed. "They might have my baby."

"Of course," Mr. Jamison said. "Perhaps I should go back to my hotel and wait for the performance this evening. I assume it's still going to be held?"

"We don't know," Elizabeth managed to say as she took a step toward Virginia and then one toward Mrs. Barker, both of whom were in tears.

"Ah, well—yes, of course." Mr. Jamison cleared his throat and then walked down the aisle and out of the schoolroom.

The three women met in the middle of the room and hugged each other until Mrs. Barker's hat fell off and Virginia's eyes grew red from crying. Elizabeth was the first to pull away.

"We have things to do while we wait," Elizabeth said. "We need to…ah…"

Surely, there were things they needed to do, Elizabeth thought. "We could bring in some wood so it'll be plenty warm when they get back."

"And I could go get some of that tonic I use to ward off a cough," Mrs. Barker said.

"First, we need to pray," Virginia said and the three women came together again. They just stood there in silence, each pleading with God.

When they parted, Elizabeth felt a need to go over to the mercantile and hold the baby. Annabelle had been tending the little one while Elizabeth was helping with the pageant, but no one was going to be rehearsing this afternoon.

Annabelle was stepping out of the mercantile when

Elizabeth was walking down the street toward the building. The other woman had the baby in her arms.

"Oh, I just heard," Annabelle said when she looked up and saw Elizabeth. "I was coming over to talk to you."

Annabelle held out the baby and Elizabeth took the little one and snuggled her to her chest.

"We can talk inside as well as anywhere," Annabelle said as she turned around and opened the door. "Business has been slow today anyway."

"Thank you," Elizabeth said as she followed the other woman inside.

Annabelle led Elizabeth back to her small parlor. "Here, make yourself comfortable. I'll heat some water for tea."

"That would be nice."

Elizabeth let the peace of Annabelle's parlor wash over her as she held the baby.

It was all happening again. And she was completely helpless. She was just starting to love this new family and God was taking it away from her.

"I don't know how you did it," Elizabeth said as Annabelle brought her a cup of tea. "How did you recover from two husbands dying?"

Annabelle sat down with her own cup of tea. "Well, it wasn't easy. It was worse with Tommy's father than with my last husband. I thought I'd never get over him."

"You must have loved him more."

Annabelle shook her head. "No, I think I loved him less. It was the guilt that made it so hard with him. It would just grind at me. I felt like if I grieved deeper it would make up for not loving him so much when he was alive."

"I know. It's the betrayal," Elizabeth said. "Me being

alive and him being dead. I know I loved Rose more than Matthew, but I think I'm going to be able to let her go. But Matthew... I just..."

"Believe me, I know."

"It seems wrong to be falling in love with Jake," Elizabeth finally said. "What does that say about Matthew?"

"Listen to me Elizabeth O'Brian Hargrove," Annabelle said. "You did your best by your Matthew. That's all you could do. Leave the rest in God's hands. You can't live in the past. Not when God's giving you a new family to love."

"Yes, but—" Elizabeth started and then blinked. Tears were starting in her eyes and she blinked again. "I'm sorry, I don't—" tears started streaming down Elizabeth's cheeks "—cry."

Annabelle stood up and came over to pat Elizabeth on the shoulder. "Of course, you cry. We all do."

"It's just that... I—I never told Jake...and now he's out there. And Spotted Fawn... I never told her. And..."

"You'll tell them," Annabelle said firmly. "They're coming back and you'll tell them how you feel. My Clarence will see that they come back. And, just in case he has a bit of trouble, we're going to sit right here and pray."

Elizabeth wiped her eyes and bowed her head.

"Lord, protect those we love," Annabelle prayed. "We know they're in Your hands. Amen."

Elizabeth looked up. "Thank you."

The bell rang out in the store and Annabelle walked to the door of her parlor. "You just sit there now and relax. I'll let you know if anyone hears something."

Elizabeth nodded. She lifted the baby up to her shoulder and rubbed the little one's back.

"God's going to bring your uncle home," she whispered to the infant. "And your big sister, too."

Elizabeth hoped she was right. She didn't care what Annabelle said. She didn't think her second loss would be easier than her first. She had barely made it through losing Matthew; she couldn't lose Jake, too. Especially not like this, with him not even knowing that she cared about him.

All of the anger she'd felt toward God didn't mean much to her right now, not when she needed Him so much.

Elizabeth sat and held the baby until she saw the first snowflake fall outside the window in Annabelle's parlor.

"Oh, dear." Elizabeth stood up. She needed to go back to the schoolhouse and make sure someone was keeping the fire up.

"I'm closing here in a half hour," Annabelle said as Elizabeth told her she was going. "I'll be over there then."

Elizabeth nodded.

"Everyone will probably be back by then anyway," Annabelle said. "The way this whole town is praying, they've just got to be back soon."

Elizabeth had snow on her and the baby when she got back to the schoolhouse. The room was nice and warm when she stepped inside. Everyone looked behind them when Elizabeth opened the door.

"It's just me," Elizabeth said as she started to brush the snow off as best she could with one hand.

The reverend had gathered the children to the front of the room and it looked as though he was reading them a story from the Bible. Virginia was sitting off to the side listening, as well.

"I didn't know it was snowing that much," Virginia said as she walked back to Elizabeth. "Colter didn't even take a coat."

"He probably has a blanket in the bedroll behind his saddle," Elizabeth said.

"I know, but—" Virginia said and then sighed. "I worry. He's my boss, you know."

Elizabeth smiled. "I know."

"Sometimes, I think…" Virginia started. "But it's impossible. Not with him believing the way he does and me—"

Elizabeth nodded. "I know."

The two women sat together and waited. Finally, Mrs. Barker came back to the schoolhouse, too.

"I was writing a letter to Elias's father," she said as she sat down with Virginia and Elizabeth. "Then I got so mad that he isn't here that I just tore it up. A boy needs his father."

"I know you miss them both," Elizabeth said.

"I noticed Elias took an old coat of his father's this morning. I should have seen that earlier. My husband always wore that coat when he went out riding with Elias at this time of year."

"At least he'll be warm," Elizabeth said. All of a sudden she wished fiercely that she'd let Spotted Fawn keep wearing those leggings of hers. They'd keep her warm in the snow better than those flimsy pantalettes and stockings that she was wearing now.

"I'm sure your girl will be fine, too," Mrs. Barker said as she put her hand on Elizabeth's arm.

"Thank you."

Virginia was the one who suggested that everyone sing some hymns. The children had been singing Christmas carols all week so they settled into the familiar sounds of their favorite hymns easily.

"Some of these children have a real love for music," Virginia said after one song. She'd come back to sit with the women while the children each had an apple fried doughnut from the basket Elizabeth had brought in that morning.

"It's too bad you can't teach them," Elizabeth said.

Virginia nodded. "Maybe someday."

"Don't wait too long," Elizabeth said. "Sometimes—"

"I know," Virginia said as she stood up. "Sometimes we wait until it's too late."

Elizabeth pulled the baby close to her again.

Chapter Nineteen

Tommy saw the horses first. Dusk was just starting to make itself known and the boy had been standing by the schoolhouse window, searching through the falling snowflakes, trying to see something before it got too dark.

"They're coming! They're coming!"

Elizabeth put the baby back in the small crib she'd fashioned out of two benches and rushed to the window to look out. She could barely see the figures in the distance.

"There are three horses," Tommy announced. He paused a minute. "I wonder what happened to..." His voice trailed off.

Oh, dear, Elizabeth thought, squinting to see better in the snow. There should be five horses. The three men and the two children. "I'm sure there's some explanation."

Unfortunately, Elizabeth could not think of an explanation that was any good.

It was silent in the schoolroom, but Elizabeth could hear the quiet sobbing of Mrs. Barker.

"They didn't find them," the other woman finally said. "My baby's gone and it's all my fault. If I hadn't made such a fuss about that Christmas tree, he would have never gone out there and—"

Elizabeth walked over to the woman. "Hush now, you had no idea at the time what would happen. We can't control everything that happens in life."

Elizabeth opened her arms and the other woman walked right into them.

"We're not God," Elizabeth finally murmured as she patted Mrs. Barker on the back. Elizabeth knew how the other woman felt; guilty for not being able to foresee what would happen to the ones she loved.

God forgive me for trying to be You, Elizabeth prayed silently as she felt her old resentments melt away.

"They're coming fast," Tommy yelled.

Both women rushed back to the window. Sure enough, Elizabeth saw, the horses were coming in at a slow gallop.

"Oh, dear, what now?" Elizabeth said as she turned to hurry out onto the porch.

The three horses came stomping up to the porch, tossing their heads and prancing a little. A cheer rose up from the children waiting on the porch. Everyone was home.

Spotted Fawn was sharing a horse with Jake and Elias was riding behind Higgins's saddle. Colter rode alone, but he wore a grin as big as the other two men did.

"Thank God," Annabelle said when the cheering died down.

"We thought you might worry once you could see us," Jake said. "So we hurried up here."

Elizabeth just looked up at her husband. He wasn't wearing his hat and his hair was blown this way and that.

The cold had made his face pale. And yet he was the most handsome man she'd ever seen. He had her heart.

"Spotted Fawn saved my life," Elias leaned around Higgins and announced from the back of the horse. "Those Indians were going to scalp me and Spotted Fawn said they had to take her hair first."

"Oh, dear Lord," Mrs. Barker gasped.

Elizabeth echoed the sentiment but she was so speechless not even a gasp escaped.

"Of course, they didn't want hers on account of who she is." Elias kept going. "She can talk to them and everything."

"Of course she can talk to them." Mrs. Barker finally got her breath back. "She's one of them."

There was a moment's silence.

"Not that," Mrs. Barker added with a reluctant little smile. "Not that she's not one of us, too, now."

"She's just got a brown skin is all," Anna said decisively from where she was standing along with the other children. "Like Elias has got that red hair of his and I have my blue eyes. It's all just different colors, but the same underneath."

"That's why they wanted my scalp," Elias said, still excited over his adventure. "That Indians said they'd never seen such red hair. It'd make a good—whatever they use them for."

Elizabeth stepped off the porch and walked over to Jake's horse. She put up her arms and Jake lifted Spotted Fawn off the horse and into them. Elizabeth gently set Spotted Fawn on the ground so she could hug the girl properly.

"I love you," Elizabeth whispered into Spotted Fawn's ear. The girl stood a little stiffly in Elizabeth's arms, but she still had a small smile on her face the whole time she was being hugged.

"What happened to the other horses?" Tommy asked as he looked around.

"We traded for them," Elias explained as he slid off Higgins's horse. "At first, Spotted Fawn offered our horses for my scalp and they were thinking about it, trying to decide if it was a good deal or not on account of my hair being so special. And then Spotted Fawn opened the saddlebag on my horse and brought out those ornaments—"

"My Christmas ornaments!" Mrs. Barker was aghast. "Don't tell me you broke those ornaments. They came from Germany."

"We didn't break them. Spotted Fawn traded them for my scalp."

"Well, what would those Indians possibly want with the things. They don't even celebrate Christmas," Mrs. Barker snapped. "They're handblown glass berries and nuts and apples and—my word, don't tell me they tried to eat the things."

Elias shook his head. "Spotted Fawn put each of the ornaments on some yarn and the Indians are wearing them around their necks. One of them even had a big grizzly paw around his neck and he took it off to wear a pear. I thought maybe he'd give me the grizzly paw, but he didn't. Anyway, they like the ornaments. But they said they weren't enough so they also got the promise of more Christmas presents."

"What presents?" Mrs. Barker looked around.

"We're supposed to go leave them presents of food in the ravine by the schoolhouse tomorrow and they'll leave us our horses back."

Mrs. Barker looked up at the men. "I thought you were supposed to get everything back."

"Spotted Fawn had already made the trade when we got there," Jake said. "It wouldn't be honorable to back down then."

"Well, I've never heard of such a thing," Mrs. Barker said.

Over the next few hours, that phrase was repeated often. Elizabeth suspected it was partially because of Elias. The tale of his nearly being scalped got bigger each time he told the story. The band of renegades grew from eight to nearly eighty. The knife grew to the size of a sword. The grizzly paw became a whole leg of the animal. And Spotted Fawn grew from being his rescuer to the one he bravely rescued.

Spotted Fawn didn't seem to mind. She was busy getting ready to be an angel for the pageant. Since all of the children were still at the schoolhouse and there had been no way to let most of the parents know about the excitement of the afternoon, it was decided they should just go ahead with the pageant.

"You're quite the angel," Elizabeth said as she straightened Spotted Fawn's wings for the tenth time. "I just don't want you to go riding out like that again."

Spotted Fawn nodded. "I don't think Elias will go."

"Yes, well, you shouldn't go with anyone, unless it's your uncle, of course. Or some other adult that your uncle and I approve of."

Spotted Fawn nodded. "Like Mr. Higgins."

"Yes, it's safe to ride to school with Mr. Higgins."

Elizabeth squared the shoulders on Spotted Fawn's white union suit and decided her daughter did look a little like an angel.

The pageant eventually started with the stars gliding onto the stage area at the front of the room. A dozen coal oil lamps were sitting on shelves and they made the whole inside of the schoolhouse look golden. The stars painted on the front wall even glistened a little. Mrs. Barker had moved the small tree from where it stood at the side of the room to the middle of the stage area, declaring it was a perfect tree for a pageant. The red calico ornaments on the tree stood out brightly since someone had hung a lamp on the ceiling over the tree.

The parents were sitting on the school benches, none of them paying attention to which side of the line they were on. The railroad man was sitting in the front row and he wasn't frowning, so Elizabeth took that as a good sign. She and Jake were in the back. Jake had brought his shoulder sling so the baby could sleep if she wanted. Elizabeth liked being able to see everyone in her family, even Spotted Fawn, who was standing so close to her friend, Anna, that their wings were probably tangled by now.

The reverend, looking dignified and solemn, walked out onstage with the stars.

"'In the time of King Herod,'" the reverend started to read from his Bible for the pageant, "wise men came from the East asking 'Where is the child who has been born King of the Jews? For we observed his star at its rising, and have come—'"

The stars were rising up and dancing while the angels began to sing.

The whole pageant was over in forty minutes. The stars finished their dancing, the shepherds heard the angels, and they all sang together of the holy night long ago. The telling of the story didn't seem as if it took much time, but Elizabeth knew the families in this community would never be the same.

Part of that was because, before the pageant, everyone had heard the story of how Spotted Fawn had gone to the rescue of Elias Barker, the boy whose mother had tried to make her an outcast. Everyone knew there would be no more talk about heathens in their midst or lines down the floor of the church.

"It's a new start for us all," Elizabeth said to Jake. The final child had just walked off the stage area and people were lining up for the food table. She and Jake were content to sit on the bench in the back of the room.

Jake nodded as he reached over and took her hand that lay on her lap.

"You're a blessing to me and the girls, Elizabeth O'Brian Hargrove."

"You're all right with me being both O'Brian and Hargrove?" Elizabeth looked up him in surprise.

"I figure if Spotted Fawn can make her peace with Elias, I can stop being jealous of a dead man."

"Oh, you have nothing to be jealous about," Elizabeth said. "You're—"

"Yes?" Jake leaned his head closer.

Elizabeth blushed. She looked around to be sure no one was listening. Even then she whispered. "You're magnificent."

Jake started to grin. "I hope that look in your eyes means you're thinking of staying with us past the spring?"

Elizabeth nodded. "It's just—"

Jake's grin started to fade. "Whatever it is, we'll work it out."

"It's not a problem," Elizabeth said. "I'd just like to

have a real wedding before—you know—so we can say the words and mean them."

Jake's grin spread as his eyes deepened. "Elizabeth, will you marry me?"

Elizabeth nodded. "It would be my pleasure."

"In that case, I'm going to kiss my fiancée," Jake said as he proceeded to do just that.

Elizabeth thought she heard clapping in the distance, but that didn't make any sense. The pageant was already over. And, since it was, there seemed little harm in having another kiss. Or two.

Epilogue

❧

Everyone gathered for the wedding on the first Sunday afternoon in May. Elizabeth had wanted to wait for a day that would be warm enough for them to have the ceremony on the banks of Dry Creek. Besides, it gave Jake time to put up the headstone he'd promised and for her to finish her mourning.

"You're a beautiful bride," Virginia said.

Elizabeth smiled over at her friend as they waited by a cottonwood tree. Virginia was her maid of honor. "Thank you. I can't believe the day is really here."

The guests were all being seated on the log benches Jake and Higgins had borrowed from the schoolhouse. Dozens of families had come from Miles City as well as some of the soldiers from the fort.

The railroad man had even ridden over. He was making his second inspection of Miles City and had already told everyone things were promising. He said he'd been impressed with the children in the town, particularly Spotted Fawn.

Elizabeth had been proud when she heard the man

talk of Spotted Fawn's bravery. She looked over to where the girls were sitting now with Annabelle and Higgins.

"I can't get used to calling the baby Mary," Elizabeth whispered. Spotted Fawn had decided her sister should be named in honor of Christmas. "I always just think of her as my baby."

Virginia followed her gaze. "She'll always be your baby, no matter what her name is."

Elizabeth nodded. "I know."

They were silent for a few minutes and then Elizabeth smoothed down the folds of her moss-green velvet dress.

"Jake always did want me to have a dress this color," Elizabeth finally said. "I think he was half-afraid I was going to wear that mourning dress if he didn't buy me something new."

"Maybe you should pass the mourning dress along to me now," Virginia said with a twist to her lips.

"Oh, don't say that." Elizabeth put her hand on her friend's arm. "Colter will come back."

Virginia shrugged. "I'm not even sure I want him to—"

Colter had left town in January, saying he had business he needed to attend to before he went forward with his life. He'd left the saloon and Danny with Virginia as well as enough money to see them settled while she turned the saloon into a studio for her piano lessons.

Just then the reverend cleared his throat. The guests were seated and Jake was waiting at the front of the aisle formed by the two rows of benches.

"We'll talk later," Elizabeth said as the two women walked forward.

"No, we won't," Virginia said. "This is your wedding

day and there's a man watching you now who looks like he's the happiest man alive."

"He does, doesn't he?" Elizabeth said as Virginia walked down the aisle ahead of her.

Jake was wearing a suit. Not a suit of buckskin. Not even a flannel shirt and wool pants. No, it was a suit that would do justice to a banker. He thought his mother would be proud, even of the red socks he wore on his feet.

Elizabeth almost floated down the aisle to him. She was beaming and he couldn't take his eyes off her. She was a vision in that green dress of hers, just as he'd known she would be. His Elizabeth was beautiful. She wore her old wedding ring around her neck on the gold chain he'd given her for Christmas; he had her new ring in his pocket.

When Elizabeth reached his side, she put her hand on his arm.

Jake had insisted on the longest ceremony possible this time. He wanted to promise everything to his wife. That he'd protect her. Comfort her. Provide for her. Love her.

He paused on that one. He especially wanted to promise to love her.

Elizabeth looked up at Jake as she repeated her vows. She almost had to shade her eyes, the sun was so bright behind him. She smiled; he looked all golden around the edges.

"You may now kiss the bride," Reverend Olson said with such satisfaction in his voice that some of the guests chuckled quietly.

"Finally," the reverend added with heartfelt enthusiasm.

Elizabeth didn't care if the whole countryside erupted in joyful laughter. It was no secret that she and Jake had walked a long path to arrive at this place. She reached up and touched his cheek as he bent his head toward her. The kiss was all she'd ever dreamed it could be.

* * * * *

As a teenager growing up in north Mississippi, **Elizabeth White** often relieved the tedium of history and science classes by losing herself in a romance novel hidden behind a textbook. Inevitably she began to write stories of her own.

Along the way Beth married her own Prince Charming and followed him through seminary into church ministry. During a season of staying home with two babies, she rediscovered her love for writing romantic stories with a Christian worldview. Her first novella saw print in 2000.

Beth now lives on the Alabama Gulf Coast with her family. She plays flute and pennywhistle in church orchestra, teaches second-grade Sunday school, paints portraits in chalk pastel, and—of course— reads everything she can get her hands on. Creating stories of faith, where two people fall in love with each other and Jesus, is her passion and source of personal spiritual growth. For more about Beth, visit her website at bethwhite.net.

Books by Elizabeth White

Love Inspired Historical

Crescent City Courtship
Redeeming Gabriel

Love Inspired Suspense

The Texas Gatekeepers
Under Cover of Darkness
Sounds of Silence
On Wings of Deliverance

REDEEMING GABRIEL

Elizabeth White

Truly I tell you, whatever you did to one of the least of these brothers and sisters of mine, you did to me.
—*Matthew* 25:40

For Hannah, who has read them all

Chapter One

Camilla Beaumont cautiously opened her bedroom window and leaned out. It was one of those inky Mobile nights when warm April air met earth still cool from winter, brewing up a fog as thick as gumbo. A night when the Union blockade crouched like a sullen watchdog far out in the bay and Confederate soldiers camped under abandoned cotton shelters at Camp Beulah just outside town. A night when any civilian with a grain of sense was tucked up asleep under the breeze of an open window.

She paused with one leg out the window and took a deep breath. With practiced ease she grabbed the knotty old wisteria vine that twined around the lattice and began the climb down.

It was amazing she hadn't been caught and sent to the prison on Ship Island. In the early days her forays had been executed with haste and blind luck. Lately, however, every move and communication were plotted with exquisite care, orchestrated by an anonymous sponsor. Camilla longed to meet him, one day when the war was over, the Yankees went home, and the Southern conscience woke up to the truth that slavery was wrong.

As she scooted into an alley behind the Battle House Hotel, a baby's cry from an open upstairs window stopped her in her tracks. She prayed there wouldn't be a baby tonight. Babies made her task twice as difficult and dangerous.

Shuddering, she continued down empty residential streets, slipping from behind one tree to the next—huge old oaks dripping with Spanish moss that tickled her face, magnolias just beginning to bud, and scratchy, richly scented cedars. She sneezed, then looked around, stricken with fear, breathing in and out. The fog was so dense she could barely see her hand in front of her face. When all remained quiet, she continued, knees trembling.

At the waterfront, noise and light from inside the buildings spilled out into the fog. She paused outside the Soldiers' Library to watch the approach of two gray-uniformed soldiers. They seemed more intent on observing the ribaldry inside the gambling saloons and oyster bars than enforcing the 9:00 p.m. slave curfew.

Slouching into a bowlegged, droop-shouldered posture, she lurched out into the road. An inebriated vagrant wandering the downtown streets in the wee hours of the morning was a common enough sight. As long as he was white.

She hesitated at the corner of Water and Theater streets, peering blindly into the mist, and nearly jumped out of her skin when cold fingers tapped her cheek. She stifled a shriek with one hand.

"Now, now, Missy, I thought you wasn't comin'." The

whining whisper was so close to her ear that she could smell the speaker's fishy breath.

"Shh! Virgil, you nearly scared the life out of me. Come here before somebody sees us." She grabbed a skinny arm and towed him deeper into the shadows.

Any passerby who chanced to see them would have found little to tell them apart. Much the same height, they wore the same disreputable costume—dark stocking cap, patched pea jacket, canvas pants of an indeterminate color and hobnailed boots.

"Where's the bag?" Camilla turned Virgil around and yanked off the burlap sack slung across his back, then placed her hands firmly on either side of his vacant face. "You forget you saw me tonight, you hear?"

Virgil nodded with childish pleasure. "I ain't seen you, Missy."

"Good." Camilla reached into her pocket for a coin and a slightly fuzzy toffee. "Get yourself something to eat, and I'll sell your papers for you."

"Yes'm, Missy." He popped the toffee into his mouth. "You'll bring my bag back when you're through?"

"Haven't I always?"

"Yes'm, shore have." Virgil grinned, then shuffled away into the fog without a backward glance.

Camilla watched him go with a mixture of pity and gratitude. Since no one considered him capable of putting two thoughts together on his own, Crazy Virgil the Birdman could come and go as he pleased. When she assumed his identity, she was virtually invisible.

Disguise complete, she stepped into the street and continued northward to where the Mobile and Tensaw rivers dumped into Mobile Bay.

Camilla could remember when the quay of Mobile

was lined with stately hulls and a forest of masts. After General Bragg forbade cotton to be shipped to the port lest the Yankees succumb to the temptation to attack, the steamers made increasingly rare appearances downriver. The docks looked embarrassingly naked these days.

But there should be at least one riverboat tied in. Camilla strained to see through the fog. There she was. The *Magnolia Princess,* flambeaux peering through the mist, bumped gently against the pier like a cat nudging her mistress's skirts.

As Camilla approached, a burst of laughter reached her ears, faded, swelled again. The *Magnolia Princess,* one of the few pleasure boats remaining in these grim days, carried a troupe of actors and singers and dancers, as well as floating card games run by professional gamblers.

Ready to hawk her newspapers should she be noticed, Camilla stole across the boat's gangway, darted across the lower deck and found the ladder down into the hold.

Wooden beams creaked all around her as she descended, and the smell of oil and burning pine from the stoke hole was suffocating. Sticky turpentine oozed from the frame of the boat and clung to her clothes and hands as she felt her way down the rickety ladder. She was nearly at the bottom when she felt strong hands clasp her around the waist and lift her down.

"Horace," she breathed in relief.

"Me and the boy both here, Miss Milla, but we got to hurry. The train, she leaving in less than two hours."

Camilla took a deep breath. "There'll be four this time."

She dropped the bulky bag full of newspapers, then with the two men began to examine the barrels crowded into the narrow space. At length Horace kicked one in disgust. "Porter say he mark ours with a *X,* but it's so dark down here I can't see a thing."

Camilla wiped her sweaty face on her coat sleeve. It would be deadly to send the wrong barrels north on the train. She hesitated, then whispered, "I know you're not supposed to make a sound, but we're running out of time, so I want you to make some little noise so we'll know where you are."

There was a moment of thick quiet. All she heard was the creaking of the boat and the slosh of water against her pontoons. Then, barely audible, came a scratching sound from the barrel upon which Camilla sat. Grinning at Willie, she hopped down. When they'd found the three others, she assisted the men in hoisting them one at a time up the ladder.

Porter, their accomplice on the boat, had done his job—keeping the crew away from this end of the deck. The thick fog aided them, as well. They spoke not a word as they worked, and Camilla flinched every time one of the barrels bumped against the ladder going up. But no sound came from within any of the barrels—until they were loading the last one onto the wagon. Losing her grip, Camilla gave a dismayed little squeak.

Just in time to keep it from bursting open on the ground, Willie grabbed her end of the barrel.

As a muffled wail came from inside the barrel, Camilla flung her arms around it. "Shh, it's all right," she whispered through the knothole near the top. "I know you're scared, but hold on. We're almost away."

Horace patted her shoulder and jerked his head toward the rail station a quarter mile or so up the quay.

Taking a shuddering breath, Camilla nodded. "All right. Let's go."

The wagon lurched into motion.

As they rattled along the waterfront, Camilla strained to see through the twining fog. The military watch was spread thin. Maybe they'd escaped.

"Hey, you there!" A hoarse voice penetrated the darkness. "Stop where you are!"

Camilla clutched the side of the wagon as Horace drew the horses to a halt. Boots crunched on damp shells as a gray-clad watchman appeared out of the fog. She and Horace and Willie waited, letting the picket make the first move. Camilla kept her head down and pulled her cap over her face.

The soldier leaned against the wagon. "What you doing out here?" He reached out and whacked Camilla on the head with a gloved hand. "What's in them barrels, boy?"

She cowered. "Nothing, sir."

Horace drew the sentry's attention. "We's just coming back from market, sir. Mistress need supplies for baking."

"In the middle of the night? I don't think so." The man laughed and walked around the wagon to plant the barrel of his musket in Horace's ear. "You all holding a voodoo ritual?"

Close to vomiting from terror, Camilla felt for her newspaper bag. "Please, sir, we been delivering—" The bag was gone. She must have left it on the boat. *Think, think, think.* She struggled to her feet, and her toe struck one of the barrels already in the wagon before they loaded the other four. "Oh, please, sir, don't look in them barrels!"

"What you got there?" the man demanded. "Moon-shine?"

Horace again drew fire away from Camilla. "That against the law, sir."

The soldier turned. "It sure is, you black rascal! But I might forget I saw you out after curfew if you let me have it."

"Sir, Colonel Abernathy get upset if we let this load go. But we might could find you some more in a couple of days."

"Colonel Abernathy, huh? Why didn't you say so?" The man shouldered his gun and stepped back. "I'm on duty ever' blasted night this week. You best deliver my load within two days, or I'll have to remember I found you running around in the middle of the night. You hear me?"

"Yes, sir," chorused Horace and Willie. Camilla was too relieved to speak. The wagon started up, pitching her on her rear, where she sat hugging the closest barrel and shaking like a blancmange.

Virgil was going to be in serious trouble if she didn't find his bag.

In the quiet darkness Gabriel Laniere—trained physician, thespian and horse wrangler who presently found himself masquerading as a minister—leaned on the rail of the aft main deck of the *Magnolia Princess*. It was the only pleasure boat docked among the shrimpers, oyster boats and merchant vessels in the quay of Mobile Bay. He'd waited out the noisy leave-takings of the last of the gamblers. The only sounds on the boat now were the snores of the crew huddled behind the boiler and a faint scraping sound coming from the direction of the gangplank—most likely a straggler meandering home after being left behind.

Gabriel touched the full-blown red camellia in his lapel. It had been tossed at him with a wink a few hours earlier by the "incomparable" Delia Matthews—billed as the "star of *Simpson and Company*," a pleasing comedy in two acts, as well as the laughable farce *The Omnibus*—a symbol of her code name. Miss Matthews had indeed proved to be an actress of some versatility and ingenuity. Gabriel hoped her courier skills would match her ability to bedazzle a theater full of drunken Southern gentlemen.

What he had to report to Admiral Farragut could not wait.

The scraping noise came again, followed by a muffled grunt. Frowning, he straightened away from the rail, but paused when a deckhand appeared out of the mist that swathed the gangplank. The man carried a soft felt bag, which he tossed from hand to hand with a soft *chink*.

Gabriel retraced his steps and found the hatch down into the hold of the boat. As he descended the narrow ladder, rumors he'd dug up in New Orleans crawled through his thoughts. Even now he could hardly believe the words he'd encoded on the paper in his pocket. *Fish boat. Underwater torpedo.* Naval warfare was undergoing radical change, literally under Farragut's nose, and Gabriel's mission began with alerting the admiral to the fact that the engineers of this dangerous vessel had moved their secret enterprise from New Orleans to the unlikely backwater of Mobile, Alabama.

Then—search and destroy.

Some two hours later, he was still sitting on a barrel that smelled of sorghum molasses, his head clearing the overhead planks by a scant quarter of an inch. The hold ran the length and breadth of the boat, but it seemed to have been designed for the undernourished roustabouts who spent sixteen of every twenty-four hours loading and unloading bales, hogsheads, sacks and crates, and firewood for the ravenous jaws of the furnace.

He had been containing his temper by reciting the human bone and muscle systems. Which made him think of Harry Martin, who never could keep straight which was the fibia and which was the tibia. Last he'd heard, Martin was serving as a field surgeon with Grant. Probably hacking off limbs right and left.

He shifted his position and began on the muscles again. Delia Matthews had better have a good explanation for her tardiness. Admiral Farragut, who had recruited and trained him, insisted that intelligence work was five percent action, twenty percent listening and seventy-five percent waiting. Most times Gabriel did it by sheer force of will. And he didn't mind when the objective was in sight. But endlessly waiting for a courier who should be right here on the boat—

A light tap of boots overhead interrupted his seething thoughts. Someone removed the square hatch cover, relieving the pitch-darkness. A pair of scratched and broken boots descended the ladder, then hesitated midway.

Gabriel slid off the barrel.

"Now where in creation is he?" The voice was lighter than he'd remembered it onstage. She was a cool one. Serve her right if he scared her.

He opened his mouth to utter the pass code, but a shadow loomed in the hatch.

"Who left the hatch open?" grumbled an unseen male voice. "Harley, I told you—"

The thumping of heavy boots, and Gabriel saw the

woman's panic in the tremor of her body. She was about to scream. He reached her in one silent lunge. Clapping one hand over her mouth, the other arm clamping her arms at her waist, he snatched her into the corner under the stairs. Sliding to the floor with the actress's shaking body held close, he waited for disaster to strike.

But the mate stood at the top of the stairs, peering down into the murky darkness and muttering. Finally he turned and stomped back up the stairway. The hatch cover clanged into place, submerging Gabriel and his captive in darkness and silence.

The slim, lithe form in his arms continued to tremble. Fearing the return of the mate, Gabriel kept his hand over Delia's mouth, his hold gentling as she relaxed. Her clothes smelled of turpentine and fish, and the small head was covered with a ragged knit cap that scratched his jaw. A good idea, as the luxuriant mass of hair would have given her away if she were seen away from the cabin area.

Squirming, she expelled a little sigh that tickled his hand.

He tightened his hold. "Oh, no, you don't," he whispered. "I'm not uncovering your pretty mouth until I'm sure you can keep it quiet."

She nipped the palm of his hand.

He released her mouth, barely containing a yelp. "Why you little—" He lowered his voice. "Are you trying to get us both hanged?"

"Who are you?"

Good, she was careful. "Joshua."

The boat breathed around them: creak of timbers, slosh of water, scent of pine resin drifting with the soft fragrance of lily of the valley. He yanked off Delia's cap, releasing a tumble of curly hair. He lifted a handful to his face and breathed in, curling his arm more snugly around her.

"Stop pawing me and tell me what you want."

He chuckled. "Try any more tricks and you'll be sorry."

Silence. Then, "I'm listening."

"Good. I've got you a sermon to deliver, and you'd best do whatever it takes to get it in the hands of the man upstairs." When she moved to get up, he tightened his arm around her. "Stay put. We have any more interruptions, I don't want to have to dive for cover again."

"Oh, all right." She shifted in discomfort.

He reached into his coat for the sermon he'd composed that afternoon, then fumbled at the side of her coat. She stiffened, but allowed him to slide the paper into her pocket. "Too bad you wasted so much time getting down here, Camellia. I'd like to stay and chat, but I've got to get ashore before daylight."

She gasped. Shoving his hand away, she snatched up her cap and crammed it down over her hair. She scrambled to his feet and backed toward the hatch. "I've got to go."

Quietly she climbed the ladder, lifted the hatch cover and peeked out. Apparently finding the coast clear, she disappeared.

Gabriel rubbed his eyes and relaxed against the rough wall. He'd give it a few minutes before he risked his own exit from the hold.

The cipher was delivered.

Camilla scrambled over the wrought-iron fence bordering the rear of the Beaumont property. Chest heaving, she tumbled spread-eagle onto the grass and stared up at the still-black sky. She'd covered the distance from the riverboat to Dauphin at Ann Street at a flat-out run.

In four years they'd never come close to getting caught. Now they'd have to find a way to supply whiskey to Colonel Abernathy as well as that dratted sentry. She threw her arm across her eyes. When the paper in her pocket crackled, she shuddered and sat up. The man had called her by name, although he'd said it kind of funny. The message had to be from Harry, who was presently in North Mississippi, as far as she knew.

After leaving Mobile at the declaration of hostilities, Harry had chosen a different way to communicate with her each time. Once he'd placed a note in the spine of a book and sent it to Jamie. Her brother approved of Harry, even if her grandmother did not.

She staggered to her feet. Harry's latest messenger boy was sorely lacking in manners. Yet she would endure the fright and indignity again to have a letter to read and dream over, to help her remember Harry's face.

She glanced up as she crept toward the house. The night seemed to have lightened a bit. Thank God for the open sky. When she'd gone back into the hold of the boat to retrieve the bag, the darkness had seemed to reach for her ankles. No wonder that deckhand nearly caught her. If the ruffian who called himself Joshua hadn't grabbed her and covered her mouth, she might've screamed.

At the edge of the porch she paused. Male voices murmured through the open windows. Papa was up late. That wasn't unusual, but the summer draperies had been closely drawn, dimming the light from the room.

She pulled back into the shadows beside the porch and peered through the lace. Her father was as attached to open windows as she was. Why would he pull the curtains on a muggy spring night?

Her father spoke again, answered by another man. Gradually the conversation began to make sense. They were discussing boats, or maybe *a* boat. Transportation was the family business. Nothing to linger over.

Then Papa's voice dropped so low she had to strain to hear. "You're sure the Yanks don't know about it?"

"I'm sure of it. We scuttled it hours before Butler followed Farragut into New Orleans."

Papa grunted. "You have the plans?"

"Hidden in the machine shop. But remember the original model wasn't fully operational. The propellers tended to lock without warning, and we hadn't tested her with a full crew." The man cleared his throat. "Finding men willing to go under water deep enough to test her distance— well, I'm not sure I'd try it myself."

"Oh, balderdash! I'd get in the thing tomorrow, if I weren't a foot too tall and twice that too wide."

"I'm sure you would, Zeke." The man sounded amused. "But even if we start building tomorrow, it'll be a month before it's ready to test again."

"You *will* start tomorrow," Papa said. "And I want it completed in three weeks. Money's no object when we've got the chance to sink Yankee gunboats without risking our own men."

"I suppose it could be done." The other man paused. "Laniere thinks he can correct the problem with the propeller. If nothing else goes wrong, we could break the blockade."

Papa chuckled. "Excellent. I intend to be situated in a place of influence when we send the Yankees back north where they belong." There was a scrape of chairs, a mutter of goodbyes, and the light was extinguished.

Camilla leaned against the house. Her father was setting himself up to make pots of money off a vessel so secret that it had to be scuttled before the Yanks could get their hands on it. It was one thing for her father to comply with the Confederate army's demands that he provide transportation for the troops—strictly a defensive service. But to invest family money in a deadly weapon…

Maybe she'd misunderstood.

On shaky legs she crept around the side of the house and climbed the wisteria. She pulled herself through the open window and collapsed onto the floor. Sitting against the window seat, she removed her filthy clothes and tossed them under the bed. The room reeked of turpentine.

She hoped Lady wouldn't take a notion to visit. Her grandmother never let a thing go by, which was how she kept the household under control, but so far she didn't know about the underground railroad. And she didn't know about Camilla's communication with Harry.

Camilla rose to light the lamp, then unbuttoned her shirt and yanked it off. With a little grunt of frustration, she picked the knots free and unwound the linen strips that bound her bosom. Gradually she could breathe more freely. She heaved a sigh of relief as the last strip fell into her lap. Then she remembered the folded paper in her pocket. Rummaging under the bed, she found it and eagerly unfolded it.

She frowned. This wasn't a letter. It was a sermon. She skimmed to the bottom. Harry always signed his name, but there was no signature here.

She read the sermon again. It was taken from the biblical account of the Israelite spies Moses sent to infiltrate the land of Canaan.

Mystified, she slipped on her nightgown and tucked the paper into the lacy ruffle of her sleeve. The stranger on the boat had said her name. And she'd never forget that voice. Smooth and deep, like the cough syrup Portia poured down her throat when she had the croup.

The familiar way he had touched her mouth and her hair had been abominable, but he'd kept her from being discovered by the deckhand. His arms had held her gently.

Cross-legged on the cushion at the open window, she touched her lips. She could still taste a faint saltiness from his hand. He'd said she had a pretty mouth. How would he know that? It had been pitch-dark almost the whole time. Maybe Harry had described her.

What did he mean by asking her to deliver the sermon to the "Man Upstairs"? The whole scene had been so bizarre and confusing. She'd forgotten all about looking for Virgil's bag. Maybe she could make him a new one. Sighing, she rose to blow out the lamp.

The doorknob rattled.

She nearly dropped the candle snuffer. She'd nearly forgotten Portia, who always brought her bathwater and something to eat after a running. She hurried to unlock the door.

Portia stomped in with a brass can of steaming water under one arm and a stack of clean linen under the other. "If ever I saw such a mess of idiots in all my born days!" She thunked the can down on the washstand and faced Camilla with a righteous glare.

Camilla shut the door, a finger to her lips. "You'll wake up Lady—you know what a light sleeper she is!"

"You two hours late, missy." Portia tossed the linen

on the bed, reached for Camilla and yanked the night-gown off over her head. "Horace says you all nearly get caught by the graycoats, then by the grace of God you get the delivery to the station—then Miss Camilla ups and takes off again without a word of explanation!" Portia's nostrils flared. "Bathe quick, before that smell sticks to you permanent. Then you can eat while you tell me where you been."

"I'm sorry, Portia." Camilla meekly began to wash.

"Hmph." Portia dug under the bed and came up with Camilla's stinking clothes. "You fall in a pigpen on the way home?"

"It's the pitch from the boat." Camilla completed her bath, hung her towel on a brass rack beside the wash-stand and picked up her hairbrush. It was going to take hours to get the tangles out of her hair.

Having already bundled the offending clothes into a canvas bag and tossed the whole thing down a laundry chute, Portia snatched the brush. "Lucky you didn't get the stuff in your hair—we'd be cuttin' it off right about now."

A haircut would be less painful than Portia's brisk strokes with the brush, but Camilla closed her eyes and endured. She deserved a certain amount of pain for her stupidity.

"You gonna tell Portia where you been for the past two hours?" The brushstrokes slowed and gentled. "I been just about out of my mind, worrying."

Camilla rested her head back against the cushion of Portia's bosom. "I had to go back to fetch something I left on the boat."

"It better been something almighty important."

"It was Virgil's news bag." Camilla waited for the

explosion that didn't come. Feeling a tremor under the back of her head, she opened her eyes.

Portia's dark face was perfectly bland, though there was an amused spark in the back of her eyes. "Girl-*child,* you're gonna put yourself out one too many times for that cockeyed old man. I sure hope the Lord makes good on that promise about 'doing it unto the least of these.'" She snorted and began to brush again. "Virgil Byrd's about the least of anything I ever seen!"

Chapter Two

Gabriel woke to the sound of a timid scratching at his door. Having long ago trained himself to sleep with one foot on the floor, he moved in one fluid step to the door, his derringer cocked and ready to fire. "Who is it?"

"Reverend Leland, it's S-Sally. Sir."

Reminded of his ministerial alter ego, he relaxed and lowered the gun. Opening the door, he found the young maid who had escorted him to his room yesterday twisting her apron into a white corkscrew. "A bit early in the day for spiritual counseling, my dear," he said dryly.

Sally's blood climbed to the ruffle of her mobcap. "Sir, I got an urgent message."

Gabriel pulled his galluses up over his shoulders. "What is it?"

"They's a lieutenant downstairs, told me to come get you on the double. Said tell you there's a lady been took by Colonel Abernathy, and she needs you right away."

Gabriel's blood froze. The only lady he knew here was Delia Matthews. "Tell the lieutenant I'm on my way, and ask him to make my—ah, cousin as comfortable as possible."

The mobcap bobbed and disappeared.

Gabriel dressed and shaved, managing to nick his chin with the razor in his haste. Irritated, he examined the cut in the mirror. Beards and mustaches were in fashion these days, but yesterday's trip to the barber was essential to his disguise. He hadn't been clean shaven since his sixteenth birthday; he hardly recognized himself. In fact, he'd forgotten about that arrow-shaped scar his brother, Johnny, had put on his upper lip when they were kids. He touched the scar. Johnny was probably dead by now. Ma always said the good died young.

Gabriel had every intention of living to be an old man.

Escorted by the young lieutenant, he fumed all the way downtown to Confederate headquarters. Delia should have been headed upriver with her troupe by now. If they'd left without her, he had no way to get the cipher into Union hands with any expediency. And what if she'd been searched?

His wait in the luxurious parlor of the Rice mansion, which housed Colonel Abernathy's staff, did nothing to cool his temper. His only consolation was the proximity of his understuffed horsehair chair to the two yawning sentries lounging on either side of the front hall. He couldn't help wondering why this war was taking so long. Grant or Sherman ought to stroll down here tomorrow and round this bunch up like so many hound dogs snoozing in the shade.

He was beginning to lose interest when the secretive note in the voice of one of the sentries brought him fully awake.

"You hear about the delivery coming in tonight?"

"Yeah. About time, too. If I'd known there wasn't

gonna be no whiskey allowed, I'd thought twice before joining up. Where's it coming from?"

"Somebody caught a couple fellas with the Birdman last night. First time anybody's actually seen 'em. Promised if they'd let 'em go they'd pass the next shipment our way."

The first sentry chortled. "The Birdman may be crackers, but he knows his blackstrap."

Hat over his face, Gabriel settled his head on the carved rosewood frame of the chair. So the Rebel army wasn't above dealing in contraband whiskey. Idly he wondered about the identity of the Birdman, but a sudden series of piercing shrieks from the upper floor of the house brought his head off the back of the chair. The sentries jumped.

The shrieks escalated in volume as a door opened and a harried-looking junior officer appeared at the bend of the stairs. He mopped at some beige-colored liquid dripping from his eyebrows and mustache. "Is there a Reverend Leland down here somewhere?"

The shrieks ceased as Gabriel stood. He had his story planned out. "I'm Reverend Leland. I see you've made my cousin's acquaintance."

The young man glanced over his shoulder. "That woman don't act like nobody's cousin—except maybe Old Nick's. I'm pretty sure she sprung straight from the gates of Hades. Colonel Abernathy wants to see you. Right this way, sir."

They found the colonel in an upstairs bedroom, which had been converted into an office with the addition of a desk and a couple of bookcases. The colonel's lank brown hair stood on end, a bit of egg yolk adorned his left sideburn, and grease stains marred the military perfection of his gray coat. He rose with an agitated scrape of his chair. "Reverend! Last night my men apprehended a young woman, and she—well, she's what you might call a bit of a handful." The colonel blushed. "She claims to be a gentlewoman, but we know she's been traveling up and down the river as an actress."

Raising a sardonic eyebrow, Gabriel took the proffered chair. "Working as an actress might not be the most respectable occupation for a woman, but it isn't illegal."

"Of course it isn't, but one of my men claims Miss Matthews was pumping him for information."

"And your man was completely sober?"

The colonel picked up a perfectly pointed quill in his inkstand and began to sharpen it. "You know as well as I do it's against army regulations to sell whiskey to military personnel."

"Of course." Gabriel sat back. "Would you mind filling me in on the circumstances of my cousin's arrest?"

The colonel huffed. "It seems Private Hubbard was enjoying a bit of leave aboard the *Magnolia Princess* last evening, and—well, Hubbard, being a strapping young man—caught Miss Matthews's attention. She invited him to her room after her performance."

Gabriel kept his tone cold and incredulous. "I think I have the picture, Colonel. The scarlet woman seduced your innocent young enlisted man, plied him with liquor to loosen his tongue and proceeded to pull information out of him in order to sell it to the enemy." The accusation sounded melodramatic and silly—the plot of a riverboat play.

"That's about it." Abernathy ran a finger around his collar. "Unless you have some other explanation."

Gabriel straightened. "I don't have to explain anything

to you. The word of my clerical office should be enough to proclaim my misguided young relative's innocence." The colonel took a breath, but Gabriel forestalled him with a raised palm. "My family history may shed some light on our current dilemma."

Abernathy nodded stiffly.

"Miss Matthews—Delia—is the daughter of my father's brother, the product of his marriage late in life to a serving woman with designs on his pocketbook. When the little girl was barely walking her mother took off with a man of heftier income." Gabriel paused to let this pathetic picture settle in his companion's mind.

Since the colonel seemed to have forgotten the breakfast tray heaved at his chest, Gabriel embroidered the story. Delia became a misunderstood soul looking for love in a callous world. She had run away to join a traveling theater troupe, and Gabriel, as her closest male relative—her father having long since expired of a broken heart—had been searching for her ever since.

"I'd only last week received a hint of her whereabouts," he concluded. "My mission is to see her restored to the bosom of her family."

The colonel looked impressed. "I declare."

Gabriel coughed delicately. "As I said, I'd nearly caught up with my cousin, and it was a simple matter to follow the trail of…shall we say, smitten officers and gentlemen."

Abernathy smiled sourly. "The lady has a way of choosing her targets."

"All the more reason to get her out of your hair, so to speak—" Gabriel eyed the egg yolk "—and return her to her home."

"I must admit I don't know quite what to do with her."

The colonel rose and went to the window. "I cannot allow my men to go unpunished when they compromise military information, and yet the lady hardly seems to have the mental discipline to remember what she heard, much less pass it into enemy hands."

"Have you questioned her?"

"I tried, but with very little intelligible response."

Gabriel grinned at the colonel's back. "Perhaps if I spoke to her in your presence I might assuage your fears."

"Yes, that's the ticket." The colonel turned. "Bowden!"

The young officer stuck his damp, sticky head around the door. "Sir?"

"Tell Miss Matthews we require her presence."

Lieutenant Bowden looked as if he'd just been requested to shave a barracuda. He shifted from one foot to the other. "Yes, sir," he said unhappily and disappeared.

Gabriel didn't have to wait long before Delia exploded into the room, followed by Bowden, who muttered a lame "Here she is, sir" and beat a strategic retreat.

Delia Matthews in broad daylight was a sight to behold. She stood seething in the center of the room, onyx eyes snapping, fists planted on her generous hips. The tight trousers and coat she'd worn last night had been replaced by a dress with an equally tight and low-cut bodice. Gabriel was hard put to keep his clerical gaze above her neck. Colonel Abernathy didn't even try.

She was the sort of woman whose company Gabriel most enjoyed—straightforward, without genteel coyness, secure in the power of her own beauty, yet sturdy and self-reliant. This was no hothouse flower of Southern aristocracy, ready to wilt at the threat of adversity and delighting in drawing blood with unexpected thorns. This woman was a gardenia, blooming in lush flamboyance—in fact, she even smelled like one.

She folded her arms. "Where have you been?"

Gabriel eyed his courier with grim admiration. "If I weren't so glad to see you I'd turn you over my knee. What kind of trouble are you in now?"

Delia glared at the colonel. "If this nincompoop thinks I give two hoots how many guns come down the pike into this stinking little mud hole, it's no wonder he's *here,* instead of where the action is!"

"See here!" yelped the colonel.

Gabriel choked down laughter. "He's just doing his job, Cousin Delia. And he said he *might* let you go, if you promise not to repeat anything Private Hubbard told you." Gabriel let one eye blink closed.

Delia's expression of outrage shifted to a blinding smile. "I told them it was a big misunderstanding. The private took me all wrong. I asked him if he was a good shot, and he started off on all this nonsense about guns. I didn't understand half what he said." She tripped across the room to take the colonel's arm. Tears glistened on the ends of yard-long black lashes as she looked over her shoulder. "Cousin Gabriel, you understand why I got just a teensy bit upset when they arrested me? It was too humiliating!"

Abernathy ran a hand around the back of his neck. "Miss, if you want to avoid misunderstandings in the future, you'd best stay away from dens of iniquity like that riverboat." He backed toward the open window. "Reverend Leland, Miss Matthews is released into your custody."

Thunderclouds formed on the actress's alabaster brow. "His *custody*—"

"Thank you, sir." Gabriel hustled Delia out of the room.

They made it back to the Battle House as inconspicuously as was possible for a woman of Delia Matthews's looks and temperament. As he secured a table in a corner of the sunny dining room of the hotel, Gabriel lost patience. "You'd best stop those languishing looks at every man in sight if you expect me to retain any scrap of credibility. We're not even supposed to meet in public, and now I've had to invent a runaway cousin."

Delia's eyes blazed with resentment. "*Your* credibility? I'm the one who's been under arrest for twelve hours."

Gabriel froze in the act of hailing a servant. "*Twelve* hours? When did they arrest you?"

She lifted one milky shoulder. "Not long after the show. Turned out that baby-faced private wasn't quite so naive as most of them."

"Less than six hours ago you were *not* in the hold of the boat." He said it out loud, hoping it was not true.

Delia spread her hands. "I've been under arrest since ten o'clock last night. Reckon there was some other woman running around loose on the boat." When he found himself incapable of answering, her fingers fluttered to her mouth. "Oh, my. You gave the sermon to the wrong person, didn't you?"

"Your perfume is gardenia. Not lily of the valley."

After a strained silence, Delia leaned her head on her hand and regarded him with a quirk to her red mouth. "Fine pair we are, *Reverend*."

"This is no laughing matter. What are we going to do?"

"We?" Delia's fine black brows lifted. "I can't deliver what I don't have. You get the *sermon* back before my troupe moves upriver, and I'll see it gets to the right hands. You don't…" She shrugged. "You're on your own."

Camilla woke up feeling eighty instead of eighteen. Her head hurt, her feet hurt, and there was an evenly spaced row of bruises under her rib cage where the iron spikes of the fence had jabbed her. She rolled onto her back with a groan.

She'd argued with Portia for thirty minutes about who was going to be responsible for getting that wagonload of whiskey to Colonel Abernathy—Portia said Horace, and Camilla said she'd do it herself. Portia had held her ground and informed Camilla that, once the whiskey was delivered, there would be no more underground railroad for the Beaumont household. The Captain said the whole business had gotten entirely too risky.

The Captain. Portia wouldn't say who arranged the transfer of slaves—first downriver into Mobile and then upstate by railroad. Probably it was some saintly old preacher who followed the teachings of Jesus and the Constitution: all men are created equal, with certain inalienable rights. Camilla pictured long, flowing white hair, maybe spectacles like Ben Franklin. A black frock covering frail shoulders and a Bible tucked under his arm. He'd preach with thunder and fire, but love everyone black and white the same. A man who'd organized the freedom runs for four years without a slipup would have to be brilliant.

"Camilla!"

Daydreams broken, she sat up. Nobody's voice but her brother Jamie's could carry up a carpeted flight of steps, down a hallway and through a thick oak door. He often forgot he wasn't on the quarter deck of the *Lady C*.

Her bare feet hit the floor with a thump. "Can't a person sleep around here?"

"It's almost noon!" Jamie barked. "I need your help if I'm going to sail for Cuba this evening."

She got moving. Caught up in the events of the past twenty-four hours, she'd almost forgotten Jamie's planned blockade run. He'd been to Cuba before and made it back safely, but it was always a chancy thing. The Yankees took it as a personal affront when a Confederate merchant ship slipped through with arms and supplies.

But people in the South had to eat, she thought as she donned her clothing. And they had to defend themselves.

Dressed in her faded indigo day dress, she plopped down at the dresser. As she pinned her curls into bunches over each ear, she prayed for Jamie. For his safety, for his health, for his wisdom in guiding the ship. He had many men under his command. So much responsibility.

She wondered if Jamie knew about the fish boat. Probably so. Papa confided in him, and he'd always been crazy about anything that moved in the water, from tadpoles to warships.

He wouldn't like that she knew about it. He was as overprotective as their father. But she was a grown woman now. As soon as Harry could come down south again without being blown to bits figuratively and literally, she was going to marry him and start her own family. She was tired of being under Papa's thumb. Tired of being bossed around by Portia and restricted by Lady's ideas of gentility.

She closed her eyes. *Please, Lord, end the war quick.*

She found Jamie in the foyer directing Horace and Willie in the disposition of several brass-bound leather trunks. He was dressed in a dark naval uniform, his fair hair spiking across his forehead in the humidity, sweat streaking his blond mustache and beard.

He looked up and grinned, swiping his sleeve across his brow. "There you are, Miss Slugabed. Knitting socks and writing letters last night wore you to a frazzle, I guess."

Camilla straightened the embossed buttons on her brother's coat. The top one hung by a thread. "Here, let me—" Her eyes widened. "Oh! Don't move, I'll be right back!"

She hurried to the parlor, where she'd spent several hours sewing before bedtime, and returned with a thickly quilted rectangle of gold-brocaded taffeta, folded several times and fastened with a frog closure. "I made this for your trip."

"Thank you. Er—what is it?"

Camilla pulled Jamie down to sit beside her on the bottom step. "Look, I'll show you." She unbuttoned the frog. "It's a housewife."

Jamie laughed. "Just what I need on a cruiser."

Camilla unfolded the fabric so he could see the row of five pockets and a flat square piece stuck through with needles and pins. "It's got everything you need to make small repairs to your uniform. All the girls are making them for their men going off to war."

At the wobble in her voice, his expression softened. "I'm not exactly going to war. Don't you want me to send this to Harry?"

"I made it for *you*." She gave him a mock frown. "And you'd better come back with it in person!"

"I plan to. No Yankee steamer's going to catch the *Lady C*."

Camilla slanted a glance at him under her lashes.

"Suppose the Yankees were able to build a boat that could attack without you seeing it."

Jamie leaned back on his elbows. "You mean like in the fog? Well, they wouldn't be able to see us, either. Nobody sails in weather like that."

"No, I mean—what if a boat could move underwater? Couldn't they blow you up before you knew they were there?"

He exploded with laughter. "A boat sailing under-water? Oh, Milla, you've been reading too many penny novels." He pulled her into an affectionate rough hug. "Either that or you truly don't have enough to occupy that fertile imagination. Thanks for the gift." Releasing Camilla, he refolded the housewife and slipped it into his coat pocket. He stood and offered her a broad, cal-lused hand. "I'll put it to good use. Now be a good girl and go pack me a lunch. Make it generous, 'cause it'll be a long time before I get Portia's sourdough bread again."

Packing him a lunch was the least she could do. He was always the soul of generosity to her. On the way to the kitchen, she touched one of the little carved coral camellias dangling at her ears—her birthday present. Jamie knew how much she adored camellias, how she waited for their blooming every winter.

Portia was up to her dimpled elbows in bread dough and was not best pleased by Camilla's interruption. "That boy picks the inconvenientest times to go sailing!"

Smiling at the anxiety behind Portia's grumpy frown, Camilla pulled bread and cheese out of the bin and began to carve thick slices of both.

Portia heaved a sigh as she added an apple tart and some sausage left over from breakfast to the hamper. "I hope those Yankees got poor eyesight tonight."

"Me, too. God preserve him."

Jamie wasn't afraid of anything, especially not a Yankee clipper. He took life exactly as it came, laughing at the worst dangers, even her question about the fish boat. Was his amusement genuine—or did it serve the purpose of hiding his thoughts? Everything with Jamie was usually right on the surface. Maybe her assumption that he knew about the boat was wrong.

She paused in the kitchen doorway, absently swinging the heavy hamper. "Portia, I heard something funny last night on my way in the house."

Portia's head whipped around. "Shush, little girl! Mind yourself!" She jerked her head toward the back door. "Come out this way, and we'll walk around the house."

As they picked their way through the kitchen vegetable garden, Portia drew close, sharing the handle of the hamper. "Why didn't you tell me last night?" she whispered.

"I forgot," Camilla retorted. "I was busy getting scolded!"

"Hmph. And didn't you deserve it. What'd you hear?"

"Did you know Papa had a man in his office in the middle of the night?"

Portia gave her an enigmatic look. "If he did, it isn't any of my business."

"They were discussing an underwater boat. Have you ever heard of such a thing?"

Portia snorted. "In the book of Jonah."

"It could happen. And Papa's planning to get rich off it."

Portia smiled. "He'd have a long way to go before—"

Camilla stamped her foot. "He's financing this—this

fish boat, to sell to the government so they can blow up Yankee ships." At Portia's quizzical look, she began to walk again. "I know it sounds incredible. They built it in New Orleans, then sank it when the Yankees took over. Now they're going to rebuild it right here in Mobile."

Camilla had half expected Portia to pooh-pooh the idea, much as Jamie had. But the housekeeper's broad, smooth brow puckered. "Men and their all-fired gadgets," she muttered. They reached the flagged walkway in Lady's flower garden. Portia abruptly stopped and handed Camilla the hamper. "Take this to your brother, and tell him I said happy sailin'."

"But what should I do? You know, about the boat?"

"You ain't a baby anymore. You heard more than's good for you, so keep your mouth shut and your eyes and ears open. Don't you do anything." Portia's fierce gaze speared Camilla. "You hear me?"

"S-so you believe me?" Portia's belief was infinitely more frightening than Jamie's amusement.

Portia's shoulders lifted. "I believe you heard your papa gettin' up to some shenanigans. We'll see how important it is."

Numb, Camilla watched Portia head back to the kitchen. Eyes and ears open would be no problem. Mouth shut was another story.

Chapter Three

Gabriel shoved through the swinging doors of Ingersoll's Oyster Bar and stood in the baking afternoon heat swinging a newspaper-laden canvas bag against his leg. Sooner or later his quarry was bound to surface.

Last night he'd returned to the riverboat with Delia and, while she went to her room to bathe and change, conducted a discreet search of the hold of the boat. This canvas sack—discovered behind the barrel he'd been sitting on as he waited in the dark for his courier—might or might not be a clue to the imposter's identity, but it was all he had.

Embarking early this morning on a search, he'd put on his overanxious-relative face and questioned the proprietor of every establishment on Water Street. Downtown Mobile abounded in oyster houses, lagerbier and wine shops, and gambling and drinking saloons. Women were plentiful in those places, but no one admitted to harboring one dressed as a man.

He was about to start over on another round of the search when a violent tugging on his coat sleeve caught his attention. He looked down.

A scrawny little man in a red knit cap danced at his feet, beady pink eyes glinting under bristling eyebrows. "N—now—" The man's head stretched and retracted as he struggled for words. "Now—where'd you get that?"

Gabriel stared at him. "Where'd I get what?"

The little man snatched at the newspaper bag. "You got it! I give it to Missy, and you stole it!"

Gabriel swung the bag out of reach and found himself pummeled in the stomach by surprisingly potent punches. "Hey!" Instinctively he hooked his attacker around the neck and secured the skinny arms. He looked around panting. Shoppers and vendors watched with varying degrees of curiosity and disapproval. "If I let you go," he said through his teeth, "will you settle down and listen to me?"

"Gimme back my bag!" howled the little man.

"I'll give you back the blasted bag. Just shut up and let me ask you some questions."

Forced to concede to Gabriel's superior size and strength, the little man relaxed.

Gabriel released him. "No use asking if you're crazy," he muttered, straightening his clothing. "What's the matter with you?"

The malevolent red-rimmed eyes fixed on his face. "You said you'd gimme the bag."

"I will, I will. Come on, and I'll buy you a meal." Gabriel led the way back into the oyster bar and ordered coffee for himself and his bizarre guest.

The man slugged down his steaming coffee in three great slurps.

Gabriel waved away a waiter offering to refill the cup. "What's your name, old man?"

The hot drink seemed to have taken some of the starch

out of the man's ire. He leaned back against the wooden booth. "Name's Byrd. Virgil Byrd."

How poetic. "What makes you think this bag is yours?"

"*Is* mine. It's marked."

"Marked? How?"

"Candy took a bite out of it one day when I forgot to feed her."

Gabriel looked at the bag. Sure enough, there was a ragged hole in the bottom about the size of a half-dollar, through which he could see the rolled newspapers. "Who's Candy?"

"That's my mule. Candy."

Gabriel had seen no evidence of any such animal. "You gave the bag to the mule?"

Byrd screwed up his face. "Naw. Candy just tried to eat it. Gave the bag to Missy. And you stoled it."

"I didn't steal it," Gabriel said patiently, rubbing his aching forehead. "I found it. I suppose Missy's some other animal in your menagerie."

"Don't know nothin' about no na-jer-ee." Pride and slavish devotion lit Byrd's rheumy eyes. "Missy's my friend."

Gabriel had no idea if this was going anywhere, but what did he have to lose? "Missy's my friend, too," he said with an encouraging smile. "Pretty little thing with a curvy figure—" Byrd nodded cautiously. "Wearing a man's outfit, smells like lily of the valley?"

Byrd cackled. "Yes, sir, that's her! Smells better 'n a *per*-fume shop!"

Gabriel leaned forward. "That's right. We were having a most interesting conversation last night. She had to leave before I could give her something. Could you tell me where I might find her?"

"Naw. Onliest time I see her is late at night when she comes to borry my bag."

"You work for the newspaper?"

Byrd nodded. "And the railroad, too."

Something popped loose in Gabriel's recent memory. *Somebody caught a couple of fellas with the Birdman last night.* The two guards at Confederate headquarters this morning, discussing a load of moonshine. *The Birdman may be crackers...*

Clues came together as he scrutinized the wizened face across the table. When Byrd longingly eyed a tray on the shoulder of a passing waiter, Gabriel waved him over. "Mr. Byrd, would you care for some oysters?"

Camilla blew a lock of hair out of her eyes and straightened her back with a creak of corsets. The heat and humidity had frizzed her hair and dampened her dress under the arms. She had set up her sewing machine in the little room off the kitchen so she could converse with Portia and still run to answer the bell if her grandmother needed her. She'd have been smarter to find a place that would catch a breeze.

She put another length of burlap under the needle and pressed the foot treadle. No telling how many sandbags it would take to construct the redoubts that General Butler had ordered to be built around the northern and western edges of the city. Nothing she did was going to end the war. But if she didn't help in these small ways, she would be considered disloyal, maybe even Lincolnite.

She shoved her spectacles higher on her nose. She had a lot of respect for Mr. Lincoln, even if he was a

Yankee. If the menfolk would talk things over and solve things without blowing each other to smithereens, the world would be a better place. Early in the war, she'd questioned Papa about his stance on secession. Why, she wanted to know, didn't they work things out through the legislative process, like the Founding Fathers intended?

At first he'd put her off, saying the whole thing was too complicated to explain to a child. When she persisted, he put down his newspaper and glared. "Because there's more of them than there are of us. They refuse to let us choose the way of life that's best for us. Every man has the right to examine his conscience and free his slaves or keep them. No Yankee lawyer or mill owner or journalist can understand the economics that drives our plantation system." Camilla must have looked as if she didn't understand it either, because her father removed his spectacles irritably. "Camilla, what's going to happen to all those field slaves when they're turned loose all of a sudden? The plantations will be bankrupt, so who's going to support the poor creatures? They're better off where they are."

Camilla knew little about economics, and it seemed to her any human being was better off free, but Papa's refusal to consider a person with black skin totally human made arguing with him pointless. She'd be switched, though, if she'd let him sell his soul by building a Confederate war vessel.

She bit off a thread and threw one more bag onto the pile growing beside her chair. The obvious solution to thwarting the construction of that boat would be to wait until it was built, then somehow sink it, like they'd done in New Orleans. Maybe the waste of time and expense would make them give up. Or maybe by then the war would be over.

A thought occurred to her that she almost pushed away. Disloyal. Crazy. Dangerous.

But she couldn't seem to shake it, no matter how furiously she ran the sewing machine and sang hymns at the top of her voice.

She was undoubtedly stirring up trouble in her own mind. God wasn't talking to her, and she couldn't spy on her own Papa.

But she had already done that, however unwittingly. And look what it was leading to.

Had God allowed her to overhear that conversation so she could do something about it? Get hold of the plans to that boat and pass it to the Yankees? How could she trust some Northern agent she didn't even know? How could she be sure he'd confiscate the submarine without destroying her family in the process?

Besides, the only Yankees she knew were Harry's family in Tennessee—and Harry himself. She had no idea where he was. No help there.

She forced herself to sit quietly and pray. *I don't know where to start. I feel like Rahab, the harlot of Jericho, must have felt, waiting for the spies to arrive. You protected her and her family, so You can do the same for me. Just show me the way. Amen.*

Sighing, she opened her eyes. In her experience, God sometimes took a long time to answer prayers, and then when He got around to it, He'd do it in strange and often uncomfortable ways.

One of the kitchen bells, attached to strings running all over the house, jangled. Camilla jumped to her feet.

"I'll see what she wants, Portia!" She hurried upstairs, running from her tangled thoughts.

Since Lady liked to have access to the everyday activities of her family and servants, her sitting-room door always stood open. Camilla skidded to a stop and made a rather breathless entrance.

A striking young man rose from his seat on Lady's pink velvet sofa. At six feet, he seemed a giant in her grandmother's small, elegant room. His bow was correct, but the hard angles of his face and the assessing gleam in his black eyes struck her as anything but polite.

Camilla dropped a curtsy and forced her gaze to her grandmother.

Lady inclined her head toward the gentleman. "Reverend Leland, I'd like to introduce my granddaughter, Camilla, who occasionally remembers her upbringing. Camilla, this is the Reverend Gabriel Leland, late of Bogue Chitto. We're going to make him welcome as he begins a new ministry here in Mobile." Lady smiled and jangled the bell again. "Close your mouth, child, and sit down. Portia will bring our tea."

Jerking the spectacles off her face and sliding them in her pocket, Camilla obeyed. This dark young man who looked like the incarnation of Lucifer himself was a *minister?*

With thinly glazed disappointment, Gabriel watched Mrs. St. Clair's young granddaughter pour tea. Virgil Byrd's information that his "Missy" lived in the big white house on the corner of Dauphin and Ann streets had given him high hopes that he'd find the mysterious woman he sought—a woman who, granted, could be anybody from daughter of the house to a kitchen maid.

To his relief, early this morning he'd been admitted as a visiting minister without question.

Mrs. St. Clair, white hair piled high, dressed from head to toe in pink, had graciously invited him into a room with porcelain butterflies floating on every surface. It always delighted her, she said, to find young people so diligent in serving the Lord and their country. At his request for an introduction to the charity hospitals and soldiers' libraries, she regretfully confessed that her health no longer permitted her to go about as she once had. She then exceeded his wildest hopes by offering to send her granddaughter to accompany him.

But instead of the clever adventuress he'd been hoping to meet, into the room had burst this little hoyden. She couldn't be more than fourteen or fifteen years old.

Mrs. St. Clair gently tapped her spoon against the fragile rim of her cup. "Tell me about your people, Reverend Leland."

Gabriel stuck to a story he'd developed over the course of the past few years. "My father's family are Louisiana indigo planters. My mother is a Faulkner from East Mississippi."

"Indeed?" Mrs. St. Clair raised finely arched brows. "Perhaps my daughter, who lives in Columbus, is acquainted with the family."

"Possibly. We've not visited there in several—" A strangled squeak from the granddaughter stopped him. "Miss St. Clair?" He stifled his impatience.

She mopped at a tea stain spreading across her lap. "I'm not Miss St. Clair," she mumbled, pink-faced.

Gabriel frowned. Southern inbreeding had evidently taken its toll on the poor creature. She didn't even know who she was.

"Camilla, the purpose of a saucer is to prevent such spills." Amusement and affection laced Mrs. St. Clair's admonition. "Reverend, I should explain that Camilla's mother was my younger daughter. She is, perhaps unfortunately, a Beaumont rather than a St. Clair."

That was when it hit him that he knew this family. Or knew *of* them. Beaumont. Harry Martin's relatives. This must be the little cousin who had tagged along behind Harry and made his life miserable.

Then the girl's expression captured his full attention. She was staring at him, mouth ajar.

For the first time, he really looked at her. His gaze went from the small capable hands clenched over the tea stain to her face. The broad, childish brow, pointed little chin, and curly hair gave her the look of a china doll. But the big caramel-colored eyes were defiant, much too knowing for a child. She recognized him. The truth began to whisper in his ear.

But how had he mistaken this underdeveloped waif for Delia Matthews?

He recovered. "Miss Beaumont, I hope I haven't said anything to upset you. Do you know something about the Faulkner family that I don't?"

Pink rose to her cheeks. "It's just that you remind me of someone I met the other day. That is, you sound like him—your voice…"

So that was it. She was a sharp one, and he'd have to watch his step. "Indeed? But that's simply not possible, as I've spent the past two days pursuing a rather delicate family matter."

Mrs. St. Clair gave him an approving smile. "Most commendable to put family duty before taking on poor dearly departed Reverend Tunstall's congregation. Is there some way in which we may be of help?"

Gabriel reluctantly gave his attention back to the older woman. "I doubt it, though I thank you. I've a female cousin who's run off to join a troupe of riverboat actors. I've taken it upon myself to bring her back to the bosom of her family." Camilla Beaumont's brow puckered a little—at his mention of the riverboat? Or was it sympathy for his worry? "Forgive me, Miss Beaumont, if I've offended you by mentioning my cousin's fallen state."

She surprised him with bubble of laughter. "Mercy, I know what goes on on a riverboat. It must be rather humiliating, though, for a man of your calling to be forced to explore the nether regions of such a vessel." The words were given a sarcastic undertone by a shrewd curling of her lips.

He met her dancing eyes and acknowledged her hit with a slight smile.

"Camilla, watch your tongue!" said her grandmother sharply. "Reverend, I believe I can help. Deplorable as it is, the soldiers spend large amounts of time and money on the riverboats, and my charitable work extends mostly in the hospitals and soldiers' libraries. Camilla will take you around to visit the soldiers there, and you may easily make inquiries as to your cousin's whereabouts."

Camilla drew back, frowning. "Lady, you know I've got to finish the sandbags before the week is out. You could provide Reverend Leland with a letter of introduction—he'll easily find his way around!"

"That hardly sounds neighborly," said Mrs. St. Clair. "I'd go myself, but these old legs aren't as spry as they used to be. The sandbags can wait."

"But, Lady—"

"Miss Beaumont," Gabriel interrupted smoothly, "I'd be honored if you'd consent to accompany me. Your charming presence could only promote my standing in the city."

Camilla responded with a skeptical glare.

Mrs. St. Clair shook an arthritic finger. "And you'll go with good grace, my girl, first thing next week."

"All right." Camilla jerked at the lace on her cuffs. "I'll do it, but I don't have to like it."

Chapter Four

Squeezed between her grandmother and her fourteen-year-old brother Schuyler in the family pew the next morning in church, Camilla watched Reverend Leland walk past, affecting a limp and leaning romantically on a Morocco cane. He stood in the aisle looking for a place to sit, until Lady called his name and invited him to sit with them.

He shook hands with Schuyler and her father, his smile grateful and a bit bashful. Oh, he knew how to charm them all.

She'd known somehow that he would be here today. His presence was entwined with God's answer to her prayer, this stranger with the beautiful face and whiskey-smooth voice. It made her afraid and angry and all mixed up, sitting here beside him in church, even with Lady seated between them.

He was all kindness and sincerity on the outside, and Lady seemed to think he was God's gift to the Christian community of Mobile. But he'd all but admitted he'd been on that boat, holding her close. And now he'd come after her.

Halfway through the service, she sneaked a glance at him. He was listening to Brother Lewis's dull-as-ditchwater sermon with rapt attention. His dark hair was slicked back, the hard angles of his face piously composed, his shirt collar white and starched.

What was she supposed to do when he tried to get her alone? Yesterday he looked like he wanted to eat her for lunch...

As if he felt her gaze, Reverend Leland suddenly looked at her. The expression in his black eyes was warm, but she still felt chilled somehow.

God protect me from this man.

He smiled and returned his attention to the minister.

After the closing hymn, Camilla stepped away from him, but Lady snagged her elbow before she could slip out of the pew.

"Reverend Leland, I hope you'll join us for dinner. Portia's pork roast and mashed potatoes are famous all over the county."

"I'd be delighted!" The reverend's white smile was made more engaging by one tooth turned slightly crooked.

Determinedly unengaged, Camilla pulled at her arm.

Lady squeezed it harder. "Camilla will keep you company on the way."

"I appreciate your hospitality." The reverend's eyes sparkled. "But I'm afraid I rode to church today. My horse might object to an extra passenger." When Lady cackled, he smiled at Camilla. "However, I will claim a carriage ride at some time in the near future."

"She will look forward to that with great pleasure." Lady shooed Camilla toward the door. "We'll go on ahead and see you as soon as you can get there."

* * *

Sunday dinner in the Beaumont household was a prolonged affair, involving much conversation and laughter. Camilla watched Reverend Leland, seated across from her, flirt gently with her grandmother, filling Jamie's absence with an agreeable mix of self-deprecation, humor and thoughtfulness. She had to admit he was fascinating in the way of a beautiful and dangerous animal.

Without compromising her own secrets, it was going to be difficult to prove Reverend Leland wasn't what he purported to be. But there had to be some way.

She cleared her throat and braced herself for the impact of his eyes. "Reverend, please forgive my curiosity, but I noticed you carry a cane. Have you perhaps sustained a war wound?"

"Camilla!" Lady frowned. "That is a very personal   "

"It's quite all right, Mrs. St. Clair. I don't mind admitting to an injury gained in honorable service of my country." The reverend smiled, a bit of a challenge in the dark eyes.

"Indeed?" Camilla said sweetly. "Perhaps you might entertain us with a description of your exploits on the battlefield."

He shook his head diffidently and rather sadly. "I don't think you'd find our humiliation at Shiloh appropriate dinner-table conversation. I was one of the few to escape with my life."

A flat and embarrassed silence fell.

Camilla's father glared at her. "Perhaps, Reverend Leland, you'd join me on the courtyard for an after-dinner cigar?"

"Certainly, sir." Reverend Leland, leaning heroically

on his cane, accompanied her father out of the room, Schuyler following on their heels.

Lady rapped a spoon against the table. "I would like to know, young lady, what brought on this disagreeable attitude toward the first presentable young man to cross our paths since the war started."

"Lady, doesn't it strike you as odd that a handsome and healthy young man would spend his life riding around the country preaching?"

"It rather strikes me as commendable." Lady wagged the spoon. "He has paid his dues in military service and now spends his time serving God. Is there some unwritten law that ministers must be short, fat and bald?"

Camilla shrugged. She refused to swallow that ridiculous story about a runaway cousin. And if he was wounded, she was Tatiana, the Queen of the Fairies.

Gabriel sprawled in a wicker chair, watching his host puff with great satisfaction on a fine Cuban cigar. Though his original strategy had been to maneuver Camilla Beaumont into a tête-à-tête, he was satisfied to spend the afternoon with a man of Ezekiel Beaumont's standing in the transportation industry.

"Terrible losses at Shiloh," Beaumont was saying. "You were lucky to escape with your life."

"Yes, sir, God was on my side." Gabriel smiled as Schuyler chose a cigar from the humidor and the elder Beaumont tweaked it out of his hand.

The boy reddened. "Do you plan on going back into service, sir?"

"I'd like to, but don't know if they'll have me anytime soon." Gabriel rubbed his upper right thigh.

"Next birthday I'm going to enlist." Schuyler visibly

ignored the sudden tide of red which suffused his father's face.

Gabriel intervened. "You'd be smarter to remain here. You and your father could do more for the war effort with the railroad than by risking your hide on a Yankee bullet."

Schuyler rolled his eyes as if he'd heard it all before. But Ezekiel jabbed the air with his cigar. "Absolutely right! I'd like to know where the army would be without a fast way to move rations, arms and men."

Gabriel smiled lazily. "So the army plans to use the Mobile and Ohio?"

Schuyler snorted. "In this little backwater?"

"Listen and you might learn something, boy," Ezekiel growled. "With Corinth in Union hands, we're the only Confederate rail link between east and west. You want to see some action this summer? Then this little backwater is the place to be!" He let out a satisfied billow of smoke.

Gabriel barely registered Schuyler's snort of disbelief. For the moment he'd said all he could without arousing suspicion, but he could see several ways to sift this family for useful information. He was going to have to do it, however, against the antagonism of Miss Camilla Beaumont. For more reasons than one, he wished he could undo his encounter with her on the riverboat.

Chapter Five

Gabriel drew up his hired calash in front of the Beaumont home. After securing the horse to the hitching post, he climbed the steps and knocked briskly at the double doors. Camilla Beaumont had avoided him for nearly a week, one excuse after the other keeping her busy. He'd had little to do but prowl the streets with an ear out for information about the fish boat.

Fortunately, Mrs. St. Clair had all but commanded her recalcitrant granddaughter to drop everything and accompany him on a tour of the military hospitals.

The butler, Horace, ushered Gabriel into the parlor, where he found Camilla—still rather schoolgirlish in appearance with a pair of dainty gold-rimmed spectacles perched on her small nose—sitting with listless boredom in a wing chair. Across the room a decorative blonde played something classical on the pianoforte.

The music stopped as the young woman lifted her hands from the mother-of-pearl keys with exaggerated confusion. Camilla stood and gave Gabriel a grudging hand to press.

"Miss Beaumont, a pleasure to see you," he murmured, taking her hand to his lips. He held it there, enjoying her pink cheeks, tight lips and futile tugs against his fingers.

Once her hand was released, she shoved it into her pocket. "Charmed," she said, teeth together.

The young woman at the pianoforte cleared her throat. "Camilla, why didn't you tell me you were expecting company?"

"My manners must have gone begging. Reverend Leland, I'd like you to meet Miss Fanny Chambliss." That social chore performed, Camilla retreated to the window.

Gabriel bowed over Miss Chambliss's hand, keeping it only for the requisite two seconds. "The Lord has seen fit to honor me this day with *two* beautiful young ladies to welcome me."

To Gabriel's amusement, Miss Chambliss accepted this as her due. Simpering, she arranged her silken skirts upon a Belter rosewood sofa whose rich wine-colored upholstery flattered her golden curls and gentian-blue eyes. "Camilla, what a charming addition to our acquaintance."

Gabriel didn't have time for pretty distractions. "If you're ready, Miss Beaumont, my carriage is waiting."

Her almost-brown eyes glittered. "I'm sure Fanny will like to join us. I'll just run get my hat."

Gabriel gently gripped her elbow. "I'm sorry, but my carriage only holds two."

Rage flared in Miss Chambliss's eyes before she looked down with sweet disappointment. "Camilla's always the lucky one. Maybe another time?" She gave Gabriel a flirtatious smile.

"I'll hold you to it." Gabriel smiled to take the sting from his rejection. "Your hat, Miss Beaumont?"

"I'll get it. See you tomorrow, Fanny." She jerked her elbow free and rushed up the stairs.

By the time Camilla returned, Fanny Chambliss had taken her reluctant leave. Gabriel eyed Camilla's outdated jocket hat as he escorted her out to the calash. The hat's round crown and curved brim emphasized her broad, smooth brow and big eyes, and he wondered if she deliberately played up her babyish looks.

As he tooled the calash down the bumpy brick street, she sat beside him stroking the fringe of her paisley shawl, refusing to meet his eyes.

"Miss Beaumont—may I call you Camilla?—it was kind of you to put aside your sandbag enterprise long enough to accompany me today."

His ironic tone brought her gaze to his face. "You may call me anything you like, if you'll just leave me alone."

"Do you always run from confrontations? I would not have thought it of you, considering your nocturnal adventures."

"Let me out of this buggy." She grasped the door handle.

Slapping the reins, he gave a whistle. The startled horse jerked into a faster gait. "Oh, no, Miss Camilla. We're going to talk, whether you like it or not."

"I thought you wanted to visit hospitals!"

"We'll do that, too, but first you're going to answer some questions. I don't know what you were doing on that boat dressed like a boy, but you've got something that belongs to me, and I want it back."

"You're the one who shoved it into my pocket, *Reverend* Leland. And, for that matter, what were *you* doing on the boat?"

Gabriel glanced at her coolly. "I told you, I was

searching for my cousin. Sometimes in order to reach the spiritually lost of this world—"

She interrupted with a rude noise. "I don't know what you are—bootlegger, slave smuggler, something else entirely for all I know—but you are no minister."

He looked at her with real admiration. "That's putting it with no bark on it. What makes you think I'm not a minister?"

"Besides the way you put your hands on me?" Her eyes sparked hot gold. "You're too young and—" She gulped and tugged her hat brim down.

Gabriel smirked. "You'd have to be the first to admit that looks can be deceiving. Did you even look at that paper I gave you very much by mistake?"

"Of course I looked at it."

"And what was it?"

"It *looked* like a sermon."

"And that's what it was. My sermon for my first service at the Methodist church this Sunday. I could write it again. But I'm asking you, as politely as I know how, to give it back to me."

"You may be a preacher, but you are no man of God."

"And you may be a female, but you are no lady."

She gasped and then grinned at him, a dimple hovering at one corner of her mouth. "You sound like my grandmother."

He stared at her for a moment, then growled, "Where's the hospital?"

"Corner of the next block. Turn here."

"That's Barton Academy."

"It was, before the war started. I thought you were from out of state." Her bright-eyed look held a challenge.

"I visited here when I was in college."

"Really? Do you know my brother Jamie?"

"Yes, but I doubt he'd know me. We ran in different circles." He drew up the horses outside the hospital livery and got down to help Camilla from the carriage. "I did meet your cousin, Harry Martin."

"Harry!" She turned and gripped both his hands. "I knew that message must have been from him! But what does it mean? Oh, please tell me how to read it!"

It took him a moment to realize she thought the sermon was a message from her cousin.

He glanced around. Military personnel, medical staff and visitors crisscrossed the hospital grounds. "This isn't a good place to talk."

Blushing, she released his hands. "It's just that it's been so long…" She straightened her shawl. "We'll go inside. Lady said I should introduce you to Dr. Kinch, the hospital administrator."

Every muscle in Gabriel's body tensed as he followed Camilla up the broad stone steps fronting the building and held the door for her. The confrontation with Dr. Kinch was inevitable. He almost looked forward to it.

Dr. Joseph Kinch shook hands with Gabriel and gave Camilla an arch smile. "Miss Beaumont and her grandmother are two of our most ardent fund-raisers and visitors to the hospital." He pinched Camilla's cheek, making her squirm. "Quite the angel of mercy."

Gabriel bowed. "The merit of your work is well-known, Doctor."

Camilla opened her mouth to ask if the men had met before, but something in Gabriel's hot gaze stopped her. Secrets. She'd better tread carefully.

Gabriel's smile had an edge. "I've heard about your

research into the causes and treatment of yellow fever. A large amount of my time is spent burying its victims and ministering to bereaved families. Seems to me the disease has carried off as many hale young fellows as the war."

Dr. Kinch inclined his leonine head. "'Tis an unfortunate truth. My goal in life is to eradicate this elusive killer. I have my suspicions of the source, but have yet to prove it."

"I pray for your success. Many of my former parishioners have expressed a desire to fund your research— when the war ceases to drain the Southern economy."

"I regret to say that the war has conscripted my most promising medical students," said Dr. Kinch. "Research is now confined to my own sporadic attempts, in between running the hospital and supplying field surgeons." He sighed. "Medicines, especially quinine, are getting harder to come by every day."

"Are the cases of yellow fever up, then, Doctor?" Camilla asked.

"I'm afraid so. Since New Orleans fell and refugees have descended on Mobile, the hospital is full to overflowing. We could hardly turn away the poor souls, and yet..."

"Your mercy is commendable." Gabriel's lips twitched.

Camilla set her teeth. "Reverend Leland, I promised to read mail to the poor soldiers here. Perhaps we should attend to our business."

The reverend gave her a sardonic look. "An angel of compassion, indeed. Dr. Kinch, it's an honor to make your acquaintance."

With Gabriel behind her, Camilla entered the ground-floor ward and led the way among the patients. These visits broke her heart, but she had to come. She had no formal nurse's training, but the doctors were glad to get any help available.

She was very conscious of Gabriel's dark presence. Once or twice he seemed about to speak, but when she turned to look at him, he avoided her gaze and clasped his hands behind his back.

Camilla stopped at the bed of a seven-year-old girl who had caught her leg in a coil of baling wire. "This is Lecy Carrolton—" She gasped as two strong hands clasped her elbows and moved her aside.

Gabriel knelt beside the cot and gently brushed the hair back from Lecy's hot forehead. Her delicate brows remained knit in pain, her eyes closed. "Hello, little one," he murmured, "having a bad dream?"

Silken lashes fluttered, then lifted. "Yes, sir," she whispered.

"How long has she been like this?" Gabriel's hands gently explored the swollen angry flesh above and below the bandage.

"Her daddy brought her in over a week ago," Camilla said, nonplussed. "She doesn't seem to be getting better, no matter what the doctors do. They're afraid they're going to have to—" She bit her lips together and brushed the little pink toes of Lecy's good foot. "We need to pray for her."

"We need to do more than pray for her." Gabriel looked around and snapped his fingers at an ancient orderly in a stain-spattered coat. "You there! Bring me some—" He caught Camilla's eye. She stared at him wide-eyed. He raked his hand through his hair.

"Who *are* you?" she whispered.

He glanced at Lecy. "If the oafs would treat their instruments with carbolic acid before they operate, most of these gangrenous infections would never occur. I've—I've followed enough field surgeons to know that."

"Dr. Kinch is one of the finest surgeons in the South. I'm sure he's doing all he can."

"He's doing all he can to line his pockets." Gabriel rose and stalked toward the doorway.

Camilla hurried after him and grabbed his arm. The muscles were corded, his expression angry. "I won't let you speak that way about the greatest doctor who's ever lived in this area. You don't know him."

His black glare scorched her. "You're right. I don't."

Camilla dropped her hand. "What's carbolic acid? It sounds dangerous."

Gabriel took a breath and looked away. "It's an antiseptic. If it's sprayed onto wounds and the instruments used to operate, it somehow keeps infections from growing. Nobody really knows why."

"Do you think we could get some? Maybe Dr. Kinch doesn't know there is such a thing."

"Maybe he doesn't." Gabriel was silent for a long moment, then gave her an enigmatic look. "Listen, Miss Camilla, I'd like to help that little girl, but I'm just a traveling preacher. If you want to inquire about carbolic spray, go right ahead, and I'll try to convince your famous doctor to try it."

Camilla stared at him, confused by his sudden coolness. "We should help Lecy if we can."

He smiled. "Ah. There's the rub. *Should* and *can* are often mutually exclusive."

As Gabriel helped her into the buggy and started the horses toward home, Camilla's heart was heavy. She hoped her unhappiness had nothing to do with the door Reverend Gabriel Leland had just very firmly shut in her face.

The sun was going down and mosquitoes were beginning to spread out from the swamps as Gabriel made his way on horseback down to his uncle Diron's shack on Dog River. He couldn't stop thinking about that little girl in the hospital with the infected foot. Maddening that, without the necessary medicines, he could do so little. He could only hope that Camilla would be able to locate the carbolic spray. Then he would think about the risk of exposing his identity by bringing himself so overtly to the attention of Dr. Kinch.

He tied Caleb to the hitching post outside, stepped over an emaciated hound lying across the doorjamb and entered the shack without bothering to knock. This time of day, Uncle Diron wouldn't be indoors anyway.

"Uncle!" He felt his way through the dark, obstacle-strewn one-room shanty. "It's Gabriel!"

He wasn't surprised that there was no answer. The old man was all but deaf.

The spring screeched as Gabriel shoved open the screen door and stepped out onto the back porch. Diron's iron-gray curls rested against the back of a cane-bottom rocker, the broken leather boots propped against one of the skinned pine posts supporting the porch. Huge, knotty hands wielded a bone-handled knife against a small chunk of cedar with delicate precision.

Gabriel approached the rocker and stepped into the pool of light cast by an oil lamp on the porch rail. The old man looked up, his rugged face lighting with pleasure as the knife blade flicked away into the handle and clamped Gabriel in an unabashed bear hug.

Then just as strongly thumped him on the ear.

"Ow!" Eyes watering, Gabriel backed up a pace. "What was that for?"

Diron's black eyes sparkled like marbles beneath bristling gray brows. "Staying away so long without writing, you good-for-nothing whelp! All that highfalutin education, and you can't even put pen to paper to let your old uncle know you're alive."

Gabriel touched his stinging ear. "Uncle, you know you can't read."

"Could always find somebody to read it to me." The old man lowered himself into the rocker with a grunt and jerked his chin toward the other chair. "Sit down, boy."

Gabriel obeyed. His father's brother had always been crusty. "I'm sorry I lost touch. I figured you'd be better off without me making trouble."

Diron snorted without bothering to deny the charge. He flicked the knife open and went back to work on the figure of his dog, Ajax. "You've grown into a man." Diron glanced at Gabriel with a sly smile. "Do the women still follow you around in droves?"

"Haven't had much time for women lately." But a vision of a curly haired, golden-eyed moppet floated through his brain. In truth, he'd thought about little in the past few days but the fact that Camilla Beaumont had assumed his sermon was a message from her cousin, Harry Martin. Which meant she had been corresponding with a Federal officer.

And her papa didn't know.

"Uncle, I've got to ask you something."

"Tell me where you been for ten years, *then* you can ask me questions!"

Gabriel sighed. "Well, for the first couple years I

roamed up and down the rivers. Gambled away what money I had left. Then I decided a job might be in order, so I went west and worked a few ranches. Punched cows so long I'm plumb bowlegged."

Diron looked skeptical. "With your education— herding cows?"

"Uncle, the cows don't care whether you spout Latin declensions or sing bawdy-house ditties." Gabriel folded his arms. "An education wasn't anything but a drawback in most of the places I've been." He held up a palm. "I don't regret it, uncle. I appreciate everything you sacrificed to help me get through college and medical school. It just—didn't work out. I'm sorry." He rose and moved to the edge of the porch, where he stood looking out at the river. "I've given up medicine for religion."

Behind him Diron gave a disbelieving snort. "What? Why?"

"They threw me out of medical school at the end, remember? No diploma, no license. I had to find another profession, so I'm riding the circuit as a preacher now." It was time to address the delicate topic of his identity. Gabriel was grateful for the darkness hiding his expression. "And I changed my name to Leland—so make sure you call me that."

"You changed your name and got religious." Resentment laced Diron's tone. "So I'm not good enough for you anymore."

"You know that's not true, uncle." Gabriel gentled his voice, tamping down the temptation to blurt out everything to his mentor and foster father. He turned and found the old man bowed over his whittling. "I mean, I am religious, and I need to distance myself from what I used to be. But you'll always be my favorite old man."

Diron grinned a little. "Some of the tales I could tell about you…"

"Uncle—"

"Aw, don't worry. I can keep a secret when I have to."

Gabriel turned sharply to study his uncle's shadowed face. He looked around more closely. Even in the uncertain light of the flickering oil lamp, he could see improvements around the old shack. New steps with fresh paint. The pier, which had been a mess last time he was here, extended gracefully out into the river, a sturdy fishing boat bobbing against it. "What've you got into around here? Fishing's never been so lucrative."

Diron shrugged and flicked his knife across the pine. "I'm doing some work for Chambliss Brothers."

Gabriel leaned against the post and stuck his hands in his pockets. "There can't be many men in this part of the country who're making money instead of losing it."

"Beckham Chambliss is a smart businessman." The old man grinned. "Strikes when the iron's hot."

Gabriel shook his head at the pun. "I suppose the war brings in machine shop trade."

"Now you're thinking. The secret's providing what the military needs." With a cagey look Diron leaned toward Gabriel. "If you're interested in investing, I could put in a word."

"I might, if the basic funding is secure."

"As secure as it gets this day and age."

"I don't know." Gabriel pretended to hesitate. "Who's the bankroller?"

"Swear you'll keep it to yourself."

Gabriel nodded.

Diron lowered his voice as if Ajax might carry tales.

"The major stockholder of the Mobile and Ohio Railroad."

Gabriel released a soundless whistle. Ezekiel Beaumont, then, was a man with not just a finger but an entire fist in the Confederate military pie.

And his daughter had intercepted a sensitive Union document. God have mercy if she let that document get into the wrong hands.

Chapter Six

Camilla found Portia in the warming kitchen, transferring hot yeast rolls into a wicker basket. The housekeeper was perched atop a wooden stool situated in a stream of sunshine pouring through the open window, her big Bible open on the table.

Camilla plopped into a rocker in the corner beside the empty fireplace and pulled a half-finished sock and a ball of yarn from a quilted bag. "Portia."

Portia glanced up. "What, honey?"

"What are you reading?"

"Galatians five—the fruit of the Spirit. Gotta remind myself every now and then."

"'Love, joy, peace, long-suffering, gentleness, goodness, faith, meekness, temperance: against such there is no law.'" Camilla sighed. "Why is it so hard to do all those things?"

"'Cause they're not things you do. It's what you *are* when you're under the Spirit's control."

Camilla knitted fiercely for a moment. Had she been under the Spirit's control yesterday when she'd been in the company of Reverend Leland? He had upset and confused her so that she'd hardly felt like herself.

She put her hand into her pocket and fingered the paper she'd been carrying around all morning. "Portia, if I tell you something, will you promise not to scold?"

"I can promise you'll be sorry if you *don't* tell me."

What had she expected? "Well, the night I heard— you know…"

Portia gave her a head-down, under-the-eyebrows stare.

"When I went back to the boat I was given this message. I think it's from Harry, but I can't make head nor tails of it."

Portia's lips tightened. "I told Mr. Jamie there wasn't no future in encouraging that Martin boy. Not when he's up there on the wrong side of the Mason-Dixon."

"But it didn't come through Jamie this time. And it's different, somehow. For one thing, he didn't sign it, and he didn't give me a key to decode it."

"Let me see." Portia took the paper Camilla handed her. "Why you got to set your heart on that rapscallion…" She frowned. "What's Joshua and the land of Canaan got to do with anything?"

"I don't know." Camilla's needles attacked the sock again. "Do you suppose he's on a spy mission? Maybe he's trying to tell me he's coming down south."

Portia smoothed the paper. "Could be. He spent a lot of time here with your family when he was in medical school. He knows the area inside out and could blend in. But I hope he's not planning to make his base here. We got troubles enough of our own."

"What do you mean?"

"Rumor says the Federals will target Mobile next,

now that New Orleans fell. Military regulations will be tighter. The colonel asked some mighty awkward questions when Willie took him the liquor. We got to be more careful than ever. The freedom runs are over 'til further notice."

"Portia, no!"

"We can't risk our station. Burn this thing. We can't take no chances." Portia slapped the Bible shut.

Camilla tucked the note back into her pocket. "Why don't you like Harry? He's on our side."

Portia picked up a knife to stem a bowl of bright red strawberries. "I got nothing against him. But it's been a long time since you've seen him, and I'm afraid you're mixing up romance with politics."

"What's that supposed to mean?"

Portia sucked in her cheeks. "Haven't you had this discussion with your grandma already?"

"Lady won't let me talk about Harry. Oh, Portia, I want… I don't even know how to tell you what I want!" Camilla stood and plucked a strawberry from the bowl. "Harry used to listen to me and teach me things Jamie and Schuyler wouldn't, and he treated me like a grown-up. He said when I got old enough, he'd marry me and take me to Tennessee where it snows on the mountains and the leaves turn orange in the fall…"

"Milla, baby, come here." Portia opened her arms and scooped Camilla into the safe harbor of her embrace. "Now listen real good and try to understand what I'm gonna say. Harry Martin's the only boy besides your brothers you've ever known. I'm not saying he's not grown into a good man, but how long's it been since you've even seen him?"

"Five years." Camilla tucked her face against Portia's

shoulder. Remembering the day Papa had found out Harry had Yankee sympathies still put a shiver between her shoulder blades.

Portia stroked her hair. "Doesn't that strike you as a long time between conversations?"

"We've stayed in touch."

"Milla." The strong, dark hands, sweet with the smell of strawberries, cupped her face. "What if he's using you?"

"Harry wouldn't—"

"What's he write to you about?"

Camilla stepped back. "He tells me he misses me! That he remembers the fun we used to have. He's interested in everything. My sewing, how the fishing's been… Schuyler's schooling, Jamie's runs to Cuba…" She hugged herself, remembering the last few letters before it had gotten so hard to get correspondence through the lines. Harry had asked questions about Papa's railroad business that she'd taken for simple family concern. Portia's wry expression forced her to wonder. "Harry wouldn't use me!"

"Maybe not. But I hope you won't waste your life waiting on a man who doesn't consider your welfare above his own." Portia went back to the strawberries. "The Lord wants to give you to a man after His own heart."

"I think Harry's that man."

Portia's shoulders lifted. "I pray you're—"

The outside door flung open. Schuyler catapulted into the room, bringing with him a distinctly horsey smell. "What's for lunch?" He snatched a roll in each hand and danced out of Portia's reach. "I'm starved!"

"You always starved." Portia rescued the rest of the rolls by setting them inside the dumbwaiter and slamming the door. "When you gonna stop growing and quit raiding my kitchen all hours of the day and night? I had a whole bucket of blackberries in the pantry last night and had to go pick more just to have enough for a cobbler!"

Schuyler laughed and picked Camilla up from behind, whirling her in a dizzy circle.

"Schuyler, quit! You're squeezing the life out of me!"

"I've been bigger than Silly-Milly for a year now." Schuyler winked at Portia. "Pretty soon I'll be able to put *you* over my shoulder!"

"That would be a sight." Portia shook a finger. "Put your sister down and go help your grandma down the stairs. I heard her bell a few minutes ago."

Schuyler dropped Camilla with a thunk that jarred her teeth. She whacked his bony shoulder, then, grumbling under her breath, picked up a heap of linen napkins waiting to be folded.

"I will, but I've got to tell you the news first. Jamie's ship's been sighted! Another blockade runner made it in last night, and the captain says the *Lady Camilla*'s going to make it into port tonight."

Camilla forgot her aggravation. "Praise God! Is the ship intact?"

Schuyler nodded. "She's coming slowly. Seems she's only sailing with a couple of sails for some reason, but the body of the ship looks fine." He shrugged. "Maybe she's overloaded with supplies."

Portia closed her eyes. "May the good Lord be with our boy."

Camilla fervently echoed the prayer.

"The meeting of the Mobile Missionary and Military Aid Society is hereby called to order," announced Mrs.

Chambliss in stentorian tones. The bird's nest in her new spring hat quivered in tandem with her three chins.

The dozen women who littered Lady's sitting room that bright Monday morning responded by putting away quilting hoops and bags of lint that they had been pulling for bandages. Under cover of the titter of feminine conversation, Camilla, who sat next to Fanny on the window seat, muttered, "I still think we ought to shorten it to 'MoMass.'" The paradoxical title of their charitable organization always struck Camilla as ridiculous and pretentious.

"Camilla, you are so crude. Where would our dear, brave soldier boys be if we women didn't cook and sew and work our fingers to the bone in their absence?" Fanny examined her perfect nails.

Camilla's reply was forestalled by the deafening thump of her grandmother's cane against the oak plank floor. All conversation came to a halt.

Lady posed the cane scepterlike beside her chair. "My son-in-law has agreed to transport the provisions we've been collecting on the next train into Mississippi. It's time to get down to the business of packing and labeling it all." Her compelling green eyes swept the room, daring anyone to find an excuse not to participate.

Even Lottie Chambliss wilted. "Where should we gather to work?"

"Since we've stored everything in the railroad warehouse, we might as well leave it there." Lady tapped a finger against her lips. "It occurs to me that one or two strong male backs would be invaluable. Camilla!"

Camilla jumped. "Ma'am?"

"You will please contact Reverend Leland and request his assistance tomorrow morning."

She'd had enough of the pretend minister's company of late. "Why don't we just get Horace and Willie to help?"

"Horace and Willie will be otherwise occupied. Besides, the dear boy has told me repeatedly to call on him if we ever needed him." Lady tapped her cheek. "Perhaps Fanny wouldn't mind asking him."

Fanny simpered, "I'll be glad to get a message to the reverend, since Camilla seems to be reluctant."

"It's not that!" Camilla passed Fanny an annoyed look. "I hesitate to take advantage of his kindness."

Fanny looked ready to fight over the reverend, but her mother intervened. "Fanny does not pursue young gentlemen for any reason." She quelled her daughter with a reproving glare. "Do you, Fanny?"

Fanny looked much struck. "Of course not." She picked up her hoop. "This quilt should be ready to auction next week. I'm confident it'll bring quite a bit for the Widows' Relief Fund."

"Yes, dear, your work is exquisite." Fanny's mother patted her hand fondly. "Lady, may I pour the tea?"

"Hold that still, boy! I know I taught you better than to jump around like a june bug in a fryin' pan!"

Gripping a set of tongs, Gabriel used his wrist to swipe at a blinding stream of sweat. It was hot as Hades in the Chambliss Brothers' Machine Shop, where he'd gotten snookered into helping Uncle Diron work on a boiler. "Uncle, you said we were coming down here to check on a new project design. You didn't tell me you planned to fire up the anvil."

Diron gave one more slam of his enormous hammer and removed the bowed sheet of metal from the anvil, his scruffy gray beard split by a grin. "When you were just a little tad, you used to spend hours with me making knives and tomahawks and horseshoes. The clerical profession's let you go all soft."

"Maybe so." Gabriel flexed his aching shoulders and looked around the shop. The oily, metallic smell of the place did bring back pleasant memories, but he didn't have time to think about them. He had arranged to meet Delia at the military's afternoon parade review. He reached for a rag and began to wipe his hands. "Speaking of my ministerial duties, uncle, you'll have to excuse me while I clean up. I've a patient in the hospital I need to visit."

Diron gave him a skeptical look, but shrugged and went back to work on the boiler.

Gabriel went to the rain barrel just outside the door and brought back a bucket of water, which he poured into the basin on a worktable at the far end of the room. As he soaped his chest and shoulders, he noticed a scrap of wrinkled paper lying on the table. It was covered with his uncle's spare but painstakingly detailed drawings, four or five views in three dimensions, all of the same object. It looked like a modified boiler, but there were significant differences between it and the boiler on the other side of the room. Finlike projectiles extended from its bottom and sides—and there seemed to be a rudder, and a hatch.

He continued to stare at the drawings. Excitement burned through every nerve ending as enlightenment dawned. *This* was the military project his uncle was building for Ezekiel Beaumont. This was the mysterious fish boat.

His hands itched to pocket the sketch. But perhaps

he would learn more by continuing to observe his uncle. Besides, he wanted to see the boat itself. He wanted to touch it and know if it really would do what he'd heard it would do.

Now, more than ever, he had reason to pursue Camilla Beaumont.

Virgil Byrd was loitering with his mule at the front steps of the Beaumont mansion later in the day when Camilla appeared for her outing. She stopped to pet the mule's whiskery muzzle and offer a gardenia from her silver posy-holder as a treat.

Virgil gave her a worshipful grin. "Candy shore does think you're the beatin'est thing she ever seen. Man alive, that there's the purtiest shirt—whatcha call it, now?"

"It's a Garibaldi blouse." Camilla plucked at one thin red sleeve, praying the buttons would hold. It was a couple of years old, but it was still one of her favorite garments. She gave Candy another flower. "Virgil, do you know Reverend Gabriel Leland?"

Virgil canted his triangular head. "Now, is that the one that rode in here couple days ago on a bay gelding? Got a Bible in one pocket and a derringer in the other?"

Camilla nodded grimly. "That's him."

"I like that fella! He was real nice to Candy." He scratched his chin. "He give me back my newspaper bag and bought me some oysters."

"What was he doing with my—your bag?"

"Dunno. But he give it back to me when I told him where you live. He shore is a nice man."

Nice was not a term Camilla would have applied to the devious reverend. "Do you know where he is?"

"He's staying at that big old hotel down on Govermit Street."

"The Battle House?"

"Yes'm. But he ain't there right now. He's gone in the hospital."

Camilla caught her breath. "He's hurt?"

"Naw!" Virgil guffawed. "He ain't *in* the hospital. He's just visiting. He ast me if I could get him some carbolic spray, so I did."

"Carbolic spray?" Camilla frowned. "Where would you get that?"

"Oh, I can get most anything if I got something to trade for it." Virgil looked anxious. "I wished I'd knowed you needed some—I done give it all to the rev'rint."

"Never mind. I suspect he'll know what to do with it much better than I would." Camilla slapped her gloves against her palm. "Virgil, I'm going to the hospital. Would you do something for me?"

"You want a ride, Missy? Candy would be pure honored—"

"No, no, thank you." Camilla hid a smile. "All I want you to do is go down to the wharf and find out if there's any news about Jamie's ship. See if he made it to port last night."

"Yes'm. Shore will. Missy?"

Camilla halted in the act of stepping down onto the boardwalk. "What is it, Virgil?"

"Candy shore thinks you look a huckleberry above a persimmon in that there Jerry-bald shirt!"

The entire city of Mobile seemed to have gone military-crazy. Gabriel paused outside Barton Academy where, as far as he could tell, people lined Government Street clear down to Royal. The Friday review was a sight to see. Patriotic fervor was high; Confederate flags fluttered from balconies and stretched across carriageways, and women had even sewn tiny replicas into the sleeves of their dresses or appliquéd them onto their hat bands. The opportunity to watch the regiments posturing and drilling was too good to miss. His next report would be filled with squadron numbers and names of commanders.

"It's nice to see you looking hale and hearty this afternoon, cousin."

Gabriel turned and gave Delia Matthews a mocking bow. "Are you enjoying the reviewing of our brave troops?"

"Oh, indeed." She slanted a provocative look from under heavy lids. "My stay in the city has been most profitable." She glanced down at the small burlap sack in his hand. "What's that?"

After meeting Crazy Virgil at the riverfront, Gabriel had come downtown with the prized carbolic spray. He hoped he wasn't too late to save the little girl.

But Delia didn't need to know he'd been wasting time chasing down chemical compounds for medicinal purposes. "It's a…gift for someone. I'm about to make a hospital visit." He frowned as he examined Delia's conservative bonnet, high-necked dress and practical shoes. If not for the lush figure and dramatic beauty of her face, she would have blended in with the mostly female crowd. "I trust you're behaving yourself?"

"I am the soul of decorum." Delia yawned. "The women you sent to keep an eye on me have been most diligent. It took some ingenuity to give Mrs. Chambliss the slip this morning. She wanted me to go with her to a quilting bee!"

Gabriel laughed. "You should've gone with her. You might have learned something."

"I already *did* learn something before—bunch of gossip-mongering biddies that they are. Word is, the riverboat raises anchor at first light tomorrow. Time's up, cousin."

"You can't go yet." Drawing close, he lowered his voice. "I could write most of that paper again, but certain things in it can't be safely duplicated. Give me two more days."

"I can't, Gabriel." Delia's eyes softened. "I'm expected."

Gabriel supposed Admiral Farragut did have a certain claim on Delia's time. She was leaving, so he'd have to get that cipher back one way or another. Even if he had to kidnap Camilla Beaumont to do it.

"All right then, I'll meet you at the wharf before dawn."

Delia bit her lip. "Don't do anything to jeopardize the mission."

He gave her an ironic smile. "I'm not the one who got myself arrested. I have something to take care of. Lie low until tonight, and I'll see you then."

"Be careful." Delia melted into a crowd of women waving to a troop of passing soldiers.

With an effort Gabriel shelved his worries about the missing cipher and turned toward the hospital.

He found the little girl named Lecy lying in her cot, playing with a doll made from a hank of yarn tied to form head, arms and legs. The child was still pale, but her eyes were bright. Gabriel looked at the end of the bed. Both legs were still intact.

Releasing a pent-up breath, he smiled. "Hello, Lecy. How are you feeling today?"

The big Irish-blue eyes lit. "Pastor Gabriel! I'm getting well. My leg quit hurting after you were here the other day. Miss Camilla came to see me again."

"That's good." Gabriel hunkered beside the cot to examine her doll. "Where's your mama?"

"Home with my brothers and sisters. I got to get well so I can keep an eye on them while Mama works outside."

"There are eight in all," said a quiet voice behind him. Camilla Beaumont moved to the other side of the cot. "Lecy's number two. The oldest isn't quite right, so her folks depend on her a lot."

Gabriel looked up Camilla, not entirely surprised to see her. A splash of sunshine from the open window made a nimbus of the gold-streaked hair curling about her face, and her ruddy blouse echoed the healthy color in her cheeks. Leaning over the bed, she looked like a guardian angel in primary colors.

He dragged his gaze back to the child. "She's doing better today, thank the Lord." Startled by the rush of gratitude that flooded him, he jerked the sheet free of the mattress so he could unwrap the bandage from the wounded leg. It was free of infection, the skin a healthy pink. "She'll be able to go home soon."

"I wasn't able to find any carbolic spray, but I've been coming by here every day to wash her wound. It seems to have helped."

He showed her the contents of the canvas sack he'd set on the floor at the end of the bed. "I'd brought some myself. I was sure she was headed for amputation." In reluctant wonder, Gabriel replaced the gauze strips around

Lecy's leg. Maybe Camilla's prayers had done some good after all.

"Young man, you overstep your bounds." The heavy voice was accompanied by angry footfalls.

Gabriel looked around, and Camilla straightened.

Dr. Kinch strode toward them, his white imperial beard jutting. He nodded at Camilla, then glared at Gabriel. "I would like to know on whose authority you endanger my patient's health."

Gabriel got to his feet, heat pumping from his gut to his extremities. "On the authority of God Almighty. Have you anything that outranks that?"

Fishlike, Dr. Kinch's mouth opened and shut.

Hiding a smile, Camilla tucked the sheet back under the mattress. "I'm sure Reverend Leland meant no harm. We were marveling over how well Lecy has recovered."

"Indeed." The doctor puffed out his lips. "But you shouldn't unwrap that bandage. Contaminated air has been known to carry mysterious miasmas into open wounds."

Gabriel offered the doctor the antiseptic he'd brought. "I've heard military doctors are using this compound now to reduce such infections. I hope you'll accept it as a token of my goodwill." He forced a conciliatory tone. "I wouldn't wish to do anything to slow down Lecy's recovery."

The doctor huffed as he accepted the sack and its contents. "I'm sure you have the best intentions, sir."

Lecy caught Camilla's hand. "You promised to bring my dolly a new dress."

Dr. Kinch examined Gabriel's neat bandaging, then excused himself to finish his rounds. With a smile Camilla produced a scrap of taffeta fashioned into a doll gown. She remained with Gabriel to carry on a cheerful conversation about the child's numerous brothers and sisters.

They wandered through the wards, stopping here and there to read a letter, pray with sick and heartsore soldiers, and rejoice with those who were almost well enough to go home or return to the front lines. Camilla's demeanor with the patients remained gentle and solicitous, but several times Gabriel caught her looking at him with a question in those clear topaz eyes.

Might as well face the music. He took her elbow and led her out onto a balcony overlooking Government Street, where the military review was winding down, clumps of butternut and gray troops dispersing toward the encampments at the edge of town. The fresh breeze off the bay blew Camilla's dark skirt against its hoop and outlined her upper body in the red blouse.

Gabriel met the wry expression in her eyes and smiled to cover his discomfiture. "Do you come to the hospital every day?"

"Not unless there's somebody in particular I need to see."

He frowned a little. "Did you follow me here today?"

"I suppose you could say that." Camilla leaned back against the balcony railing, an irritated glint in her eyes. "My grandmother wants to know if you'd like to help prepare some boxes for shipment out into the rural areas where food and supplies are needed."

"Your grandmother apparently thinks I'm having trouble filling my time." He grinned. "And you'd rather she found someone else to deliver her messages. Miss Camilla, you wound me."

"I'm sure you couldn't care less whether or not I like

you." She presented him with a clean, indifferent profile. "Shall I tell her you'll come?"

"Where and when?"

"Tomorrow morning, at the M & O depot. There's an empty car on a train heading north at noon. Papa says it'll be the last one for the week."

"I'll be glad to help."

"Good." The amber eyes turned to him. "Reverend Leland—Gabriel, I've been wanting to ask you something."

"What is it?" He moved as close to her as her great hooped skirt would allow.

She sighed and twisted a little pearl ring around her pinky finger. "My cousin Harry…please tell me if he's well. Is he happy? Does he think of me?"

Gabriel wished for an insane moment that he were in Harry Martin's shoes. To have a girl like Camilla Beaumont in love with him…

He shook his head. "I never answered your question about whether he wrote the sermon I gave you, but you must believe me when I say he did not." He hardened his voice. "I haven't seen him in a long time, and I don't know where he is. Our political views don't jibe."

"I suppose they don't." She stared at him for a silent moment, her body gradually stiffening with disappointment and grief. "Would you explain to me how you justify bribing information out of a poor, innocent vagrant like Virgil?"

Delia was right. Compassion was getting him in trouble. Over the past few weeks, questions of his own had begun to interfere with his sleep. The possibility that he was being directed by some unseen hand was disturbing on a level he couldn't begin to explain, even to himself. "First of all, that old man is about as innocent as a water moccasin. I didn't bribe him—I simply bought him a good solid meal, and he mentioned that he knew you." Camilla sniffed, but he didn't care whether she believed him or not. "I found his bag in the hold of the boat, he recognized it, and I returned it."

She regarded him shrewdly, but before she could question him further, a great caterwauling arose beneath the balcony, accompanied by a hideous and earsplitting braying. Gabriel and Camilla both leaned over the rail. Directly below, Virgil Byrd was struggling to restrain a very unhappy mule at the grand white granite entryway of the hospital. It was unclear whether they were trying to get in or out.

Gabriel put two fingers to his mouth and whistled.

The mule slumped and fell silent. Camilla looked at Gabriel wide-eyed, both hands over her ears. A hospital orderly shut the door from the inside.

Byrd grinned from ear to ear, his unkempt head thrown back. "Rev'rint Gabe! Missy! I knowed you was in there somewhere!"

Camilla burst into infectious giggles.

Gabriel glanced at her smiling. "Get that flea-bitten animal out to the street!" he shouted down at Byrd. "We'll be right down."

Gabriel and Camilla hurried down the stairs and back through the wards, then bid farewell to the harassed orderly guarding the front door against marauding enemies and recalcitrant mules. They crossed the yard and found Byrd sitting in the shade of a huge mossy oak by the street. Candy was hunkered beside him, munching placidly on a playbill from the theater down the street.

Camilla planted herself in front of Byrd, hoops swaying with the force of her sudden halt. "Virgil, you know you can't bring Candy into the hospital!"

Byrd shuffled his feet. "She don't like to get left behind. It hurts her feelings."

"What if she decided to eat a chart or—or kick over a bedpan?" Camilla sighed at Byrd's uncomprehending, hangdog expression.

"What's your business, Byrd?" Gabriel asked impatiently.

The old man brightened, puffing out his chest. "Missy told me to find out about Mr. Jamie's ship. The *Lady Camilla*'s in port, just like you said. But they ain't lettin' nobody off the ship, 'cause they's all come down with the yeller fever."

Camilla gasped.

Gabriel put a hand under her trembling elbow. "Byrd, where's the ship?"

"Down to Fort Morgan. They say the whole crew's bound to die, 'cause they ain't no quinine in a hunnerd miles of here. Besides, ain't nobody in their right mind gonna board a ship full of yeller fever."

"But yellow fever's spread by—" Gabriel stopped himself just in time. "So the ship's cargo hasn't even been unloaded?"

"Who cares about that?" Camilla frowned. "We can't let those men die! I'm going to figure out some way to find some quinine. Virgil, go back to the waterfront and see what you can find out." She pulled her elbow free of Gabriel's hold. "My grandmother will expect you tomorrow morning at the M & O station. Good day, Reverend Leland."

Gabriel watched Camilla hurry across the street as Byrd hauled the mule off in the direction of the waterfront. Too bad their momentary camaraderie had been disrupted. Now he'd have to start all over to gain her confidence. She had something he wanted. But if he could get hold of something she needed with equal passion, they might come to an agreement. Perhaps he could use her ignorance about the treatment of yellow fever to his advantage.

Whistling, he sauntered after Crazy Virgil the Birdman.

Chapter Seven

By the dim light of the moon, Camilla placed one di-
lapidated boot on her cedar chest to tie the laces. It had
taken what was left of the afternoon to locate her slave-
running costume, for Portia had stuffed it behind the
washtub in the laundry room. She hoped she could get
out of the house without waking Portia, or worse, Lady.
Virgil had been unable to find quinine at the docks today,
but she had to go to Jamie anyway. Perhaps there was
something she could do for him. Laces tied, she opened
the window casement and slid her leg across the sill.

And nearly knocked Gabriel Leland off the wisteria vine.

He choked out a surprised exclamation and grabbed
her ankle. Fortunately, she had a good grip on the curtain.

"Let go!" she hissed.

"Pardon me if I decline," he returned. "If you would
be so kind as to haul us both back inside—"

"Hush! Do you want my grandmother to hear us?"

"Now that would be a fascinating turn of—"

Camilla gave a mighty shove of her boot that would

have sent her gentleman caller tumbling, if he hadn't had the agility of an orangutan. He dodged sideways, grabbed the windowsill, and pushed Camilla inside the room, where they fell, panting, side by side on the floor.

He pushed himself to his elbows and rolled slightly toward her. She found herself staring at his mouth, a strong, full mouth, with an oddly shaped little scar interrupting the curve of the upper lip.

He seemed to be listening for something, head to one side, his dark hair flung into half-closed eyes. "It's all right." He relaxed. Smiling, he plucked the cap off her head, and her hair sprang forth in Medusa-like abandon.

"All right?" She struggled to her elbows. "If I scream, my papa will shoot you dead."

"After he ships you off to a convent."

He had a point. "What do you want?"

"My sermon."

"You can't possibly believe I think that's a sermon."

"I don't care what you think. I'm proposing something you understand. A trade."

"Ha! What would you have that would interest me?"

"Quinine."

The word rumbled through her, sharpening her panic. She searched his deep-set eyes for mockery or braggadocio but found only matter-of-fact calm. And a glint of something else that might have been admiration.

"How'd you get it? Virgil says there isn't any."

"Let's just say I have other connections."

She scrambled to her feet and pressed the heels of her hands to her eyes. "I don't know who you are, and I certainly don't trust you. *Where* is the quinine?"

Gabriel sighed, rolling to his feet. "My uncle has it. He's quite the accomplished smuggler, it turns out."

Camilla lowered her hands, reluctantly meeting his gaze. "Your uncle? Then you have family here?"

"No one you'd know." His mouth twisted.

Trembling, she considered her dilemma from every angle. She'd been praying for a way to help Jamie, but would God send her help in the form of this diabolical man?

He looked at her steadily. Clearly he was aware of her indecision, but he made no move to coerce her either physically or verbally. That fact somehow reassured her. "All right," she said. "But before I give you the sermon we deliver the quinine to Jamie."

"I might have known you'd insist on coming." He sighed. "You are quite out of your mind, you know. What if your grandmother, whom you seem to regard with such fear and trembling, discovers you're traipsing around in the middle of the night in those clothes?"

"I don't care. I'm coming with you. I want to see Jamie for myself. This might be the last—" She swallowed. "Take me with you. Please." Humiliating to beg. She held his gaze, breath hitching in spite of her efforts to steady it.

Suddenly he turned and pulled the curtain aside. "Come on, then. We'd best hurry."

Camilla took two steps for every one of Gabriel's as they hurried through the quiet, misty downtown streets. "Do you really believe what you preach?"

He expelled an impatient breath. "We don't have time to discuss religion."

"See?" She stumbled over a rut in the road. "I knew you were no minister!"

Steadying her with an arm around her waist, Gabriel

chuckled. "Come to my church this Sunday if you want my opinions on God."

She persisted. "What's that sermon about? Why don't you just write it again?"

"I threw away my notes."

"But why—"

"You ask too many questions." Gabriel jerked Camilla to a halt and lowered his voice. "Take my word for it, I've got to get it back tonight."

"You owe me the truth, Gabriel Leland."

"As you well know, the truth is a dangerous commodity in wartime."

The grim set of Gabriel's dark features and the implication of his words crystallized her suspicions. "You know, don't you?" She felt as if she might faint. "You were sent down here to trap me and—and the rest of us!"

Music blared as someone opened the door of a nearby tavern. The light exposed a flare of triumph in Gabriel's eyes. He stepped into the shadow of the building. "You might as well give me the details."

"I'm not telling you anything."

"Then maybe I should tell your papa you're sending whiskey barrels up the rails behind his back. Bet he'd like to know his house slaves are selling liquor to the military." His voice came out of the darkness, relentless. "He'll likely choose Virgil Byrd as the scapegoat. What are you planning to do with the money? Your wardrobe getting outdated?"

Camilla raised a hand to slap the accusations out of his mouth, but he caught her wrist and had her snugged against him back to front before she could blink.

"I hate you, you—hypocrite!" She struggled against

his strong arms, panting. "Whenever you don't want to answer questions you go on the attack."

"That's right. A useful lesson for you, my lovely little smuggler. Where's the whiskey coming from? Byrd can't be producing it all by himself."

"I'm not telling you anything!"

"Fine. Byrd will tell me. He loves that stupid mule almost as much as he loves you—"

"Leave him alone!" Camilla cried desperately. "He didn't have anything to do with it. There wasn't any whiskey in those barrels—it was people!" She felt Gabriel's tension against her back but could no longer contain her anger and fear. "The railroad operations are over now, so you can have me arrested if that'll satisfy you. But I beg you in the name of mercy to leave Portia and Horace and Virgil out of it!" She sagged in his arms, her head rolling back against his shoulder.

Gradually Camilla became aware that the grip on her wrist had loosened, and she was being supported rather than crushed. She felt Gabriel lean back against the tavern wall and slide down it until they were crumpled together in the weeds and mud.

"You're an abolitionist." His voice was a hoarse whisper.

She turned her head and nodded, her temple scraping against the stubble on his chin. "Yes."

"Can you prove it?"

"Do I have to? You've been following me around for two weeks now."

Gabriel sat silent. She listened to the steady thump of his heart under her ear. He held in his hands not only her life but those of all the people she loved. If she was arrested, her entire family would be implicated. She'd known that from the beginning. Portia had warned her often enough.

And he still had the quinine.

She felt Gabriel's chest lift and fall with a huge breath. "My name is Gabriel Laniere," he said quietly. "That's the truth. I can't tell you anything more, but you can trust me not to turn you in." When she tipped her head back to look up at his shadowed face, he shook his head. "No time for explanations now. We've got to get that sermon to the *Magnolia Princess* before it weighs anchor at dawn."

Gabriel could hear Camilla trotting behind him down the street. He didn't slow down. Delia would not wait for him for long.

As the tall warehouses of the quay loomed, Camilla tugged at his coat sleeve. "Don't you know there's a curfew?" she whispered. "What if we get stopped?"

Gabriel shrugged. "I have a pass."

"A pass? Where'd you get a pass?"

He chuckled. "The provost marshal is a member of my church. Since I could be called to a deathbed at any hour of the day or night, Mr. Parker thinks my movements should be unrestricted."

"So that's how you've been able to sashay around here with nobody questioning you." She grabbed his arm. "This is the banana dock. What are we doing here?"

He scanned the horizon. The faint pink glow over the water told him that dawn wasn't far off, and the *Magnolia Princess* would begin her return trip upriver. He looked sharply at his companion. "Is this where your 'railroad' connects?"

"Used to. But not anymore." She pressed her lips together. "Since the Yankees took Pensacola and New Orleans, everybody's in a panic that they'll attack here next."

"What's that got to do with the 'railroad'?"

"I suppose I have no choice but to trust you." When she took her hand from his arm he felt the loss of physical warmth, but more, her emotional detachment.

So what? he asked himself. What difference did it make if a little girl with big, guileless eyes trusted him? It only mattered because he needed to know what she knew. Still he felt a bit sick. "Of course you can trust me."

"Of course." She gave him a small, bitter smile. "I'm sure you've heard rumors that a new commander's on his way to Mobile."

Gabriel nodded. "I've heard. Do you know who it is?"

"General Forney. He was wounded at Dranesville, so they're sending him down here to recover. Restrictions are being tightened, which means operations are suspended until it's safe again."

"Who's running the operation?"

"I'm not telling you any more until you tell me what's in that sermon and what you plan to do with it."

What could he safely tell her? She was abolitionist, he was now sure, and she clearly knew the value of keeping secrets. But she was also practically a child—albeit an intrepid one—and the daughter of a military bankroller. "I'm sending it north."

"But—"

The sound of quick footsteps approached out of the mist behind them. They both turned as a figure almost identical in size and shape to Camilla hurried toward them.

Gabriel let Delia come close before he addressed her. "Did anyone see you leaving the boat?"

"Of course not. Who is this?"

"Delia Matthews, Camilla Beaumont." The two women nodded warily, and Gabriel smiled in black amusement. "Camilla's been safeguarding our cipher all this time. She came to see it on its way upriver."

Delia's brows snapped together. "We'll be lucky if I make it back in time. Where's the cipher?"

Camilla reached into her blouse and, with obvious misgivings, handed the paper to Gabriel. "You know how important this is, don't you?"

"Yes, Reverend, you're not the only bean in this stew." Delia took the sermon with a sassy flip of her wrist. "Charmed, Miss Beaumont," she tossed over her shoulder as she disappeared into the fog.

"Well!" Camilla planted her fists on her hips. "I gather you had intended to meet that—that *woman* in the boat the night you gave me the sermon."

Gabriel shrugged. "No flies on you, missy."

"How could you mistake me for her?"

He looked her up and down and sighed. "You don't know how many times I've asked myself that very question."

"Are you an agent? I mean from—" She gestured vaguely.

"What do you think?" He turned toward the hotel.

Camilla followed. "So if you are…can you get a message to Harry for me?"

"I've got more important things to do than be your messenger boy." Harry was a good man, but Gabriel found it irritating that she seemed so enamored with her cousin.

"Of course you do." Camilla dodged in front of him and stopped, boots planted wide and chin in the air. "You sit around in ladies' parlors drinking tea and deliver long, pious homilies on Sunday mornings." She poked him in the chest. "You obviously know a lot about medicine— why don't you at least share that gift, like Harry does, instead of wasting it?"

"I don't have a license. Not that it's any of your business." He stepped around her and turned onto Government Street.

She came after him. "That doesn't make any sense. You cared about Lecy Carrolton, enough to go to the trouble and expense of getting hold of that medicine. And I saw the way you touched her and smiled at her. You can't fool children—" She tripped over an uneven brick in the pavement and went sprawling.

Gabriel stood with his back to her, listening to her sobbing breaths. He should walk away. Camilla Beaumont and her underground railroad and her plague-stricken Secesh brother were complications he didn't need. Even though the cipher was delivered, he still had to find that underwater vessel. But he'd given her his word.

He turned around and found her sitting with her head cradled on her knees. He extended his hand. "Come on, we have to go after the quinine."

She looked up at him wordlessly.

He knelt and touched her shoulder. "Are you all right?" The words came out more gruffly than he'd intended.

"I've got to know what side you're on, Gabriel. I think God sent you here to help me, but I've got to know."

A chill walked up the back of Gabriel's neck, but he made himself remain on one knee, grounded by the threadbare texture of her shirt and the faint scent of lily of the valley. "I'm on the right side."

"What's right, Gabriel? Is it right to hold another

human being in bondage? Is it right to murder fellow countrymen over property? Is it right to starve people out and keep medical supplies from entering a port?" She dropped her head, and a long curl at the back of her neck blew against his hand.

He twined the curl around his finger and found himself just as inexorably bound to the woman. Maybe she was right, and God had sent him to her. He only knew he couldn't walk away from her.

"What's right is holding this nation together. Those black folks you love so much are never going to be free if the United States splits."

"But Papa says they eventually *will* be freed—when we're left alone to make that decision in our own way."

"You honestly think a rich plantation owner's going to bankrupt himself for the benefit of a bunch of people he thinks of as animals? Would your papa do it?"

"I don't know. I hope so! What difference does it make what *I* think?" She shut her eyes.

"Look at me!" When the heavy black lashes lifted, he poured all the force of his will into her eyes. "It makes all the difference in the world. I'm putting my life in your hands right now. I have to discover everything I can about gray military activity in this area, including development of a boat that travels underwater, and I need your help."

"Oh, Lord Jesus," she whispered, and he knew it was a prayer.

"Camilla, listen." He took her hands to press his advantage. "You may not want to admit it, but it appears we share some philosophical, if not religious, views. We're just going about it in different ways." He took a breath and released it. "Now I need to enlist you to *help* me. That boat—"

"I know about it," she whispered.

"What?" He stared at her, dumbfounded.

"I know about the fish boat. I heard my father and Mr. Chambliss talking about it the night I met you on the riverboat."

Chapter Eight

Camilla rode astride the tall gray gelding behind Gabriel, holding awkwardly to his waist and trying not to lean against him. A lady should retain some measure of distance, despite the night's bizarre events.

They followed a wooded track along the coastline that led south toward the two forts guarding the entrance to the harbor: Fort Gaines on the elbow of Dauphin Island to the west, and Fort Morgan on the eastern tip of the bay, where the blockade runners found sanctuary. Jamie was there, and she would see him sometime today.

Gabriel held his peace, apparently understanding she needed time to absorb the burden of his confidences. He wasn't a real minister, but he wasn't a bootlegger, either. He was the Union agent she had so ignorantly prayed for.

She was going to spy on her own family. She was going to bring this medicine to Jamie and aid a Yankee spy's entry into a Confederate fort.

Camilla shuddered.

Gabriel slowed the gelding and looked over his shoulder. "Are you cold? We're almost to Uncle Diron's."

She shook her head. "Just tired." She leaned her aching forehead against his back as he chirruped to the horse.

Sometime later she awoke as someone lifted her down. Sunlight fell against her eyelids. Drowsily she lifted her arms to hang on and snuggled her cheek into Gabriel's shoulder.

Her eyes popped open. "I'm going to be in so much trouble."

Gabriel shook his head, eyes amused. "I sent a message from the hotel when we got the horse." He carried her up the steps of a weather-beaten river shack and across the porch. She smelled sausage, heard someone whistling with a beautiful, warbling tremolo.

"Put me down." When he did so, she stared up at him. "What did you tell my papa?"

"The truth. That we managed to get hold of some quinine, and we're taking it to your brother." He spread his hands. "How could he object? I'm the preacher. Besides, I'll have you back home by sundown."

"It's a long way down to the fort."

"Not by boat. The steam packet makes a stop at Deer River Point." He placed a hand against the doorjamb and bent close to her. "Uncle doesn't know I'm blue. So keep your tongue between your teeth. We're going to get the quinine and go."

Camilla nodded and removed her cap. One more person to deceive.

Gabriel's uncle looked like a man who could move a mountain if he'd a mind to. Yet his face was kind and open, and he greeted her with an elaborate old-fashioned bow. She laughed as his mustache tickled her hand when he kissed it.

She looked for Gabriel and found him sprawled comfortably in a basketlike chair surrounded by a clutter of fishing equipment, an artist's easel and an odd assortment of musical instruments and pots of brushes and paints. He was already sound asleep.

Diron sent a droll glance toward his nephew. "Gabriel's a young man of simple needs."

Camilla surveyed the crowded room. "He didn't tell me he has family in Mobile. I thought he was from— well, not from here." Her stomach growled. "Is that sausage I smell?"

Diron chuckled. "And grits. Come on back, and I'll feed you." He led the way toward the back of the long, narrow room, where a cast-iron cookstove squatted. He dusted a wooden chair with a rag and seated Camilla with great courtesy.

She might have been dressed in her finest taffeta ball gown, instead of her brother's breeches and boots. "Thank you." She smiled.

Diron hadn't forgotten her implied question. "Gabriel ain't big on letting folks into his brain box, though when he was a little fella he'd chatter your ear off, asking questions." He filled a plate for Camilla and handed it to her. "He's got lots of family in the area, but they're on the reservation across the state line. Doubt you'd know 'em."

Camilla swallowed a bite of biscuit. "Reservation? There's an Indian reservation near here?"

Diron sat across the scarred little table, a spatterware mug of coffee clamped in his big paw. "They moved the last of the Creeks over there in thirty-six, the year Gabriel was born."

"So Gabriel's Creek Indian." That explained the deepset dark eyes, bronzed skin and high cheekbones. "How did he end up living here with you?"

"Kind of a long story." Diron shrugged. "My brother and I are French-Canadian by birth. We came downriver to trade and ended up staying. Jean married an Indian girl, but after they moved the Creeks off Alabama land, she missed her family and wanted to follow. Turned out he couldn't stick it. He went off on a trading expedition and never came back."

His words stung Camilla's heart. "Gabriel's mother was left with a baby to raise by herself?"

"Three. Johnny was two, Gabriel an infant and Sara still in the womb when their father left."

"My soul, what kind of man would abandon his wife and children?"

"A very young and self-centered one." Diron sighed. "Jean loved Little Flower in his own way, but he never adjusted to the coastal climate. Reckon he knew, between me and the Indian family system, his wife and kids would be cared for." He paused and folded brawny arms, watching his nephew sleep. "Reckon they were."

Camilla pushed away her plate. "Didn't you have a family of your own?"

Diron colored to the ears. "Never had the manners nor inclination to keep a woman." He chuckled. "Besides, once I had young Gabriel running around here raisin' the roof, wouldn't no woman come within a mile of the place."

"Why would Gabriel's mother send only him to live with you? Why not the older boy, too?"

"Oh, Johnny was getting along just fine. But Gabriel was—I guess you could say a bit of a handful. He was reading and writing by the time he was four, and talking like a college professor. If he wanted to know how something worked, he'd take it apart and put it back together, sometimes in better shape than it was to start with. Anything he's seen one time, he'll never forget." Diron shook his curly gray head. "He could think of more questions than his poor mama had time to answer in a lifetime. She sent him to me out of pure self-defense. Didn't take me long to realize he needed more education than I could give him. The Catholic schools didn't have room for him, so I talked the Methodist missionaries into taking him on. Gabriel finished Barton Academy when he was only fifteen and won a scholarship to medical college."

Camilla leaned forward. "And that's where he met—"

"Uncle, you gossip like an old woman." The subject of their discussion reached over Camilla's shoulder to pluck a biscuit from her plate.

She jumped. "I just wanted to know—"

"I know what you wanted to know. It's ancient history." He towered over her, chewing, his expression bland. "Uncle, where's that bundle of stuff I brought you to keep for me a few days ago?"

Diron set his mug down with a thump. "I put it away, but you owe me some explanations before I hand it over." He eyed Gabriel's travel-stained suit and Camilla's boy's clothes. "I ain't asked no questions, figured you'd tell me why you show up here at daybreak with this pretty little lady." His grizzled brows slammed together. "Her papa ain't comin' after you with a shotgun—"

Gabriel shouted with laughter, and Camilla found her breath snatched away. Gabriel Laniere with a genuine grin on his face was a sight to see.

"I imagine her papa'd be glad to get rid of her." He chuckled at the indignant lift of her chin. "We're on our way to Fort Morgan to take medicine to Camilla's brother. I'm no cradle robber," he added with unnecessary relish.

Camilla bristled. "I'm a grown woman, and I come and go as I please. It's easier to travel in boy's clothes, and Gabriel is kind enough to escort me."

"Yep, young Gabe's the soul of kindness." Tongue in cheek, the older man got to his feet. "Sit down, boy, while I fix you a plate."

Gabriel shook his head, pilfering another biscuit and a couple of sausage links. "We've got to get on our way. Camilla's daddy *will* pull out the shotgun if I don't have her back by sundown."

Diron nodded. "Serve you right, you scalawag. I'll get your bundle." He set the remains of his breakfast on the porch, just outside the back door. "Come and get it, Ajax!" A blue tick hound, snoozing peacefully under a mimosa, lifted his head and lumbered to his feet.

While Diron climbed a ladder into a tiny sleeping loft, Camilla wandered around the room. She picked up a small hand-carved wooden replica of the hound slavering over his breakfast on the porch. It was cunning, lifelike and crafted with a loving hand. "I've never met anyone quite like your uncle." She looked up to find Gabriel leaning against the kitchen table, watching her with hooded eyes. "What is it?"

"We'll have to get on that packet down to the fort. Uncle's right—you'll raise some eyebrows dressed like that."

She shrugged. "I'll put my cap back on. Nobody'll know I'm a girl."

"Hope you're right. But remember we'll be in broad daylight, so keep your hands in your pockets."

Camilla replaced the figure of the dog and examined

her small, smooth hands. "Only you would notice something that minor."

"Anybody with a grain of sense would notice it."

She scowled. He was worse than either of her brothers.

Diron looked over the edge of the loft and cleared his throat loudly. "Anybody interested in this here quinine bag?"

Feet propped on the rail, Gabriel lounged under the striped canvas awning on the upper deck of the western bay steam packet. After leaving Caleb at a livery near the quay at Deer River Point shortly after seven, he and Camilla had boarded one of the little thirty-foot steamers that slogged up and down the coastline. The shallow-draft boat had dodged sandbars and trees and stumps embedded in silt and reeds for nearly an hour, and another two remained before they would reach Grant's Pass.

Except for pretty villas dotting the low, wooded shore, the monotonous coastline had changed little from the days Gabriel had spent as a boy hunting and fishing with his uncle. He found himself interested in watching Camilla, who stood at the rail looking pensively out over the water. Her nose was getting pink.

He nudged her elbow with his foot. "Better rest while you've got the chance. Don't want you fainting on me before we get home."

She lifted her face to the breeze blowing fresh off the water and hugged the leather sack holding the bottle of quinine to her stomach. "I like the sun, and I'm not tired." She turned to look at Gabriel, anxiety filling her eyes. "How long does it take for yellow fever to kill a man?"

"Depends how long they've been down with it. Cuba's rife with the stuff."

"When is somebody going to find a way to prevent it?"

Gabriel felt the old bitterness take hold. "Maybe somebody's already found what causes it. Maybe nobody else is listening."

"My brother's such a good man, and he loves the Lord so much. He doesn't deserve to die."

"Camilla, nobody deserves to die. It just happens. Remember, we're in the middle of a war. A *civil* war, God help us. Your brother's a blockade runner. He knew the risk he took."

"There's something you don't understand." Camilla met Gabriel's eyes, her chin set against its trembling. "My mama was carried off by yellow fever when I was four. I'm not losing Jamie the same way."

As the packet hauled up alongside a jetty off the eastern tip of Dauphin Island, Gabriel told himself it was just as well he didn't have time to think about Camilla's disclosure. He and Camilla threaded their way among the civilian passengers headed for the tatty-looking masonry shell of Fort Gaines. The wharf swarmed with army and navy personnel, businessmen and fishermen. The few women in the crowd looked to be of the strumpet variety. Gabriel was relieved that Camilla chose not to draw attention to herself.

The fort was surrounded by a hot wasteland of sand and tents. A former commander had ordered removal of the trees in order to clear the line of approach from any direction. Much of the activity today, however, seemed to center more around food than defense. Cook fires were in abundance, and the scent of coffee, fried salt pork and hardtack made Gabriel's mouth water.

Camilla had to be hungry, too, but she trudged beside

him up the hill to the fort without complaint. Though her shoulders drooped, she allowed him to take the heavy bag of quinine from her with obvious reluctance.

As civilians desiring passage on the ferry to Fort Morgan, Gabriel and Camilla were required to show the pass signed by Provost Marshal G. M. Parker to the commander of the fort. Major Hallonquist, a delicate-looking man with a middle-aged paunch and a shallow chin camouflaged by sparse whiskers, stood as his visitors came into his office a rough table and three straight-backed chairs in a large tent.

Camilla swept the cap from her head, spilling long, gold-shot curls in every direction. "Good afternoon, Major. I'm Captain James Beaumont's sister. I've come to take some quinine out to his ship, the *Lady Camilla*, which is quarantined at Fort Morgan."

Major Hallonquist gaped.

Hiding his dismay at her brashness, Gabriel said smoothly, "And I'm Reverend Gabriel Leland, come to give Miss Beaumont my aid and escort." He spread his hands, as one reasonable man to another. "Please forgive our intrusion and odd attire, sir. Miss Beaumont was anxious to get to her brother as quickly and with as little attention to herself as possible."

"My brother's very ill," she added.

"Your brother is a hero to us all, Miss Beaumont." Major Hallonquist smiled. "We're anxious to obtain the supplies and arms he's brought in. But he must remain in quarantine for the full two weeks. I can't risk endangering an entire garrison with that fever."

"But I've got quinine right here!" Camilla held out the bag of medicine. "Let us take the ferry over to Fort Morgan. We'll find a way to get out to the *Lady C* somehow."

The major shook his head, but Gabriel held up a hand. "Sir, if there's even one man still infected with the fever on that ship, I promise we'll not come back through here. We'll find a way to get back to Mobile on our own."

"Please, sir," Camilla said with dignity, "you know how valuable that cargo is. If my brother dies, you may never see it."

Hallonquist sighed, reaching into an overflowing crate beside the table. "Very well." He scribbled on a scrap of paper. "This will get you on the ferry, but it's Colonel Powell's decision whether to let you into Fort Morgan."

"Oh, thank you, sir!" Camilla beamed.

Gabriel took her elbow. "Come on, before we miss the ferry. Thank you, sir."

The major shook his head. "Just don't come back here with that fever!"

Chapter Nine

"Have you lost your mind?" Gabriel kept his voice low, though he felt like howling.

Camilla tossed her head, oblivious to fellow passengers on the ferry goggling at the brazen hussy dressed in pants. Her hair fluttered like a wavy banner in the gulf breeze.

"You should have let me handle the major. There was no need to make such a display."

Camilla set her white teeth. "My brother's dying, and I wasn't going to shuffle around in the background while you took all day to get to the point."

He bent close to her ear. "A little patience and self-restraint go a long way to getting you what you want!"

"Major Hallonquist was impressed with my daring and devotion to my brother." The dimple beside her mouth gave her a self-mocking appearance.

Gabriel grunted. "I grant you, he was taken in. But don't pull a stunt like that again without checking with me first."

She slanted a look up at him. "You're the boss, right?"

"Yes." He stared her down.

She gave him a slow and completely female smile. "We'll see about that."

As the lighthouse at Mobile Point came into view, Gabriel began to take mental notes. Admiral Farragut would need detailed information in order to plan any future invasion of the port.

What Gabriel had seen so far assured him that Mobile would fall like an overripe peach whenever Farragut was given clearance to attack. Competition between Rebel gulf coast army and navy command had led to confusion and jealousy, a deadly combination in any war effort. Troops were enthusiastic, but poorly armed and sketchily trained. The fort on Dauphin Island was a disaster, though Major Hallonquist seemed to be struggling to correct the mess. It remained to be seen if Fort Morgan, under Colonel William Powell's command, would be any better.

Gabriel and Camilla disembarked at the engineer's wharf, along with a small wagonload of supplies and building materials. The parapet wall along the top of the star-shaped fort appeared to be in excellent repair. Cannons poked through the small embrasures in the corner bastions. Only a swift and strong naval force would bluster past this Confederate stronghold.

The two gray-clad soldiers in charge of moving the wagon onto the wharf nudged one another and grinned behind Camilla's back as she strode toward the glacis— the cleared ground sloping upward toward the fort. Gabriel, following at a more leisurely pace, paid little attention until one of the men whistled.

"Hey, honey bunch," the man called, "you want a ride in on my wagon?"

Camilla walked faster. She had almost reached the

tunnel that led through the glacis, when the loudmouthed soldier caught a handful of her hair and jerked her to a stop. Her eyes widened.

Gabriel quickened his pace.

"Let me go." Camilla pulled at the big hand holding her hair. "I've got business in the fort."

The soldier looked at his snickering friend. "Let's see your pass, sweetheart."

As the man poked into Camilla's pockets, Gabriel approached. "The lady's with me. Let her go."

The soldier reluctantly released Camilla's hair. "Some lady. Dressed like a— Ow!"

Camilla had stomped hard on the man's instep. She stalked into the sandy tunnel without a word of thanks to Gabriel. He followed, catching up to her just as she exited the postern into the dry ditch surrounding the fort.

"Don't say it!" She whirled to face him.

"Don't say what?"

"You know what. I could have handled that oaf! I'm only letting you come along because I might need your help to get out to Jamie's ship. But don't get the idea that you're in charge. You hear me?"

Gabriel took the last step, put a gently cupped fist under her chin, and bent so close that he could have kissed her—if he'd had a mind to get his ears boxed. "I see it this way. You and I need each other. Now, you may not approve of my methods, and I sure don't approve of yours. But we can get a lot more accomplished if we work together." He let her think that through and watched her expression go from mutiny to reluctant agreement. "There's a certain underwater vessel that I believe your father is bankrolling. I hope my helping your brother will make your daddy trust me enough to give me access to his business ventures. If you're on my side, like you claim to be, you've got to trust me, you've got to *help* me—not keep balking every step of the way. Do *you* hear *me?*"

"I hear you." When she curled her hand around his wrist, he felt it down to his bones. "Gabriel, I'm scared for Jamie, and I'm scared for my papa."

He dropped his hand, breaking her hold on his wrist. "You've got good reason to be scared. But I think I can help. Let's see if we can find—" he consulted the pass given to him by Major Hallonquist "—Colonel Powell."

Though she would never have admitted it, Camilla had been shaken by those two soldiers handling her so familiarly. When Gabriel introduced her to the garrison commander as the sister of Captain Beaumont, she nodded and faded into the background, allowing Gabriel's glib tongue to finagle a small rowboat to take them out to Jamie's ship.

On the water again, Camilla sat in the bow of the boat and watched Gabriel pull the oars. He had removed his coat and rolled up his sleeves, and the bunching and stretching of his muscles gave her an odd feeling in the pit of her stomach. She couldn't help thinking about the way he'd looked at her after he'd protected her from those men outside the fort. He must be a successful agent for the United States. He seemed to have an uncanny knack for getting what he wanted.

And what he wanted, among other things, was information about that fish boat. Camilla sighed, trailing her hand in the water.

Gabriel caught her gaze. "How long has your brother been running the blockade?"

"It's his third run. He got through easily the first time,

but the second was a close call. The blockade's tightening."

"You'd think food and supplies would be less readily available if the blockade was really effective."

"What do you mean?"

Gabriel flexed his big shoulders. "I wonder if there's some kind of collusion between the blockaders and the runners. By all rights, your brother ought to be at the bottom of the gulf."

"You're heartless!" Camilla glared at him.

He lifted an arm to wipe the sweat off his nose. "I told you, there's a difference between war and medicine."

"That's absurd. Jamie's not a Confederate officer. He's just a merchant captain. Why should he be under attack?"

Gabriel gave her a dry look. "Surely you don't think the only thing on that ship is food and clothing."

"Maybe not, but—" Camilla floundered, then brightened. "Look, we're almost there!"

She could scarcely sit still as they neared the *Lady Camilla*. The sixty-foot light-draft vessel had a twelve-inch hole right above her waterline. Her boats were shot-riddled; the fore topmast and fore gaff were cut away, and the rigging sagged like a toy some child had thrown down in a tantrum. She appeared to have been hulled again and again. It was amazing the ship had survived the attack.

As she and Gabriel hauled up alongside the *Lady C,* several excited and scruffy-looking sailors leaned over the lower deck rail. A rope ladder plopped over the side. Camilla scrambled up it, glad of her male attire. Managing skirts and crinolines on such a venture would have been next to impossible. As it was, she nimbly landed on her feet on deck and shook hands with a grinning mate, leaving Gabriel to his own devices.

"Miss Camilla!" The mate's rust-colored hair was bound out of his eyes with a bandanna. "What are you doing out here? Cap'n Beaumont didn't say nothing about you coming!"

"How is he, Rudy?" Camilla scanned the gaunt face of the *Lady C*'s first officer. "How are you?"

"Gettin' better, thank you, miss. The cap'n ain't doing so well, though. And he'll hide me for lettin' you on board. We'll be under quarantine for another week at least."

Gabriel interrupted. "I think he'll be glad to see us. We brought quinine."

Camilla caught his sleeve, pulling him forward. "Rudy, this is Gabriel Leland. He purchased the medicine and escorted me from Mobile."

Rudy Van Zandt frowned, despite his obvious pleasure in seeing Camilla. "Your papa knows where you are?"

"Of course he does. Reverend Gabriel is a friend of the family."

"Hmph. We'll see what the cap'n has to say." Rudy led the way to the captain's stateroom, muttering to himself and sending Gabriel dark looks. Camilla's heart nearly stopped when she saw that the cabin wall had been smashed by a shell, then roughly patched. Had Jamie been wounded?

Rudy knocked on the door and waited for an answer. At Jamie's "Come!" the mate stuck his head in. "Visitors, sir!"

"Tell them to get off this ship immediately!"

Camilla shoved past Rudy and faced her brother, who

sat at a small desk making notes. "I've come all the way from Mobile to bring you some medicine, Jamie Beaumont. You'd better find your manners, whether you're dying or not!" She held on to her anger to keep from sobbing at the sight of his pale and exhausted face.

"Camilla! What are you doing here?"

"I told you, I brought you some medicine."

"Well, turn around and go home the same way you got here." Jamie went back to his notes as if the discussion were over.

"I can't. They won't let us back into the fort."

Jamie stood, hanging on to the back of his chair. "What idiot gave a lone woman a pass into the fort?"

"I'm not—"

"She's with me." Gabriel moved to stand beside her, an amused quirk to his mouth.

"And who are you?"

Gabriel reached around Camilla to extend his hand to Jamie. "Gabriel Leland. Your reputation speaks highly of you, Captain Beaumont."

Jamie shook hands, but his expression remained suspicious. "Mr. Leland."

"*Reverend* Leland," Camilla put in. "The new Methodist minister. He arrived a day or two after you went to sea."

Jamie wobbled. "Excuse me if I sit, Reverend Leland. Still a mite weak at the knees."

"Call me Gabriel."

Jamie nodded. "We can use the medicine, but I must say, I don't appreciate your exposing my sister to infection."

"Have you ever made your sister stay put when she wanted to go somewhere?"

Jamie laughed. "Only once that I can think of."

Camilla scowled. "And you paid dearly for it, didn't you?"

"Sounds like a story I'd like to hear." Gabriel looked down at Camilla, eyebrows raised.

She shook her head and hopped up onto Jamie's desk. "It's not a pleasant memory." She laid her palm gently against her brother's bearded face. "How are you feeling?"

"I'm past the worst of it, but several of my men were killed by the Federals, and many more are still ill from the fever. I've done what I can for them, which God knows wasn't much." He leaned his head in his hand.

"You need rest." Camilla squeezed his slumped shoulder. "You should stay in your bunk and let Rudy take command."

"I'm captain." Jamie straightened, his gray eyes hardening. "I brought us through the blockade, and I'll take us into port."

"How did you slip through?" Gabriel asked.

Jamie smiled. "Would have been easy as pie, if it hadn't been for that dang rooster we picked up in Cardenas."

Camilla leaned back on her hands, giddy with relief now that she was sure Jamie wasn't going to expire before her eyes. "What were you doing with a rooster on board?"

"We've got a hold full of chickens. Mr. Chambliss—"

"He hires the ship," Camilla informed Gabriel. "You met his daughter, Fanny."

"Right. Anyway," continued Jamie, "he was convinced he could make a killing off chickens and eggs, so he insisted we buy some when we stopped in Bermuda. I forgot about the rooster until we'd just entered the Gulf Stream, and were almost past the blockaders."

Gabriel's smiled broadened into a grin. "How long did it take you to wring the bird's neck?"

"About thirty seconds. Then, danged if we didn't hear another cock-a-doodle-doo a minute later. It was so dark we'd killed the wrong bird!"

Camilla laughed. "From the looks of the *Lady C*, the Federals resented their early wake-up call."

Jamie sobered. "I'm just sorry my guns weren't rigged to return fire."

Gabriel looked interested. "Why weren't they?"

"We had less than eighteen hours to transfer guns, ammunition and equipment from a British schooner just off the coast of Nassau." Jamie snorted. "I was already down with the fever and couldn't be everywhere. Little things like rammers, sponges, sights, locks and elevating screws got left behind."

Camilla regarded her brother with horror. "You were virtually defenseless!"

"Remarkable that you got through," Gabriel murmured.

Camilla thought of his conspiracy theory. But Jamie wouldn't be in collusion with the Yankees any more than—well, come to think of it, her own loyalties were divided. Anything was possible. She met Gabriel's sideways look, then glanced away.

"The good Lord was on our side." Jamie got to his feet, looking weary. "Since you came all this way with that medicine, we might as well put it to use. Where is it?"

"Left it with your first officer," Gabriel said. "Seems to be a capable chap."

"Best of the best." Jamie nodded. "He'll know what to do with it. Not to be inhospitable, but you'd better get my sister home."

Camilla caught his hand. "But, Jamie—"

Jamie shook his head. "Tell Father I'll be home in a sennight, thanks to you and the preacher." He nodded at Gabriel, then paused, a sudden frown between his sandy brows. "You look familiar. Have we met before?"

Gabriel smiled. "I don't see how. My family's all from Mississippi."

Jamie moved to close the door. "You look a lot like a wild-eyed half-breed my cousin Harry used to run around with in medical school. Small world, I suppose." He winked at Camilla. "Tell Van Zandt if he lets any more visitors on board he'll be demoted to cabin boy!"

"Major Hallonquist said after we left Jamie's ship we weren't to come back to Fort Gaines." Camilla gave Gabriel a troubled look as the ferry shoved off into the choppy late-afternoon waters of Pelican Bay, which separated the two forts. In concession to the sun, rapidly falling in the west but still shooting a blinding glare off the water, she'd taken refuge in a canvas chair under the canopy.

Gabriel leaned against the rail. "We're going to skirt around the fort—the major will never see us. Besides, we couldn't give anybody yellow fever if we wanted to."

"But we were right there with all those poor sailors— and Jamie was still sick as could be."

"You don't get the fever from people, Camilla. It's carried by mosquitoes."

"Everybody knows it's one of the most contagious—"

"Everybody *doesn't* know it. If you asked your erudite Dr. Kinch, he'd tell you he's been trying for years to prove a theory advanced by one of his former medical students." He shrugged. "Who knows what blunders he's made in his experiments."

Camilla's pretty mouth was ajar. "Are you telling me you were a student of Dr. Kinch? And you can prove what causes yellow fever?"

"I was on my way to proving it. But there was a... scandal that discredited my work. For two years, Professor Kinch ridiculed my theory. Then, before I left medical college, he confiscated my papers. I don't know what he did with them."

"How is it that he hasn't recognized you?"

"I had a full beard and mustache then, and much longer hair. I was younger and skinnier." Gabriel lifted his hands. "You have to understand, too, that I was the charity case. You should've seen my clothes. Kinch was the dean of the college and did his best not to see me."

Camilla sat silent, staring at the water. Despite the heat, she'd replaced her cap and still wore her baggy coat. Faint dewy drops lay on her upper lip, and her eyelids drooped. She'd endured tremendous discomfort in the past twenty-four hours for her brother's sake.

And they weren't home yet, by any means.

She looked up at him, frowning. "Did Harry know about your theories and experiments?"

"Harry was more interested in doing what was necessary to graduate than messing around with mosquitoes in a laboratory."

"That would be Harry." Camilla smiled faintly.

"He didn't laugh at me, like most people did, but he had other things to occupy his time. Your family, for one thing."

"He was at our house a lot, of course, but he was always bringing someone with him. Why didn't you…"

"He invited me, but I chose not to accept." Gabriel smiled at her discomfort. "You saw my uncle's house. I didn't have the money or the inclination to dress or behave in a way that would have been acceptable to your family."

"I'd have welcomed any friend of Harry's."

"You were a schoolgirl at the time." He cast her an assessing look. "Your big brother once put me in my place, you know."

She leaned forward, elbows on knees. "He seemed to recognize you."

"Probably would have, if I'd been wearing the war paint they smeared all over me that night."

She drew a sharp breath. "Jamie wouldn't be so cruel!"

"It was a joke." He shrugged. "To give your brother credit, he tried to get the others to stop. But he and I were both about thirty pounds lighter, and—it was over pretty quick."

"Where was Harry?"

Her patent horror sent a rush of gratitude flooding through Gabriel. "Poking feathers in my hair. He thought the whole thing was hilarious."

Camilla closed her eyes and swallowed.

"Look." He took her wrist and surprised them both by dropping a brief kiss on her knuckles. She stared at him wide-eyed. "I wouldn't change anything that's happened to me, because it made me strong and self-reliant. Nothing and nobody surprises me anymore. Remember this, Camilla Beaumont—you can't trust *anyone*." He couldn't quite trust her, either. Yet he'd given more truth to her in the past two days than he'd given to another living soul. He dropped her hand. "I wish I could have proved the mosquito theory."

"Didn't anybody believe you?"

"People believe what they want to believe."

"You could still prove it—"

"Dr. Kinch or somebody else eventually will." Gabriel turned his gaze toward the reddening sun, against which the sandy beach of Dauphin Island and the flags of Fort Gaines began to appear. "We'll be docking in a few minutes." He started to rise.

"Gabriel, are you a believer?"

The tone of Camilla's voice more than her words stopped him. "I believe in the United States of America. I believe in the strong protecting and defending the weak. I believe in myself."

"Those are good things." She hesitated, her gaze intent on his face. "But do you believe God has a purpose for you—that He loves you enough to give His Son for you?"

The glow of Camilla's face, the simple question filled with power and eloquence, caught him. He'd heard several hundred hellfire-and-brimstone sermons in his lifetime, but preachers didn't often mention God and love and purpose in the same sentence.

He avoided Camilla's tender eyes. She made him want to believe. "We'd better get moving. I've got to figure out a way to get us on the northbound packet without crossing paths with the military." He stood abruptly.

Camilla bowed her head.

As they slipped across the gangplank of the ferry, Gabriel glanced at his companion. Her face was composed, but a couple of telltale streaks tracked through the dust on her cheeks.

He told himself it was time she grew up.

Chapter Ten

By the time the packet chugged through Pinto Pass, just off the quay of Mobile, heavy clouds had moved off the gulf, hiding the setting sun and threatening to dump their contents on the city. The leaden atmosphere suited Camilla's mood.

People believe what they want to believe.

Gabriel's cynical observation clanged through her thoughts. If it was true, then there was no hope for anyone. All mankind must be captive to experience. Where did faith fit in? Where did God Himself fit in?

Camilla followed Gabriel along Water Street, hurrying to keep pace with his loose, swinging stride. He'd insisted on accompanying her home. They both knew there was going to be trouble when they got there. Camilla's stomach clenched with apprehension.

"What am I going to do about my clothes?" She tugged Gabriel's coat sleeve. Except for a shadow of beard, he looked the picture of immaculate propriety. She knew she must look like a proper wild woman.

Gabriel stopped to survey her in the twilight. They had entered the residential block of Government Street, and the noise of Saturday night downtown had faded until the only sounds were cicadas singing in the trees and leaves rustling with the brewing storm. "You *are* a mite dirty, Miss Beaumont."

"You know what I mean! Lady will lock me in my room for a month if I come in dressed like this. I should go in through my window, change my clothes—"

"You should march in and tell the truth. The more lies you tell, the worse it gets."

She raised her eyebrows. "Says the arbiter of the truth himself!"

"Absolutely." He grinned. "Come on, I'll be right there with you." He bounded up the front steps and pulled the brass knob of the doorbell.

Portia swung the great mahogany door wide. "Reverend Gabriel! Miss Camilla!" She fisted her hands at her hips. "Where in the name of Jehoshaphat you been all day? Your papa's fit to be tied!"

Camilla heard her grandmother call from the direction of the drawing room. "If that's Camilla, tell her to present herself immediately."

She looked at Gabriel. "We're in for it now."

He gave her a gentle shove toward the doorway. "Remember, tell the truth."

Camilla lifted her chin, swept off her cap and marched toward the drawing room. Her boots thunked loudly on the hardwood floors, the sound of Gabriel's footsteps behind her comforting.

She burst into the drawing room. "Lady, I'm sorry I missed the meeting, but Reverend Gabriel and I— Oh, gracious..."

Several gray-clad officers stared at her, teacups halted halfway to whiskery faces. Scones and brightly colored jellies and delicate petits fours filled a flowered tray on the center table.

She found her grandmother, a splash of saffron amidst the sober uniforms of the men, seated in the Sleepy Hollow chair, a silken fan hiding her expression. After several beats of silence, Lady snapped the fan shut. "Camilla, as you can see, we have houseguests." She turned to a gentleman with an enormous amount of braid decorating his uniform. "General Forney, I'd like you to meet my granddaughter. Camilla is quite famous for her grand entrances."

Camilla sat across the Sunday-morning breakfast table from her grandmother. Head propped against her hand, she idly moved her grits from one side of her plate to the other.

Lady cleared her throat. "You look lovely this morning."

Camilla looked up with a small smile. "Thank you, Lady." She wore her best jonquil gauze gown, with her mother's locket fastened round her throat and the camellia earrings dangling from her lobes. Her curls were caught at her nape with a pearl clasp. Certainly she was in better looks than last Saturday evening when she had humiliated herself in front of all those soldiers.

The grits took another excursion across the plate.

"You've been as blue as a barefoot Eskimo ever since you got back from Fort Morgan," said Lady with a frown. "I hope you're not coming down with the fever."

Camilla shook her head. "I'm just tired. It's an honor to have General Forney recovering here with us, but two invalids—him and Jamie—is a lot of extra work."

Lady reached over and lifted Camilla's chin. "I don't think it's fatigue causing that pensive face."

Camilla felt her cheeks heat.

Lady sat up. "It's Reverend Leland, isn't it?"

Camilla turned her face away to hide her chagrin. "He could have come to inquire after Jamie."

"As a matter of fact, he did and asked if he could talk to you at your earliest convenience."

"Why didn't you tell me?"

Lady sniffed. "I just did. I suggested he take you out this very afternoon after church, for a drive down the Bay Shell Road and a picnic."

"Without asking me? Jamie will expect me to read to him this afternoon—"

"As church starts in less than an hour, it's too late to back out." Lady held out a hand. "May I borrow your butter knife, dear? Mine seems to have disappeared."

Camilla picked up the knife and gasped. It was upside-down. Portia had been passing "railroad" messages to her this way for years.

Lady frowned. "What is it?"

"Nothing." Camilla pushed back her chair. "I'm not feeling well. You go on to church without me."

Lady forestalled Camilla as she started to rise with a commanding hand on her arm. "What's in that knife?"

"Nothing!"

"Give it here."

"Don't be silly, it's just a knife."

"Then you won't mind letting me see it."

The day she'd dreaded for years had arrived without warning. With a shaking hand, Camilla laid the knife in her grandmother's soft palm.

Lady deftly unscrewed the blade of the knife. She

held the halves in her two hands and looked at Camilla, who waited, lips pressed together. Lady pulled a small roll of paper from the handle. She scanned it, then held it out to Camilla.

Swallowing tears, Camilla shook her head. "I left my spectacles upstairs. Will you read it to me?"

Surprise flickered in Lady's eyes. She hesitated, then unrolled the paper again. "'My dear Camilla, I pray that this letter reaches your eyes only—'"

Camilla snatched the paper and tried in vain to read the cramped script. Tears of relief further blurred her vision, but Harry's signature swam at her from the bottom of the page. Lady's discovery of her correspondence with her cousin was very bad indeed, but at least the secret of the underground railroad was still safe. "It's from Harry," she said foolishly, handing the letter back to her grandmother.

Lady smiled slightly and smoothed the paper. "'Your eyes only,'" she repeated, "'for my entire regiment could be endangered if this falls into the wrong hands. But I knew you would be wondering what has become of me since our last communication. I know it must be difficult for you to keep our secret. I trust that your affections have not changed. Mine have only grown stronger as the months have passed and as the danger has increased.'

"'Rumor says Grant has set his sights on Pascagoula. This causes me great anxiety, since it is uncomfortably near Mobile. Grant is an ambitious and intrepid commander. I pray your family will remain safe, and that Uncle Ezekiel will have the sense to evacuate in the event of attack.'" Lady's voice faltered. "'Corinth was a bloodbath, as you can imagine—' Camilla, he was at Corinth!"

"Was he hurt?" Camilla held her stomach in an agony of suspense.

"No, he says, 'I was kept miraculously from harm. I have been working around the clock, sewing bodies back together and removing parts that could not be redeemed. Oh, Camilla, may God spare you from sights that I have seen these past three days! I am worn to the bone, but as soon as the wounded have been posted to the nearest hospital, I will join my regiment in the march south. Grant is determined to control Southern waterways. I can think of nothing more horrible than invading a part of the country almost as dear to me as my home county in Tennessee. But, my dearest Camilla, I cannot deny my duty to country. I beg you to flee, should our Union forces threaten Mobile. I will pray for you every day until I hear that you are safe. Meantime, remember me to our Father in heaven. Your Harry.'"

Camilla pressed the back of her hand to her mouth. She blinked tears away and realized Lady had dropped the letter.

Her grandmother's closed eyes looked sunken with age, the lids thin as parchment. "That it should come to family marching against family. A healer turned soldier."

"I'm sorry," Camilla said in agony. "You know I've always loved him."

"Like a brother," Lady said harshly. "But he left us and went back to Union Tennessee. Harry made his choice, Camilla. He chose the other side."

"That doesn't change his love for us—his love for me." Camilla felt the blood flow to her cheeks.

"Look at me, Camilla." Her grandmother's pale eyes were fierce. "Remember this—war changes more things than you can comprehend. If we come to the end of this nightmare, and your estimation of Harry has not changed—if you can revere him above any man you've ever known, if you're convinced he's God's best choice for you—then you may marry him with my blessing. But please, my dear one, do not let pity or sentiment or even loyalty cheat you of that best choice. Do you understand me?"

"Yes, Lady." But Camilla wondered if she did understand.

Gabriel handed Camilla down from the high seat of the open gig he'd hired from the Battle House livery, then tied the horse to a mimosa bending close to the shell road leading out to Spring Hill.

"Lovely weather for a picnic," she said primly and marched toward the creek meandering a few yards away.

"Indeed it is." Gabriel tossed his felt hat into the rear of the gig, removed his coat and followed Camilla with a blanket and picnic basket hooked over one arm. He flipped the blanket across the grass and began to set out the lunch that Portia had packed while the family was at church. "If your conversation continues to take this scintillating tack, however, I may be enveloped in the arms of Morpheus before lunch rather than after."

She put her hands on her hips. "Oh, stuff it."

"I plan to, as soon as you join me on the blanket." He smiled at her, squatting with an arm resting across one knee. "Camilla, I'm getting awfully hungry."

She hesitated, then plopped to her knees in a billow of yellow gauze. "What's in the basket?"

They feasted on fried chicken, biscuits with strawberry preserves and dewberry cobbler still warm from the oven. When every bone had been picked clean and every crumb rescued, Gabriel leaned against a tree trunk, hands clasped across his stomach. Camilla reclined on her elbows, feet tucked beneath her skirt.

She pulled a small feathered and beaded fan from her pocket. Gabriel looked ready to fall asleep, yet she knew he could be alert in an instant. "Why did you invite me out today?"

He opened one eye. "Wanted to see what you've been up to. Climbed out any windows lately?"

"No. But I'm surprised you didn't know that."

"I've kept an eye on you, but I've been busy this week. Weddings, funerals, hospitals… Just pure wore me out."

"Lady said you came to see Jamie." Camilla couldn't keep a trace of resentment from her voice. "You didn't even say hello."

"You were out running errands, I believe." A faint smile curved his lips. "So you missed me?"

"Like I miss a toothache!" He laughed, and Camilla hitched a little closer to him. "Seriously, Gabriel, a lot has happened, and I needed to talk to you."

Both eyes opened. "You send word to me day or night and I'll come." Though his lazy posture didn't change, she knew she had his full attention. "You hear me?"

She nodded.

"Good. Now what is it?"

"I've been thinking about this boat thing."

"The boat? You mean the torpedo boat? What do you know about it?"

"Not much. The night you and I met—you remember—"

"Believe me, that night is forever limned on my memory."

"Well, as I was entering the house, I passed an open

window, and heard my papa talking about a machine shop. That's where the plans are. They called it a fish boat."

Gabriel sat up, eyes on fire. "What else did you hear?"

"They said they'd already scuttled one prototype of the boat when the Yanks took New Orleans. They're rebuilding it here, and—and they did mention one other name." Camilla hesitated. The more she'd thought about it the less sense it made. Maybe she'd misunderstood. "The other man said somebody named Laniere was working on fixing a propeller problem."

Gabriel stared at her. "My uncle Diron is involved somehow. I think he's engineering the metal construction. I saw the plans on his worktable at the foundry a couple of weeks ago."

Camilla picked up a napkin and began to pleat it. "You've got to spy on your uncle, and I have to spy on my papa."

Gabriel pressed his lips together. Apparently he had some sort of conscience after all.

She sighed. "What do you want me to do?"

"Keep your mouth shut and your ears open." He gave her a sharp look. "You haven't said anything about this to anyone else, have you?"

"I asked Jamie if he'd ever heard of such a thing, but he busted out laughing."

Gabriel let out a breath. "Who else?"

"I asked Portia if she knew anything about it—"

"You asked your mammy about an underwater boat?"

"For your information Portia is one of the smartest people I know! She's got more rank than I do, for that matter, in the 'railroad' organization." Camilla frowned at Gabriel. "You of all people shouldn't be prejudiced."

He raised his brows. "The woman is an uneducated slave. What would she know about a complicated military machine?"

"She's as educated as I am." At Gabriel's snort, she stiffened. "Lady taught her to read and write, and she's memorized big chunks of the Bible."

"That's certainly practical information."

"You're hopeless." Camilla bounced to her knees and threw the napkin at him. "Why should I tell you anything else?"

"All right, cool down." Gabriel propped his arms on his bent knees. "Let me think. Your brother probably paid no attention to you, and Portia has her own reasons to keep quiet. But in the future you've got to keep this between you and me. You understand?"

"Yes. But I want to help."

"Then you've got to get me into your papa's office. I don't know where they're building the vessel, and I can't get Uncle Diron to talk. I want to find out where it is, look at it, see if it's really a threat. And if it is…"

"What are you going to do?"

"I'm going to destroy it—and the builders and financiers—and take the plans to Washington, so they can build one of their own."

Camilla stared at him. "But that means Papa and your uncle!"

He looked away. "Do you think the general is involved in any way?"

"General Forney? I don't know. We've hardly seen him since he came, he's been so ill from his wounds. His personal staff cares for him, for the most part."

"I need you to try to find out any orders he has from Richmond, plans he's making for fortification of the city, particularly the forts down at the gulf." Gabriel rubbed his temples. "You're in a strategic position to gather intelligence, Camilla."

Swallowing the lump in her throat, she nodded. "There's something else, Gabriel."

"What?"

"It's Harry. I got a letter from him this morning. Lady intercepted it."

His hand shot out to grasp her wrist. "How did that happen?"

"Portia sometimes passes me important communication inside a hollow butter knife at breakfast. Lady must have suspected for some time—I don't know, she just grabbed it and opened it."

"So your family didn't know you'd been corresponding with him. What did the old lady say?"

"It was strange. She didn't seem near as mad as she was when I came home last Saturday wearing trousers. I think she almost felt sorry for me."

"So as far as she's concerned, it's just a forbidden romance." Gabriel's lip curled.

"That's right," Camilla said evenly. "Harry's in Corinth, preparing to march south with Grant."

"He's well, then?"

She nodded. "Yes, but he's tired. He thinks Grant may attack Pascagoula, then Mobile."

Gabriel shrugged. "Unlikely. Not enough at stake down here, as far as I can tell." His black eyes glinted. "Except maybe for that fish boat."

Chapter Eleven

"How are you feeling this morning?" Camilla stood at the doorway of Jamie's room with a breakfast tray, bringing with her the smell of sausage and eggs and Portia's biscuits. She walked in, noting the fading yellowish cast of her brother's face and the slight droop of his eyelids. The entire family was concerned that after a week he hadn't completely rebounded from the fever. He spent most of the day in his bed looking out the window.

Still, Jamie was home, and he would recover. They were lucky he was alive. She touched the locket at her throat.

Jamie brightened as he looked up from his book. "My appetite must be coming back. That smells wonderful."

"Oh, good!" Camilla beamed at him. He had eaten but little since Horace and Willie had half carried him up the stairs. Gabriel said hunger was a good sign.

She set the tray across his lap and pulled a ladder-backed chair close to the bed. The room, from curtains to furniture, was designed on Spartan lines. Navy checks on the bed and at the windows, simple braided rugs on the floors, plain pine dresser and armoire, and uncushioned wooden chairs. Her brother was a sailor through and through.

Jamie uncovered the plate and tucked into his breakfast with initial gusto, but his shrunken stomach filled quickly. "I can't hold any more," he said. He wearily laid down his fork and leaned back against the pillow.

"Portia's going to come stomping in here and accuse me of starving you." Camilla moved the tray to the dresser. "She'd force-feed you herself, if she weren't so busy with the general and his staff." When he smiled without opening his eyes, Camilla smoothed the sandy, unkempt hair from his forehead. "You need a haircut. I could get my scissors…"

Jamie opened one eye. "Did you come in here to cheer me up, or is this your way of sending me to an early grave from sheer irritation?"

Giving his hair a gentle tug, she sat down. "Jamie, please tell me you're not going out again, with the blockade so tight. You almost didn't make it through this time!"

"The Yankees can't keep the *Lady C* from sailing. Chambliss pays me good money to make sure they don't."

"Is it true General Forney ordered all cotton to be burned or moved to the interior? Won't that weaken our trade relationship with Europe?"

Jamie's eyebrows climbed. "What's got you worrying your pretty little head about trade deficits? General Forney knows what he's doing."

"But it doesn't make any sense!"

Jamie sighed. "He's afraid any cotton left down here will encourage the Federals to attack. I'd heard the general's first inclination was to evacuate, but he's promised to defend the city."

Camilla picked up her brother's spyglass propped against a water pitcher on the bedside table and aimed it at the open window. "My goodness, this is amazing! You can see all the way into— Jamie! That's Mayella Honeycutt's bedroom!"

He snatched the glass from her hand. "Believe me, I don't feel like peeping into anybody's bedroom." He collapsed the instrument and placed it in the drawer of the table. "What were you going to say?"

Distracted by the possibilities of a spyglass, Camilla stared blankly at Jamie for a moment, then blinked. "You don't think the Yankees will attack here, do you? I heard rumors in church Sunday that Grant's marching south through Mississippi."

Jamie sobered. "I heard that, too, but I doubt he'll make it this far."

Camilla swallowed hard. "What if Harry's with him? Doesn't the idea of fighting against your cousin—your best friend—give you the willies?"

"Harry chose his side." His words echoed Lady's. "And I chose mine. I choose to fight for independence and states' rights. I didn't vote for Mr. Abe Lincoln, and he's not going to tell me how to run my life."

"But what about Horace and Portia and Willie? Don't you see that we're doing the same thing to them? Running their lives without their say-so?"

Jamie's wintry eyes told her she'd gone too far. "You don't know what you're saying."

Frightened, she backpedaled. "Maybe not... I just wondered."

"Camilla, you leave political maneuvering to your menfolk." Jamie closed his eyes again. "I believe I'll have one more biscuit before you take the tray. Oh, and ask Papa to stop in when he gets home tonight."

Camilla squelched the urge to fling the tray at her brother's head. Menfolk. If they were as quick to listen as they were to give orders, the world would be a better place.

The soil was still moist from an early afternoon rain shower as Camilla set her bucket of fertilizer on the garden path and pulled on a pair of work gloves. Dressed in her oldest gown, a faded black-and-yellow plaid two-piece protected by a white cotton apron, she knelt in front of her grandmother's prize day lilies.

Lady supervised from the screened porch, one foot propped on a gout stool. "Don't stint on the fish heads, miss!" she called.

Trying not to breathe, Camilla dug in.

Several days had passed since her conversation with Jamie. He'd given her a sharp look once or twice when the subject of the general's plans to defend Mobile came up at family dinners; however, as his health returned, Jamie's impatience to be back aboard his ship took precedence over concern for Camilla.

Relieved, she found other avenues of gathering information. The military personnel who tracked in and out of General Forney's temporary quarters either ignored or patronized the slaves—and Camilla, too, for that matter. They spoke freely and disparagingly of Flag Officer Randolph's "cockleshell gunboats" stationed near the city, wondering loudly if they would withstand a Federal attack.

There was talk, too, of a massive movement of Confederate troops through the city by rail. Camilla, a railroad man's daughter, understood more of their conversation than they realized. Now that Corinth had fallen to the Union, the M & O was literally the only Confederate link by rail between east and west.

She stopped digging to shove her spectacles upward with the back of her wrist. The trouble was, she didn't understand the implications of all the intelligence she absorbed. She'd memorized numbers of troops, commanders' names, and often slipped back to her room to draw little maps of fortifications she heard described. To her untrained mind, however, it was mostly a soup of unrelated scraps of data.

Then there was the underwater boat. Short of rifling Papa's study, she couldn't see any way to discover its whereabouts, as Gabriel had asked her to. Portia refused to discuss it, Jamie was for obvious reasons out of the question, and Lady—

"Young man!" shrieked that matron with a sudden thunk of the cane against the wooden porch floor. "I'll thank you to take those oversize boots out of my flower garden, if you please!"

A startled young officer murdered one more day lily before leaping onto the flagged path beside Camilla. Flushing, he met her eyes. "Sorry, miss—ma'am?"

"It's quite all right. One less mouth for me to feed, so to speak." She nodded toward the porch, where Lady sat drumming her fingers on the arm of her chair. "It's my grandmother who's rather attached to the little blighters."

He pulled out a handkerchief and mopped his face. "I wasn't watching—I'm newly appointed to the general's staff and thought I'd take a shortcut   ma'am? Miss? Do you live here?" Admiration filled his blue eyes.

Camilla glanced down at her muddy dress and stinking gloves. "I do. I'm Miss Camilla Beaumont."

He didn't seem to mind that she had declined to offer her hand. "I'm Second Lieutenant Israel Duvall." He grinned and bowed. "And I'm going to be *Private* Duvall if I don't hurry. But, *miss,* I hope to see you again—very soon!" He turned to Lady with another engaging grin. "Sorry, ma'am!" Whistling, he continued around toward the front of the house, keeping to the path.

When he was out of sight, Camilla burst into giggles.

Lady contented herself with a dry smile as she leaned her chin on the knob of her cane. "You're slow on the uptake, my girl."

"What do you mean?" Camilla picked up her trowel again.

"Fanny Chambliss would have secured an afternoon drive at the very least."

Camilla scowled. "I could do better than that."

"Prove it to me. We'll host a subscription ball—for the benefit of the troops, of course. The first girl to obtain a waltz with the lieutenant will be crowned queen of the ball."

"That would hardly be fair, since I've already met him!"

Lady raised her thin brows. "And you think Fanny hasn't? My dear, you greatly underestimate your foe."

Wearing a new black frock coat, ruffled white shirt with starched collar and evening trousers, Gabriel stood at the Beaumonts' front door. After Horace admitted him and took his hat, Gabriel stopped at the pier-glass mirror that dominated one wall of the grand foyer to straighten the knot of his black cravat. He had to credit Camilla for following through on her promise to get him into the house with the chance to rub shoulders with relaxed and—if he was lucky—slightly drunk Confederate officers.

He eased his way through the garden of ruffled hoop skirts that crowded the ballroom and stopped to take his bearings. The Beaumonts showed more taste than most nouveau riche Southern aristocrats. A rather fine military orchestra, stowed in a minstrel's gallery overhead, was playing a lilting waltz. Great banks of flowers filled every surface and every corner, helping to cover the scents of so many warm bodies. Greek Revival-style columns, polished to a gleam, supported the ten-foot-high ceiling at wide intervals. The burgundy-colored silk draperies at the windows were woven with gold threads that glittered in the light of the magnificent crystal chandeliers. Expensive but not gaudy.

He scanned the room, hoping to catch sight of the master of the house. Mrs. St. Clair held court in one corner, rose-striped skirts spread about her. An officer in general's uniform—presumably General Forney—sat beside her, receiving the addresses of several well-dressed ladies.

Gabriel waited for the set to end, then crossed the room, greeting acquaintances as he went. As he stopped to exchange pleasantries with an acquaintance, Gabriel felt a hand rest on his shoulder. He turned to find Jamie Beaumont, resplendent in black evening dress, grinning at him.

"Beaumont!" Gabriel smiled and offered his hand. "Good to see you up and about."

Jamie shook hands. "Thanks to you and Camilla, I'm almost ready to take the *Lady C* out to sea again."

"Glad to hear it, though I suspect you were on the

mend already. Sounds like you've got another run through the blockade planned. Is that wise?"

Jamie frowned. "Why? Have you heard something?"

"No." Gabriel shrugged. "It seems a man of your talents would choose to invest them more directly in the Confederate cause. There has to be a naval force down here at the gulf—"

Jamie's amiable expression vanished. "I am excessively tired of the questioning of my family's loyalty to the South."

"But, my dear fellow—"

"The fact that my cousin chose to join the Union is no reflection on our—"

Gabriel lifted a palm. "What cousin?"

"Camilla didn't tell you we have a cousin who is a Union army surgeon?" Jamie looked sheepish.

"She didn't, but even if she had, it's obvious your family is above reproach."

Beaumont relaxed, though the expression in his gray eyes remained guarded.

Gabriel pursued the subject. "I simply wondered if— considering the tightening of the blockade, you know— there might be more profitable ventures closer to home."

"As to that, my father will keep me busy, I'm sure." Jamie looked down.

"I'd hoped to speak to him tonight."

"I'm afraid railroad business took him to the central part of the state. He should return within a few days."

"I see." Gabriel tried to look disappointed. "I found a fine Cuban cigar I wished to gain his opinion of, but I'll save it for another time."

"He'll appreciate that, I'm sure. Have you met our

houseguest?" Jamie nodded toward his grandmother's corner, where sets for a quadrille were being formed.

Gabriel hesitated. "We met briefly two weeks ago."

"Ah. Then you'll need no introduction."

Gabriel followed his host, who seemed oblivious to the young ladies gazing hopefully in his wake.

General John Forney shook hands with Gabriel. "Please forgive me, Reverend, if I'm not able to stand." Forney, a handsome man with a wiry dark beard, silver temples and piercing light green eyes, gave him a tired smile. "I had looked forward to the entertainment tonight, but I'd best conserve my strength."

"I understand." Gabriel assessed the general as a formidable force. He had distinguished himself with bravery at First Manassas and at Dranesville, and Richmond had consequently rewarded him with a promotion and the Mobile command. "Our congregation prays for your continued recovery."

Forney produced a dry smile. "I'd be grateful for any intervention with the Almighty you can send my way." He indicated Gabriel's cane. "It seems you owe your own existence to prayer. Mrs. St. Clair tells me you were at Shiloh."

"In a minor role. My leg hardly pains me at all these days."

"I daresay all it needs is a little exercise." Mrs. St. Clair deftly used her own cane to send Gabriel's clattering to the polished wood floor.

He instinctively found his balance, his startled gaze flicking to his hostess's bland countenance.

"Why, Reverend!" In a lesser individual, he would have called her expression a smirk. "I believe a miracle has occurred. Perhaps in celebration you could take my granddaughter onto the dance floor."

Camilla, hovering just within earshot, had been quietly giving instructions to one of the many servants hired for the occasion. At her grandmother's shocking behavior she shooed away the servant and turned, hands planted at her tiny waist.

Gabriel was hard put to keep his eyes in his head. Tonight, Camilla hardly looked like anybody's little sister. The lacy folds of the bertha collar of her gown draped gently below her shoulders, exposing a vast expanse of snowy throat and bosom.

He lifted his gaze to her face and found there an ironic smile very similar to her grandmother's. He gave her a jerky bow. "Miss Beaumont, I'd be honored."

The misplaced dimple appeared as she curtsied. Surrendering his cane to a servant, Gabriel took Camilla's gloved hand and escorted her into the formation of the quadrille.

"Are you sure you're up to this?" She peeped up at him as they waited for the music to start.

He surveyed her as thoroughly as he dared. She was exquisite tonight. Her hair, caught loosely off her face in a silken snood, was threaded at the top and sides with tiny white flowers and seed pearls. Her eyes were bright with mischief, her cheeks flushed with the warmth of the room.

"I imagine I can keep up with you," he said.

She seemed discomposed by his examination, her full lower lip caught by white teeth, cheeks stained an even brighter pink. He placed his thumb in the palm of her hand, pressed gently and held her gaze.

It was a small gesture, but shockingly intimate. Her

lips parted, and her eyes widened. With a down sweep of lashes as old as time, she flipped open her fan. "Why, Reverend, how can you keep up with someone who's not going anywhere?"

For the entirety of the dance, he found himself wondering what she meant. None the wiser by the end, he returned her to her grandmother's side, bowed and retrieved his cane. Leaning against the wall, the cane clamped under his arm, he watched Camilla accept a waltz with a young second lieutenant. They twirled gaily around the room, separated only by the width of Camilla's great hooped silk skirt. The lieutenant held the same hand Gabriel had just pressed, and she didn't seem to mind one bit. The boy's other hand rested lightly at her waist.

Camilla's hair was coming down as usual, curling wildly around her face. She looked, Gabriel thought, like a little hoyden. Well, no, to be fair, she looked—

He caught his thoughts going round in circles. It didn't make any difference how Camilla Beaumont looked, as long as she somehow got him into her father's study before the night was over.

As she circled the ballroom in Israel Duvall's arms, Camilla took perverse satisfaction in Gabriel Laniere's continued avoidance of her gaze. She could still feel the pressure of his callused finger in the center of her lace mitt.

But that was ridiculous. She gave Israel a dazzling smile and checked to make sure Gabriel saw.

Though he didn't seem to be looking, his lips tightened. Satisfied, Camilla allowed Second Lieutenant Duvall to dance her to the opposite end of the ballroom.

At the end of the waltz, the officer returned Camilla to her grandmother's side and bowed over her hand. As he straightened, his gaze slid over Camilla's shoulder. His blue eyes widened.

Camilla turned and sighed. Fanny Chambliss stood chatting with the general, delicately plying her embroidered fan. She looked like a fairy, her silvery tresses smoothly parted and arranged in complicated plaits at the back of her head. Her gown was icy blue, matching her eyes. Fanny had, of course, worn the same gown at every formal gathering within the past year—as had most women of the city, including Camilla—but Second Lieutenant Duvall wouldn't know that.

"Wh-who is that?" he stammered. "Will you introduce me?"

Camilla might have had the first waltz, but it looked like the last one would go to Fanny.

Suddenly a door slammed at the front of the house. Loud voices approached the ballroom. Camilla stood on tiptoe, craning to see over the heads of the men between her and the open doorway. The babble of questions and exclamations made her even more determined to discover the source of the excitement, which seemed to be making its way toward the general.

Lifting her skirts, she dodged across the crowded ballroom. As she reached her grandmother's side, a uniformed adjutant hastily removed his cap as he saluted his superior officer.

"Sir! Flag Officer Randolph sent me to inform you the Yankees have moved in on Fort Morgan."

At the sudden burst of consternation from the assembled crowd, General Forney stood painfully. "The Federals have been sitting in the gulf for six months, Sergeant.

What makes Captain Randolph think we're in imminent danger?"

"These aren't just blockaders. Looks like an iron-clad—maybe even two, best we can tell." The sergeant gulped. "He's afraid it might be Farragut, sir!"

A collective gasp muffled the general's calm response. Before Camilla could gain more than a vague under-standing that Randolph was to bring his squadron into the city, she sensed a tall, dark presence just over her left shoulder.

She looked up to find Gabriel Laniere's gaze mov-ing from her face to the doorway of the ballroom. It was time.

Without looking again at Gabriel, Camilla eased through the crowd. In the general air of hysteria pro-voked by the news from Fort Morgan, she attracted little attention. She waited outside the door for perhaps three minutes before Gabriel joined her.

"Didn't want to be seen leaving together," he said. "We've got to hurry."

She led the way toward the stairs. "Papa always locks his study. I don't know how we're going to get in."

"Show me the room, and I'll worry about that."

The ballroom, dining room and several parlors took up the first-floor entry level; the ground floor contained the breakfast room and other less formal family rooms, including her father's study.

When Camilla hesitated before the door, Gabriel waited for her to move aside. She stood looking up at him with her back to the door, hands on the doorknob.

He was all business, a frown marking two lines be-tween his brows. This man was ruthless, and she was about to expose her father to whatever he chose to do.

"Maybe this isn't a good time," she said. "What if somebody comes looking for me?"

"You can go back to the ball and cover for me." When she still refused to move, Gabriel expelled an impatient breath, picked her up by the waist and plunked her to the side. "Go on."

"No, I—if you find something, I want to know about it."

"Suit yourself." He shrugged and slipped a slim piece of steel that he had produced from a pocket into the keyhole. With a soft *snick,* the lock gave.

Camilla followed Gabriel into the dark room. "Should I lock the door back?"

"Yes." He lit an oil lamp resting on a table just inside the door and began to open desk drawers, methodically thumbing through papers and books.

Camilla sidled toward a big red chair and sat down with a creak of leather that sounded loud in the quiet room. She whispered, "What's going to happen to my father if you find what you're looking for?"

Gabriel closed the bottom right-hand drawer and stood up, dusting the knees of his trousers. He began to search through the clutter on the desktop. "I don't know. Depends on what I find."

"If, for example, you see that it's not such a dangerous thing after all, maybe it won't do what you think, or it costs too much or…something…will you go away and leave us alone?"

Gabriel set a marble paperweight down, then leaned across the desk, both hands flat. "You can get that out of your head right now. I know my uncle Diron's skills well enough to know that this vessel will do what they say it will do. As to how financially practicable it is—

well, that's something only your papa would know." He jerked his head toward the bookshelves that covered one whole wall. "So if you'll quit interrupting me—maybe even lend a hand—perhaps I'll discover that information before the sun comes up."

Camilla sat in offended silence for a minute. The sooner Gabriel found what he was looking for, the sooner they could get back to the ball. He was crouched at a bottom-row shelf, systematically removing books to search them one by one. She decided to start at the top.

She pulled the rolling ladder from its space beside the window, set it on the far side of the shelves from Gabriel and climbed, holding to the rail to balance her wide, bell-shaped crinoline.

After unsuccessfully searching the top shelf, Camilla moved her oil lamp down to the second and gave a squeak of excitement. Papa's ledgers—thick, heavy leather volumes, cracked and well-worn—were organized by date in bold black letters on the spines. She moved her finger down the row until she reached the last one, bearing a current date: *April, 1862.*

"Gabriel! Come look."

"What is it?" He looked up, the lamplight casting weird shadows across his cheeks and forehead.

She shivered. "I found Papa's ledgers. Maybe there's something about the fish boat in them."

"Maybe." He looked skeptical. "If I were him, I wouldn't keep a secret in so obvious a place." But he stood and crossed to the ladder. Before Camilla could object, Gabriel shoved her skirt to one side and climbed the narrow ladder to stand directly below her.

"What are you doing?" she gasped as he reached around her to the shelf she'd been searching.

"Which one?" His breath tickled her ear. He fingered the volumes.

Camilla pulled down the correct ledger and placed it in Gabriel's hands. Still embracing her, looking over her shoulder, he opened the book and thumbed through it. After a moment he slapped a forefinger onto a page. "Chambliss Brothers Machine Shop and—Skates Foundry. That must be where they're building the main body of the boat."

"Oh, my." Without her spectacles, Camilla could only take his word for it. "How much money…"

"Enough. Your papa's pretty full of lettuce, it seems."

Camilla let that settle hard. They'd been scrimping on household expenses for some time, at Papa's insistence, while he'd been funneling the family income into some torpedo boat that might or might not do what it was supposed to do.

Still, she reminded herself, he *was* her papa, a man filled with wisdom. He was only doing what he thought best for his family and his country.

"What are you going to do?" she asked, staring at the blurry ledger page.

Gabriel's sigh sent shivers racing through her. This surely was not proper, particularly with her undergarments exposed on one side. "I wonder if there are other backers for this project." He closed the ledger and replaced it, bracing his hands on the shelf. "How can I find out?"

Camilla turned her head and found Gabriel's shadowy face less than an inch from hers. "Wh-what?"

"Does your father have close business partners? Anyone else who'd have the wealth to invest in the boat?"

"I don't know. Why?"

"Because if they have the resources to rebuild it, there's little point in destroying the prototype. We have to get the plans across Confederate lines, then go after the source of the money."

"Then you *are* planning to ruin my family!"

"What did you think I was going to do? Invite him to a Sunday-school picnic?"

Camilla was startled by the rattle of the doorknob and a swift banging.

"Camilla! Are you in there?"

Jamie's voice. Camilla felt her stomach flip. "Oh, heavens!" she whispered. She pushed against Gabriel's arms, nearly sending them both off the ladder. "We've got to get out of here!"

"There's no time to go through the window. Come here!" He jumped lightly off the ladder, then reached up to catch Camilla by the waist and swing her to the floor. Just as the door swung inward, Gabriel swooped.

Camilla found herself lifted off the floor and most thoroughly kissed.

Chapter Twelve

Gabriel felt Camilla jerk, struggle as the study door opened, spilling full light into the room.

"Leland!" barked Jamie Beaumont. "Release my sister!"

Just as he let Camilla go, Jamie grabbed his shoulder and spun him around.

Beaumont looked as if he didn't know who to light into first. "Camilla, have you lost your mind? Are you all right?"

"You're wasting sympathy on the wrong party." Gabriel pressed the back of his hand to his bleeding lower lip.

Camilla brushed at a spot of blood on her bodice. "If you've ruined my best dress I'll never speak to you again!"

"I am certain, Jamie dear, that what we have just witnessed was a betrothal kiss."

Gabriel's head whipped around. All amusement fled.

Delythia St. Clair stumped into the room, wagging an arthritic finger at Jamie. "Exceedingly bad manners, my boy, to draw pistols on one's prospective brother-in-law."

* * *

Gabriel sat squirming on the edge of the red leather chair, facing Jamie Beaumont's basilisk glare and Mrs. St. Clair's triumphant gleam. What had seemed like an excellent idea at the time now seemed to be the height of idiocy. Surely they were not going to insist on an engagement just because he had kissed the little hoyden.

He glanced at Camilla, seated on a horsehair sofa under the window. She stared at her lap, touching a finger to her red lips. No help there.

"Did Camilla agree to marry you?" Jamie paced in front of the fireplace. "When my father returns, he'll have something to say about that."

Ezekiel Beaumont would never throw his only daughter away on a penniless circuit-riding preacher. Gabriel contrived to look upset. "Surely he'll allow Camilla to marry where her heart is engaged—"

"And my heart is very much engaged elsewhere." Camilla jumped to her feet. "Lady, you know I'm going to marry Harry!"

"Sit down, miss!" Mrs. St. Clair thumped her cane so hard the lamps shook. "Reverend Leland is clearly under the impression that you have accepted his suit. Considering the outrageous behavior your brother and I witnessed, your options have narrowed to one—you will consider yourself betrothed, or your reputation will be in tatters."

Camilla stuck her chin in the air. "Lady, you are so old-fashioned! Besides, nobody saw but you and Jamie."

Mrs. St. Clair's tone was perfectly enunciated. "No gentlewoman allows hcrsclf to be intimately embraced outside of marriage, as you very well know."

Camilla frowned. "Why aren't you shouting at *him?*"

Gabriel hid his amusement. "Miss Beaumont, the

nearness of your beauty overcame my good sense. As a man of God and a gentleman of honor, I am fully prepared to offer you the protection of my name."

"You are quite forgiven, but I would prefer that we pretend it never happened."

Jamie wheeled and halted. "Excellent notion."

"Certainly not." Mrs. St. Clair tapped her fan against her palm.

Gabriel hesitated. If he insisted on a betrothal, he stood in danger of being shackled for life. On the other hand, he would have almost unlimited access to Confederate high command, as well as the chance to dismantle the underwater boat project.

He would just have to make sure the tie was temporary.

"I refuse to abandon my obligation to duty." Ignoring Camilla's pleading look, Gabriel rose and bowed to Mrs. St. Clair. "Would you allow your granddaughter and me a moment alone to seal our commitment?"

"In a pig's eye!" Jamie burst out.

But his grandmother nodded with grave dignity. "Certainly, Reverend. James, you will escort me back to the ballroom. And I will expect to see the two of you back there in five minutes or less."

Gabriel bowed again as Jamie reluctantly accompanied his grandmother from the room, leaving the door open a discreet inch.

"This is a fine disaster!" Camilla said through her teeth.

Gabriel bumped the door shut. "It could be worse. If your brother had caught us going through those ledgers—"

"Yes, but did you have to—" She pressed her lips together and looked away.

"I was beginning to think you a free-thinking young woman," he chided.

Tears swam in her eyes. "You're the most heartless person I've ever met. You don't care about my family, and you certainly don't care about me. You don't have any morals of your own, so you make fun of those who do, and—and—you use that false title 'man of God' to cover your trickery and cynicism!"

Everything she said was true, but he wasn't going to feel guilty about doing his job and enjoying a stolen kiss.

She blinked away her tears. "I think you're afraid of real faith."

He smiled to cover his discomfort. "I'm not afraid of anything, though the charge of cynicism is perhaps true. I doubt God is much interested in our mission."

"God is interested in *everything* we do. I trust Him to take care of me." Camilla stared at Gabriel with calm assurance. "What's more, I believe He loves you enough to send you to Mobile, Alabama, to reveal Himself to you."

Something pierced his armor of doubt. What if she was right? "No skin off my nose if you want to believe that." He moved toward the desk, putting space between himself and Camilla. "I'm sorry if you're not happy with our engagement, but I think it'll serve our purpose very well."

"There have got to be less…personal ways for me to help you."

"Why, Miss Beaumont, one would almost think you are afraid of me." The accusation hung in silence for a moment or two before Gabriel shrugged. "It docsn't matter. I want unlimited access to your father and his military houseguests, so we're going through with it." He allowed a delicate pause to underscore his determination. "Otherwise I might be tempted to indulge in a bit of...bragging."

"You are despicable," Camilla said between her teeth. "I'll go along with it, but I promise you my papa won't like it."

Gabriel laughed. "I'm counting on that."

"Milla! Miss Milla!"

Camilla struggled out of a dream in which she walked down an aisle, dressed in a wedding gown so enormously belled that it brushed the ends of the pews on either side. The groom's face was obscured by her lacy veil and by the fact that her spectacles were perched on top of her head rather than on her nose. But when she reached his side, Papa lifted her veil to reveal that it wasn't Harry at all but Gabriel Laniere, regarding her with an I-told-you-so smirk.

Harry stood before them with a prayer book open in his hands. "Dearly beloved..."

"Miss Milla, roust out of there and get your clothes on! Your grandmama's upset."

Camilla squinted at Portia, who had jerked aside the mosquito netting as well as the window draperies. Sunshine poured across the carpet, setting dust motes into flight. "What time is it?"

"It's 'most nine o'clock. She had breakfast a long time ago, and she can't understand why everybody don't get up with the chickens." Portia opened the armoire and sorted through Camilla's pitiful array of gowns, shaking her head. "Girl-child, you done outgrown half of what's in here."

Camilla struggled to her elbows and yawned. "I'll let one of them out this afternoon."

"Looks to me like all the let's done out." Portia examined the seams of the dress she had selected. "Never mind. Just hurry, before Lady has an apoplexy."

Camilla rolled out of bed and started to wash. "It was nearly two in the morning before the last of the soldiers left." She rinsed her mouth and spat. "My feet hurt."

"I hear you was quite the belle of the ball." Portia helped Camilla into camisole, chemise, corset, hoops, petticoat and finally the too-small dress. She worked in tight-lipped silence.

Camilla sighed. "What's the matter, Portia?"

"Nothing," Portia said, then burst out, "I suppose you think it's not important to tell me you done got engaged to that foreign preacherman." She found several snarls in Camilla's curls that needed her vigorous attention.

"Oh." In the mirror Camilla studied the neat plaits that bound Portia's beautiful head. "You heard about that."

"Is there anything happen around here I don't hear about?"

"I suppose not." She regretted Portia's anxiety. "Portia, he's not foreign."

Portia snorted. "Don't know what lies he's fed you, but that boy don't come from nowhere, if you ask me. Too good-lookin', too smooth, too much of everything! You mark my words. That's one load of trouble you're takin' on."

Camilla met Portia's wise dark eyes in the mirror, wondering if she dared invest Gabriel's secret in her mentor. Something restrained her. She shrugged. "Can't go back now."

Portia sighed, gave Camilla a brief hug and shooed her out of the room. "Go see what your grandmama wants."

Camilla found Lady in her sitting room poring over a stack of fashion magazines.

"Where are your spectacles?" Lady demanded as Camilla entered the room.

"In my pocket—"

"Put them on and come look here. I think this train of Mechlin lace would look exquisite over—"

"Lady, what are you doing?"

Lady paused with fingers marking several pages in the top book. "We're going to plan your trousseau, of course." She smiled. "I remember when Thomas asked for my hand, I couldn't wait. Camilla, what is it?" She pushed the magazines off her gout stool so that Camilla could sit before her. "If you're worried about your father, I can bring him around."

"It's not that." Camilla sighed. "Well, maybe it is, a little. But it's mostly Harry. I promised him…"

"Dear one, we all make promises when we're young, and time can alter the conditions of those promises." Shaking her head, Lady took Camilla's hands. "It's time to face the reality that Harry might not even make it through the war alive—"

"Stop it!" Camilla tried to pull her hands away. "Don't say that!"

"Camilla, look at me. Mobile seems to be a safe place, but there's no guarantee of protection." Lady's voice was harsh. "It has come to me lately that you're a woman grown. Having known the blessing of a Christian husband, I want the same for you."

"I don't know what you're afraid of, Lady, but Papa and Jamie will take care of us—" Camilla stopped when Lady pressed her fingers to her eyes. "What *is* it? What do you think is going to happen?"

After a moment her grandmother's hands fell to her

lap. "Something just tells me to be on guard." Lady closed her eyes.

Camilla was more frightened by the resignation she had glimpsed there than by any of the events of the past month. Then a rumble of thunder shook the house, and she realized that the morning's sunshine had been overtaken by one of the sudden squalls that came off the gulf. Shadows slid into the room.

Camilla felt her way through confusion. "Do you truly want me wed to one man when I'm promised to another? Surely that can't be God's will."

"Your commitment to Harry is commendable, my dear." Lady's eyes opened, shrewd and bright. "But if your attachment to him were as deep as you say, that scene last night would never have taken place."

Camilla blushed, unable to defend herself.

"Reverend Leland is a very attractive man."

"I suppose he is."

"I'm curious. Whose idea was it to find an empty room in which to converse? Yours or his?"

"I don't remember!" Camilla grabbed a copy of *Godey's Lady's Book* and randomly flipped it open. "Portia says I'm going to split a seam if I don't do something about my dresses. What do you think about this new style?"

The rain came behind the thunder, falling as if God upended an enormous heavenly mop bucket. That afternoon Camilla sat in the front parlor with her feet drawn up and a small lap desk across her knees. She looked up when Schuyler slopped through the front door, bringing with him mud, wet leaves, and a steamy, swampy odor. Shaking his damp head like a gangly sheepdog, he slung water all over Portia's spotless oak floor, creating a soupy, sandy mess under his dirty boots.

Camilla scowled as the ink ran on her journal page.

"Where's the general?" Schuyler dropped his oilskin slicker right where he shrugged it off and snagged an orange from the basket at Camilla's elbow. He headed toward the stairs.

"Lady's in her—"

"Not *that* general!" Schuyler grinned over his shoulder. "General Forney!"

Camilla slammed the journal shut and set the desk aside. "Why?"

"Jamie sent me. Word's come up from the gulf that the Yankees have backed off from Fort Morgan. Can't handle our choppy seas."

"Praise God!" Camilla sat back in relief. "General Forney is working in his room, I believe." As Schuyler pounded up the stairs, she went back to her journal. *The storm seems to be a blessing after all....*

The parlor was quiet for a long time, the silence broken only by the scratch of her pen, the occasional crack of thunder and the hiss and spatter of rain against the window. She found herself staring into space, chin in hand, pen waggling. There had to be some way to contact Harry.

Something happened night before last....

She scratched out the words. Too private to put on paper. Jamie and Lady had both seen it, but no one could see her feelings. No one but God.

What did He think about her unladylike behavior?

True, Gabriel had started it, but she'd been in no hurry to end it. She'd been no better than that actress, Delia Matthews, Gabriel's partner.

Camilla was Gabriel's partner now, too. A rush of unbidden pleasure filled her. To share a secret with a man was, she suspected, the beginning of the sort of relationship enjoyed by husbands and wives. Kissing him had only increased that intimacy.

But it seemed like an excellent excuse for her and Gabriel's presence in Papa's study.

What was Gabriel going to do about that ledger entry? He'd said he would go after the source of the money. He could hardly ruin Papa, as most of the family money was tied up in the railroad. As far as she knew, there was no cash lying around to steal.

She tapped her pen against the inkwell. Of course, there were ways to make sure a man's source of income dried up. She knew of families convicted of treason, stripped of every asset and committed to prison. In some cases the head of the household had even been tried and hanged.

Papa's loyalty to the Confederacy had been unquestioned since its inception. But Papa's first cousin—Harry's mother—had married Union. That left the entire Beaumont family open to suspicion. Camilla wondered sometimes if that wasn't the reason for Papa's zealous service to the Confederacy.

What would happen if authorities found out his daughter had been involved for four years in an underground railroad operation?

Bowing her head over her journal, Camilla prayed that Gabriel would honor his promise to keep her secret.

Feet dangling off the wharf at Uncle Diron's place on the river, Gabriel blew a wailing riff on his harmonica. Yellow Jack's domain was a dangerous place to be at sundown. Even if nobody else believed it, he knew that if a mosquito infected with yellow fever bit him, he could be dead inside a week.

But there was a certain peace that could only be found at the water's edge, with the full magenta, carmine and indigo glory spread out like a flame in the distance. As a youngster he would pretend to fly off on a strip of cloud into that infinity of color. He even thought he could meet the Creator if he sat there long enough.

It never bothered him that he had no ma and pa. After all, he had Uncle Diron, who was better than a dozen parents put together. But he was aware of something odd about himself, something that made people look at him sharply. He knew he asked a lot of questions—Uncle Diron told him so. He had an insatiable desire to know everything. How did things work? Why were things put together as they were? What would happen if…?

Then he'd learned that if you asked too many questions and supposed too much, life itself would blow up in your face. The Creator apparently couldn't care less about truth and those who pursued it. Gabriel made it his personal mission in life to answer his own questions, make his own truth, and to blazes with anyone who got in his way. Only since returning to Mobile and becoming acquainted with Camilla Beaumont had he begun to rethink his self-imposed spiritual exile.

The sun disappeared into the water. He slipped the harmonica into his pocket and took out a little brown bottle of tonic he'd found in his uncle's shack. He'd hoped that coming back to Mobile would bring justification, if not revenge. So far, however, all he'd run into was more complication.

For one thing, there was no underwater boat under

construction at the Skates Foundry. Just mundane items such as anchors and buttons and railroad spikes—the sort of things a man with business interests in ships and railroads would order.

So all that business with Camilla in her father's study had led to nothing. Maybe she could still be useful, but he wished he hadn't agreed to that crazy engagement. Her papa had yet to return from his business trip, and when he did…

Gabriel took another pull from the bottle and felt the burn all the way down to his gut. Nothing would wash away the nagging guilt he felt about what he planned to do to Ezekiel Beaumont. Had to be done, but Camilla would be sacrificed in the process.

She would be the means to the end.

He shouldn't worry about her; in the past she had proved capable of protecting herself. He chuckled at the mental image of Camilla in boy's clothes, trying to shove him out her window. She'd almost broken his neck.

Then he thought about the way she'd looked on the night of the ball, dressed like a princess and kissing him with startled abandon. He groaned. Nothing good came of courting good girls. It hadn't taken her thirty minutes to start preaching at him. *God loves you,* she'd said with that unshakable certainty he found so hard to contradict.

Some part of him, maybe the little boy who loved sunsets, wanted to believe her. But the man who had been at Shiloh found it difficult.

He tossed the bottle into the water, heard it land with a solid plunk and watched it float off in the moonlight.

Chapter Thirteen

Late Tuesday evening, Camilla reluctantly followed Lady to the door of her father's study. "Zeke, Camilla has something she wants to tell you." Her grandmother paused for barely a moment before sailing in without an invitation.

"I still think we should wait until he's had a chance to eat supper," Camilla whispered as her father looked up from his paperwork with a frown.

"No point putting off a difficult task." Lady seated herself in one of the two chairs facing the desk. When Camilla hovered beside her, she snapped her fingers. "Sit down, miss. You'll give your father a crick in his neck."

Papa glared as if the pain in his neck were seated across from him. "Whatever you two have up your sleeves can wait until morning. It's nearly ten, and I can't go to bed until I check this bill of lading."

Lady merely chuckled. "Rough week, Ezekiel?"

Papa pushed up his spectacles to rub his eyes. "I've been traveling for eight days. I haven't eaten since this morning, and I'm very busy." His gaze rested on Camilla and softened somewhat. "What *is* it, Milla?"

She squirmed. "Something happened while you were gone. We had a ball..."

"For which I am very thankful." He smiled. "That I was gone, I mean. I presume everyone had a good time?"

"Yes, sir, I mean, until we heard the Yanks were firing on Fort Morgan."

Papa pressed his fingers against his temple. "Camilla, you didn't come in here to tell me something that's been in the papers for nigh on a week."

"No, sir, but you asked—"

"Oh, for goodness' sake." Lady banged her cane against the floor. "Quit pussyfooting around and tell your papa—"

"Tell me *what?*" Ezekiel barked.

"That I'm betrothed," blurted Camilla.

Ezekiel dropped the pen in his hand, splattering ink everywhere. "To who?"

"To Reverend Leland." Camilla looked down at her fingers twisting in her lap. "It was Lady's idea."

"How could your engagement be your grandmother's idea?"

Lady bristled. "Somebody had to take charge—with you gallivanting all over Alabama, the house full of company, and your daughter in a locked room kissing the preacher!"

Papa's face purpled as he turned on Lady. "I had assumed that by this time you would have taught the girl some deportment."

"Now just a minute, Ezekiel Beaumont—"

"Lady! Papa!" Camilla kept her voice soft but gave it an edge that caused both her father and her grandmother to halt their angry words. She rose with as much dignity as she could muster, hands laced in front of her, and took a deep breath. "I'm not a baby or a toy for the two of you to argue over anymore. *If* I choose to enter into a betrothal with Reverend Leland, it's nobody's business but mine and his. Of course I'll listen to your counsel, but in the end—" She shrugged with eloquent simplicity. "It's my decision. Papa, I apologize for interrupting your work. We can talk more in the morning."

Ezekiel stared at his daughter, speechless, as she kissed his cheek. Much subdued, Lady offered her cheek as well.

"Good night, Papa. Good night, Lady."

As she walked to the door, Camilla heard her grandmother say smugly, "*That,* Ezekiel, is a lady."

Camilla spent the next two days trying to figure out a way to change the shape of her two day dresses. Her rather embarrassing growth spurts in certain areas had made it in the nature of an emergency. Eventually she realized she was going to have to swallow her pride and ask Papa for money for a new one.

She stood outside the study door, hand raised to knock.

The problem was, after her grandiose speech the other night, she hadn't had the courage to broach the subject of her engagement with him. Besides, he was rarely at home. She'd had a note from Gabriel yesterday, saying he'd requested an appointment with her father, but she'd heard nothing from either of them after that. It would be just like two men to arrange her life without consulting her.

She refused to let that happen. She rapped on the door.

"Who's there?" Papa's voice was impatient.

"It's me, Papa."

Camilla waited for a moment, then the door opened. "What is it?" Over Papa's shoulder she saw Fanny's father seated across the room in front of the desk. Mr. Chambliss had been here a lot the past couple of days. The men weren't close friends, but they had occasional business dealings. The fish boat, for example.

"Papa, it's time we talked," she said steadily. "I see you have company now, but you're never alone anymore, and it's—important."

Her father sighed and rubbed the back of his neck. "Now's not a good time. I'll come find you before I go out for the afternoon." He started to shut the door, but Camilla put out a hand to stop him.

"Please, Papa, I—I'm fixin' to go out, myself. That is, I need to buy fabric for a new dress, and I need some money."

He reddened and glanced around to make sure Mr. Chambliss couldn't hear. "Sweetheart, I just gave the last of my cash to your brother." He cleared his throat. "You look grand, anyway. Why, that dress looks practically new." He chucked her under the chin. "Run along, now."

The door shut in Camilla's face.

Her throat clogged with tears.

Later that afternoon, wearing the dress that her father had admired—which had been made three years earlier for her straight-line fifteen-year-old body—Camilla slipped out the front door carrying an empty burlap flour sack. If there was no money for a dress, then there was no money for a dress. She'd have to occupy herself otherwise and pray she wouldn't burst any buttons. She wasn't going to sit home and wait for Gabriel to come calling.

She looked around as a familiar whistling whine

hailed her from the street. Virgil Byrd trotted toward her in a small dogcart pulled by his mule. "Missy!" One skinny arm flailed above his head. "Wait for me!"

"Virgil! How have you been?"

"Slicker'n a bucket full of oysters!" He drew the cart up beside her. "Where you going? I'd be mighty happy to give you a ride."

The cart looked none too clean and smelled of sour mash. It was half full of rolled-up newspapers. "Where'd you get the wagon?"

"Mr. Hastings at the newspaper office give it to me for my route." Virgil beamed.

Camilla gathered her skirts and hoisted herself onto the narrow plank seat. "This is a pleasant surprise. I was headed to the docks. Can you drop me at the St. Anthony Street Warehouse?"

Virgil gave her one of his astonishingly shrewd looks. "Yore papa'd skin me if I's to let you off there by yore-self. No, sir. I better take you to the hospital or the church instead."

Camilla did her best to hide her exasperated amusement. "I want to scavenge the warehouses for rope."

"You can't go in them warehouses. You want a rope, I can find you a rope."

Camilla held on as they bumped across a rut in the road. "I don't want *a* rope. I want to fill this sack up with leftover rope pieces, so we can card it to make surgical gauze." When he looked uncomprehending, Camilla said firmly, "My papa said I could go. To the warehouses."

"All right, but don't blame me if you get in big trouble." Virgil drove in injured silence for perhaps a minute before he gave her a sidelong look. "You ain't borried my bag in a long time. I didn't never think that was right—

you runnin' around in the middle of the night in them boy's clothes."

"You never told anybody, did you?"

"What you take me for? You said don't tell nobody, so I didn't tell nobody."

"Good."

"'Cept Revrint Gabe."

Camilla jerked on the reins, halting the cart in the middle of the street. "So that's how he knew! Virgil, I'll never trust you again."

He blinked at her in innocent alarm. "Revrint Gabe's yore friend. He said he was, and he told me thangs he wouldn't never of knowed if he wasn't." He gave her a hangdog look from under those preposterous eyebrows.

"You still shouldn't have told him anything."

Virgil looked repentant. "If I tolt *you* a secret, would you fergive me?"

She sighed. "All right, what is it?"

"The other night me and Candy was walkin' down Church Street, lookin' in the garbage piles for somethin' to eat." Virgil looked around. "We got to the old Bethel Church—the one the 'Piscopals left empty when they moved to their new building—and dang if it wasn't empty."

"You mean it *was* empty?"

"Naw! It *wasn't* empty! There was this big metal thing in there and a couple fellas bangin' on it and climbin' in it. Ain't never seen nothin' like it in my life!"

"How big? What did it look like?"

"Big as a fishin' boat. But it looked kinda like a boiler."

Camilla covered her mouth and stared at Virgil. He'd found the fish boat!

But before she could respond, she spied Fanny Chambliss walking down the street with her beau, Wendell Nelson. Fanny turned to look in the window of the corner jeweler's store, but Wendell saw Camilla and waved. A short argument ensued, then Wendell shook off Fanny's hand on his arm and crossed the street.

After a moment of indecision, Fanny hurried after him. By the time she reached the dogcart, Camilla had introduced Wendell to Virgil.

Virgil pumped Wendell's dubiously offered hand. "I'm mighty pleased to meet you. Any friend of Missy's is a friend of mine."

"Camilla, what are you doing?" With unerring skill Fanny brought attention back to herself. "You can't stop in the middle of the street like this."

Wendell looked around. "Indeed, we're blocking traffic. Miss Beaumont, may I offer you my escort?"

Camilla shook her head. "Thank you, Mr. Nelson, but it appears you're already engaged with Fanny. I'm only going down to the docks to collect hemp—you can see the warehouses from here." When Wendell opened his mouth to protest, she smiled. "Really. Mr. Byrd will keep me company."

Fanny's lip curled. "You can collect rope anytime, Camilla. Come help Wendell and me choose my birthday present."

Something in Fanny's tone alerted Camilla to potential mischief on the part of her friend. She stroked the mule's rabbitlike ears. "Thank you very much for the ride, Virgil. You were right—maybe I shouldn't go to the warehouses until Schuyler or someone can go with me. I'll talk to you later."

Virgil grinned. "Shore enough. You have a good time

in that there joolry shop!" He hopped aboard the cart and clucked to the mule.

Fanny released a breath. "Shall we remove ourselves from the street?" They headed back toward the jeweler's, one young lady on each of Wendell's gangly arms. "Camilla, why do you have to expose yourself to that man's company? It's simply not good for your reputation."

"How could Virgil Byrd's company be bad for my reputation?"

"Everybody knows he's a bootlegger."

"He's no such thing! Fanny Chambliss, you're repeating gossip."

Wendell cleared his throat. "Miss Beaumont, the man does seem to be an odd acquaintance for a lady such as yourself."

"Virgil has more kindness in his heart than most people I know. I don't pick my friends because of how they dress or how well they can read or—"

"Oh, pooh, such excitement over a garbage-picker." Fanny shrugged. "Wendell and I were wondering if you've recovered from the interruption of your ball last week. I noticed how overset you were. In fact, the whole family disappeared for quite some time."

Camilla moistened her lips. "Yes, it was very distressing. But the Yanks seem to have given up on Fort Morgan for the time being."

Fanny refused to be sidetracked. "Wendell and I were quite concerned about you. It appeared Reverend Leland was, as well."

Camilla suddenly wished she'd chosen to pursue her rope-picking errand. "Reverend Leland is a very kind man."

Wendell seemed to be uncomfortably aware of the tension between his two companions. He cleared his throat. "Look, here's the jeweler's."

Giving Camilla a narrow look, Fanny led the way into the cluttered shop. Wendell stopped to talk with Mr. Alexander, the proprietor. Camilla trailed behind as Fanny lingered in front of a display containing a brooch, earrings and bracelet of hand-carved coral.

Fanny touched the silver clasp of the bracelet. "Oh, how pretty."

Camilla murmured agreement.

Fanny draped the beads around her wrist. "Papa says we'll all be dripping in jewels pretty soon."

"I doubt that." Camilla brushed a hand down the threadbare waistline seam of her dress.

"Oh, I think it's fairly certain."

Camilla frowned. "What do you mean?"

"Haven't you noticed our fathers spending quite a bit of time lately talking business?" Fanny cast a furtive glance at Wendell, who was still occupied with garrulous Mr. Alexander. "I think they're working on some secret project."

"What project?" Camilla whispered.

"Don't tell me you don't know."

"Of course I know," Camilla said quickly. "But I thought it was a military project, not a private business venture."

Fanny leaned over to examine the coral more closely. "It *is* a military project, but we all stand to profit if it's delivered safely."

"The boat, you mean?"

"Boat? What boat? I'm talking about the cotton, goose!"

"Cotton?"

"I thought you knew all about it." Fanny gave Camilla a superior smile. "Our papas contrived to find a Northern buyer for all that cotton General Forney ordered out of the city, and the payment's coming down on a train any day now." She lowered her voice. "Eight hundred thousand dollars' worth of silver!"

Camilla blinked. But before she could respond to Fanny's staggering announcement, she realized Mr. Alexander was peering at her earbobs, his monocle enlarging one eye to fishlike proportions.

"W-what's the matter?" she stammered.

"I say, that's a fine example of native carving, my dear. If you ever decide to sell them I would be happy to broker."

"Oh, I could never—"

"I understand." The pudgy jeweler sighed. "Sentimental value and all that. Pity." He turned to Fanny. "Miss Chambliss, would you care to try on this set?"

Ezekiel Beaumont flipped open the door of his cigar case and offered Gabriel his choice. Spinning the carousel-like contraption, Gabriel chose a fine Cuban panatela.

"Sit down, boy." Ezekiel jabbed his own cigar in the direction of the most uncomfortable chair in the small, sparsely furnished office.

Ignoring the order, Gabriel tucked the cigar in his pocket. "I'll save it for later." After a couple of days of unanswered messages, Gabriel had assumed the old man was avoiding the issue of his daughter's betrothal and run Ezekiel down at the M & O depot on Lipscomb Street. But the jumble of letters, maps, bills of lading and other assorted paperwork littering the big desk indicated Ezekiel had simply been too busy to respond. "I appreciate your time, sir," Gabriel said with fine irony.

Beaumont huffed into his chair, picking up a stack of correspondence. "The station manager's at home recovering from a malady of the lungs, and most of our able-bodied men are at work on the entrenchments. Pardon my bluntness, Reverend, but this ain't a good time to sit around jawing about church work."

"I haven't come to talk about church work."

Beaumont waved a hand. "If it's that business about Camilla, there's no need to hash that over again. All is forgiven. We'll forget it ever happened."

Gabriel struggled not to let his mouth unhinge. "But, sir, I've come to offer for your daughter's hand in marriage."

"No need to be hasty. Camilla's a pretty girl, but she's not been bred up to the hardships of a circuit preacher's life. Frivolous little thing like her—she'd drive you mad inside of a week. Just the other day she was after me again for dress money. No notion of the value of a dollar."

In spite of his preconceived ideas about society princesses, Camilla Beaumont was one of the least frivolous young women Gabriel had ever met. "Let me understand you, sir," he said softly. "You seem to consider your daughter and me to be socially unequal. Do you think I'm more interested in your business holdings than in her?"

Beaumont countered. "I'm looking out for both your best interests. Camilla doesn't seem to be all that keen on the attachment. I know for a fact she's been pining for that good-for-nothing Yankee cousin of hers since she was old enough to toddle along after him."

"You don't strike me as the type of man to give his daughter her head in such an important decision."

"True." The cigar again prodded the air. "But neither will I be manipulated by the first young jackanapes who backs the girl into a corner and steals a kiss."

Gabriel stiffened. "Mr. Beaumont—"

"Now, don't take offense. If Camilla's heart is engaged, and you can prove you're able to care for her in the manner she's accustomed to, then by all means court her." Beaumont stood and laid his massive hands flat on the desk. He speared Gabriel with eyes as hard and gray as his eldest son's. "If, however, I find you're using my daughter for any purpose other than cherishing her for the treasure she is, you'll find yourself tossed into the gulf and left for shark bait." He slammed his hands on the desk with a solid crash. "Is that clear?"

Gabriel nodded, tight-lipped. "It's clear, sir."

He had underestimated Ezekiel Beaumont.

Chapter Fourteen

Gabriel found Delia, still dressed in her costume from *The Lucky Buck,* sitting on a sack of corn husks in the hold of the *Magnolia Princess.* Judging by her thundercloud expression, she was not happy that he'd made her wait past the appointed time.

Without bothering to apologize, Gabriel crouched beside her. "What have you got for me?"

She pulled a scrap of paper from her blouse and slapped it into his palm. "Things are heating up in North Mississippi. The blockade's working, because the Johnnies are getting low on supplies. There are signs that some kind of action's coming down the M & O, and Washington wants to know what it is."

"Tell them I have an informant inside a household including a bankroller of the M & O and the commander of the gulf coast forces. I suspect they're moving troops down through here, then back up another line toward East Tennessee, but I don't have numbers yet." He hesitated. "There's something else. In New Orleans I discovered the development of an underwater torpedo boat that the builders scuttled before I could get more than a glimpse. They're reconstructing it here in Mobile."

"Have you seen it?"

"No, but I have confirmation that it exists. Camilla Beaumont is helping me find it."

Delia scowled. "The society belle with you on the pier? Who *is* she?"

"The daughter of Ezekiel Beaumont, who happens to have his finger in lots of Confederate pies, including the railroad and this torpedo boat. She's not pro-Union, but she's abolitionist. I'm talking her around."

Delia stiffened. "You're going to get us all killed!"

"I know what I'm doing. Make sure Farragut knows what I'm onto and ask for more time. Did you find out about the fifty-third Tennessee cavalry that was at Corinth?"

"Yes, but it's not good news. They were detached to Tupelo, got caught in a little skirmish and were out-maneuvered because they overestimated the enemy's strength." Delia snorted. "McClellan is the biggest horse's behind you ever met in your life."

"McClellan? I thought they were under Grant."

"Grant moved on to try for Vicksburg."

Gabriel sat quiet for a moment. "How many left in that company?" He knew most of them.

"Almost all wiped out, I'm afraid. The ones in the rear caring for the wounded were taken prisoner."

Gabriel took her wrist. "Any names?"

"No. I could probably find out, if you want."

"Harry Martin, a field surgeon. First lieutenant, I think."

Delia sighed and shook her hand free. "All right. I'll

do my best. Don't get your hopes up, and be careful what you tell the Beaumont girl."

"If I didn't know better, I'd say you were jealous."

Delia rolled her eyes, then flounced up the ladder.

Gabriel chuckled, waited a suitable amount of time and followed.

Camilla stopped for a moment in the open doorway of Chambliss Brothers Machine Shop and watched Gabriel and his uncle shape a carriage wheel. Diron held the metal to the anvil, while Gabriel swung an enormous hammer with practiced ease. He grunted as the hammer slammed against the metal with a deafening final clang, then stepped back and wiped his face against his forearm. As he looked up and caught her gaze, he slowly lowered his arm.

Camilla swallowed. The temperature in this place must be at least a hundred and ten. That would explain why her midsection felt so hollow and squishy. She backed out onto the sidewalk.

Gabriel followed, yanking a bandanna from a back pocket and wiping his face. "Were you looking for me?"

"I haven't seen you since the ball," she said breathlessly. "I was just wondering if you'd talked to Papa yet."

A teasing glint appeared in his eyes. "Last I heard, you didn't think this engagement was such a good idea. Change your mind?"

"N-not exactly." She twisted her ring. "I've learned something. Something important."

Gabriel glanced over his shoulder at his uncle, who was picking over some scrap iron. "We can't talk here. Where are you headed?"

"Lady asked me to deliver some supplies to the hospital, then pick up a box at the train depot. If you're finished, maybe you could come with me?"

He ruefully looked down at his dirty hands and sooty, sweat-soaked clothes. "You'd better come talk to uncle while I clean up."

Camilla followed Gabriel into the machine shop, which smelled of oil and metal and cinders. "Do you work here often?" She watched Gabriel pick up a huge hunk of iron and chunk it into a corner.

He grinned over his shoulder as he walked toward a curtained-off section of the huge room. "A man can't sit around writing sermons all day long."

She made a face at his broad back, then smiled at Diron. "Hello, Mr. Laniere."

He wiped his grimy hands on his even grimier apron and offered her a massive paw. "Pleased to see you, Miss Camilla." He looked her up and down with an appreciative whistle. "You were pretty, got up like a boy, but you're an eye-knocker in a dress." He winked. "Gabriel tells me your papa gave him permission to court you. Amazing how that boy manages to land on his feet."

Camilla blushed. "He obviously gets his charm from you."

"Don't know about that." Diron pulled a tobacco pouch out of his shirt pocket. "Boy'll feed you a load of malarkey sooner'n look at you." He crammed a wad of tobacco inside his cheek.

"I know Gabriel loves you."

"Not too long ago I would've said he didn't love nobody but hisself." He expertly sent a stream of tobacco juice into a nearby spittoon. "Now I ain't so sure."

"Wh-what makes you think that?"

"Never saw him look at nobody like he looks at you."

Diron crossed his arms. "And I can tell he ain't quite figured you out yet. That boy does love a mystery." He leered. "Might want to remember that."

Camilla grinned. Diron Laniere was a rascal, maybe more so than his nephew. But she suspected he was right. If she were crazy enough to contemplate a real marriage with Gabriel, she'd have to be on her toes to keep from being run over like a watermelon on a train track.

Her amusement dimmed as she reminded herself that they were only playacting. As soon as she told Gabriel where the fish boat was, he would find a way to inspect it. Would he destroy it? Would he simply copy the design? Could he do either one single-handedly? And what on earth would happen to her own father if the vessel were destroyed?

Where did her loyalty to her father end and patriotism begin? She was very much afraid patriotism was being colored with a broad brush by her own tenderness for a certain Union spy—a tenderness she could not afford. When Gabriel Laniere got what he wanted, he would be gone.

Behind the patched canvas curtain, Gabriel slopped water from the chipped pitcher into its mismatched bowl, then splashed his face and upper body. He was so glad to see Camilla Beaumont that it scared him. He was almost ready to ride out of town right now, torpedo boat or no torpedo boat.

No telling what brought her searching for him. He jerked on a clean shirt and tucked it into his trousers. Deciding against a jacket because of the heat, he wet-combed his hair and started to shove aside the curtain. But long habit made him stand quietly, half-concealed.

Camilla was regaling uncle with the tale of the trip down the bay to deliver the quinine. "You never saw a ship so full of holes in your life. And it was all because of a rooster!"

Diron sat with his booted feet hooked over the top rung of a stool, enjoying his tobacco. He chuckled. "Wouldn't have been so funny, though, if the ship had gone down."

"That's true." Camilla's eyes met Gabriel's, but he put a finger to his lips, and she maintained a flirtatious lilt in her voice. "I've been meaning to thank you for obtaining the quinine. You're quite a hero yourself!"

"Pshaw! An old scoun'l like me?" Diron turned his head and hit the spittoon with dead aim. "Not much I wouldn't do for the Confederacy."

"I know." Camilla lowered her voice. "Papa says you've been quite a genius in the design of the—you know, the boat." Camilla put her palms together in a swimming motion.

Diron frowned. "What boat?"

Camilla blinked. "Why, the boat my brother captains, of course."

"It ain't common knowledge he's the captain," Diron said slowly. "You better not say that to just anybody."

Gabriel's skin prickled. He'd been trying unsuccessfully to worm information out of his uncle for weeks, and Camilla had uncorked the old man in a matter of minutes.

Camilla smiled. "Papa says Jamie must have some pirate blood in him. He's patriotic, of course, but he's not interested in any sea venture that won't bring him a good profit."

"This one'll make him a hero, for sure, and likely make us all rich."

"Y-you mean Papa and Mr. Chambliss?" Camilla seemed to realize the conversation had bobbed into heavy undercurrents. She pulled her small spectacles out of her pocket and slipped them on, concealing her agitation. She wandered over to Diron's workbench, where she began to poke around.

Gabriel frowned. What did Chambliss have to do with it?

"He's an investor, sure. But your family stands to gain the most."

"I think it's thrilling Jamie gets to captain the boat." Camilla picked up a pearl-handled knife and brushed its blade against her thumb. "He can't wait to test it."

It was all Gabriel could do not to whistle at her audacity. How did she know the thing hadn't already been tested?

Diron leaned forward and gestured with his knife. "Tomorrow night we'll know."

Gabriel watched Camilla's hand jerk, and a line of scarlet traced the pad of her thumb. Her stricken eyes met his.

He jerked the curtain aside and crossed the room to take the little pearl-handled knife out of her shaking hand. "What do you think you're doing?" He pinched the cut together to stop the flow of blood.

Her skin was waxen as camellia petals. "I guess I wasn't paying attention."

"Uncle, don't you have a clean rag around here somewhere? Sit down, Camilla, before you faint." He hooked a stool with his foot, picked her up by the waist and plopped her onto it.

Shaking his head, Diron produced a clean cloth. Gabriel tore a strip off it and tied it around Camilla's thumb.

He stood frowning at her, holding her by the wrist, while she took a couple of deep breaths. "You all right?"

"Yes, I…that was very silly, wasn't it?"

"Very. We'd better get out of here before you do some real damage. Ready to go?"

Camilla nodded, the smile returning to her eyes as she looked at Diron. "I hope I didn't ruin your knife."

"Shouldn't leave it lying around. Wash that wound in clean water when you get home, Miss Camilla."

Gabriel released Camilla's wrist and helped her off the stool. "I'm staying in town tonight, uncle. I've an appointment early in the morning."

Diron grunted an acknowledgment and went back to work.

Gabriel offered Camilla his elbow. She clung to it tightly as they left the shop and walked across the street, where she'd left the wagon hitched. Once they were rattling down the street, Gabriel glanced at Camilla. She was staring at her bandaged thumb. "To the depot, or do you want to go home?"

Answering seemed to take a huge effort. "The depot. Lady'll have a fit if I don't get these supplies delivered."

"Why didn't she send one of the servants?"

"I offered to go because I needed to talk to you. Where have you been for the past week?"

He shrugged. "Trying to catch up with your father. He's been avoiding me."

"I suspected he might. He and Lady have been arguing over our betrothal."

"I finally talked to your papa. He's slippery as a gar. Never said I couldn't court you, but he let me know I'd better not get ideas above my station."

"That doesn't sound like Papa."

"He was being protective of his only daughter. I'd probably do the same." *I must be getting soft,* Gabriel told himself in disgust. He jerked the reins sharply as they turned onto Government Street. Camilla's shoulder jounced against his.

"Papa's protecting something, but I'm not sure it's me. He and Beckham Chambliss have been dabbling in confiscated cotton, selling it somewhere up north."

"What?" Gabriel turned sharply. "How do you know that?"

"Fanny Chambliss told me yesterday."

"Are you sure it's true?"

"It makes sense, doesn't it? Papa and Mr. Chambliss have been in business together off and on for years. I'm sure that was him I heard with Papa that night, discussing the fish boat."

"From what uncle just said, it most certainly was." Gabriel gripped the reins. "They need money to finance the thing, and if the blockade and the war are eating into railroad profits, that would be a perfect way to make a little fast cash."

"It may be more than a little." Camilla leaned close. "Fanny said there's a shipment of eight hundred thousand dollars in silver coming down this way soon."

Dumbfounded, Gabriel stared into the sparkling gold of Camilla's eyes.

"And that's not all." Camilla put her lips to Gabriel's ear. "Virgil Byrd has seen the boat."

"Where? I've got to see it for myself."

"It's in the old Bethel Church, but Papa's got guards posted all around the property."

"How did Byrd get close enough to see it?"

"He wanders around where he pleases, and nobody says a word to him."

Gabriel drew a breath. "Let's deliver these supplies." He flapped the reins to hurry the horses. "I *will* get close to that boat, Camilla, one way or another."

At the M & O depot people milled about—officers and enlisted men, slaves engaged in hauling and loading, and the odd gentleman of business. Gabriel was surprised at the number of women executing errands in the absence of their menfolk. The depot itself was so new that the raw boards had not yet been painted.

Gabriel rounded the wagon to assist Camilla to the ground, then swung along beside her as she lifted her skirts and picked her way across weeds, oyster shells and muddy red clay toward the transport office.

Gabriel took Camilla's elbow. "How long has the station been open?"

"About a year. Papa convinced the state legislature to fund the railroad just before hostilities in South Carolina started." She lowered her voice. "The folks in Richmond have made good use of the rail line, but haven't been forthcoming with cash for the upkeep. You can see why Papa's a bit anxious about profits."

"Surely your father's not the only stockholder."

"Of course not, but he's sunk a goodly sum into the enterprise."

So the outcome of the war would determine the Beaumont family fortunes on multiple levels. If the secessionists won, Ezekiel stood to gain thousands in debt retirement from the Confederate government. In the opposite case, the Beaumonts would lose everything.

Gabriel handed Camilla up the steps onto the broad

porch of the ticket office. What would he do if it came to a choice between protecting her and discharging his duty? Prayer suddenly seemed like a very good idea.

"Mr. Havard!" Camilla rushed toward the road agent's counter. "Lady says there's a delivery for us come in on the morning train."

"Oh, yes. It's from a Mr. Shoat, up in Benton's Mills. Very peculiar shape and quite heavy. If I didn't know your papa better, I'd say he's routing dead bodies up and down the line!" Mr. Havard laughed at his joke. "Do you need help loading it onto your wagon?"

"No, thank you. Reverend Leland here will help me." Camilla signed for the delivery and received a stamped bill of lading. "Give my regards to Mrs. Havard and the children."

"Certainly, Miss Camilla. It's good to have seen you."

"You have some useful connections." Gabriel accompanied Camilla to a large, noisy warehouse close to the tracks, where slaves and white hired men were unloading and reloading cars. "Do you suppose you could get him to feed you military use of the railroad? Troop movement in and out of here, numbers, provisions and such?"

She gave him a troubled look. "I don't like to use people who trust me."

That sounded like an accusation. "Do you understand you don't have a choice anymore? You're in this whether you like it or not, and it's too late to back out." The moment the words were out of his mouth, he wished them back.

Camilla's luminous tea-colored eyes filled. She jerked her arm out of his hand and hurried toward the warehouse.

"Camilla!" Gabriel strode after her. "I didn't mean—"

"Leave me alone." Her back was a straight, angry line. Hiking her skirts well above her ankles, she stepped over steel beams and sacks of salt, dodged towering stacks of crates and elbowed past piles of unclaimed furniture and machinery. She was going to trip over something and get hurt if he didn't do something. Helplessly he followed.

She came to the end of the warehouse, walked into a corner behind a leftover bale of cotton and stood with her forehead pressed against the rough pine planks, hands flat on either side of her head. Her bonnet hung from its ribbons, and her eyes were squeezed shut.

He stood a short distance away, castigating himself for a fool.

"I'd have done anything for you, Gabriel, if you'd just asked," she choked out. "Haven't you learned *anything* yet?"

"I suppose not." He took off his hat. "You're new territory."

Camilla turned her face so that the tear-streaked curve of her cheek glowed in a shaft of light. "I'll help you, but you've got to let me do it my way."

"There's not time." He moved around the cotton bale. "Uncle knows you're involved, Fanny Chambliss, too, and God knows who else." He paused. "There's something I've got to tell you."

"What is it?" She turned, back to the wall, eyes wide.

She was afraid of him. He wanted to hold her and convince her that— What? That he was a hero like her cousin or her brother or any number of young men she knew and admired? That he hadn't come here to overthrow her country and destroy her family's way of life?

He took a breath. "Delia Matthews told me Harry's

regiment was in a skirmish outside of Tupelo, Mississippi, and they couldn't hold out."

"Is he dead?" Her voice was high, almost inaudible.

"We don't know for sure. Rebels took the survivors prisoner. Delia says she can find out."

Camilla's head fell back against the wall.

He moved to pull her into his arms. She flung her arms about his waist and buried her face against his chest. He endured her clinging, knowing she wept for another man who was—or perhaps used to be—his closest friend. What a grand joke on Gabriel Laniere. When had it happened? When had he fallen in love with Camilla Beaumont?

"I don't know what to do," she whispered. "How can I go to Harry when you're here, and Jamie's going to test that horrid boat tomorrow night, and Papa's selling illegal cotton…"

Gabriel put his hand to the back of Camilla's head. She lifted her face, eyes closed. Tears were smeared across her cheeks, those ridiculous little spectacles skewed to the side. He took them off and slipped them into his pocket.

With the slow inevitability of a coastal tide drawn to the moon, Gabriel bent to kiss her lips, swollen and salty from weeping and innocent as dew on rose petals. For a moment he felt her respond before she shoved at his chest.

"Gabriel, stop. I can't do this."

His heart thudded in his throat. "I'm not going to apologize."

"I know, my fault." She averted her face.

He set her away from him, plunked her bonnet on her head and began to tie the ribbons. "You look like a fright," he said gruffly, as if his world had not just been turned inside out by less than half a kiss. "Where's this delivery we're supposed to pick up?"

"We'll have to find the freight agent, but—"

"Then let's go." He walked off.

"Gabriel!"

Releasing a breath, he turned. "In two days I'm gone, Camilla." He waited a beat, while she looked at him with tear-filled eyes. "Nothing's changed."

Chapter Fifteen

Camilla trailed behind Gabriel as they went in search of Percy Cleveland, the road agent. How could she be falling in love with this pigheaded *Yankee?* He didn't have a heart for the Lord. He was not, as Lady would say, her "right man." And Portia would preach for a week if she knew what he really was.

Nothing's changed. That might be true for him, but her life had just been turned inside out.

To Gabriel she was a tool, someone he could use to further his mission. The knowledge was bittersweet. She wanted to help end slavery, and aiding the Union was the best way to do it. But more than that, she wanted with her whole heart to work side by side with Gabriel. She wanted to belong to him. She wanted him spiritually whole. She wanted him *alive.*

But that wasn't going to happen unless God Himself intervened.

The drive home was silent, Camilla and Gabriel both absorbed in thought. When he pulled the wagon up behind the house, Portia appeared at the kitchen entrance, hands on hips.

"Thought you'd gone to Fort Morgan and back again." She skewered Gabriel with a look. "Y'all drive on down to the smokehouse. I'll get Willie to meet you there."

Gabriel started the wagon again. "Who died and crowned her queen? The woman's going to freeze me into a pillar of salt one of these days."

"She's just protective."

"Whole family is."

Camilla couldn't dispute that.

When they got to the smokehouse, a little white-washed building situated several hundred yards from the main house, Gabriel and Willie unloaded the wagon. Then Willie picked up a crowbar and, with matter-of-fact efficiency, pried the lid off the "coffin."

Camilla put her hand to her mouth and began to giggle.

Gabriel shouted with laughter. "Looks like Mr. Shoat himself came down the line."

With a broad grin, Willie began to unpack two hundred pounds of bacon, ham and salt pork. "Mister Zeke gonna find a way to get hisself some bacon for breakfast, General Pemberton or no General Pemberton."

Gabriel walked with Camilla back up to the house. "Your papa's a scoundrel, you know that? The rules are for everybody but him."

She had to acknowledge the truth of that statement. "I'd stop him if I could, but that seems like such a minor thing compared to—"

"Camilla, I never claimed to be a saint." Gabriel made a wry face. "But at least I admit what I am. These people who talk out of both sides of their mouths—they just get under my skin."

Camilla stood with one hand on the doorknob, looking up at him. "Papa's not perfect, but he's a good man. I love him very much."

He stared at her a moment. "I know you do." He turned to go, but she caught his sleeve.

"Gabriel, what are you going to do?"

He picked up her hand and pressed her fingers. "I won't let anything happen to you."

She watched him stride down the drive path. He'd never once looked her in the eyes.

Shortly after midnight, with denouement on his mind, Gabriel leaned against an oak at the corner of Conception and Church, listening to the racket coming from the saloons and lagerbier shops. He remembered when he and Harry had celebrated passing their first medical-school examination and had awakened the next morning to find themselves incarcerated in the city jail, both with crashing hangovers. Later they'd slithered into class together, more than green around the gills.

Odd to think Camilla had been not too far away that day, playing with her dolls. Or, more likely, sneaking off to go fishing.

Ever since they'd parted ways earlier in the day, Gabriel had been considering how best to extricate himself from an unendurable situation. The job he could do. What he could not do was stare into a pair of gold-streaked brown eyes and continue to hold himself aloof.

He fingered the watch in his pocket. He was going to have to stop thinking about her every other breath, wondering what she was doing, what she was thinking.

He straightened as he heard soft, shuffling footsteps and labored breathing.

The Birdman appeared, empty newspaper bag slung

over a bony shoulder. "Now, you ain't got no call to come snooping around here in the dead of night, Revrint. Missy said for me to come get her if you—"

"Keep your voice down, Byrd. Camilla sent me herself. How else would I know where you'd be?"

The old man rubbed his nose. "You ain't gonna get me in no trouble, are you?"

"Byrd, I'm convinced you've got a whole troop of angels watching out for you." Gabriel cast about for some way to allay the man's suspicions. "If you don't help me get into that church, Camilla's the one who'll suffer."

Confusion flitted across the emaciated features. "She said I weren't supposed to tell nobody but you, and she wanted to know if you come down here to look."

"Byrd." Gabriel shared a man-to-man look. "We've got to protect Camilla from that thing in there. You're the only one who can help me."

Byrd shifted, tugging at his cap. "I don't want nothing to happen to Missy. What you want me to do?"

Ten minutes later, a small fire burned merrily in a weedy field less than a hundred yards from the munitions dump on Water Street. Byrd, leading his sleepy mule on an impromptu trip to the creek for a drink of water, raised a hue and cry. Startled out of its stupor, the mule brayed loud enough to resurrect every inhabitant of Bethel cemetery.

The sentries posted at the property on Church Street came running, but by the time they got there the fire, now a roaring blaze, had spread dangerously close to the munitions dump.

Meanwhile, Gabriel slipped through the back entrance of the church and lit a small oil lamp. He wished he had time to savor the moment. His heart pumped as he walked toward the vessel in the center of the room, which had been cleared of all furniture, the windows boarded.

He held the lamp high as he walked around the cigar-shaped cylinder boiler. This little tin can was going to sink a Union gunboat? By his best estimate, it was somewhere between thirty and thirty-five feet long, four feet wide and five feet deep. Six-foot-long fins on each side gave it a sharklike appearance. Small for its purpose, the boat would barely fit through the double doors of the church's front entrance. The builders would have to be careful to get it out of here without drawing attention.

He touched the smooth, darkly gleaming metal. The seams were expertly joined; at least it appeared seaworthy.

A brief glance around the room produced a ladder, which he dragged over. Once he was high enough to examine the top of the boat, Gabriel saw at either end a seacock valve with a pump, opening into water-ballast tanks. That answered the question of submersion. In the center of the boat, two elliptical hatches were fitted like corks in a bottle, just large enough for a man to slip through.

It took him several precious moments to figure out how to release the central hatch cover. Sweating, he pulled it back on its hinge, settled it with a soft metallic clink, and lightly vaulted on top of the boat. Taking a deep breath, he eased into the hatch. No problem to the waist, but his shoulders barely fit through the opening. He stood with his body in, head out, and reached for the lamp, which he'd set on top of the ladder. Holding it high, he crouched.

The interior of the boat had a tomblike closeness. It was hard enough to breathe now—how on earth could a crew survive underwater for any length of time? It gave him the shudders to think about it. Gabriel faced the port side, where a long metal bench ran the length of the vessel. A pole fitted with eight hand-cranks ran toward the propeller. Ingenious.

Turning cautiously so as not to bump into anything, he moved forward crabwise. He couldn't resist turning the wheel, which controlled the rudder. A finely crafted mercury gauge, which would ascertain the depth of the craft, was fixed to a wooden panel to the left, with a compass beside it.

He mentally sketched everything he saw, including a couple of four-foot lengths of pipe, whose purpose he couldn't immediately determine. After examining every inch of the vessel's interior, Gabriel emerged from the hatch and noiselessly hoisted himself out. One more thing he needed to do before he left the building.

He approached the sea-cock valves.

Camilla awoke sometime in the night, feeling as though someone had been tapping her on the shoulder. The Holy Spirit often woke her to pray in the quiet darkness, the perfect time to hear that still, strong voice. Sometimes He brought someone to mind, someone with a need, someone hurting. In these days of war there were many of those.

She listened, waiting.

She had been dreaming about Gabriel. The image of his dark, inscrutable face, the intent way he looked at her, made her stir restlessly. *Father, he's Yours. I can't change him. Make him yearn for You. Whatever he's doing now, let it lead him to You.*

Turning over, she covered her head with the pillow. What should she do about Harry? She didn't know if he was dead or alive, could hardly remember what he looked like. She was afraid to go to him, had no idea how to find him. And what about Jamie? Should she warn him not to get in that awful boat?

The answer came clearly in the form of a Bible verse. *Have I not commanded thee? Be strong and of a good courage; be not afraid, neither be thou dismayed; for the Lord thy God is with thee whithersoever thou goest.*

It was a verse she'd learned as a child at her grandmother's knee, and she'd been reminded of it again in Gabriel's sermon from the book of Joshua. She lay in the dark, allowing her spirit to be filled and strengthened. Gradually her shivers ceased.

With a deep breath, she flung the covers back and reached for a flint to light the oil lamp.

Weak early morning light was breaking over the bay as Camilla silently boarded the *Magnolia Princess*. She found the correct cabin door and firmly knocked. Something hit the other side of the door and bounced onto the floor with a soft thud.

She smiled and knocked louder. "Miss Matthews?"

There was a soft expletive from inside the cabin. "I'm not receiving callers this morning."

"Miss Matthews, I'm sorry, but I've got to talk to you."

After a moment of silence Delia Matthews, clad in nothing but a rumpled negligee, yanked open the door. "What do you want?"

Camilla took a deep breath. "Gabriel says you know where Harry Martin's regiment is."

Delia leaned against the door frame and yawned. "Does your mama know where you are?"

"My mama's dead, but she taught me some manners before she passed on. Are you going to let me in or not?"

"Maybe. Depends on what I get in return."

"If I tell you how you can get hold of eight hundred thousand dollars in silver, would that be enough?"

Delia straightened, sleep gone from her dark eyes. "Would you mind saying that again, please?"

"Can I come in so we can talk privately?" Camilla struggled not to let her embarrassment show. She needed this woman's help, and it wouldn't do to antagonize her. Besides, she'd been thinking about judgmental attitudes. She'd been proud of her generosity toward Virgil, but it wasn't easy to extend the same toward a beautiful woman who had some claim to Gabriel's attention.

"I have a roommate. Let me get dressed, and I'll come with you." Delia shut the door firmly in Camilla's face.

A few minutes later, the door opened and Delia came out wearing a modest blue two-piece dress. In the careless way of beautiful women, her heavy dark hair was bundled in a thick knot at the back of her head. She looked stylish but demure.

Camilla followed Delia into a gambling parlor abandoned during daylight hours.

Delia seated herself in one of two red velvet slipper chairs and gestured for Camilla to follow suit. "How do you know about this silver shipment?"

"It's coming to my father." Camilla moistened her lips. "I suppose Gabriel told you about the fish boat?"

"He mentioned it."

"I don't know where the money's coming from, just that it's intended to finance the boat. I think I can help you get it."

"Why should you do that?"

"Didn't you hear me? I want you to take me to my cousin."

"I can't just up and leave."

"I think you could leave whenever you felt like it. Especially for eight hundred thousand U.S. dollars."

Delia laughed. "You're not as stupid as you look. Does Gabriel know you're planning to fly the coop?"

"He wouldn't have told me Harry's in trouble if he didn't want me to go to him." Camilla frowned. How did she know Gabriel had told her the truth? To him, truth was a commodity for sale, and he was likely to dilute or embroider it for his own purposes.

Delia leaned back and tucked her feet up. "I don't know your cousin."

"But Gabriel said—"

"Maybe Gabriel didn't think you'd have the nerve to come and question me. What did he tell you?"

"That Harry's regiment was in a skirmish and the survivors were taken prisoner."

"That much is true." Delia's tone softened. "But we don't know if your cousin survived."

"Harry's a surgeon. He wouldn't have been directly in the line of fire."

"Miss Beaumont, have you ever seen a real battle?"

"No, but—"

"I'll put it to you this way. The science of aiming a cannon is far from perfected."

Camilla blinked back her tears. "So he might be dead. But I've got to know for sure. If you could tell me where to go, who to ask…"

Delia tapped a fingernail against her teeth. "I could tell you where the battle site is, but you'll get in all sorts of trouble, asking after a Yankee surgeon. Even if he's alive, he'll be in a prison camp somewhere."

Camilla clenched her hands in her lap, praying for wisdom. "I've got to try. I'll offer myself as a nurse and look for Harry as I go. It would be easier if you were with me, but I'll do it alone if I have to." She hesitated. "Is Gabriel going to sabotage the fish boat?"

Delia looked at her with half-closed eyes. "What do you think?"

"I don't trust either one of you." Camilla rubbed her temple. "But if my brother is hurt, you'll never get one more bit of information out of me."

"Gabriel's stingy about what he tells me. I don't know what he plans to do with that boat. But if I were you, I'd make sure anybody I care about stays away from it." Delia sat up, swinging her feet to the floor. "Now tell me about that silver."

Chapter Sixteen

"Lady, I'm all set to leave. Don't make this any harder." Camilla stood before her grandmother on the side porch, a bandbox in one hand and a portmanteau at her feet. "General Forney signed a pass to get me through any lines I might cross. They're desperate for nurses."

Lady set her favorite rocker into angry motion. "George Havard won't sell you a ticket if your father tells him not to."

Camilla sighed and set down the bandbox. She sank to her knees, taking her grandmother's hand in both of hers. "You've got to make Papa let me go. I love Harry." Her feelings had somehow shifted to brotherly affection, but Lady needn't know that.

Lady looked away.

"I'm eighteen now. You taught me to seek what God would have me do. Lady, the Lord woke me up last night to pray, and I heard His voice as clearly as I've heard anything."

"What I've taught you is to go to God's Word when you need direction. People who hear voices in the night—"

"It *was* God's Word. You've had me memorizing verses since I was a baby. What was it for, if not to guide me when I have to make a decision? Sometimes God's people have to move on faith, and this is one of those times for me." Camilla laid her cheek against Lady's hand. "Can't you see I don't want to disobey you, but I can't disobey my heavenly Father either?"

Her grandmother's hand turned to cup Camilla's chin. "I fear for you, child."

"I'm afraid, too." Camilla looked up. "But the Lord has promised to go before me and protect me."

Lady sat quietly for a moment, then muttered, "This is not at all wise." She reached for her reticule lying on a table near her elbow. "You'll need money."

Camilla smiled. "Thank you, Lady."

Lady sat in injured silence as Camilla kissed her cheek and gathered her bags.

Why did obedience to the Lord so often rupture relationships, leaving one feeling uncertain and lonely? Where was the joy Jesus had so often promised? Sighing, Camilla entered the house to say goodbye to Portia.

Camilla arrived at the station with barely enough time to purchase her ticket while Horace arranged for the disposition of her luggage. As she waited in line, she couldn't stop praying for Harry and worrying about whether Delia had told her the truth.

Watching the train chugging on the tracks, heaving and spitting sparks, she noticed a bedraggled band of soldiers being herded off a freight car some distance down the line. Unkempt and dirty, stumbling with wounds and exhaustion, they must have been bound for the hospital.

As they came closer, she realized the uniforms were neither gray nor butternut.

Blue. The uniforms were dark, Union blue.

"Nasty Yankee dogs!" someone behind her jeered. "Blueback baby killers!" There were other, worse epithets shouted.

She put her hands over her ears as she strained to see over the gathering crowd.

"Miss Milla!" She felt Horace's hand at her elbow. "You gonna get trampled. Let's get you on board."

"No, wait." She pushed through the restless, muttering body of people blocking her view of the Union soldiers. By the time she had fought her way to the outside of the crowd, the clump of blue-uniformed men had been shoved toward the station house, where they stood shuffling, shoulders hunched and caps pulled low, in the shade of a sycamore tree.

She was vaguely aware of the conductor calling, "All-l-l abo-o-oard!"

As she rushed toward them, a gray-clad arm snatched her around the waist. "Here, miss, stay back, now. Them's dangerous fellows."

Camilla looked up into a grim bearded face. "Oh, please let me go! One of those men might be my cousin."

"I wouldn't be claiming him. These fellas are headed for a trade against some of our men on Ship Island." The officer gave the prisoners a pointed glance. "If they make it that far."

Struggling against the guard's arm, she scanned the obscured faces of the bluecoats. "I only want to speak to them."

She staggered as she was suddenly released.

"Sir!" The officer saluted someone behind Camilla.

"Corporal, you may permit Miss Beaumont to approach the prisoners. I'll make sure she comes to no harm."

"Yes, sir!"

She looked around and returned the speculative stare of Israel Duvall, the young officer with whom she'd danced at the subscription ball.

He bowed.

The train blasted a warning whistle, and the rhythm of the engine increased. She glanced at the prisoners, then back at Duvall.

She was just about to dash for the train when one of the prisoners, leaning weakly against the outer wall of the station house, squinted up at the merciless afternoon sun. Something about the tilt of his head made her catch her breath. He caught her gaze and broke out into a familiar lopsided grin.

Camilla picked up her skirts and ran.

The train pulled away from the station with a squeal of brakes and an explosion of steam.

She was gone.

Gabriel listened to the rhythm of his boots crunching on the shell drive path of the hospital and repeated it like a litany: *She's gone, she's gone, she's gone.*

Camilla was safely on a train headed out of town. He stared at the imposing facade of the hospital building, wishing he could go after her to protect her and ensure her happiness. He felt more alone than he'd ever felt in his life. No amount of heroics or pleasure-seeking would fill this great, gaping hole in his life. *Vanity, vanity, all is vanity.* Indeed.

All he'd ever wanted to be was a doctor, a healer.

All he'd managed to become was a liar.

Gabriel jammed his fists into his pockets and climbed the hospital steps. One thing he knew for sure. He couldn't stomach much more of this preaching thing. To stand in a pulpit and mouth platitudes he neither fully understood nor believed was a refined sort of torture.

As he opened the heavy front door, the medicinal smells smacked him in the face. He breathed deeply, feeling the pull of his calling. He'd been drawn here as if by a force beyond himself. Camilla had said the Lord had brought him to Mobile to show him— What was it? That God had a purpose for Gabriel Laniere, that He loved him. It had sounded unlikely at the time, even more so now.

He wandered into one of the ground-floor wards. Faint moans came from the cots lining the room. Sick women, wounded men, mangled children. Where was God, after all?

Be still and know that I am God.

Gabriel looked around, thinking someone had spoken aloud, but saw no one, heard only his own heartbeat.

A sudden commotion of voices and heavy boots passed the open door of the ward. By the time Gabriel reached the hallway, the noise had passed into a nearby surgical ward. He could hear the deep groans of a patient, shouts for a doctor, then, as he got closer, the voice of a woman underneath like a sweet ostinato. Gabriel strode into the surgery uninvited.

Camilla hovered beside a patient writhing on the surgery table, while two Confederate officers tried to hold him down. She should have been halfway to Malbis by now. Her traveling costume of navy merino wool indicated that she had been on her way but abandoned the trip for this man.

Camilla looked up at the closest officer. "Where's the doctor?"

Gabriel recognized one of General Forney's staff officers, Second Lieutenant Duvall.

"I don't know." Duvall bore down on the patient's wiry arms. "Miss Beaumont, you have no business here. The man's all but dead anyway."

Camilla's expression darkened, but before she could respond, Gabriel strode forward. "Perhaps I could be of assistance."

Duvall looked annoyed, but Camilla's face lit. "Gabe—Reverend Leland! Thank God you're here!"

Gabriel glanced at the man on the operating table. It took every bit of self-control he possessed to show no more than bland concern.

A million questions swarmed into his mind, but he walked toward the table as if he'd never seen the man thrashing feebly against the soldier's restraining hands. Ignoring Duvall and the aide, Gabriel laid his hand against Harry's forehead. He found it dry and burning with fever. Harry's face was haggard, darkly bearded, the eye sockets pronounced and the cheeks sunken.

Gabriel looked at Camilla. "I agree with the lieutenant that you don't belong here, Miss Beaumont. Perhaps you could explain your concern for a Federal…prisoner, I assume?"

"Yes, he's a prisoner." She gave him a hot, indignant look. "He needed medical attention, so I—I insisted!"

Harry fainted, his lanky body going limp. Gabriel would guess he suffered from simple malnutrition and exhaustion rather than any serious disease.

He folded his arms and met Camilla's eyes. "Miss Beaumont, your humanitarian impulses are going to get you in serious trouble. This man obviously suffers from Septigarius disease."

Both officers backed away from the table. "Are you sure? How do you know?" Duvall brushed his hands against his coat.

"I've preached many a funeral for the victims of this malady."

Duvall grasped Camilla's elbow. "Miss Beaumont, I insist you allow me to escort you home."

She resisted. "You may return to the guard and inform him this man is too ill to leave the hospital. Reverend Leland and I will see that he's returned to prison when he's well enough."

"But—"

"Lieutenant, a dead prisoner is no good to you in an exchange," she pointed out. "You have a duty to discharge, and I have nothing else to do."

Amused, Gabriel put on a show of reluctance. "Your grandmother wouldn't want you to stay here where you might contract any miasma floating in this contaminated air."

Camilla rolled her eyes. "I come here nearly every day. But you may tell my grandmother my trip has been postponed and I'll be home as soon as possible."

Duvall bowed stiffly. "I hope you know what you're doing." He gestured for the other officer to follow him from the ward.

When they were gone, Camilla hurried to shut the door. She returned to Harry's bedside and took his limp hand. She rounded on Gabriel. "Don't just stand there— do something for him!"

"What do you suggest I do?"

"I don't know, you're the doctor."

"I'm not a—"

"Oh, horse-puckey! You *are* a doctor, whatever you're pretending to be at the moment."

"Keep your voice down."

"I'll keep it down when you do something for Harry."

They glared at one another as the sounds of people and horses on the street passed the open window.

Gabriel shrugged and bent close to Harry's chest, listening for several moments, wishing for some of the instruments he used to own. He lifted one of the closed eyelids and examined the pupil. "What's he doing here?"

"I don't know." She watched every movement of Gabriel's hands. "I was about to board the train when about a dozen prisoners were herded off a freight car and made to stand in the heat outside the depot." She shuddered. "I almost didn't recognize Harry."

"Did he recognize you?"

"I think so." Camilla stroked Harry's bearded cheek. "What's wrong with him?"

"Not much that a long, cold drink, a few hot meals and a week's sleep won't cure."

"What about the Septagarius—"

Gabriel gave a bark of laughter. "No such thing."

She stared at him, then dissolved into giggles. "Mercy, you had me scared to death."

"Good. Maybe it'll make you think before you do something like this again."

"I'd do it again, Gabriel."

And that was the heartbeat of her. Unselfish to a fault. A dangerous fault.

He grunted and finished his examination. Eventually

he looked up and met Camilla's worried eyes. "I'd give a lot to know what he's been through. Don't know exactly how to treat him. Trouble is, he's in such shock, he may not wake up for days. By then he could be dead."

"I thought you weren't worried." When he shrugged, Camilla bit her lip. "I'm taking him home."

"Are you out of your mind? You can't take a Union prisoner into your father's house!"

"Papa wouldn't turn Harry away. Jamie wouldn't let him."

"Camilla, think. Isn't General Forney still billeted in your home?"

"Well, yes, but—"

"Besides, why would the Rebs release a prisoner to you? Your family would be implicated as Union sympathizers."

"My grandmother is rabid Secesh. My father's financing Confederate transportation. And my brother has been running arms into port, for heaven's sake. Surely the presence of one very sick relative, even if he's in a blue uniform, wouldn't make us suspect."

Gabriel thought of his interviews with the Vigilance Committee before he'd been allowed to enter the city. Camilla couldn't know what a precarious situation her family was in.

He tried another tack. "Then think of Harry's safety—"

"I *am* thinking of him. He'll die if he doesn't get proper care. Gabriel, you've got to help get him released into my custody. I know you've got the influence to do it."

Maybe he did. Maybe if he kept the situation under control, he could avert disaster. The situation was getting more complicated every day. The advantages of working in a place where one was known always traded in pitfalls.

Gabriel scrubbed both hands down his face. "All right. I'll see what I can do." The joy that lit Camilla's face sank a stone in the pit of his stomach. She loved Harry. He swallowed, closing his eyes to the pain. *God, if you're there, we need you.*

He looked up when Camilla gasped. "Lady!"

"What in the name of Adam's house cat is going on here?" Delythia St. Clair stood in the doorway, leaning on the arm of General Forney himself. Tugging at the general's arm, she advanced into the ward. "Was leaving the city on a whim not enough to upset the entire household, but you decide to compound the embarrassment by adopting Yankee prisoners?"

Camilla straightened her backbone. She bore an uncanny resemblance to her grandmother in that moment. "Lady, do you know who this is?"

"Reverend Leland." Lady nodded regally.

Camilla stamped her foot. "This isn't just some stray Yankee. It's Harry!"

A frown descended on the matriarch's countenance. "My dear, you've taken leave of your senses."

Gabriel intervened. "Mrs. St. Clair, perhaps you should come closer and see if this man is indeed your grandson."

"No grandson of mine wears an enemy uniform!" She looked up at General Forney, who patted her hand in sympathy. "It's Ezekiel's side of the family that spawned such traitors." She hobbled over to the surgical table to peer at the patient. "I've never seen this man before in my life. Camilla, you will go home. Reverend Leland, will you see to it that this man is treated humanely and returned to wherever he came from?"

Gabriel frowned. "The Bible commands us to love our enemies and pray for those who persecute us, ma'am, but even I balk at harboring Yankee soldiers."

"Lady, I swear to you if you turn this man away I'll get on the next train headed north and never come home again." Camilla was white with emotion.

Gabriel wanted to pick her up and kiss her senseless. He looked at General Forney, who had remained in the background, listening acutely to the exchange. "General, perhaps we might reach a compromise. It's my understanding this man is a trained surgeon. As such he would be a valuable hostage for exchange purposes."

Forney's eyes widened with interest. "Really?"

Gabriel nodded. "Would you agree to my taking him into personal custody, with Miss Beaumont as nurse, until he is well enough to survive the trip to Ship Island?"

"A suggestion of great merit." Forney stroked his lower lip. "But are you willing to risk catching whatever ails the man?"

"I would deem it an honor to put my life on the line again for my country." Gabriel bowed.

Mrs. St. Clair thumped her cane against the floor. "Camilla, if you insist on this mad venture, you will at least pursue it from the safety of our home. Reverend, I will send one of the servants to transfer your belongings to Beaumont House this evening."

Gabriel chewed the inside of his lip to keep from shouting victory. He'd be quartered in the same house with the top local Confederate command. At the same time he could watch over both Camilla and Harry. Possibly he could even facilitate their escape if the situation required it.

Perhaps God had been listening to him after all.

They all accompanied the stretcher bearing Harry Martin's supine body from the hospital, Mrs. St. Clair leaning on the general's arm, Camilla walking beside her cousin—her love?—trying not to expose her emotions. Gabriel almost pitied her.

As Harry was loaded into the back of an ambulance wagon, Camilla anxiously attending him, Gabriel assisted Mrs. St. Clair into the carriage she'd left waiting under the hospital portico.

The grande-dame touched his shoulder. "Thank you, Gabriel."

He looked up at her in surprise. "Ma'am?"

She smiled at him grimly. "It's time you and I had a talk, young man. I'll expect you in my sitting room this evening after dinner."

Chapter Seventeen

The cut-glass gasolier suspended above the dining table illuminated a splendid array of heavy shining silver, delicate bone china and sparkling crystal. Camilla found herself unable to work up any sort of interest in the forthcoming meal. She wanted to be at Harry's bedside.

Still, she couldn't squelch a frisson of awareness as Gabriel held her chair. His fingers brushed her arm as she seated herself, and she looked up to find him staring at her with a possessive, almost hungry expression in his eyes.

His eyes shuttered as he leaned down. "Where's your brother?"

"Schuyler's always late for dinner."

"Not Schuyler. Jamie."

"He's been gone for several days."

"Gone?" Gabriel's black gaze sharpened.

Camilla shifted her shoulders. "I haven't had time to ask questions."

"Here comes the general. Make the most of the opportunity." Gabriel touched Camilla's bare shoulder with an infinitesimal pressure that had her burning to the eyebrows, then moved to his place three seats down the long table.

Camilla managed to keep up a laughing banter with General Forney on her left and watch Gabriel flirt with her grandmother. What an amazing ball of complications he was—but how reassuring his presence. She'd put them all in a dangerous position by bringing Harry home, but somehow she knew it was the right thing to do. She would trust the Lord and Gabriel to keep Harry safe.

Camilla smiled at the general's attempt to conceal a yawn. "You must be keeping long hours, sir."

Forney chuckled. "Forgive my poor manners, my dear. I would not miss this for the world. Your grandmother sets a fine table. One could almost forget the Yankees clamoring on our doorstep."

Camilla shuddered. "What do you think are our chances of repelling the enemy?"

"With the loyal backing of families such as yours and the bravery of our gallant Southern men, we must prevail."

"I'm very proud of my father's and my older brother's involvement in the effort."

Forney smiled. "Your papa has perhaps the most useful talent of all—that of making money."

Camilla looked at the general over the top of her water goblet. "Papa and his machines." She smiled. "Someday he's going to pay somebody to invent a craft that will take off into the air."

Forney frowned. "Does your father discuss his projects with the family?"

"Of course it's a closely guarded secret." Camilla set down the goblet. "If anyone stole the plans, Papa would lose all that lovely money he's going to make off it. Besides, I don't pretend to understand how the thing works." She flicked a glance upward at the general, who was pulling thoughtfully at his mustache. "Will they be testing it soon?"

"I'm not sure to which project you refer."

Camilla made a diving and swimming motion with her hand. Over the general's shoulder she caught Gabriel's eye. He frowned, shook his head slightly.

Forney pushed away from the table, rose and bowed to Camilla. "Miss Beaumont, I must ask you to keep this conversation in strict confidence and refrain from questioning anyone else about your father's project. Your brother's life could depend on your discretion. Excuse me." He gestured to his adjutant, seated next to Schuyler, and the two of them walked from the dining room.

Camilla twisted her ring. The general clearly knew what she'd been talking about. Jamie was testing that underwater boat soon, maybe tonight. She closed her eyes and breathed a prayer for her brother.

For the moment she could do nothing to help him, but Harry lay, still unconscious, on a cot in the warming kitchen. Portia was sitting with him, with instructions to fetch Camilla if he awakened.

Camilla rose, straightening the lacy shawl about her shoulders. "Lady, please excuse me," she called softly. "I'm needed in the kitchen."

Lady nodded in an abstracted fashion as she allowed Gabriel to help her from her chair. "Reverend Leland and I will be in my pink sitting room. We are not to be disturbed." She took up her cane and, leaning on Gabriel's arm, accompanied him out of the dining room.

Camilla hesitated, frowning. Odd, most odd. But Harry needed her. She hurried toward the kitchen.

* * *

Gabriel helped Mrs. St. Clair into a chair, then seated himself across from her. His hand went to his inside coat pocket, but stopped as he caught the old lady's sardonic gaze.

"Feel free to indulge in your after-dinner cigar, Reverend—may I call you Gabriel?"

"Of course." Gabriel pulled out his cigar case and chose a cheroot.

"I've come to think of you quite as one of my own grandsons, you know." His hostess sat ramrod straight, hands atop the cane, regarding him with a Camilla-like stare. "Perhaps you won't mind if I regale you with a bit of family history." She inhaled deeply as he lit the cigar. "I do love the smell of a cigar. Used to smoke myself, before I had the responsibility of my grandchildren."

Gabriel grinned. "Would you care for one, ma'am?"

The birdlike head canted. "Don't mind if I do."

When the two of them were contentedly puffing up a haze of fragrant smoke, Gabriel leaned back against the sofa. "I assume this history has something to do with the young man in the kitchen?"

"Why would you assume that?"

"He *is* Camilla's cousin."

"I haven't seen Harry in—oh, five years or so. I doubt I'd recognize him if I met him face-to-face." Lady waved her cigar. "No, my boy, the history I wish to discuss goes back a bit further than five years. Back to a time when Southern Mississippi and Alabama were sparsely settled. 1812, to be precise."

"Fifty years ago." Gabriel frowned. "America was at war with England at the time."

"Oh, yes, but this is a much more personal history

than that. My parents were missionaries, you know, to the Indians."

"I didn't know." Gabriel blew a lazy smoke ring.

"Yes. In 1812 I was sixteen years old and deeply in love."

"Camilla's grandfather was a lucky man."

"Indeed, he was." The old lady grinned. "But he was not my first love."

"You astonish me."

"I'm sure I do. My sweetheart was a young chief of the Creek nation known as Red Eagle."

Gabriel sat up straight, choking on a carelessly indrawn huff of smoke.

"We were not allowed to marry," Lady continued, ignoring Gabriel's watering eyes and attempts to regain his breath. "I was sent to live with relatives in Mississippi. Red Eagle, as I discovered later, eventually took to wife a young kinswoman of his. That same year he led the Creeks in a revolt against settlers encroaching on their land. It was a bloody conflict that lasted several years."

Gabriel, wheezing, was unable to answer.

"Though I, too, married and became mistress of my own household, I followed the dispersal of the Indians to Oklahoma after they succumbed to white authority. Red Eagle's daughter, however, remained with a remnant of the tribe on a reservation in Mississippi. She married a French trader named Jean Laniere."

"A very interesting history, ma'am, but—"

"Jean Laniere was your father."

There was a long, taut silence.

The old woman returned his look calmly. "You have much the look of your grandfather, my dear."

"Indian blood is not the recommended entrée into society," he muttered.

"I know. That's why I made sure you were accepted into medical school."

Gabriel could not control his expression. "*You* made sure? Why?"

Lady examined the ash at the end of her cigar, the thick brown of the tobacco an absurd contrast to the papery whiteness of her fingers. "Maybe it was a way to make up for the loss of Red Eagle." She looked up. Tears stood in her eyes. "I suppose I never got over him, though I did love my husband. When my daughter died, I came back to Mobile to help raise her children. I chanced to see you with your uncle one day at the market—you couldn't have been much more than twelve or thirteen." Her smile was both tender and wistful. "I knew immediately who you must be."

Gabriel surged to his feet and prowled toward the blackness of the window. All this time there had been someone watching over him, someone concerned for his welfare, not just on his own behalf but because of his grandfather.

He turned with a jerk. "Why tell me this now?"

"I've seen the way you look at Camilla." He flushed, but before he could reply the old lady held up a hand. "Do you wonder why I never invited you into our home, particularly when your friendship with Harry developed?"

"That's not so hard to figure." Gabriel sneered. "Half-Indian kid like me, with hardly a complete suit of clothes to my name. Did Uncle Diron know where the scholarship came from?"

Lady shook her head. "I gave it anonymously. Gabriel, I wanted you to have a chance."

"I had a chance, all right." The old anger swamped Gabriel so that he wanted to put a fist through the window. "I thought I'd earned it myself. And look what came of it in the end—disgrace, exile, humiliation—"

"Yes, just look." Lady struggled to her feet. "Look what you've done. You saw that maniac Joseph Kinch using mental patients for medical research and did everything in your power to stop him. You sacrificed your reputation and your career trying to prove that mosquitoes, not human contact, cause the spread of yellow fever. If you were my own son I couldn't be prouder of you." Her hands trembled atop the cane, and her face contorted with a fierce twining of anger, pride and exultation.

Gabriel's fury evaporated. Taking her cane, he helped her back into her chair, then knelt with his forehead on her knee. He felt her hand on his head like a queen blessing one of her knights. "You know I'm a fraud, don't you?"

Lady sighed. "I love you, Gabriel. Not for Red Eagle's sake, but for your own. And the Lord loves you, too. He's reserved you for some wonderful purpose—He's just waiting for you to invite Him into your life."

How could she see his emptiness? He felt like a man standing inside a dark room refusing to enter the sunshine for fear it would blind him. He thought of the men he'd killed, the women he'd used, the friendships betrayed in the name of duty. Was there really hope of forgiveness and redemption? "Camilla keeps saying that, but until now I've seen no evidence there's a purpose to anything."

Lady's frail hand slipped to his shoulder. "Evidence is all around you, but what is required is an act of faith."

"Faith in what?" Gabriel lifted his head. "Even someone like me can pretend to be a Christian and get away with it. But good people every day are bought and sold and beaten and murdered. Where's the justice of that?"

"God is always patient, slow to anger. But herein is love: in that while we were yet sinners, Christ died for us."

"I won't argue that I'm a sinner. But I've always been responsible for my own debts."

Tenderness filled the old woman's eyes. "Until you abandon that debt to Christ, your life will have no ultimate meaning. Live for Him, Gabriel, and find peace."

Control. Hard-won control. He was supposed to fling it away in a moment?

He thought of the night he'd watched the sunset from Uncle Diron's dock. Yes, the moment had come now, but the decision had been building for some time. God flung colors and music and love at him from every unexpected direction. He'd be a fool to stay in the dark room.

"All right," he said simply. "I will."

And the light came on.

Camilla sat on a low stool beside Harry's cot, turning the pages of a dog-eared copy of *The Pilgrim's Progress*. She'd sent Portia to help remove the remains of dinner and had been passing the time contentedly for some thirty minutes.

"'Lo, Silly-Milly."

At the husky murmur her gaze flew to Harry's gaunt face. With a glad cry she cast herself on his chest. His arms closed feebly around her, and she gave in to tears. "Oh, Harry, I was so worried about you." She searched his tired gray-blue eyes. "How dare you scare us all so badly?"

"I'll wager Lady wanted to toss me into the bay." Harry smiled faintly.

"She says she's never seen you before." Camilla smiled in return. "Maybe she didn't get a good look at you."

"Maybe she didn't." Harry turned his head with an obvious effort, taking in his surroundings. "Never thought I'd be in this room again. Not that I'm complaining, but how did I get here? And where are the guards?"

"It's a long story, and you need food and rest." Camilla stroked his bearded cheek, then reached for a pitcher of water on the nearby sewing table and poured a little into a glass. "Here, can you drink this?" She slid her arm under Harry's head and lifted it, holding the glass to his parched lips.

"Thank you." He closed his eyes. "It's good to be in a real bed. Clean sheets are a miracle."

Throat clogged, Camilla rose. "Portia left some broth on the fire. I'll be right back with it."

"I'm not going anywhere."

When she returned, Harry's breathing was deep and regular, his eyes closed. But before she could set down the bowl of broth he turned his head. "Milla. You smell so heavenly."

"Are you sure it's not the broth?"

His eyes opened. "Sometimes I dream of lily of the valley."

Blushing, Camilla began to feed him tiny spoonfuls of broth.

Harry quickly tired and pushed the spoon away. "Thank you, no more. Camilla, when we were in the hospital I thought I heard—" He licked parched lips. "That doctor sounded like an old friend of mine."

Camilla caught her breath. "I don't know how to tell you this, Harry, but—"

"You've gotten yourself into a pickle as usual and expect me to get you out of it." Gabriel's deep voice came from the doorway.

Camilla's head jerked around.

Gabriel filled the room with his negligent, contained energy. "It's me, Harry. What have you got to say for yourself?"

Harry tried to smile. "Hullo, old man. Thought I was hallucinating when I heard your voice. How'd you turn up here again?"

"It's a long story." Gabriel laid the back of his hand against Harry's brow. "You were headed for Ship Island for exchange, but I doubt you'd have made it in this condition. Camilla saved your life." He sounded a mite regretful.

Camilla bristled. "What else was I supposed to do?"

"Camilla's been my angel on more than one occasion." Harry glanced at her fondly.

"I'm sure she has." Gabriel straightened. "Do you realize what a mortal fix you've gotten her into?"

"Would you prefer that I had died instead?" Mottled color flooded Harry's face.

"Stop it!" Camilla rose to face Gabriel. "If you're not going to be any help, get out of here and go back to your actress. I'm sick of you interfering!"

"Delia's gone. And I didn't say I wasn't going to help."

"Then help me figure out how to get Harry out of here alive."

"I told you—" he shrugged "—he's just malnourished, not sick or wounded. Give him a day or two here, and the Rebs will take him on down to exchange, then he'll be home free."

Camilla's jaw set. "I don't want him back in Rebel custody at all."

Harry cleared his throat. "Would you two quit talking about me as if I were a child? I ought to have some say in the matter."

Gabriel gave him an impatient glance. "You're in no condition to make decisions. You've caused nothing but trouble as it is."

Camilla knelt beside the cot. "If we let them take you again, you might never make it to the exchange. They didn't feed you before—"

"They didn't know I'm a surgeon. Now that they do, they'll be more likely to take care of me. What if I offered my skills for a time here, in return for special treatment?"

Gabriel's lip curled. "Only you would think of that—"

"That's a wonderful plan." Camilla looked up at Gabriel. "Maybe he could be an extra pair of eyes and ears for us in the hospital."

"What good would that do?" Gabriel clenched his teeth. "Besides, if you're so concerned for his safety, you don't want him here in Confederate territory."

"I think you're jealous, old man."

Gabriel turned away. "Do whatever you want, Camilla. You haven't listened to me yet—why should I expect you to start now?" He stalked out of the room.

Camilla looked after him, biting her lip. "He's just angry because I won't grovel to him."

Harry took her hand to his lips. "Milla, look at me." When she did, she was astonished to see tears standing in his eyes. "I thought of you every day while I was on the march, and sometimes the only thing that kept me going was knowing you were here at home, safe with your family. I dreamed of your hair and your eyes and your laugh." He smiled and reached up to touch one of her curls.

"Harry—"

"No, listen. If you'd found someone else while I was gone, I'd be crushed, but—but I could understand. You were so young when I left for Tennessee." Harry's bony hand slipped down her arm to grip her elbow with surprising strength. "But not Gabriel. I know him too well. He's a renegade and a rolling stone. An infidel."

Camilla searched his eyes, overwhelmed with feelings she could neither define nor control. Uppermost was the desire not to hurt Harry. But something about his appeal bothered her.

"Why did you…" She hesitated. "Why didn't you bring Gabriel home to our family when you were in medical school? We would have welcomed him, perhaps introduced him to the Lord."

"Gabe can be charming when he wants. But he was brought up by that crazy uncle of his and has no other family to speak of, so his morals are lacking, to say the least." Harry grimaced. "He never acknowledged any authority beyond his own intellect. He's got a way with women, and he's brilliant at getting what he wants. Maybe I was afraid you'd be attracted to him." Harry sighed and looked away.

Camilla spoke over the threat of tears. "I'd never give my heart to a man who owes no allegiance to God." She leaned toward Harry. "But you and I have been apart for a long time. I'm not the same little girl you used to know. Please…be patient with me, Harry."

Camilla closed her eyes against the disappointment in his haggard countenance. But Gabriel Laniere's dark, scornful face only appeared in its place.

Chapter Eighteen

Sometime in the wee hours of the morning, Byrd tied Candy to a gardenia bush outside the newspaper office. "Stay right there and be quiet," he said and shuffled toward Church Street.

Candy was getting tired of that gardenia bush. He hoped whatever was going to happen would happen fast, so he could get back to his still. Business was going to slack off if he left it much longer.

The old lady said if he'd watch Mr. Jamie and let her know when he got ready to set sail in that contraption, she'd find him a table to go in his shed. She'd offered to pay him a lot of money, but he didn't want no money. Candy sure would like to eat off a table, though.

Byrd shook his head as he trudged along. Maybe he should've told Missy what he was doing. Missy was right fond of her brother. But the old lady said not to tell Missy 'cause it would upset her, and Byrd wouldn't want to upset her no way.

Sometimes it was hard to know what was right. He wished he could read the Good Book for hisself so he could know. Maybe instead of a table he should ask for a copy of the Good Book. Maybe Missy would even teach him to read—if she wasn't too mad at him.

He quickened his steps and slipped into the yard of Bethel Church. The windows were darkened, as they had been since early spring, but a crack of light split under the bottom of the one nearest the door. Whatever that Thing was, it took a powerful lot of banging and scraping in the wee hours of the night.

He crept toward the building and jumped to see through the sliver of open window, but he wasn't quite tall enough. He slid to the ground, tugged his cap over his ears and settled down to wait. The old lady said not to go to sleep, because something might happen. He wished something would happen quick.

Then he almost missed it because they were so quiet. But a creak of the big double doors at the back of the church startled him awake. He jumped to his feet.

"Where's the wagon?"

"Coming. Look, there it is."

Out of the darkness a flatbed wagon rattled up, pulled by two draft horses. Only the military could afford to pay for that.

The two men went back inside the church and returned with three others. They helped the wagon driver carry the Thing out of the church. Byrd listened hard and picked out Mr. Jamie's voice as the man who had first spoken. He seemed to be in charge.

"Laniere," said Mr. Jamie, "I want you here at the stern. Protect the rudder, because if it bends we'll be starting all over."

The six men climbed into the wagon with the Thing. Byrd craned his neck, trying to see it as they tied it down. It hadn't changed much since the last time he'd seen it.

Maybe narrower at one end. Maybe an extra bump on top. He couldn't hardly tell, it was so dark.

He was going to have to follow. He wished he had Candy so he could keep up better, but then again maybe not. Candy never could keep a secret.

The wagon lurched into motion, and Byrd followed on foot. He had on a brand-new pair of boots the old lady had given him, so his feet didn't hurt so bad. He could also walk faster than he used to. The wagon went slowly, so he kept up pretty well until he passed the newspaper office.

He didn't know how she did it, because that was a dang strong-smelling gardenia bush, but Candy caught wind of Byrd as he passed her. She set up a braying you could've heard all the way to Pelican Point.

Byrd froze. The wagon jerked to a halt.

"What's that?" one of the men on the wagon asked.

"Sounds like a mule!"

"Where is it?"

"Somebody shoot it!"

"And wake the neighborhood? Just grab it and shut it up."

Byrd hauled at the rope that tied Candy to her bush. It was tangled in a twisted limb and refused to come loose. Candy continued to hee-haw in spite of Byrd's whispered apologies.

He almost had her loose when he felt a heavy hand on his shoulder, lifting him and shaking him like a dead rat.

"What do you think you're doing, old man?"

Byrd ducked his head and kicked his feet. "Lemme go!"

"Hey, Beaumont, that's the Birdman," said someone on the wagon, "he's harmless."

Byrd felt his head return to normal position. His feet touched the ground.

Mr. Jamie kept hold of his shoulder. "Shut that mule up."

"I 'spect she's hungry," Byrd said. "Got any paper?"

"Chambliss, get that newspaper over there—hurry."

Candy was shortly chewing on the newspaper in injured silence. Byrd worked the rope free from the bush, while the men on the wagon looked around to make sure the disturbance hadn't brought down the watch.

Mr. Jamie's face was shadowed, but Byrd could feel his anger. If he didn't kill him, the old lady would. But maybe if he was dead Missy would forgive him.

"Here, give me that rope," Mr. Jamie said.

"But Candy'll run away—"

"I don't give a rat's ear about the mule! Give me the rope!"

Byrd obeyed.

Then found himself bound and tossed into the back of the wagon with the Thing. Some finlike part of it dug into his back.

"Keep him from tattling all over town about what he saw." Mr. Jamie climbed onto the front seat with the driver.

"But I wouldn't tell nobody—"

"Shut up!"

Byrd shut up.

The wagon bumped and jostled several hundred yards, then turned left. After a right-hand turn Byrd could smell the river. The wagon drew up. He heard water flowing past pilings and all the other night noises of a riverbank. Someone hauled him up by his jacket and the seat of his pants and tossed him into the mud several yards away from the wagon. Byrd could see boots and the wagon's wheels and not much else. He was afraid if he made any noise they might shoot him. He'd seen a gun in the waistband of one of the men.

He rolled over. Best he could tell, they were at the foot of Theater Street. The water of the bay was shallow and choppy here, because the wind blew through unobstructed by trees. They'd have a hard time sailing anything.

He scooted off to the side unnoticed by the men, who were busy unloading the Thing. Looked like a dang shark. A real big one. Byrd shuddered, thinking about Jonah in the Good Book.

He rolled closer and saw a long pier sloping into the water. Straining against the weight of the metal, the men carried the Thing across the pier and pushed it off into the water. He wondered why it didn't float off, but then he saw it was tied to a piling with a thick rope.

How were they going to sail it? No mast, no sails, not even a place to stand on it. It was round as a barrel and slick as glass. It bobbed like a cork in the rough water.

"You got the candle?" asked Laniere, and Mr. Jamie grunted. "Good. Now remember, when the candle goes out, that means your air's gone, and it's time to surface. Pump the water out of the ballast tank as fast as you can."

"I will." Mr. Jamie sounded impatient. "We've been through this a hundred times."

"I know, but we don't want to toss the whole project with any careless moves." Laniere spread his big, hammy hands. "Wish I was small enough to go with you."

"Well, you're not. I can handle it."

"Did you check—"

"I checked everything! We've got to go before daylight. Come on, men." Mr. Jamie approached the Thing, and the other men followed.

Stiff with terror, Byrd watched as Mr. Jamie raised one of the bumps on top of the Thing, like it was some kind of lid.

He wanted to go get the old lady, tell her what her grandson was doing. But he was trussed up like a chicken over a spit, and if he rolled much farther downhill he'd land in the river. He watched all the men but Laniere disappear, one by one, inside the top of the Thing.

Laniere untied the rope and gave it a shove with his boot. It floated away, picking up speed as if something inside gave it life. Before Byrd's goggling eyes, it began to submerge. Within a frog's spit, it disappeared underwater. Out on the pier, Laniere danced a little jig, then, arms folded, started to tramp up and down the pier.

Byrd didn't know how long he lay on the hard damp ground watching Laniere, but his arms and legs got numb and he got a crick in his neck. He almost yelled out, but Laniere halted at the end of the pier, staring out across the water. Laniere pulled out a pocket watch and held it up to the moonlight.

After another eternity of waiting, wondering what happened to the Thing, Byrd couldn't stand the pain in his limbs anymore. "Can't you come let me loose?" he called. "I promise I won't tell nobody."

Camilla sat straight up in bed. She had been dreaming again, the wedding dream. Jamie had escorted her down the aisle toward Gabriel Laniere. Gabriel calmly pointed a long, cold Colt .45 at Jamie's heart. He was laughing.

With trembling hands Camilla yanked off her nightcap and shoved her fingers into the wet ringlets at her temples.

She was going crazy.

Since she was awake, she ought to check on Harry.

She ignored the dressing gown lying across the foot of the bed and padded across to the door. It was too hot to put on extra clothes. Anyway, Harry would be asleep. She'd look in on him and come right back to bed.

Wearily pushing the long full sleeves of her gown to her elbows, she descended the stairs. She thought about last night as she left the kitchen, the way she'd turned her head at the last minute before kissing Harry on the cheek. He'd looked disappointed, but she hadn't been in a kissing mood after Gabriel left the room. Gabriel had closeted himself with Schuyler in the game room for the rest of the night, and she hadn't seen him since.

She stepped through diamond-shaped patches of moonlight cast by the mullioned windows above the front entryway, then headed through the central hallway toward the kitchen. It seemed to be a clear night. Maybe she'd step outside and cool her hot face before she checked on Harry.

She passed the dark, quiet little sewing room and stepped out onto the screened porch. Odd to think that Gabriel was asleep in a guest room in her own house. Or maybe he was out spying on somebody else—although, as far as she knew, anybody he might want to spy on was right here in the house.

Except Jamie. *Father, bring Jamie home.*

She sat in Lady's rocker and tucked her feet up inside her gown. A sweet peace enveloped her as she prayed for her brothers, for her father and grandmother. For Harry and Gabriel. For the men giving their lives in the foolishness of war. Fretting wasn't going to change anything. Only God could resolve the conflict.

Sometime later she heard odd noises coming from the back drive path. She got up and shoved open the screen door. It sounded like a horse clopping with a staggering gait down the path, its breath heaving.

"That you, Missy? I come to tell you—"

Heart pounding in her throat, Camilla hurried down the steps while Virgil caught his breath. "What is it?" She snatched Candy's tattered rope harness.

"It's Mr. Jamie—the Thing swallowed him!"

"What thing?"

"That shark-thing. He went down in it and never come back up!"

Camilla's knees buckled. Jamie had been in the fish boat. "Where did it go down?"

"Down at the end of Theater Street. They was a man named Laniere there, but he untied me and took off. Said for me to come get yore papa."

Virgil had been tied up at the river by Gabriel's uncle? Camilla had no idea what he was talking about, but she'd better do something. "Virgil, go wake up Horace and Willie. Tell them to get the wagon out and meet us at the place where the—where Jamie went down." Running toward the porch, she threw over her shoulder, "I'll be there soon as I can dress."

As she reached for the kitchen doorknob, it turned under her hand. She slammed full tilt into Gabriel's chest.

Gabriel had seen Camilla in men's pants, in a ball gown and in everyday working garb. The sight of her in a white cotton nightgown, limned by moonlight, her long curly hair glittering against her shoulders, knocked the breath out of him.

He steadied her, gripping her forearms against his chest. "I heard voices. What are you doing out here?"

"Get out of my way."

"Not until you tell me what's going on. Where's Harry?"

She jerked against his grasp. "As far as I know he's sound asleep."

Gabriel let go of her to push her hair out of her face, cool silk against his fingers. "You're upset. What's wrong?"

Trembling, Camilla closed her eyes, and tears seeped from under the thick lashes. "I need you, Gabriel. I need your help. Byrd just came to tell me the boat sank." She began to shudder violently.

"The torpedo boat?" Gabriel cupped her shoulders. "But that can't be—I—"

"Virgil saw you looking at it two nights ago." Camilla's eyes flew open as she grasped his wrists. "Did you do something to it? Sabotage it? You knew my brother would be on it!"

"Camilla, no—"

"I hate you!" She wrenched away from him. "You have no conscience, and you'd rather tell lies than eat. You've used me and my family. Don't ever ask me to trust you again."

Gabriel allowed her to shoulder past him. He stood there staring at his own trembling hands. Hands that in the past had done despicable things. He'd entered the church that night, intending to loosen one of the ballast tank valves—just enough that the pump wouldn't function properly.

But he hadn't been able to bring himself to jeopardize the life of Jamie Beaumont. Something else had gone wrong with the blasted vessel. He hadn't done his job, yet he was going to pay the consequences anyway in the most hideous way possible.

Looking up, he lowered his fisted hands. *God, are You there?*

He shook his head. Since when did God talk in audible voices anyway? He shoved open the outside screen door and headed toward the carriage house.

The building was lit by pine knots burning in iron baskets. The wagon was already hitched, with Horace at the reins and Willie helping his mother into the back. Good to know he'd have help, though the responsibility of the rescue lay on his shoulders.

Portia gave Gabriel a murderous glare as he vaulted into the wagon. "Where you think you're going, preacherman?"

Gabriel ignored her. "Let's go." Horace started the horses, and Gabriel glanced at him. "Any of the three of you swim?"

Portia and Willie exchanged an uncomfortable glance. "Naw, sir," Willie said.

"Didn't think so. Where are we headed?"

"Theater Street." Portia's tone was still surly. "Just hope it isn't too late."

"Where'd the old man go?"

Portia snorted. "The Birdman? Scared to death. Said he was going to check on his still."

Gabriel grabbed the side of the wagon as it lurched over a pothole. "I might've known."

The remainder of the short trip was accomplished in silence until they turned onto Theater Street, which dead-ended at the river. As the wagon rolled to a stop, Gabriel and Willie jumped to the ground and ran toward the pier.

With the dawn beginning to spread across the horizon Gabriel distinguished a prone figure at the end of the pier. Uncle Diron.

Diron looked up, face ravaged by tears, pushed himself up onto his knees and clutched his head. "This is my fault, Gabriel. They've been down too long. They're dead."

Chapter Nineteen

Gabriel took a shallow dive off the end of the pier. He swam hard and swift out into the center of the river, where Uncle Diron had said the boat disappeared. No telling how far it got before the air inside dissipated. He'd have to simply guess which direction Beaumont had steered the boat.

He came up for air, tired by the current forcing him downstream. It seemed the height of idiocy that they would have tested the vessel in such shallow water, especially in the dark. Gabriel could only assume that Jamie, having grown up fishing these waters, trusted his own navigational skills. The men had probably also feared that the farther they had to transport the boat, the greater their chances of discovery.

The current would have affected the course of the little underwater boat. Treading water, Gabriel took his bearings. Lights from downtown cast a misty glow above the warehouses lining the water's edge, while trees on the opposite side of the river shrouded the moon, casting deep shadows across the water.

Please, God, give me success, he prayed and started swimming again.

Gabriel swam and dove, searching, until his strength was all but gone. On the point of giving up as his uncle had done, something told him to try one more time. He stayed under until his lungs seemed about to burst, then as he turned to push to the surface, his foot brushed something hard and metallic.

He surfaced for air, panting. If by any chance those men were still alive, the minute he opened the hatch, four of them would die. He couldn't rescue more than one. Jamie Beaumont would be forward at the helm, nearly impossible for him to reach.

He heard a shout, looked toward the shore and saw a small fishing boat approaching with two men aboard. One of the figures he recognized as his uncle. If he could work quickly, they might be able to bring up more than one man. He dove again.

Thank God he'd explored the boat so carefully that night. He found the central hatch cover, lifted the latch and heard the horrid bubbling sound of water pouring into the interior of the boat. He entered, praying for grace. This was too much like going into a grave alive.

He felt his way forward, past four bodies floating against the hull. He reached the helm and felt for Jamie Beaumont's body. He grasped the captain's lax body and pulled him toward the hatch. It seemed they would never make it and Gabriel would die, too. He forced down his panic.

Almighty God, if You love me—if You love Camilla— help me get her brother to the surface.

After an agonizing struggle to squeeze past the mechanical apparatus of the boat, Gabriel pulled himself through the hatch, maintaining a tenuous hold on Jamie's collar. When they were both through, Gabriel shoved with his feet against the boat and swam one-armed toward the surface, towing Jamie Beaumont's dead weight.

Sweet, blessed air. Gasping, Gabriel filled his lungs with it, at the same time looking for the boat. "Uncle!" he shouted hoarsely and swam toward it.

With the last of his strength he clambered into the boat and helped his rescuers pull Jamie's body aboard. Coughing and sucking in great lungfuls of dank air, Gabriel flipped Jamie onto his back. He began to force oxygen into his lungs.

After several minutes he sat back on his heels and felt for a pulse, any twitch or sign of life. Nothing.

"He's dead, isn't he?" The trembling little voice came from behind his back.

One hand on Jamie's sodden chest, Gabriel twisted his head. Camilla stared at him, eyes like black holes. "What are you doing here?"

"Never mind that," she said. "Try again."

It was hopeless, but he bent to shove air into Jamie's lungs. The moment he moved away in despair, to his utter astonishment Jamie suddenly jerked, lifted his head, heaved and coughed. Water spewed out of his mouth, wetting Gabriel's already sopping chest.

"God, my God," Gabriel whispered in a delirious prayer of thanks, clutching the sides of the boat. He looked at Camilla.

She flung herself on her brother, who continued to heave water out of his lungs with single-minded concentration. "Jamie—oh, Jamie," she groaned over and over, patting him on the back, kissing his shoulder, wiping her eyes. "Oh, thank God."

Overcome, Gabriel gathered his wits. "Uncle, take us back to shore. We need to get him dried out and in bed."

Nodding, Diron began to ply the oars. "Brave little girl you got here. Them three was too scared to get out on the water, so the little one insisted on coming with me. I figured they'd all be dead. Can't believe you found the boat—"

"Uncle, how could you let her come?" Gabriel rounded on his uncle.

"I didn't make them boys get in that thing. They was all being well paid, and they wasn't supposed to get this far out from shore."

Camilla collapsed, weeping across Jamie's shivering body. "You did this, Gabriel. Four men dead, and we almost lost Jamie."

There was nothing Gabriel could say that would bring those men back to life. At least Camilla had her brother, but she clearly hated his very soul. Misery swamped him.

Only the quiet dip of the oars broke the silence. As the boat neared the pier where Portia and Willie and Horace waited, Camilla refused to look at Gabriel. After they tied in at the dock, she assisted in moving Jamie from the boat to the wagon. She climbed in, leaned into Portia's embrace and sat staring into Jamie's slack face. He had fallen into a sort of stupor.

Gabriel turned to his uncle. "Round up whoever else is in on this little project with you and get those other men out before daylight. Notify their families that there was a fishing accident."

Diron nodded and headed toward town on foot.

Gabriel turned to Willie, who stood beside the wagon.

"Ride Camilla's horse home. We'll meet you there." After Willie was gone, he climbed onto the seat beside Horace.

The ride back to Dauphin Street was accomplished in tense silence. Jamie's body had undergone enormous trauma. They could lose him yet.

As they drew up at the rear of the house, the sun was peeking over the ridge of trees to the east. Gabriel took charge, watching Camilla and hoping she would speak to him, absolve him of his part in the accident. Her eyes were glazed and dry as she allowed him to lift her from the wagon, while Portia and Horace took Jamie through the kitchen entrance.

"Camilla—"

"I've got to tell Papa and make sure Jamie's settled." She looked away. "Let me go."

Gabriel held her shoulders. "Jamie knew there was a risk."

"Yes. I should have stopped it."

"How?"

"I don't know." She looked up, her unfocused gaze so full of worry he would gladly have soaked it into himself. "*You* could have stopped it."

"Camilla, listen to me. This is war. You and I have been pulled in whether we like it or not. I can't stop this thing overnight. All I can do is accomplish my mission the best I know how. I'm beginning to believe…" He found himself thinking the impossible, wanting to offer her the fragile seed of his new faith. He didn't know how, and she wouldn't believe him now. He brushed a thumb across her cheek. "I've got to believe there's hope. That somehow you and I will come out of this alive and together. I swear I didn't sabotage the boat."

Her eyes filled and her soft mouth trembled. "Of course you'd say that." She pulled away from his hands and strode into the house.

He stared at the door of the screen porch. *Oh, God, where are You now?*

On an overcast afternoon two days later, Camilla stood with her family in the church cemetery, watching Pastor Lewis crumble a handful of dirt into each of the four graves before the men plied their shovels. General Forney and his staff had insisted on attending the service, lending military dignity and a sense of protection. But it was a false security. In fact, there was nothing real about this scene.

Back home in his bedroom, Jamie still lay at death's door with Portia attending him. His body, weakened from the bout with yellow fever, had yet to shake off the damage to his lungs, and he tossed and turned with feverish mutterings. Camilla and Lady had taken turns nursing him, but she'd found herself unable to sleep even when she was in her room alone at night. Horrible images of Gabriel Laniere heaving Jamie into the boat beside her kept circling her mind until she wanted to claw them out. One more minute under the water and the pastor would have been burying Jamie as well.

As the last shovelful of dirt fell, she backed out of the family circle and walked over to lean against a broad, mossy oak tree. She closed her eyes. Her legs felt like pudding.

"I'll take you home if you want, Camilla."

She looked up at Gabriel's dark, somber face. Since the accident, he'd left her alone for the most part, though she often felt his concerned gaze. She wanted to shriek at him.

Instead she took a deep breath. "I've thought a lot about that night, Gabriel. I can't figure out what Virgil was doing out there by the river. Did you send him to watch?"

"If I wanted a spy I wouldn't pick someone with the mental capacity of a five-year-old. I told you I didn't have anything to do with it."

"He said he saw you go in." Camilla's voice rose in spite of her determination to maintain control. "And you told me yourself you were going to destroy it."

"I'd planned to, but I decided it would be more worthwhile to steal it."

"I don't believe you," Camilla ground out. "You've lied to me from the beginning. Harry told me he was the one who kept you out of trouble in medical school, not the other way around, and that it was *his* research Dr. Kinch was interested in."

Gabriel's lips thinned. "And of course you'd believe him."

"He didn't want to tell me, but I made him. I could tell something was weighing on his mind last night." Camilla gave a short laugh. "He's afraid you'll talk me into doing something I shouldn't."

"God forbid Camilla Beaumont should do anything ill-advised." Gabriel took a step toward her.

There was a crunching sound nearby. Gabriel whirled, and Camilla sidestepped to see around the tree.

"There you are, Camilla!" Fanny Chambliss stood there, huffing as if out of breath. "Mother sent me to look for you."

Camilla glanced at Gabriel. "What is it?"

Fanny patted her bosom. "We decided we should get up a set of tableaux—in memory of the men who died. I know they'd not want us to pine away."

"Go ahead, if you want to." Camilla lifted a shoulder.

"Oh, but we—Mother and I—think you should participate, as well. After all, you can't be that busy."

"Fanny, I don't think—"

"Reverend Leland, tell her what a grand idea it is! People will be so overcome by sympathy for Camilla that— Oh my, we're bound to raise lots of money for the war effort."

Gabriel frowned.

"Besides," Fanny continued hastily, "if you take part, General Forney will lend his support. Wouldn't it be grand to have soldiers in a scene or two?"

Camilla closed her eyes, unutterably exhausted. She just wanted Fanny to leave her alone. "Oh, all right," she muttered, turning away.

Fanny caught her arm. "But perhaps you should try some tincture of rose water to put some color in your cheeks. You're looking a mite peaked."

Camilla stood before the pier-glass mirror in the foyer, vigorously rubbing her cheeks. She wished she had some of Delia Matthews's rouge so the hectic color now blooming would stay put all night. She wore her favorite mint-colored dress, but she still felt as if she were slogging through an anxious fog.

Behind her she heard footsteps bounding down the stairs and a whistle that sounded like Jamie's. She turned with a catch of her heart.

It was Schuyler, jerking at his cravat. "Hullo, Milla, let me at the mirror, would you?" He elbowed Camilla aside and craned his neck, examining a nick on his Adam's apple.

"You look very handsome." He'd grown older somehow in the week since Jamie's accident, his gaunt, coltish features seeming to have hardened and sharpened toward manhood. He'd just celebrated his fifteenth birthday.

"Thanks." His grin in the mirror turned sly. "You look slick yourself. Don't you wish old Harry could go to the party with you?"

She frowned. "Harry can't show his face outside the house, and if you tell anybody he's here—"

"It's common knowledge we've taken in a stray convalescent—with the general's blessing."

"What?"

"Don't worry, Lady's made sure nobody knows he's a relative." He grimaced. "Who'd contradict her?"

"I hope you're right. Come here." Camilla turned her brother and tugged his cravat straight. "Maybe you should check on the carriage."

"All right. Hope the Chamblisses have oysters." He jerked open the front door.

Camilla had told Harry she'd say goodbye before she left. It seemed ridiculous to attend any sort of celebration while Jamie was so sick, but Lady had insisted she needed to get out of the house, that she herself would attend Jamie.

She found Gabriel in the kitchen, sitting in a chair tipped back on two legs, feet propped on the end of Harry's cot. He was warbling on a harmonica as Harry finished off a supper of peas and corn bread.

Gabriel turned to see what had caused Harry's sudden grin. His lids drooped as he surveyed her full hooped skirts, low neckline and neatly coiffed hair. "Well," he drawled, "if it isn't Princess Camilla herself, come down to commingle with the peasants."

Camilla smiled at Harry. "Call Portia if you need anything while I'm gone. How're you feeling?"

"Much better, sweetheart, now that my appetite's back." Harry rubbed his still-lean middle.

Gabriel's chair hit the floor as he surged to his feet. "He'll be out of here in no time. See you later, old man—have to go dance with the flowers of the Confederacy." He whacked Harry on the shoulder, then took a step toward Camilla. He looked as solid and ungiving as a stone wall. And beautiful in the way of a dark angel.

She sidestepped. Gabriel followed, blocking the doorway. Planting her fists on her hips, Camilla leaned to see around him. "Harry, I'll look in on you when I get home tonight."

"I'll be looking forward—"

Gabriel turned Camilla and propelled her out on the dark screen porch. He pressed her against the wall, flattening her hoops, framing her face with his hands. She felt his breath on her mouth, smelled the clean scent of his linen, heard the singing of the mosquitoes beyond the screen.

"I can't watch you do that," Gabriel muttered. "Every day he stays, it gets more dangerous—"

"More dangerous than having a spy living in my house? At least Harry came in wearing a uniform." She grabbed his wrists. "You don't want anybody stepping in on your territory."

"Maybe." His voice came closer. "You said you'd marry me, Camilla."

"You know that was just a—"

He cut off her words, his mouth fierce against hers.

Within seconds she was angrily kissing him back. They broke apart, panting, and Gabriel set his forehead against hers. "See?"

Sweetness still speared through her. "I don't see anything. All I know is we both have responsibilities that don't include…well, what just happened."

"What's wrong with what just happened? Why not take whatever pleasure comes in the middle of this nightmare?"

"If that's what you want—pleasure for the moment—then go find Delia Matthews."

"I don't want Delia."

"Why, Gabriel?" She closed her eyed. "Why do you want me? Sometimes I think you don't even like me—and I know you don't like my family or anything they stand for! Please explain it to me."

"I can't explain it. You're the last person I ever thought—" Gabriel's voice splintered. "There's something—I don't know, shining about you that draws me, and—all *I* know is, I love you and I want you."

The raw emotion in his voice nearly undid her. "Here's what I want, just in case you care. I want a godly husband who'll love me and give me children and stay with me the rest of our lives."

"You know there aren't any guarantees in wartime."

"I don't have to have guarantees, but I do want commitment."

"And you think Harry Martin is going to give you that?"

"He already has. We've been betrothed since we were children."

"I can't believe you'd be stupid enough to marry one man when you're in love with someone else."

"Oh! You conceited, self-absorbed—"

"I know, I know. That didn't come out like I meant it." He took a breath, his hold gentling. "I told you I love you, Camilla. I mean it. And I did what you asked. I gave my life to God."

"You're just saying that to make me—make me believe you're different."

"You know better than that. I'd never lie to you."

There was something frightening in his tone. Something like truth. But she was afraid to trust it. She'd trusted too much already. "Let me go."

He released her and stepped back. "What do I have to do to prove it?"

"I don't know. It's just too much…" Camilla blinked away tears of confusion and rushed into the kitchen. "Schuyler, let's go!"

She heard the outside screen door slam hard. Gabriel was gone.

Chapter Twenty

At a discreet scratch on the door, Lady looked up from her journal. "Come." She hastily wiped her pen and put the book away.

Portia entered the room. Her dark brown eyes met Lady's with mutual trust and respect. "Ma'am."

"Are the children off to the party?"

"Yes. Heard some mighty loud fussin' out on the screen porch right before Camilla and Schuyler left."

"Indeed?"

Portia grinned a little. "I expect Reverend Leland got his ears boxed."

"Keep an eye on them, Portia. I don't want things getting out of hand."

"You know I will. But here's what I come to tell you." Tension sharpened Portia's voice. "Willie's been watching Mr. Zeke. He and Beckham Chambliss and that no-account Diron Laniere have pulled the fish boat out of the river, pumped the water out of it and started working on it again. They talking about moving it out of Mobile."

Lady closed her eyes briefly. "That machine already killed four men and nearly took my grandson. I cannot understand Ezekiel's fascination..." She drew a deep breath. "Does the general know?"

"I think he's looking the other way. Seems that boat's just as important to him as catching the spy." Portia tipped her beautiful, regal head. "Something else. Don't it strike you a mite odd the Rebs are so easy about Mr. Harry being here?"

Lady frowned. "The general is a kind man. He appreciates family loyalty."

"But he ain't stupid. And he's visited Mr. Harry himself a time or two. Late at night."

"What are you saying? You think Forney's trying to force Harry to turn coat?"

Portia folded her lips together. "This might be a chicken don't need no turning."

Lady returned her old friend's grim look. It had never occurred to her to distrust Harry, though she of all people knew how deceiving appearances could be. "I've got to talk to him."

"I thought you would."

"Watch him, Portia. I'll be down later."

Gabriel expelled a cloud of cigar smoke. From the darkness of the terrace outside the Chamblisses' grand ballroom he watched the company inside laughing and chattering as they enjoyed an array of expensive hors d'oeuvres. Earlier, he'd applauded the stultifyingly insipid tableaux celebrating the beauty and patriotism of the South's young women, the gallantry of its young men. As soon as it was over, he'd stepped outside for a smoke.

Somehow he had to find out what had caused the torpedo boat to sink and what had happened to it since the night of the accident—and not just for Camilla's sake. If they were that determined to get the thing running, they were desperate. Farragut would want to know.

The closest source of information at this point was Camilla's father. Uncle Diron had disappeared sometime during the past two weeks since. Gabriel had ridden down to the river shack and found it deserted. Ajax had greeted him with undisguised hero worship and insisted on following him back to town. Feeling sorry for the abandoned hound, Gabriel had lifted him onto the saddle and carried him, dangling like a carcass, all the way home.

He supposed he shouldn't call the Beaumont mansion *home*. Truth was, he'd begun to enjoy verbally fencing with the old lady, sharing a smoke with Ezekiel after dinner, playing billiards with Schuyler. He'd even managed a time or two to coax a gleam of amusement into Portia's disapproving dark eyes by filching her angel biscuits between meals.

Through the window now, he watched Camilla flirting her eyes at that second lieutenant who always seemed to be around lately. The hardest thing about staying in the Beaumont house was hearing Camilla's voice every day, watching her nurse Harry and her brother back to health, sensing her anger with him.

Harry calling her *sweetheart* tonight had taken him beyond objectivity where she was concerned. Or maybe he'd been past it for a long time. Stupid to blurt out his love for her, his conversion experience, in that awkward way. He could only dream about coming back after the war to see if he still had a chance. Maybe he could even offer that commitment she wanted so badly.

He studied the glowing tip of his cigar, smiling. Marriage for Gabriel Laniere. Maybe humility was a good thing.

Leaning against the French door, he watched Camilla's vivid heart-shaped face as she accepted Duvall's teasing. Funny, he'd not considered her beautiful the first time he saw her. Now—just the turn of her cheek brought a catch to his breath. He watched her gaze drift away as if she wasn't really listening. The worry at the back of her expression reminded him of the day of the funeral. He wished he could chase it away.

But it looked as if somebody else had already done so. As he opened the door to reenter the house, Camilla flushed and straightened. Duvall looked amused.

As Gabriel stepped inside the room, Camilla stared at the lieutenant, chin up. "You can't have really done that."

Duvall smirked. "It was necessary to maintain the discipline of the troops. We couldn't let that old man funnel moonshine into the ranks without check."

Gabriel stood behind Camilla's shoulder. "What old man?"

Duvall flicked an impatient glance at Gabriel. "Virgil Byrd—the Birdman, as he's known. Reverend, I'm sure you'll approve of removing another source of contraband whiskey."

Camilla knotted her fingers. "Couldn't you destroy Virgil's still without taking him to jail?"

Duvall shrugged. "Byrd's been seen at some deuced odd places at all hours of the night. We suspect his activities may involve rather more than bootlegging."

Gabriel studied the young lieutenant. If the Rebs had been watching Byrd, then he and Camilla were in trouble, too. "Miss Beaumont, it's my privilege and responsibility to visit those who are sick and in prison. At the first opportunity, I'll be happy to ascertain Mr. Byrd's well-being."

"Thank you, but—oh, Virgil will be so scared!" Camilla hurried toward the door.

A satisfied smile curved the lieutenant's mouth.

Gabriel pushed his way through the crowd, following Camilla. As he reached the doorway, Fanny Chambliss stepped into his path. "Reverend Leland—Gabriel, where are you going in such a hurry? You must come and meet my papa."

Gabriel watched Camilla's disappearing figure. "I'm sorry, but—"

"Weren't you asking me just the other day about Papa's donation to the needy in our town?" Fanny pouted.

Gabriel hesitated. Camilla couldn't get into trouble in the ten minutes it would take him to get rid of Fanny. He bowed. "Miss Chambliss, I am at your disposal."

"He's asleep, Willie." Through a hole in the roof of the jail Camilla looked down at Virgil, slumped directly below, snoring. How he'd slept through the noise they'd made removing the tiles was a mystery. She moved to slide feetfirst into the hole, and a rain of disintegrated mortar fell into the cell.

Virgil sat up, coughing and brushing at his face. "Missy!"

"Shh! You'll wake the guard!"

Camilla lowered herself, hung by her hands for a moment, then dropped lightly onto the floor. She brushed at her stinging hands.

Virgil struggled to his feet. "I knowed you'd come."

"Why didn't you stay out at Caswell Springs?"

"I was afraid you'd need me." He touched her shoulder. "It's gonna be all right. I been trusting in God."

"It's not that s—" She swallowed hard. "Oh, Virgil." His faith was an example she ought to follow.

The filtered starlight was blocked by a dark face peering through the hole in the roof. "Miss Milla! You all right?"

Camilla looked up. "Willie! Do you have the rope ready?"

"Yes'm. Here it comes."

"Virgil, you first. Once you're out, go get Candy. I found her wandering around and tied her up behind the newspaper office. Go straight to Caswell Springs and stay there until I come for you." She shook her finger in his face. "You hear me?"

"Yes, ma'am." Virgil took hold of the thick rope hanging beside his head. It jerked him off his feet and pulled him upward.

Left alone, Camilla began to pray.

Lady paused outside Ezekiel's study. Confronting him had never been easy, but in these days of war—with resources and tempers stretched thin—she dreaded adding to his worry. Drawing herself up, she rapped smartly on the door with her cane.

An indistinguishable growl was her answer.

"Ezekiel, I need to speak with you."

"I'm sorry, Lady, but this is not a good time."

"Oh, pish." She opened the door.

General Forney, seated at Ezekiel's desk, immediately got to his feet. Ezekiel stood at the fireplace, puffing away on a cigar.

She wished she had one. "I beg your pardon, gentlemen," she said without a trace of regret.

The general bowed as Ezekiel took the cigar out of his mouth. "Lady! Are you not at the Chambliss ball?"

"Clearly I'm not," she said tartly. "I wasn't feeling quite the thing. But I've recovered enough to venture down to the kitchen to check on our...guest."

"How is he?" Ezekiel glanced uneasily at the general, who looked, she thought, a bit conscience-stricken.

"Well enough to eat a good meal and make eyes at your daughter. It's high time we had him escorted to his rendezvous with the appropriate authorities on Ship Island. Don't you agree, General?"

Forney pulled at his mustache. "Indeed I do. We shall make arrangements at the first opportunity."

"Lady, your interference is unnecessary. I know the boy is no direct relation to you, but there is no reason for this heartless—"

Forney tapped the desk. "Beaumont, you may rest easy. The boy will be treated with every consideration."

Ezekiel started to speak, but something in the general's intent expression seemed to stay further protest. He walked to the door and bowed to Lady with exaggerated courtesy. "If you're satisfied, ma'am, the general and I were discussing important business. We'll not keep you any longer."

Repressing the urge to poke her son-in-law's round stomach with the end of her cane, she smiled at Forney. "Thank you, General. I depend on your attention to duty." She curtsied and quit the office. As soon as she heard the door shut, she headed for Camilla's room directly above the office.

* * *

Gabriel took the Jack and the Beanstalk route to Camilla's room via the wisteria vine. The urgency of catching her before she went after Byrd outweighed his fear of the damage Fanny Chambliss's jealous suspicions could cause. Camilla had a good thirty-minute lead on him.

He pushed open the sheers inside the window, then stepped over the window seat, listening to the silence of the room.

The bed gleamed with white lace in the moonlight. As part of his brain conjured up a picture of Camilla in her nightgown, her hair streaming across her shoulders, a different sort of knot developed in his gut. He should make a noise and warn her. Or climb back down the wisteria. If her father should find him here—

"Well, Gabriel, you are certainly one for creative entrances." A candle flared in the corner, revealing Lady enthroned in Camilla's chair. She smiled like a pirate. "I suppose I should question your familiarity with my granddaughter's bedroom."

He opened his mouth to speak.

"Never mind." She slashed an imperious gesture. "What are you doing here?"

He glanced at the window. "Where's Camilla?"

The rocking chair stilled. "She's not at the party?"

"She left thirty minutes ago. You haven't seen her?"

"No, I'd only been here a few minutes myself when you arrived." Lady reached for her cane and struggled to her feet. "What happened?"

"It's a long story." Gabriel turned back to the window. "I've got to go after her."

Before he could blink, the cane hooked his ankle. Gabriel found himself flat on his back on the floor, a knife at the end of the cane grazing his temple. "Not so fast," Lady said calmly. "I want the whole story, if you please."

He lay silent, reviewing his options.

Lady sighed. "If you hadn't guessed by now, I am the Camellia. I'm the one who's been giving you your spying orders. I can't help you if you won't tell me what's wrong."

Gabriel's head swam. He'd been chasing all over the United States, not to mention the C.S.A., at the behest of a hundred-pound grandmother who'd been in love with his grandfather.

"Move the cane so I can sit up," he gasped.

Lady chuckled and retracted the blade.

Gabriel got to his feet. "Does Camilla know who you are?"

"For her safety I've kept it from her, though the servants know." She shrugged. "My sympathies were with the North from the beginning, because of my parents' antislavery beliefs. I had no control over my husband's plantation until he died, when I freed the field hands and moved in here with my daughter's family. Portia, Horace and Willie insisted on following me."

Gabriel folded his arms. "So you taught Camilla to be abolitionist."

The old woman snorted. "The subject caused such disruption when the children were small that Ezekiel and I agreed to wait until they were older to discuss it. Events took care of themselves."

"What do you mean?"

"When Camilla was about fourteen, she went fishing one day when she was supposed to be in school. She happened across a slave woman who had escaped with her baby in a whiskey barrel. The woman was dead, but Camilla and Portia managed to get the baby away."

"My God."

"Yes, God was very much in control." Lady smiled wryly. "Portia came to me. Though I was very angry with her for involving my granddaughter, the damage was done. I could see that if Camilla was to be kept from disaster, I would have to help her." She shrugged again. "Over the years we've developed an unofficial station of the underground railroad. Camilla is quite good at what she does."

"I can't believe you would let her—"

"Gabriel, have you yet succeeded in preventing Camilla from doing what seems right to her?"

He had to smile. "You should have told me long ago who you are."

"It's a complicated situation. I met Farragut years before hostilities broke out. Afterwards, I saw that I was in a position to provide intelligence. Women hear things that men don't realize is useful. I got word to Farragut, and he agreed that I might help. I've gradually taken on more responsibility. But—as you know, trust has to be earned."

"Working blind is not my idea of effective intelligence. I've wasted enough time here." Gabriel edged toward the window, steering clear of that lethal cane. "The Rebs caught the Birdman selling liquor to the enlisted men, and Camilla seems to have gone to his rescue."

Lady sat down hard on the window seat. "I just overheard a conversation between my son-in-law and the general. The silver shipment that came in this week wasn't for cotton. There's been a trade for the torpedo boat, and Forney is having the vessel moved from Mobile to Charleston."

"When?"

"Tonight. Union forces are crossing the line into Mississippi and will be in Pass Christian later today." Lady shook her head. "Forney's afraid if they don't move the vessel now it will be confiscated."

"The Federals are in Mississippi? I suppose that's why Forney's men left the ball early."

"I'm sure. Which means there will be military personnel all over town tonight. You've got to stop Camilla."

"Precisely. So if you don't mind…"

Lady moved aside. Gabriel climbed out the window and found a foothold on the vine. Camilla's lead was now close to an hour. It would be a miracle if he caught her before she walked into trouble.

Chapter Twenty-One

Camilla rubbed her arms as she waited for Willie to drop the rope. The cell made her skin crawl. No windows, a heavy oak door braced with iron bars, smelly earth floor. She kept her face turned up to the hole in the roof.

The Lord is my light and my salvation, she reminded herself, craning her neck to see the stars.

At last she heard a scraping sound, then the rope fell, brushing her shoulder. "Willie?" When he grunted in response, she grabbed the lifeline. "I've got it. Pull me up."

With a small jerk she was on her way up. She scratched her face coming out of the hole, and the rope burned her hands, but the feel of moist open air was a blessing. She lay for a moment with her cheek against the shingles, her legs still dangling inside the jail.

She took a breath and looked around for Willie. There was a big figure crouched beside her, his face shadowed by his hat.

"Miss Beaumont. How charming to meet you here." The hat tipped back, and Gabriel's teeth gleamed white in the darkness. "I believe you owe me a dance."

She pulled herself out onto the roof. "You're worse than a wagon dog following me around."

He clicked his tongue. "You wound me. A little gratitude wouldn't be out of place."

Sitting up, she jerked the rope out of his hands and began to coil it around her arm. "How'd you know where to find me?"

"Ah. See, that's where observation pays off. I asked myself, 'Reverend Leland, if you were a brave but hare-brained little girl who wanted to commit an act of treason, what would you do?'" He tilted his head and deepened his voice in self-mockery. "'Why, I believe I would go home, change into my brother's clothes and talk one of my servants—who happens to possess as little sense as I do—into assisting me.'" He returned to his natural voice. "And bless me, Miss Beaumont, if you haven't done just that." He sat balanced on his haunches as comfortably as if he were drinking tea in Lady's pink parlor.

Scoundrel. "Where's Willie?"

"I sent him on with Byrd." Gabriel took the heavy rope off her shoulder and proceeded to undo her work. He efficiently tied one end to a stovepipe poking out of the roof, then tossed the other over the edge. "Told him I would get you out of here safely."

Of course Willie would obey *him* instead of Camilla. With a sigh, she pulled the roofing slates back across the hole. "I can get myself home."

"You're not going home."

"What are you talking about?"

"Camilla, the omnipresent Lieutenant Duvall will know exactly who deprived him of his prisoner. Why do you think he told you about it? Since you took the bait and managed to get here before I could stop you, the only recourse is sending you to Union territory."

She struggled to keep her voice down. "Are you mad? I'm not leaving my home and everybody I—"

"Yes. You are. I've managed to avoid suspicion myself, but Duvall is aware you're not the butter-wouldn't-melt-in-your-mouth society miss you claim to be. I'm surprised he's not here already."

Camilla stared at him, the breath knocked out of her. "Gabriel, I can't leave without saying goodbye—"

"If you go home, you'll be arrested for treason along with your entire family."

She crouched before him, suffocated by the truth. He was right. Part of this terrible coil could be directly attributed to Gabriel's machinations—but not all. Her own decisions, her own mistakes, had led her and her loved ones into mortal danger. Despite his harsh words, she sensed his compassion.

Compassion? Where did that fit with this spy, this liar?

She drew herself together. "All right," she muttered. "Then let's go. I'll get word to them later."

"Good girl." Relief colored Gabriel's deep voice. "I'll go down first, you follow. Be careful." He backed spider fashion down the sloping roof, hands and feet clinging to the shingles.

Camilla wasn't afraid of heights, but the steep descent was tricky. Scooting on her rear, she inched down while Gabriel grabbed the rope and went over the edge. By the time she reached the eaves, Gabriel was standing on the ground holding the rope taut. Taking a deep breath for courage, she slid onto her stomach and shimmied down.

Gabriel caught her by the waist before she reached

the bottom and set her on her feet. To her surprise, he immediately released her and stepped back.

She gave him a questioning look, but he reached for the rope and flung it up onto the roof out of sight.

"Where are we going?" she whispered. Government Street was deserted, but she didn't want to draw the attention of any random sentry who might be out and about.

"Rail station. There's to be a trade tonight. Turns out the eight hundred thousand in silver your friend Fanny has been counting on has nothing to do with contraband cotton. It's earmarked to pay for the fish boat. Forney's going to send it by rail over to Charleston."

"They got it working again?"

Gabriel nodded, putting a finger over his lips. He pulled Camilla into the shadow between two buildings. "Sentry," he whispered in her ear.

They waited, Camilla hardly daring to breathe but aware of Gabriel's solid shoulder just above hers. A gray-clad sentry sauntered by, whistling, gun propped across one shoulder. He looked neither right nor left and disappeared around the next corner.

Gabriel touched Camilla's arm. "Come on."

They zigzagged through town without further alarm, approaching the depot from behind the warehouse. The river ran behind them, silent in midnight somnolence. A few boats tied in at the dock rocked gently with the current, their owners and captains long gone for the night.

Camilla's heart pounded, though she hid her reluctance. At last she was going to see with her own eyes this contraption that had nearly killed Jamie. If only there were some way she could make sure it never killed another sailor, whether Union or Confederate. Nobody ought to suffer the way her family had suffered for such an evil cause.

Gabriel slipped around the side of the warehouse on the balls of his feet, carefully stepping on tufts of grass and mud, so as not to crush the oyster shells underfoot. She followed as best she could, nearly slamming into him when he stopped suddenly at the corner.

He peered around the building. Camilla held her breath.

No sound but the chirr of mosquitoes and tree frogs. The damp reek of the river. Rough plank walls against her shoulder. She looked up at the moon, sailing like a virgin's halo into a bank of clouds.

"There's not a soul here," Gabriel breathed. "What's going on?"

"Maybe they changed their minds."

"Your grandmother said—"

Camilla started to laugh out loud, but caught herself and crammed a fist against her mouth. "What's *Lady* got to do with it?" she whispered.

There was a long pause. "You didn't know?"

She looked up at him, expecting him to explain the joke. The night was very dark indeed, and she'd left her glasses at home. But her eyes had somewhat adjusted to the gloom, and there was no sign of amusement in his posture or manner. "Gabriel?"

"Your grandmother's the brains behind everything. The underground railroad, setting up my couriers, communication with the admiral." He paused. "Everything."

In a night full of surprises, this one took over her breath, her thoughts, the strength in her legs.

Gabriel caught her around the waist. "Easy now." He gave her a moment to recover. "She said your father and the general were to meet my uncle and Mr. Chambliss here at midnight, to arrange sending the torpedo boat east. I've got to make sure that doesn't happen."

"How are you going to—" She gasped at the sound of approaching footsteps.

"I told you the rudder was bent." It was Diron Laniere's rough voice. "We couldn't send it to Carolina without putting it back through the forge."

"So your faulty work is to blame for nearly losing eight hundred thousand dollars' worth of inventory." The cultured drawl sounded like Fanny's father, Mr. Chambliss. The two men paused just beyond the corner behind which Gabriel and Camilla waited.

"The boat was perfect," growled Diron. "Only thing that would do that much damage would be if got caught on something underneath the water while it was in operation. Threw the balance off so it waggled in circles instead of coming to the surface."

Mr. Chambliss grunted, but Camilla couldn't hear the rest of his answer. There was a jingling of keys as somebody opened the warehouse door. The men's voices retreated inside the building.

For the moment Camilla didn't care. *The rudder was bent.* The boat had been destroyed while in operation—not before.

Gabriel had nothing to do with Jamie's accident.

"Camilla!" Gabriel gave her a slight shake, bringing her back to herself. "Are you all right?"

"I'm..." She passed a hand across her brow. "I'm so sorry, Gabriel."

"About what? Not knowing about your grandma?"

"No, about... I thought you..." She seized his hands. "You didn't sabotage that boat, did you?"

"I told you." He searched her face with gruff tenderness. "I was going to loosen a ballast tank valve, but at the last minute I just couldn't do it. That's why it's so important that I succeed this time."

"So the other thing you told me…the thing about giving your life to God? Was that the truth, too?"

"It's the absolute truth. And it has nothing to do with you. Well, of course, in a sense it does, because I'd never had found Him without you. But maybe I *would* have, because it seems He's been pursuing me since I was ten years—"

Camilla launched herself at him, stopping his incoherent whisper with her lips.

Lady carried a candle into the dark sewing room off the kitchen and found Harry sound asleep on his cot. When she touched his shoulder, he grunted and rolled over, swiping a hand across his face.

"Lady?" His voice was rough with lingering sleep. In the flickering light of the candle she thought his blue uniform still hung loosely on his thin frame, but he seemed recovered from whatever malady had overtaken him. He lifted his head. "What are you doing here? What time is it?"

"After midnight." She set the candle on the sewing machine table and dragged Camilla's little stool close to the cot.

A dimple creased Harry's rough cheek. "To what do I owe the pleasure of this unexpected condescension?"

"As you very well know, charm will get you nowhere with me." She frowned at him.

"It's the middle of the night," Harry complained. "You could at least be cordial. Why did you never like me?"

"I don't dislike you, Harry. I simply wish you wouldn't take advantage of Camilla's hero worship. She deserves a chance to meet other young men before she ties herself to you."

"Yes, but even when we were children—"

"Even when you were children I could see it coming. Leave her alone, Harry."

He sat up, injury on every line of his thin, handsome face. "Uncle Zeke thinks I'm good enough for her. Jamie, too."

"I didn't bring you here to argue over Camilla. I want to know what you've been telling General Forney."

Harry's expression was innocent. "We've discussed the terms of my exchange. That's all."

"And just what are those terms?"

"You're a meddlesome woman, do you know that?" Harry smiled gently.

"Have you turned Camilla pro-Union?"

"I don't discuss politics with Camilla."

"Well, you're going to discuss politics with me. I won't have my granddaughter jeopardized by your checkerboard loyalties." Lady was pleased to see Harry's eyes flicker. "If you've got any notion of taking Camilla with you when you leave Mobile, you have another think coming." She paused. "And if you love her, you *are* leaving Mobile."

Harry sat white-faced and wordless for a moment. "I'm not sure what you mean."

Lady unfastened Camilla's locket from about her neck. "I have a proposition for you, my dear."

Delia held her breath as the stable door opened, admitting a small pool of candlelight. For more than an hour, she'd been sitting on a bale of hay in the first stall, absorbing the unfamiliar odors of leather, feed and manure, her pulse accelerating with every passing moment.

She'd never laid eyes on the house servant who'd brought her the Camellia's note. But he'd spoken the code word and waited respectfully while she responded. The instructions he brought were both odd and downright inconvenient, considering she'd been entertaining a highly placed officer with connections to the lower Mississippi command. But she didn't dare defy a direct order.

So she'd rid herself of her visitor, changed into her *Omnibus* costume and skipped off the riverboat. Hurrying through the stifling, silent streets of Mobile, she'd wondered at this sudden development. She'd thought Gabriel had the situation well in hand and hadn't expected to meet him again.

But the candle's flame revealed a much thinner frame than the erstwhile minister's muscular body. Delia shrank into the shadows of the stall. Who was this? Under the broad brim of the man's hat, she could see nothing but an angular jaw.

He lifted the candle. "Camellia?" The voice was soft and deep, almost cultured. Southern in inflection.

"Who are you?" She stayed in the shadow, waiting to see what he'd do.

"Harry Martin. Lady sent me." His gaze found the stall, and he began to edge toward her. "Come on out."

"Stop right there. I have a gun." She let him hear the click of shot engaging. "Where's Gabriel?"

"I gather he's in need of assistance. That's where you and I come in."

Nothing seemed right about this. Strange man, strange meeting place, vague orders. But still...orders. She opened the stall door and moved into the aisle, the little derringer clasped in both hands.

Harry Martin moved closer, spilling candlelight on her face. His eyes widened in admiration, his lips forming a soundless whistle.

She aimed the gun at his heart. "I have the wagon ready. Where's the silver?"

"They're bringing it down to the kitchen entrance. Would you mind pointing that popgun somewhere besides my person? You're making me a tad nervous."

"I'm not too calm myself," she said grimly. "I don't know why we're doing this."

"Because you and I are expendable, my dear." Martin smiled faintly. "And—presuming we manage to evade capture—we stand to come out of this much richer than we went in. How does that sound?"

Delia hesitated, then lowered the gun. Harry Martin might not have the palpable charisma of Gabriel Laniere, but there was a certain wicked charm in that crooked smile. And the opportunistic flair appealed to her sense of adventure.

"It sounds like you and I are in for an interesting evening. Come help me hitch these horses."

Gabriel would have been much happier if he'd been able to finish this job without worrying about Camilla's safety. The bravest of cohorts, she would never slow him down on purpose, but she was flagging. She'd been through a lot today, and they had a long night ahead.

The two of them skulked in a ditch below the tracks, where an eastbound train chugged in the dark like some jolly monster. They'd watched Beckham Chambliss pace along the rails while Gabriel's uncle and a small crew of roustabouts strained to lever the boat from a wagon into an open railroad car. Uncle Diron's profane remonstrations to "Watch out, you boneheads!" had punctuated the men's grunts and curses for several hair-raising minutes before the vessel was safely disposed in its home on wheels.

It appeared that Diron was to be the only guard assigned to the boat. The rowdies scattered as he clambered into the car, wiping his sweating face on a rag. He stood scowling down at Chambliss in the yellow light of a lantern swinging from his large fist. "You're sure the payment's secure—"

"I told you, Laniere, you'll receive your share on your return." Chambliss backed away, as if he were afraid the big man would charge him like the bear he resembled. "Just get this thing delivered. Then it'll be their responsibility."

Diron glanced at the shadowy hulk of the boat behind him. "I'm gonna miss her. I might stay and make sure she does her job."

Chambliss shrugged. "What you do from here is your business—as long as the merchandise reaches the buyer. I'm going to report to Beaumont and the general." Waving away Diron's growl of assent, he turned and staggered toward the empty wagon.

Gabriel felt for Camilla's hand. "Now's our chance. Come on." He stood cautiously, making sure she was on her feet before he moved toward the train.

Diron had taken the lamp inside, and Gabriel avoided its dull glow as he flattened himself beside the open door. "Uncle!" he called softly. "It's me."

Diron's curly gray head appeared in the opening of the boxcar. "Gabe? What the—"

"Shh! Give me a hand up, will you?" Gabriel allowed his uncle to pull him into the car, stifling more profane exclamations with a raised hand. He turned and leaned out to help Camilla in. "Up you go."

She landed on her feet, raising her chin as Diron lifted the lantern and squinted at her.

"Well, if it ain't my little quinine lady." The old man shook his head.

"How are you, sir?" she said as politely as if she were still dressed in ball gown and hoops. Gabriel half expected her to curtsy.

Diron scratched his head. "I'm confused. What're you two up to this time?" He peered at Gabriel, nearly blinding him with the lantern.

"Douse the light, uncle. I need to talk to you."

Diron's expression shifted from good-humored curiosity to suspicion. "What have you got yourself into now, boy?" He blew out the lamp, and darkness blanketed the rail car.

Gabriel reached for Camilla's hand. "Camilla and I are eloping."

She gave a little squeak, which he silenced by squeezing her hand.

"Her pa coming after her? I don't want to get on the bad side of Ezekiel Beaumont."

"As far as I know, he isn't." Gabriel forbore to mention the possibility that, before the night was over, they would be followed by half the military command of Mobile. "They won't miss her until morning. By then we'll be halfway to South Carolina."

"You got rocks in your head? You can't run off with the daughter of one of the richest men in Mobile!"

"Keep your voice down, uncle."

"Papa isn't rich." Camilla's voice trembled slightly, but Gabriel was glad to hear a bit of her usual pertness assert itself. "And I'm old enough to marry who I want."

"Then go ahead and marry him, but don't involve me in your havey-cavey business." Diron's voice took on a note of importance. "And your papa may not have been rich before, but this thing right here—it's made us all a pretty good pile of money tonight."

"Is that— Is it the torpedo boat?" As Camilla drew closer to Gabriel he could feel her shiver. "I thought it was at the bottom of the river."

"We raised it. I wasn't supposed to tell, but since you seen it, there's no point keeping quiet."

"Four men died in that thing, uncle. You should've left it where it was."

"Works better than ever now," Diron said stubbornly. "And it's faster and tighter than the one those idiots sank in New Orleans."

Gabriel slid an arm around Camilla. If she fell apart, Uncle Diron might call down the watch. As of yet, he seemed to have no idea of Gabriel's true mission.

Gabriel should have known his little love was built of sterner stuff than most women.

She took a shuddering breath. "My brother nearly died trying to make this boat operable, Gabriel. We need to help whatever way we can."

The click of a gun from the vicinity of the doorway made the hair on Gabriel's arms rise. He turned, reaching for his derringer.

"I wouldn't advise that, Laniere." Lieutenant Duvall's tall figure wavered, a shadow just beyond the open doorway of the rail car. A gun glinted in his hand. He pointed it at Camilla's head. "Such a fine sentiment, Miss Beaumont. But I wonder how the judge will interpret it in light of your collusion with a known Union spy. Your friend Miss Chambliss has confirmed extremely suspect behavior, including your relationships with Harry Martin and Virgil Byrd."

Chapter Twenty-Two

Delia clutched the wagon seat as it rocked over the rutted downtown streets. Harry Martin seemed to mind neither the bone-jarring impact of wooden wheels on hard-baked red clay nor the ominous rumble of thunder overhead. Summer thunderstorms were apt to burst open without a moment's notice, and—though she was no wilting flower to be overset by damp clothing—delivering their cargo to its destination over flooded streets would be dangerous as well as uncomfortable.

So far the journey from Dauphin to Lipscomb streets had been accomplished with a minimum of fuss. Harry seemed disposed to address her with a mixture of ironic courtesy and genuine masculine admiration—piquing her pride but in no way putting her out of countenance.

She had no doubt, however, that given time she could properly enslave him.

All thoughts of conquest were jolted right out of her head when a peremptory voice rang out, "Halt there! Your pass, if you please!"

Delia tensed as Harry reined in the horses.

A young graycoat officer approached holding a lantern. He yawned and shifted his gun to the opposite shoulder. "Y'all are out late. Where you going?"

"The depot." Pulling his hat low over his face, Harry reached into his coat pocket. "Here's my pass."

Frowning, the sentry scanned the paper. "Looks like General Forney's signature." He sent Delia an appreciative look. "Haven't I seen you before?"

She fluttered her lashes. "Maybe."

The sentry rewarded her with a smile. "What's in the wagon?"

"Take a look if you want," Harry said, sounding bored. "You saw the pass. It's the general's commission."

The sentry turned toward the rear of the wagon. "Run into anybody else on your way?"

Harry shook his head, but Delia caught the odd inflection in the question. "You looking for somebody?"

The young man hesitated. "Deuced odd things going on down at the station tonight. Too much activity for a Sunday morning." He shrugged. "But who am I to question the general's orders? Y'all go on. Just be careful. The bottom's fixing to fall out."

As if to verify this sage prediction, thunder rolled and a few heavy drops spattered onto Delia's knitted cap.

Harry flapped the reins, and they were in motion. Moments later the wagon bumped across an intersection of rails, and the depot came into sight. Harry circled the wagon toward the river, stopping on an elevated stretch of ground that was rapidly turning to mud. By now, the rain was coming down in earnest.

Delia peered up at her grim-faced escort. "What now?"

"See that train over there?"

She wiped her face with her hand. "Yeah."

"We're going to search every car until we find Camilla and Gabriel."

Terror strangling her, Camilla stared into the black eye of Duvall's pistol. Cold sweat dampened the front of her shirt and popped out on her upper lip. She captured thoughts fluttering like frightened birds and offered them in prayer. *Oh, God, the lion's den. Are You here?*

He was. She knew it—and glancing at Gabriel's tense face, she felt his knowledge, too. The comfort of his solid presence, his oneness of spirit with her, bolstered her courage.

"Miss Beaumont, please put your hands behind your back. Laniere, tie her up." Duvall detached a rope dangling from his waist and tossed it to Diron. When he hesitated, Duvall gave a small shrug. "Or I will shoot her."

Camilla's knees trembled, but she obeyed. Gabriel would not hurt her.

"Uncle?" Gabriel glanced at Diron as he moved behind Camilla to reluctantly wrap the rope around her wrists.

Diron looked away, flapping his hands. "I hoped you wouldn't come. But, boy, I can't let you take away everything I've worked the past two years for. Why couldn't you just stay out west where you were happy?"

"Shut up, old man." Duvall jerked the gun. "You'll get your money for building your contraption, and I'll get the reward for running in a couple of spies. You got the other rope?"

"You're mistaken about the girl," said Gabriel as his uncle bound his hands tightly behind his back.

Camilla blinked at the cold droop of his eyelids, the almost bored set of his mouth.

"Oh, I don't think so." Duvall checked his captives' bonds, then stepped back satisfied. "I watched every move the two of you made tonight. Who'd think a little flower like her could shinny up a tree and climb through a roof?"

"She was just playing a game to see if she could disobey her papa." Gabriel sent Camilla a contemptuous look, startling in its intensity. "You think I'd let a silly young woman like her in on what I was doing?"

"I think you'd use a mule and a halfwit if it'd get you the information you were looking for." Duvall laughed. "In fact, I'm pretty sure you did exactly that on more than one occasion."

Tears stung Camilla's eyes. "Gabriel—"

"Oh, come, Camilla." Gabriel released an irritated sigh. "Surely you didn't think I was serious about that engagement. Uncle, please tell the overzealous lieutenant I work entirely alone. You can let Miss Beaumont go home. She has no idea what you're talking about."

The tears threatened to choke her. He was protecting her, and she loved him for it, but clearly Duvall was having none of Gabriel's nonsense.

The lieutenant stood feet braced apart, head tilted with interest. "I can see why you've been so successful in the past, Laniere. Your activities in New Orleans nearly went unnoticed. But fortunately someone was able to describe you before you slipped away. I've been following you for quite some time, determined to prove your identity and stop the leaks undermining our defenses down here."

Gabriel's response was a maddening smile. "Pity your efforts have been such a waste of time."

534   Redeeming Gabriel

Duvall scowled. But before he could move, an arm reached out of the darkness and snagged him around the neck. Camilla watched, astonished, as he struggled against a white cloth clamped over his mouth and nose. Within seconds, the lieutenant went limp.

Harry stepped into the light, waving the kerchief in one hand and Duvall's pistol in the other. He looked over his shoulder. "Miss Matthews, I trust you have the old man covered?"

"You bet I do. Sit down and be quiet, grandpa." Delia Matthews, clutching a small derringer, sauntered up and met Camilla's wide-eyed gaze. "Miss Beaumont, I see you were determined to make that train trip after all."

"It's about time you two made an appearance," Gabriel said dryly. "I was beginning to think I'd have to resort to violence." He glanced at Duvall's body sprawled in the weeds. "Ether, I assume. How long will he be out?"

"An hour or two. I'll tie him up in a minute and slide him down in the ditch." Harry vaulted into the car. "Here, Camilla, turn around. I'll get your hands."

After he untied her, she stood rubbing her chafed wrists. "Harry—"

"No time for explanations." Harry set to work on Gabriel's bonds. "Here's the plan. Lady said you're to take the pass and the wagon—"

Camilla grasped Harry's arm. "Does she know where I am?"

"I told you, she knows everything." Gabriel picked up the discarded ropes and efficiently bound his protesting uncle's hands and feet. He then took Harry's cloth and gagged poor Diron, who quickly passed out, then fished in the old man's pockets.

As he straightened, Camilla eyed the roll of papers in his hands. "Are those the plans for the boat?"

"Yes." He stuffed them into his pocket and climbed on top of the fish boat. "One more thing before we go." He opened its hatch and disappeared.

Camilla looked at Harry. "What are you and Delia going to do?"

"Stay with the train and get off in Meridian. I'll make my way back to my regiment, and…" Harry glanced at Delia. "What *do* you have in mind?"

The beautiful actress looked at Harry wide-eyed. "Would you like some company?"

"That would be delightful." Harry turned a rueful gaze on Camilla. "Clearly you have no intention of honoring our engagement, my dear cousin. I wish you and Gabriel a happy life."

She blushed, but just then Gabriel reappeared and climbed down from the boat. He patted his pocket with satisfaction. "All right, let's switch clothes, then we'll go."

"Switch clothes?" Camilla grimaced. "Is that necessary?"

Delia shrugged. "Better safe than sorry."

Gabriel and Harry jumped down from the boxcar to exchange clothes in the dark, while the women remained inside. A few moments later, Camilla leaned out. "We're finished."

"Good girl. That was fast." Gabriel, standing in the rain as if he enjoyed it, smiled up at her. He turned to extend a hand to Harry. "I don't know how to thank you."

"Keep Camilla safe." Harry lowered his voice. "One final order from our little general. The cargo in the wagon is to be used for your travel expenses and the rest delivered to Colonel Birch in Pass Christian. He'll be expecting it."

"Birch? Then the Federals have crossed the Mississippi state line?"

"Lady says so."

Gabriel nodded. "All right, old man. We're off, then. Godspeed." He reached up to assist Camilla to the ground. He briefly caressed her cheek before looking up at his former partner. "Goodbye, Delia. You're a first-class courier. I'll recommend you to the admiral."

"Stay out of the dark, cousin." Delia gave him a cheeky grin and gave Harry a hand up.

"All right, stay low," Gabriel murmured in Camilla's ear. "Let's go."

In Gabriel's mind the driving rain was a godsend, since it kept any curious sentries or railroad roustabouts indoors. He and Camilla made it safely to the wagon around 3:00 a.m., then began the nerve-racking journey out of the city. Every so often he glanced at Camilla, knowing it wasn't just the rain that had her wiping her eyes every few moments. He'd have done anything to assuage the grief that was so obviously tearing her apart. The only thing he could do for her was pray.

As he turned the horses out of the vicinity of the rail station, he also prayed awkwardly for their continued safety. The good Lord had provided them with a means of escape when the situation had been all but hopeless; surely He would protect the two of them the rest of the way.

He was beginning to think the rain had indeed delivered them completely when a hoarse shout gave him pause. He had a choice: bolt or brazen it out.

A glance at Camilla's white face under her stocking

cap made up his mind. "Whoa." He drew the horses to a halt.

A young sentry sauntered over, collar turned up against the rain. "You folks take care of your business?"

Gabriel could feel Camilla trembling so hard the seat shook. "Yeah." Brief and to the point. He could mimic Harry's accent to a point, but he'd rather not push it.

The sentry frowned as Camilla bent double, pressing her hands to her stomach. "What's the matter, lady?"

"Not feeling well," she mumbled.

"I'd better get her back to the riverboat. She's gotta work tomorrow." Gabriel touched his hat and clicked his tongue to the horses. "Good night, Lieutenant."

"Wait a minute." The sentry grabbed the near horse's bridle. "*Magnolia Princess* is that way." He jerked a thumb over his shoulder.

"Yeah, but we got a delivery to make first."

The sentry hesitated for an excruciating moment during which Gabriel desperately practiced his newfound prayer life.

At last the fellow stepped back, releasing the bridle. He cursed as he stepped into a deep puddle of water. "All right. Give the general my regards." He executed an ironic salute and let them go.

A few minutes later, Camilla looked up. Her wet face was ashen. "I think I'm going to throw up."

"We don't have time. When we get outside the city, you can have all the hysterics you want."

Camilla sighed and sat up. "If this is your idea of an adventure, I'm finding a new partner."

Before they reached the western outskirts of town, Gabriel was required to show the pass three more times.

Camilla had stopped shivering, but her anxiety and sorrow at leaving behind all she held dear had not faded. They were still not out of the woods, either literally or figuratively. Old Government Street had become a meandering track that skirted several miles of farms and pastureland, then gave way to pine and oak forest dripping in the rain.

Sometime around six o'clock the sun began to smear thick, oily shades of orange and crimson across the heavens, providing enough light to reveal Gabriel's frowning profile. His worry tightened the knot in her stomach. They were still half a day from Pass Christian. Her prayers continued a familiar plea for rescue.

Lord, may we never forget where our help comes from.

Gabriel had stopped the wagon. Jolted from her thoughts, she looked around. The road was empty in both directions. Only the sound of birdsong broke the stillness. "What's the matter?"

"I was going to wait until we reached Union lines, but I can't..." He heaved a sigh. "Camilla, we have to settle something."

Heaviness pressed on her heart. She'd known it was coming. Harry had warned her.

Gabriel's a rolling stone. He's got a way with women, and he's brilliant at getting what he wants.

Yes. Better now than later.

She gave him a bright smile. "Oh, Gabriel, I know it was just playacting to get through the fix we were in. Don't give it another thought."

Those handsome brows pinched even farther together. "Huh. Well, maybe I should show you something before you shove me completely out of the boat."

"Show me…what?"

He reached into his coat, removed a sheet of paper and unfolded it.

She plucked it out of his hand. "That looks like a page from Lady's journal."

He nodded. "It was folded in the pass Harry gave me."

Camilla scanned the fragile sheet. "It's a passage copied from the book of Ruth." Puzzled, she looked up at Gabriel. "What does it mean?"

"It's a cipher, the same type I used for my reports to Farragut. I think your grandmother must be the one who devised the code." He licked his lips, his expression inscrutable. "It gives me new orders. But they…rather depend on you."

"Me?" Camilla's heart bounced. "Why?"

"I'm to escort you as far as New Orleans to wait out the war. Apparently the admiral thinks I'll be more useful to the navy as a physician. I'm to complete my training at the medical college at government expense."

"Ah." She took a breath. "I'm thrilled for your opportunity, Gabriel."

He swallowed, playing with the reins in his hand. "And she says if we spend a night on the road, we're to report immediately to a minister and make our betrothal a marriage."

Camilla stiffened. She couldn't look at him. "Don't be ridiculous. The conventions don't apply in these circumstances. Not a soul in New Orleans will know or care if we've been together alone. I certainly won't hold you obligated to protect my reputation. Please. Don't give it another thought."

"Camilla." He wrapped the reins around the hook on the seat and caught her hands, warm in his. "I didn't say what I've wanted to say. You know I've made a disaster of every chance I've had to tell you. Please, love, look at me."

She shook her head and tried to disengage her hands. "It's not necessary. Besides I'm already—"

"If you tell me you're engaged to Harry one more time, I just may shoot myself."

She looked at him, startled.

He smiled. "You and I both know your cousin is no more capable of keeping you from bolting headlong into trouble than Byrd can keep his mule from eating paper. At least if you accept me, the world may be a safer place."

She opened her mouth to protest, but the diffident expression in those onyx eyes made the back of her nose sting. She looked down and twisted her pearl ring. "Lady really wishes us to marry?"

He shrugged. "Only if you want to."

Why wouldn't he grab her and kiss her as he'd done before? Why wasn't he shouting that he loved her?

This entire procedure was too civilized. Too sterile.

She stood up. The wagon lurched as she leaped and landed lightly on her feet. She began walking toward Pass Christian.

"Camilla!" She heard springs creak behind her as Gabriel jumped to the ground.

She began to run.

"Camilla! Come back here!"

He caught her as she jumped over a puddle in the muddy road and hauled her back against him.

She pushed at his arms folded around her middle. "I wouldn't marry you if you were Boaz himself!"

"Which is a good thing, since as I understand it, he was pretty taken with Ruth." His hold gentled as he laughed in her ear. "Camilla, I adore you. I can't make it through medical school without you. Please quit kicking my shins."

She laid her head back against his shoulder. "Did you say you adore me?"

He seemed to catch on. He nuzzled her ear, and she went liquid. "I'm not an easy fellow to love, but it looks like the Lord has charged you with reforming me."

Turning in his arms, she caught his face, rough with a day's beard, between her hands. She stared into the dark eyes. "I love you as you are, Gabriel. I love your intelligence and your wit and the way you follow me into trouble. And I love the man the Lord is making of you." She offered him her lips and came up breathless a minute or so later. "And I *do* want to marry you, if you please."

He picked her up and carried her back to the wagon, kissing her all the way.

* * * * *

When Bethany Zook's childhood friend returns to Amish country a widower, with an adorable little girl in tow, she'll help him any way she can. But there's just one thing Andrew Yoder needs—a mother for little Mari. And he's convinced a marriage of convenience to Bethany is the perfect solution.

Read on for a sneak preview of
Convenient Amish Proposal *by Jan Drexler*
available February 2019 from Love Inspired Historical!

Andrew shifted Mari in his arms. She had laid her head on his shoulder and her eyes were nearly closed. "I hope you weren't embarrassed by the man thinking that the three of us are a family."

Bethany felt her face heat, but with her bonnet on it was easy to avoid Andrew's gaze. *Ja*, the man's comment had been embarrassing, but only because she felt like they had misled him. Being mistaken for Andrew's wife and Mari's mother made her feel like she was finally where she belonged.

"Not embarrassed as much as ashamed that he thought something that was untrue."

Andrew stepped closer to her. "It doesn't have to be untrue. Have you thought about what I asked you?"

Bethany nodded. She had thought of nothing else since yesterday afternoon. "Do you think we could have a good marriage, even in these circumstances?" She looked into Andrew's eyes. They were open and frank, with no shadows in the depths.

"You and I have always made a good team." Andrew glanced at the people walking past them, but no one was paying